# The Chocolatier's Ghost

## Cindy Lynn Speer

Dragonwell Publishing

Copyright © 2017 by Cindy Lynn Speer
Cover art by Howard David Johnson
Maps by Mont Richard Bowser
Interior design by Cindy Lynn Speer


Published by Dragonwell Publishing
www.dragonwellpublishing.com


ISBN 978-1-940076-39-3

Also by Cindy Lynn Speer:


*The Chocolatier's Wife*


*Wishes and Sorrows*

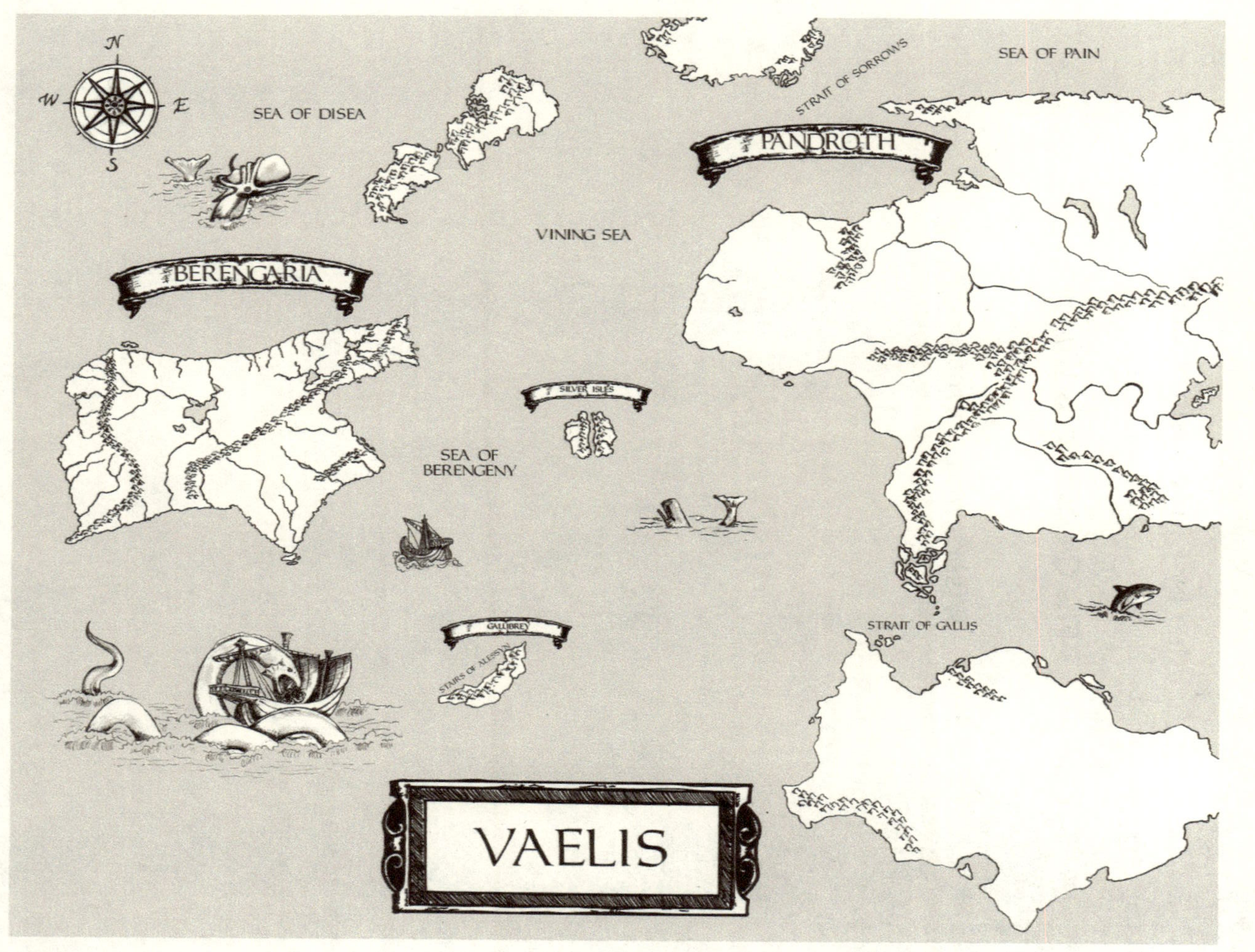
N
W
E
S
SEA OF DISEA
STRAIT OF SORROWS
SEA OF PAIN
PANDROTH
VINING SEA
BERENGARIA
SILVER ISLES
SEA OF
BERENGENY
GALLBREY
STAIRS OF ALESSIN
STRAIT OF GALLIS
VAELIS

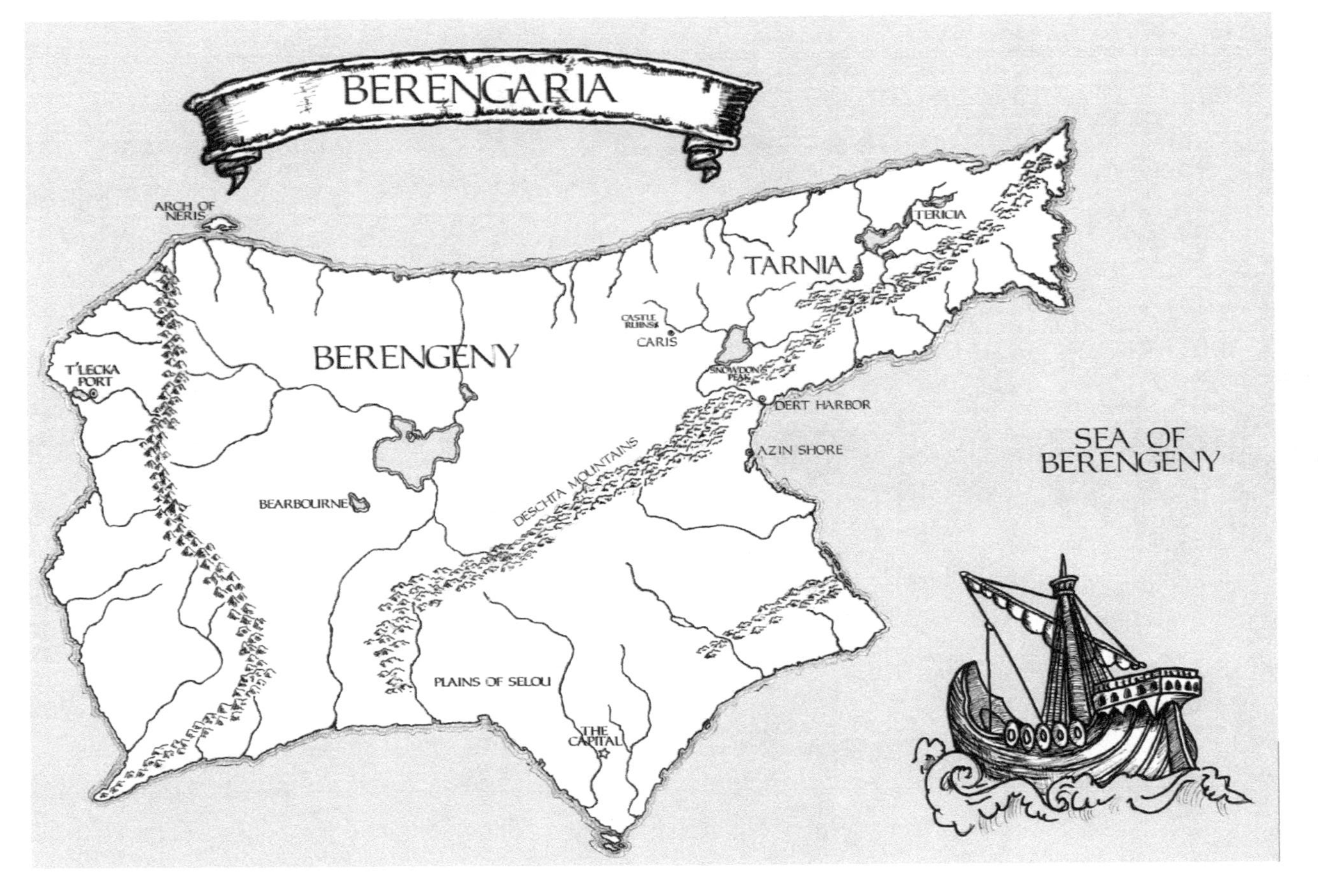
BERENGARIA
ARCH OF NERIS
TARNIA
TERICIA
CASTLE RUINS
CARIS
BERENGENY
SNOWDON'S PEAK
DERT HARBOR
AZIN SHORE
SEA OF BERENGENY
T'LECKA PORT
DESCHTA MOUNTAINS
BEARBOURNE
PLAINS OF SELOU
THE CAPITAL

# The Chocolatier's Ghost

# Prologue

"I know it is here," Franny said to Tasmin. "I can feel it. The wind, the rain, the raging sea." And she could feel it, feel the power.

*A few threats, and she'll crumble. Threaten William, and you will be able to do what you wish.* Franny thought of her beloved Eric Lavoussier, who was now holding William hostage while she got the amulet that they required. He would have his revenge and they would have true power.

And she was right. Tasmin, who stood square jawed and ready to challenge, drooped a little and she went into a hidden room, bringing forth the Heart of Ithalia, a prison of one of the most powerful Sea Witches that ever lived.

It was gray and lumpen. She snatched it from the other woman's hands and pressed it to her chest, sinking herself in, trying to hear the call. Oh, this would be worth an awful lot of money. Eric would do away with his enemies, and they would flee. They would start a new life, her and her lover.

"No, shush, I'm trying to hear what she's saying," Franny said to some foolish thing Tasmin asked her. It was annoying. She could hear nothing, but she was not going to admit that to *her*. If William, who was about as magical as a brick, could sense something when he held the amulet, surely she must?

"She's saying you made a mistake, angering my sprites, and a worse one, when you angered me." Tasmin said, and flicked something at her. A pin, long and dark, struck through the webbing between her fingers to the stone. She could feel blood being pulled from the tiny wound, she felt as if she were being drained.

"The stone absorbs life and magic," Tasmin was saying, but all she could think of was the pin. She yanked it out and dropped it, the hole in the stone was starting to glow. Franny tried to pull free of the stone, but she was stuck fast. Shaking it did not work, and when she grabbed the stone with her other hand to yank herself free, the skin of her hand seemed to fuse with the surface of the stone. "I can't let go of it! It won't let me go!"

It pulled at her. Her bones ached, and she could feel herself crumbling. The roaring in her ears blocked out everything, and the light from the stone was so very bright. She was being pulled, sucked into that tiny, tiny little hole the iron pin melted into the amulet.

And then, there was silence. Just floating in the black.

"Eric?" she whispered. She waited in the darkness a long time, whispering his name. What would happen now? Would he kill William and his worthless brother? Would they have revenge? She hoped so. Oh, she hoped so.

"Revenge and love. I understand revenge and love," a voice said.

"Help me," she whispered. The silence after that almost felt like a *thinking* silence. It was comforting and terrifying at the same time.

The world shifted, the blackness rolled away like fog, and she was laying on the floor of the cave. She placed her hands on it to help her up, but it did not feel cold or rough, just there. She could push against it, and she did.

She stumbled in the darkness, turning, trying to get a sense of place. A tiny speck of light drew her gaze, a hole the size of a pin. It winked and disappeared.

"Love and revenge. I have forgotten much, but not those concepts." The voice behind her was like the whisper of the water lapping against a stony beach. Franny turned toward it. The woman that stood there, head tilted, had been beautiful. Her face, or half of it at least, had a soft, other worldly perfection. On the other half, the skin had been flayed away, and all that was left were bones made of coral; rough, twisted, filled with holes. A ghost of a fish flicked into sight between cheek and jaw, then flickered away, showed up in the empty eye socket and swam back and forth as if caught.

Franny straightened up. Something about this woman made her want to be on her best behavior. "I am sorry to have intruded, but..."

"One does not intrude in a prison." She spoke slowly, as if unused to it.

Franny felt at a loss. She tried again, explaining herself to the woman who stood, quiet and formidable, in the center of the room. She looked over her shoulder, hoping a miracle had happened and that the wall had opened again. She looked back at the woman who was studying her, head tilted, expressionless.

Finally, she asked, "Am I really dead?"

# Chapter One

You may recall that there was a time in the Kingdom of Berengeny that a retired Sea Captain married a Herb Mistress, and that they lived, more happily than not, in the rooms above a chocolate shop. The shop was in the sea-port of Azin Shore, far to the South of the kingdom, away from the easy magic of the North.

Wise women were not thick on the ground, so banging on the door at all hours of the night was no longer a surprise. This night, the knocking was accompanied by panicked yelling. Tasmin opened one eye, groaned, and slowly pulled herself up.

"I shall see what they want," William said, already stumbling across the floor to open the window. Cold air flooded the room, making her long even more to snuggle back down into bed and go back to sleep.

Instead, Tasmin rubbed her eyes and yawned hugely before taking the cover off the light stones, their bright glow telling. "We've not been abed long," she muttered, stretching. A foot reached out from under the covers and onto the cold boards of the floor, and she flinched, and flung herself from the bed with a will.

"Aye?" William half yelled, half whispered out the window in deference to people not married to the only person who could serve in the Wise Woman's place.

"'Tis my wife, William. She's having the baby!" Joe, a large boned, earnest man had no such care for the neighbors.

"And why are you not talking to Dr. Havelock, just down the street?" The time, just coming on to two, Tasmin noticed, was not making him charitable. She pulled on her clothes right over her night dress, shaking her head to try and wake herself up. The buttons did not want to go in their holes.

"A man helping to give birth? Are you mad, William?" was the response. "Can your wife not come?"

"A traditionalist, I see." Tasmin said. "Tell him I shall be but a moment."

"We will be down shortly." His hand stroked her shoulder as he reached for the breeches folded over the back of her chair.

Tasmin was wiggling her feet into her shoes as quickly as she could. "Oh, sweetheart, go back to bed."

"You shouldn't be going out by yourself," he said, stuffing his night shirt into the waistband of his breeches. She hooked her fingers around his, forestalling him.

"Joe can protect me on the way to his wife perfectly well," she said with a smile. "Besides, 'tis her first time and if the baby is born before the dawn I shall be pleasantly surprised. If I need, I shall find someone to guide me home."

A little body landed on her shoulder. She could not see it, but she sensed one of her clan of wind sprites nestling into her hair. "And no, you shall all stay home," she said to the sprite. "Last thing the young woman needs is to think ghosts are invading her birthing room." She put her hair up in a messy bun. "All of you, to bed. I shall be fine."

William kissed her on the cheek, then pushed a pin into her hair a little better. "I do have to be up early, if you are sure...?" She rolled her eyes at him and he laughed. "Thank you."

"Sleep well." She grabbed her cloak and ran into her workroom, where she threw some useful items into a basket. "And I meant everyone..." she said to a sprite worrying at her hair. "There is no sense in anyone else in the family being discommoded."

Joe grabbed her arm the second she opened the front door and started pulling her away, barely giving her time to secure the lock. "I can't believe it, Mistress Tasmin, I can't believe I'm about to be a father," he said as they raced down the cobbles. She was tempted to ask him to slow down, but one look at his face, and she knew it would do no good. "It's been years since we married, we'd given up hope."

The second time she almost tripped she pulled her arm out of his grip with a hard wrench. "If I am dead by the time I get there, I will be of little use to Meggin."

He stared at her, his eyes weighing her. She took a step back, warding him off with her basket. "And no, you will not carry me. We will walk at a pace that assures that I will arrive in breath and in one piece." She walked under her own steam, quickly as she could as she was not a heartless woman, while Joe hovered around her as if he could usher her along.

The moon was but a sliver in the sky, creating a dim, gray light that made the night seem even colder. She tried to adjust her cloak as they went, down the hill and towards where the houses gathered closer together. The yards slowly became smaller, but the homes were well taken care of, and you got the feeling that those who lived there did alright for themselves. Not well to do, precisely, but not impoverished.

Still, it was dark and lonely, and not for the first time Tasmin thought about the town's real Wise Woman. *I hope Cherise is alright. No word for weeks...I only hope she has not been harmed and the rumors that she took off because she was overwhelmed are true, rather than anything more sinister...*

Joe's small house was half way between Dockyard Hill and the merchant district and shared walls with others on either side. Not that she had much time to study the place. Joe pretty much pushed her into the house, and she had to watch her feet to keep from stumbling on the sill.

The basket was deposited on the floor. She plucked her gloves off and tossed them, and the cloak, on a chair next to the door, trying to get herself in the proper frame of mind. *I do so hate being a midwife. But there is no one else until Cherise returns, or they declare her gone.* She and Cherise hadn't had much to do with each other, true, even though Tasmin was a herbalist and their knowledge overlapped. Cherise did not have much interest in befriending a woman she saw as competition, even though Tasmin had tried her best to reassure her that this was not the case. In their few interactions, she found the other woman shy, uncomfortable, and terribly green, but Tasmin dearly wished she was here to do her job.

She shook herself, and put on her kindest and most reassuring mien, and got to the task at hand. " Now, Meggin, let's see how things look." She smiled at the mother to be, patting her knees.

She was wrong, about the length of time she would be busy. Meggin was a natural, her mother was a great deal of help, and even Joe, rambling back and forth, was not completely without his uses. Soon, it seemed, Tasmin was carefully looking over the baby before letting the new grandmother take the baby away to swaddle it. She smiled when the new baby boy was handed over to the overjoyed parents, and turned to the things that needed doing. Cleaning up the necessary mess associated with childbirth, making sure all was well. Joe was beaming, stroking his wife's hair, holding his little son reverently. It had not been nearly as unpleasant as Tasmin had feared. This was the third baby she had delivered, and each time she went to the task with some dread in the back of her mind, as if she would make some horrid mistake. But, all was well, her dress wasn't ruined like the first time...that was the Night That Shall

Never Be Mentioned; no arguments over who the real father was, like the second. Maybe things did get easier with practice.

She went out into the kitchen with the newly minted grandmother. "Good birthers in my family," the older woman said. "I knew it wouldn't be any trouble at all."

"It was well done," Tasmin said delicately, she could almost feel the next question out of the other woman's mouth, and wanted to duck out before it came.

"So, you and your William will be having a baby soon, I suspect?"

"No," Tasmin said, "not for a little while yet." She smiled to cover up the awkward silence her words had produced and to keep the smart remark that started to form at bay. "I will be back in a few days to do the Mating Spell."

"I thought you had to do it on the birthday?"

"Oh, that's just tradition. We'll do it on his birthday next year, but we can get started in a few days. Less traumatic for the little one."

The woman thought this over, then nodded in approval, to Tasmin's relief. She wasn't sure if she could do a spell right now, she was so tired. "I'll get Joe to walk you home, then."

"Oh, 'tisn't far. I don't want to drag him from his new family." *Or wait for him.* "I am quite comfortable making my own way. Let me know if you need anything..." and she was out the door before she had to argue any further, wrapping herself in her cloak, holding her basket firmly in hand. She looked around her. Nothing but emptiness all around. Good. The only light was the moon, in this part of town no one wasted money by putting candles in the windows. Light Stones were plentiful (if slightly expensive) in the North, but somewhat ruinously expensive and hard to get in the South. She had had as many as she needed when she was teaching at the university in Tarnia, and her parents had brought her and William some as a wedding present, which she was grateful for. They were safer than candles, and, in the long run, cheaper since one did not have to replace them, just maintain them. Still, it would have been nice to have a little more light. *Up the hill there will be some torch stones, perhaps they have not faded yet.* Torch stones were cheaper because they were roasted in fires to bring the light out of them, and put in tall torch stands. The heat worked down the iron posts and were a favorite place for people to stop and warm their hands. *Not likely to be warm this time of night, though.*

She sighed. She was concentrating on trivialities, but to be honest, she was a bit bothered. *Three months. I have only been married three months, and already…'tis like my only purpose in this life is to give birth.* The idea of childbirth made her uneasy, and not just because she was seeing, up close and personal, how messy and painful and dangerous it could be. She was uneasy because she did not feel like she had really settled in yet. The shop was adorned by bottles of cordials and tea blends, her contribution to the family business, but her studies were suffering. *I simply need to balance it all out. Once everything is sorted, I shall be able to get back to my work.* She was happy. Her husband encouraged her studies, and was gratifyingly pleased when she did something directly related to the shop. He was loving, kind, and sweet, and would make a wonderful father, but the idea of actually having a child filled her with the desire to run away screaming.

Tasmin turned at the end of the street. An unseasonably late snow made the sidewalk icy under her feet. She took her time making her way up the steep hill. *Do I miss home, I wonder?* She slipped a little on the stones, so she stepped into the gravel and dirt that lined the roads, her feet crunching in the ice and grime, but feeling much more secure. She played with the thought in her head, remembering her old office, gone now to her replacement, longing for the vast libraries of the university where one could easily get lost for hours. *But in the end, I would always rather have William.* Thinking of snuggling next to him in the warmth of their bed made her move a little quicker. It was gone four, and she fancied the sky out towards the water was lightening, but the truth was that it was very dark, very bitterly cold and very quiet. *Mayhaps I should have gotten Joe to walk me back after all,* she thought, wishing she had someone strong to help her up the hill. But she had been…and still was…impatient to get back to her bed, which would be wonderfully warm since sleeping next to William was like sleeping with a small furnace. He didn't even seem to mind when she put her cold feet on him, which she was quite eagerly contemplating, since her toes felt like they would shatter if she stomped her feet too hard.

The rumble of icicles sliding off roof edges and crashing to the paving stones made her jump. Her foot slipped and she reached for one of the torch stands. She pulled herself up, clinging to the rough iron. She was right, the light had died out, and the post held but a little heat to fortify her. Her spine straightened, shivering as if cold fingers had worked their way into her clothes. It wasn't just the cold of the night. Something felt off, and all her senses reached out, trying to figure out what it was.

The wind picked up, whipping and whirling around her. It felt different, alive was not the right word, but aware. She tilted her head, feeling for her wind sprites, but she could not sense their warmth and spirit. It had teeth, and texture, and purpose. She pushed herself away from the post, shivering, but no longer from cold. Something very basic inside of her, something very small and primitive, wanted her very much to start running. Instead, she picked up her basket, took a deep breath, and started walking again.

At the top of the hill, the snow spun and shimmered in the cruel wind. As she neared it, she slowed. Tasmin didn't want to step into that whirling, dancing wall of snow, but she mentally kicked herself and kept going. *Home and warmth, Tasmin. Not so far, now. Just stop letting your imagination draw strange fancies where nothing is.*

She crested the hill, and the wind fell silent. The snow fell away, except for one spot, where it swirled and settled, drawing details that glowed faintly in the darkness to become the figure of a woman. Her head turned slowly, looking over her shoulder at Tasmin, and then the rest of her followed suit, the snow falling and lifting and resettling on the curves and folds that outlined the silvery figure. She stared at Tasmin, moving her head this way and that, as if trying to focus on the face in front of her, considering.

The ghost tilted her head, reaching out one hand slowly, making as if she would touch Tasmin. Tasmin backed up a step. The hand was getting closer, and she panicked. No herbs, no amulets would help her, but she did have another talent, thin and unpracticed, but still there.

She raised a fist, palm towards the figure, and opened it quickly, warding the touch away. "Forbidden," she whispered, and a spear of air shattered through the snow. The ghost disappeared, and the world seemed to right itself, the wind died down and everything seemed to be normal.

She stepped carefully around the newly formed pile of snow and continued her walk home. Determined not to think any more about it, she stripped off her clothes and fell into bed, half wondering if her exhausted mind had not conjured the whole thing.

# Chapter Two

While Tasmin was sleeping off her adventure, Ailiani was waking up. She could feel the dawn, in the back of her mind, come creeping closer, and so she sighed, pushed aside a pile of covers deep enough to smother most people, and slid her feet into cold boots.

She wrapped herself in her cloak, warm from being one of the layers of covers on her bed, and crept out of her tiny room. Miss Dovlington's boarding house was exclusively for ladies, and as she went down the narrow hall she could tell that most of the world was still deep in sleep. She reached out and touched the doors on either side of her, the hall so narrow that she had to bend her arms close. She counted the doors, as she always did, to help her wake up. She knew each sleeping form well, had spent time with them, and knew their stories. Some were here because it was the only place a woman can stay alone and keep her reputation. A few were the so-called fallen, a few widows, like herself. All women who were trying to make it in the world without the protection of a man. Ailiani privately thought that this was where the all-important Mating Spell failed the people of Berengeny, leaving good women broken on the crags of unforgiving rules.

The kitchen was warmer than the rest of the house, and the place's namesake was sitting in the corner. The first bread of the day was baking. The older woman looked over her glasses and nodded at Ailiani, who smiled, walked out the back door.

It was all part of the ritual.

The path down to the ocean was a thin band of light sand against the rise of grasses on either side. She walked the familiar way, counting off steps.

She had always been a morning woman; her father, a great shaman, had woken her and her brother up early every day. They drank sweetened narajilla juice and spoke about the importance of the Prayer Cycles. The Dawn Prayer Cycle was a cycle for hope. "Even women can pray," her father said, "if there is no shaman there."

And so she was taught.

Ailiani looked out at the stretch of clean, smooth sand, dawn only a faint glimmer. "A couple of days ago I did the peace prayer. Yesterday was prosperity. So, today is the prayer of rest." At Alessyn it was believed that your family watched after you, so it was perfectly fine to speak aloud, not a sign of madness. She only spoke to her long-dead family when she was praying. It was the only time of day when she allowed herself to miss them.

She threw off her cloak, and the cold cut into her. *These prayers were definitely created for warmer climates*, she thought as she slipped off her shoes and stepped onto the sand.

Dancing the Prayer was simple, each turn, each movement of the foot, every time she dragged her toe across the sand, contributed to a pattern that someone thought, many years ago, was pleasing to God. The dance was not as important as the pattern it drew, the studied leap that took her from one whorl to the next, creating the symbols of rest and quiet. She made the movements a little faster than strictly normal, but thought God would forgive her, for though it did little to warm her, the momentum kept her going.

But something did stop her, a flicker of white, filmy and soft, out of the corner of her eye. She paused on a pivot that was meant to create a dot in the middle of the circle, carefully placed a toe in the rut that created the outline of the circle for balance.

*Was that a ghost?* She frowned, looked around as much as she dared. She had not seen a ghost in ages. *I don't even know if they get ghosts here. Stairs of Alessyn, yes.* Ghosts were one reason why she was not anxious to return home.

She finished the pattern, watching carefully, then she leapt out of the pattern, left the symbols on the strand behind her as she looked for a spot that was wave-swept and unmarked by man. She was starting to hurt quite badly. The cold made the bones in her feet ache, and she was clamping her teeth to keep them from rattling together, but she had to know.

There were common prayer-patterns, ones that it was perfectly fine for a woman to know. Some were so common that ordinary villagers could be seen using them, tracing them on the prow of boats, on bed boards.

But there were some only the shamans knew. Her father had taught them to her brother, making it clear that they were for the shaman alone to know, but Ailiani watched, and remembered.

She used her right foot to draw a straight, hard line, starting into the spirit prayer.

She was pivoting dots at the corners of the crooked sided box when she saw the flicker again. A quick, small jump to one of the edges, and she transitioned to a point where she could start on another box, open this time. Once, she nearly lost her balance and had to put her foot down. Her balance was shaky, and the lines were losing their perfection.

She reached out with a toe, feeling a little bit of fear. Not for the flicker of the ghost light here, there. She could deal with that, if not today, then tomorrow or the day after. It was, irrationally, because she knew she was going to fail this pattern. The last time she'd failed a pattern, she had been ten years old and nervous.

Another line done. She had drawn it a little closer than usual...but if she evened it out, it would be equal distant on the other side, the pattern would still have balance. She stepped to the next line.

It was when she was mid-step, off balance, that she felt two gusts of wind hard at her back, and she twisted and landed on her side, the pattern destroyed. She froze where she was for a moment. That was no mere gust of wind. *They don't have ghosts here. You are being silly.*

Ailiani rolled onto her back quickly but she saw no one else, just the spirit fragments drifting around her. She could not deny what her senses were telling her. *Ghosts can't touch...* Whatever that had been, it had been purposeful.

She righted herself as quickly as she could. The cold had gotten to her, and she wrapped herself back up in her cloak. Her feet were so numb she could not tell if they were properly back in her shoes, but still she walked, swiftly, back to the house.

Miss Dovlington took one look at her and helped her up to her bed, and a moment later she was putting hot bricks at the end to warm her feet.

The dreams she had afterward were troubled. But, she was not the only creature who was uneasy.

The Ghost did not know who she was. She wandered the streets, the wind following her, swirls of snow passing through her. She could feel it, almost, trails of cold that faded quickly into nothingness.

Shop windows gave her no reflection. She pressed her hands upon them, looking, looking, and after a moment the surface tension would break, and she would slip through. She would lift those same hands to the lights...torch light, moon light, candle light, and the results were the same...nothing. She existed. She was. But she had to accept that she did not breathe, she did not eat. She made no sound.

"How long have I been dead?" she said, and it came out like a low moan, like the sound of the wind bending the trees. Franny, when she broke into her prison, had described a world so different from what the Ghost knew that she knew she must have been dead for a very long time. "I had sisters," she said. "A lover. Where are they now?" But there were no answers for her. She could feel magic, at the edges of her existence, soft and old. A remnant of what she had been. *If I use it, my sisters might know. I am not prepared to face either of them.* The thought surprised her, but felt right. Deep in her soul, she knew she had to avoid them no matter what.

*Very well,* she thought, *I exist again. I don't know how, but I am free of my prison. What can I do with what I have?* She had slept, mostly, to keep herself sane, and thought came slowly to her. Memories were sluggish, as if time had buried them in the deep, relentless silt of the sea. *I am alone. I don't even know where that Franny creature is.* The Ghost had been in her safe little haven, avoiding the other woman as much as possible, wandering through the rooms she had created with her imagination and will and then, suddenly, there had been a great pressure. She remembered that. A crushing pressure that pushed her out of the prison, as if there had no longer been room for her.

Which seemed impossible. Souls were not tangible. You did not run out of space for a soul. You could have imprisoned thousands of souls within the amulet and each could have imagined their own palace. It would not have mattered. It should not have mattered.

*I make no sense. I might as well not even exist. I am nothing. There is nothing to know.*

The thought made her very sad, inconsolable, and she wandered around, the wind flinging snow and sometimes ice against the walls and windows of houses.

During the day, she slept, though the term sleep was not a correct one. She just stopped pretending to be anything. Her thoughts shut down, she merely attached herself to a corner and let herself cease. She let herself be again at night, wandering when there were fewer people about, for people made her feel worse, angry and regretful and bitter, so she was surprised to see the Woman trudging up the slope of the road with a basket in one hand, her other clutching at her cloak. Magic, familiar magic, came to her, the magic of wind, wind over water, over earth. The ghost shuddered, came closer, like one would come closer to the fire on a night such as this.

She stopped in front of the woman, gathering more ice and snow around her, trying to give herself an outline. The woman stopped abruptly, pale breath curling like smoke from her lips, eyes wide but watchful.

*If I could touch her, I could speak to her.*

The woman stopped, tilted her head. She did not look afraid, but curious. The Ghost could feel magic beating, deep inside of her, thrumming through her veins in time to the beating of her heart.

She brought up one hand. She did not need to stay with the physical form, head, arms, legs, but she found it both comforting and grounding. *Slowly. Slowly.*

The woman's eyes widened more, and she flung out her hand. Air slammed into her like a hammer, shattering the illusion of snow and ice that she'd been pulling to her, scattering her. She reformed, invisible now. The hand that had reached out to defend was slowly retracted, and the woman clutched the cloak closer, looking afraid and confused.

*Interesting.* She watched the living trudge away...the woman even looked over her shoulder, once, then shook her head and kept going.

*Time to go and visit the sea again.* The sea-side was the only place she felt comfortable, close to being herself. She let herself go again, and when she opened her eyes she found she had drifted to the shore. She was lonely, and she hurt, oh, she hurt so much. She hated the people in the houses behind her, hated their eating and sleeping and breathing and talking and seeing themselves. They seemed particularly selfish, being happy and alive while she was powerless and dead.

Powerless. Yes. That bothered her. *The woman. Maybe she is the solution. Power so much like my own.*

She turned the thought over, considering it, as she drifted to the water. There was something comforting about the sea. It seemed to know her. She drifted as far as she could, but when the land fell away and the water got too deep she was stopped and could go no further. Her connection to the land was too strong, so she went back, feeling less thin and tenuous the closer she got to land. She continued on down the beach, looking over the water, wondering what she should do next.

Another witch-woman was on the shore, tattoos like thin swirls of power on her skin. Other ghosts were gathered, wispy, more like faint echoes than ghosts, gathered to watch the tattooed woman dance, drawn to the magic she created, the glow of the pattern on the sand. She drew close. She could almost feel the woman's warmth, her power. *If I could get inside that warmth,* she thought desperately, and pushed forward. The dark-skinned woman stumbled as the ghost tumbled backward like a leaf. The dancing woman rolled over, looking around wildly.

*I need a body. It will all be fine, if I can just find a body.*

# Chapter Three

When William opened his eyes again the sun was just painting the horizon gold and lavender. The roof line of the shops opposite blocked most of it, but it was enough for him to see that the day would probably be bright and sunny. *Good. We could use some sun.* He turned over slowly, listening to his wife's breathing. Her long dark hair was in a messy braid that curled over her shoulder. The skin under her eyes looked a little bruised from lack of sleep, so he was even more determined to take care not to wake her. Gingerly he turned towards the edge of the bed, untangling himself, which involved slowly lifting her arm and gently placing it on the nest of blankets that covered her. It was murder, tearing himself from that sleep-warm form. Tasmin made a sound of protest and snuggled against him, her slender arm returning around his waist to keep him on the bed. "Now, now," he whispered. "No use protesting, your heat source needs to get up." It was tempting, to go back and curl against her, just to hold her for a little longer before the day intruded. It would be a lie to say that he had slept well the night before, every sound jolted him out of his sleep. Eventually he heard the door shut, the soft sound of her steps as she came up the stairs as quietly as possible. Once in the bedroom she'd knocked into something and muttered a soft apology, stripped off her clothes and slipped safely into his arms. Finally he was able to sleep.

Now, in the morning light, she groaned softly, but did not protest when he gently moved her arm and stood. He adjusted the curtain so the light was not shining on her face.

He paused only to take up his clothes and boots from their place before creeping out to dress in another room. The upper floor of their home was divided into three rooms. The main bedroom, which doubled as a living room, and two (much) smaller rooms. One had a bed for guests, but was being saved with an eye towards being transformed into a nursery, the other was Tasmin's study. There was also an attic, and someday Tasmin wanted to save enough money to have it refurbished. There was nothing up there at all, not even a proper floor, just the floor joists. He'd been up there once, smelled the scent of must and mouse, and hadn't felt any need to return since.

As he dressed, he could smell the chocolate rising up from the kitchen below. He itched to get to work in the kitchen, but he, too, was filling in for someone and he wanted to be at the docks as soon as possible.

Even the wind sprites seemed to be asleep as he crept downstairs, boots in hand. He peeked out into the shop proper, the sun making the stained glass frame around the large shop windows dance with color. He breathed in deeply. He wasn't quite used to it, by some miracle, and you would think that after three months or so he would be, but the smell of his shop, the soft polished glow of the wood display cases, still had a way of making him feel utterly content.

He went out the back, through the kitchen, lingering only long enough to down the roll he had kept aside for his breakfast. Soon he was striding down the steep hill that led to the docks, ships dotting the bright blue water below. The puffing of the sails still caught at his heart a little. Somewhere below, his old command would be at dock, being made ready for a voyage. He'd been a captain of the Tregaurde for his father's merchant fleet before giving it up to be a shop keeper, and as much as he loved his life, sometimes he felt the pull of the tides in his blood.

And he ignored it, for many reasons.

His brother, Andrew, had taken a vacation from the family business, and as a favor William agreed (knowing not doing so would only get his brother in trouble and spark another month-long argument with his family), but only if he could keep his own hours. *It will do him good to be away. Perhaps clear his head and help him figure out what to do about Bonny.*

Around the time William was getting married, his brother's marriage was falling apart. Bonny had committed adultery, a nearly impossible thing because of the Mating Spell they all lived by, and the talk had gotten to be too much for him. Now Bonny was in prison, serving a sentence of one year.

William took what their parents would both consider his proper place in the business again, splitting his time between paperwork and missing his little brother. They were giving him wages for his efforts, at least, the sum starting to form a small, comfortable amount. *Maybe I shall consider refurbishing the attic sooner rather than later, making Tasmin a proper work space.* The hardest part would be sacrificing space in one of the rooms for a set of stairs, rather than the ladder one had to set up every time one wanted up into the attic.

The main warehouse was close to the water, built of stone and wood, the Almsley Family coat of arms painted in fresh blue and gold paint above the main doors. There was a magnificent doorway that faced the town, leading to the main floor where merchants came to claim their things; William skipped it, taking the steep stone steps along the side down to the portside entrance, closer to the shore.

The scarred old desk that served as his workspace was not too far from the doors, and while the light was better, it was colder. A brazier had already been lit, he was grateful to see as he took off his overcoat, folded it, and hung it on the back of the chair. Between the brazier and his walk, he would be warm enough. "Good morning, Mister Boyd. What have we today?"

Boyd stepped up, placing a heavy book and a stack of papers in front of him. "I have the manifests for yesterday's shipments, if you would like to check over my work?"

William nodded. Boyd was good, so he was not overly worried. "What do we have this morning?"

"Two ships from the Emerald Line. That's what you see now, the majority of yesterday's items have already gone out. We have two carts that will need to be taken to the Capital, they requested extra guards."

William nodded, and once he double-checked the other man's work, he was soon elbow deep in silks and books and spices. Comparing manifests and opening crates to verify contents before sending them on, or sending notes to those who wished to save themselves the delivery fee to let them know their things had arrived.

He fell into the routine. He checked things off, confirmed them, Boyd sent the things away. He did not like the paperwork part of it...too much double-checking and repeating...but he liked being in the warehouse, with the boxes of mysterious goods all waiting for their new owners. He even loved the smell, wood, spices, the salt of the sea.

Early in his task he saw the crates with the familiar symbol of his favorite cacao grower but ignored it. If he did them last then there would be no harm sending a carter to his shop, should one be available.

Finally, he took a crowbar to the crates, looking forward to seeing the cocoa nibs. He pulled the lid of the first crate, then drew a bright blue bag out of the straw. It was Shaba-cloth, spelled to keep the mold out. He inspected the contents, which looked like brownish-red stones of various sizes, and smiled.

"Is that what you make chocolate out of, sir?" Boyd asked when William poured some onto his palm and held it out to the other man.

"Aye. I'd love to get the fruit and ferment the nibs myself, but I don't have the space for it. Also, transporting the fruit would be impractical."

Boyd took a nib and bit into it, then shuddered and tried to cover up his distaste to be polite. William smiled and put the pouch away, counting the rest that were in the crate, then marking them off. "It takes a lot of work to make them taste like chocolate, but 'tis worth it."

"If you say so," Boyd said quietly, pulling forward another crate and working off the lid.

Whatever reservations the other man had, William was pleased, very pleased, with the product and more eager than ever to get back to his shop.

"Sir?" Boyd looked at his lists again, then up, at one crate off to the side. It was half hidden by shadows. "We have everything marked off, but there's another crate."

William was not overly worried. This was not the first time they'd had a left-over crate, a quick look at the manifests would find something not checked off. He crossed over to it, looking for a mark on the rough-hewn wood. "Not something well regarded," he muttered, bending over to inspect the side closer, certain that there must be some mark. Nothing would have entered the warehouse without some sort of marking on it, from a ship, from a merchant, something. The crate was of poor quality. As he leaned close and breathed deeply, he caught, much to his dismay, the undertone of death.

"Oh, dear," he whispered. "Mr. Boyd, the bar, if you please?" He held out his hand, unable to stop looking at the crate. He grasped the cold metal as it touched his palm and looked for the first nail.

"I have a light, sir," Boyd said, raising it high as William pried the crate's lid open. It wasn't hard: only a handful of nails, poorly hammered in, secured the lid.

The woman had not been lovely in life, she had been too fretful, too scattered. Tasmin had called her a handful of leaves on the wind, and it had suited the former Wise Woman.

They had been gentle, whomever they were; had laid her on leaves and straw covered by a tattered old blanket, crossed her hands over her chest. Death made Cherise pretty, for her features were smoothed out, quiet. Her hair was neatly braided. He would have rathered the leaves on the wind, the fretful, forgetful absentmindedness of life.

"Oh, Light take her, poor girl," Boyd said softly.

"William?" Tasmin's voice echoed through the warehouse. He could hear her feet tapping on the stone floor as she approached. He turned quickly to meet her, unsure that he wanted his wife to see the dead woman's body. He was fairly sure, given the chance, he would gladly give up the experience himself. "Wait there, dear," he called to her. "Mister Boyd, the Magistrate, if you please. Send your quickest lad. And no speaking of this, the less said, the better."

The now pale face nodded. Boyd handed him the lantern with a shaking hand as he left to do William's bidding.

"The Magistrate?" Tasmin was running her finger along the edge of his desk. He abandoned the crate and set the lantern down on the edge of the desk.

"I am afraid that the body of Cherise has finally been recovered."

"Oh, William," she said softly. "Oh, dear William. Not again."

Only three months ago William had narrowly avoided the hangman when he'd been accused of murder. It seemed terribly suspicious to find another body in his place of work, and he was worried that he would have to go through the same hell again.

"Well, hopefully they won't arrest me, this time," he said. "I suppose we shall have to hope the new Magistrate likes me better than the old one."

"He won't have to like you much more," she said, smiling weakly. "But if Cherise is dead, what about Mistress Anne?"

Anne was the Wise Woman before Cherise. She had even performed the Mating Spell for William, when he was a child, to determine who he would marry. She left to go and visit family, but never returned, and Cherise had taken her place.

"It was never clear, what happened, only clear that Mistress Anne would not be returning. I don't know why."

Tasmin nodded, then took up the lantern.

"What are you about, my dear?" he asked as she headed back towards the crate.

"I wish to take a look at her—see if there is anything interesting or obvious."

He got up and placed a gentle hand on her arm. "We will be in trouble enough, without an unseemly interest in the body."

She looked up at him with clear, calm gray eyes. "Your experiences with Lavoussier have jaded you, my love. I don't see why this new gentleman would be sorry for our help."

He arched an eyebrow and she tossed her head. The point became moot, anyway, for but a moment later Master Carys was introduced to them.

He was not like Lavoussier. He was not tall and handsome, rather, he was just about Tasmin's height, balding, paying just enough attention to fashion to look well enough put together but not giving the impression that he actually cared. That, too, was completely different.

"Master Carys, well met. I am William of the House of Almsley. May I present my wife, Herb Mistress Tasmin Almsley?"

"I have heard of your involvement with my predecessor, if that's the right word..." Carys murmured. "Show me the body, if you please?"

"This way," William said, leading him to the crate.

"Have you checked the other crates?"

"Aye, all the cargo has been opened and accounted for. But, as you will see, there are no identifying marks on this one. I am not sure that this crate was ever on a ship."

Carys nodded, then took the lantern, peering in at the late Wise Woman. "We shall need a cart and a horse. Can you spare one?"

"Of course." William looked over his shoulder at Mister Boyd, who nodded.

"I will oversee the moving of the body. No one is to do a thing without me here," William started to agree, but Carys interrupted him. "How well did you know Mistress Cherise?"

"Not well at all. She came to my shop from time to time, but that was about it."

Carys looked at him. "You did not need her services?"

"Why would he?" Tasmin asked. "I am as well trained as she, if he needed the services of a Wise Woman, he would need look no further than me."

He looked amused. "Just asking questions, Mistress Almsley."

"Then I shall tell you that I only met her a few times, myself," Tasmin said. "I served her once at the shop, and another time I gave her some herbs that she was short of. I did not know her long enough to feel anything more than kindly disposed towards her."

He tipped his head at her and turned over the lid of the crate, studying it closely. "You must admit, it is suspect that she was discovered in your warehouse, Mister Almsley."

"Not at all! And to be honest, if I had anything to do with her demise, I most certainly would not have put her here."

Carys looked at him a little wryly. "It could be a clever ruse."

"Clever ruses of this sort are best done with men with the funds for it. A stain to my reputation of any sort will do neither this business, nor my own, any good."

Carys gave no indication of what he thought of that, and instead asked, "Are you missing any crates? Surely you have shipping crates."

"We do, but those are not the type of crate we would use. This crate would not stand up to any kind of abuse, and trust me, even the most careful of shipping will abuse a crate a great deal. I would not use that crate to transport goods next door, let alone across the sea."

"I did not mean to insult your family's crates, Mister Almsley," he said lightly, and Tasmin coughed to cover up what sounded suspiciously like a laugh. William shot his wife a glare and she pretended to look penitent.

"Indeed, but my point was that the crate probably didn't come from any of the merchants along the docks. I don't know where it could have come from. We use the same crates to transport things towards the Capital as we do to ship them across the ocean. Crates are often interchanged between us, paint over one set of marks, add another, and all is well. This one is completely mark-free."

"We will need to discuss your security. Who guards the premises at night?"

"I will have the captain of our guards come and speak with you," William said.

Carys shook his head. "Ask him to come to me at the barracks. If you would be so kind as to provide me with that cart, now, I and Mistress Cherise will be on our way."

William inclined his head. Tasmin has already turned and taken her basket from the floor next to his desk.

"I'll see to the removals, sir," Boyd said. "As soon as a cart is free, I'll have your cacao delivered, never you worry."

"Thank you. I'll see you the day after tomorrow then."

He offered his wife his arm, and they walked out of the warehouse in silence. He let the sun soak into him, through the wool of his coat, and sighed. "I wonder what this will mean for the town? They will need a new Wise Woman, unless you think they would keep you in your current role."

"They would not be permitted to. I am a married woman. I can act, in the meantime, because I am better than nothing at all, but I am afraid that tradition forbids me to take the title and the position." She shrugged, looking out towards the waves. The water was a beautiful color, deep green and clear. Still, the loveliness of the day did nothing to soothe her thoughts. "William, do you believe in ghosts?"

"I used to be a man of the sea, of course I believe in ghosts." He grinned, then shook his head to belie his words.

"I think that perhaps I do," she said distantly, looking out towards the harbor.

"You? Why just the other month you were quite displeased that I was reading..."

"That horrid book of stories of "real" occurrences from around the world? Of course I was, you know how I feel about such quackery. Ruins the reputations of sensible mages everywhere. Creighton should be ashamed."

He was trying not to grin, and he patted the hand that rested on his arm. "And so, you must understand why I am quite shocked at this revelation, that my eminently practical and sensible bride might believe in *ghosts*."

"Well, it is not completely beyond the pale, mind you. After all, there are the Ghost Winds. They quite ravage the people with madness to the North and West, and they are believed to be caused by restless or unavenged spirits."

"I always rather thought those were caused by bits of wild, uncontrolled magic from the mage wars. They are said to have started from about then."

"It sounds sensible, but...well, magic is a bit like snow, or lightning, it fades away, goes back into the ground. Storms of wild magic just randomly forming and running wild through towns every once in a great while just don't really work for me..."

"And the spirits of angry murder victims does?" He said it without mocking, he was genuinely curious.

She shook her head and shrugged.

"Why did you come to visit this morning?"

"Because," she said wryly, "I saw a ghost last night, as I was walking home, and don't get grumpy, but yes, I was alone. I guess the best word for it would be shade, for though I have never had an occasion to see a ghost or believe in one, I saw something that will do until a real one comes along. The figure was female, but the face was not easy to make out."

"Did she say or do anything?" he asked, filing away the fact that she came home alone. It did not make him grumpy, but he rather hoped she would not make a habit of it. He looked toward the warehouse, where even now the crate with Cherise's body would be making its way to the barracks, where Carys kept his offices. He shivered despite himself.

"It tried to touch me and I panicked and banished it." She sighed. "Stupid of me, but what can you do?"

"Oh, yes, so foolish not to let some unknown being touch you."

"Well, I could have backed away. Though it was easy to banish, I simply reached in and controlled the air around the snow for a second and took it apart."

"Perhaps you did not really banish it at all." He tried not to let the books that Tasmin had just disparaged fill his mind with dread imaginings.

"And perhaps I did not actually see anything. It seems both very clear and very surreal. 'Tis why I was able to pop right back into bed and go to sleep. I didn't really allow myself to think about it."

"And is it better now, in the bright morning light?"

"Not really, no." She stopped and looked up at him. "I think something is happening to the Wise Women of Azin Shore. Cherise disappeared rather suddenly a few weeks ago, leaving all of her things behind, only to be discovered in your family's warehouse. Mistress Anne went North to visit family no one knew she had, again leaving everything behind, and not one person can be found who has heard from her since."

"That is right. She left before you got here, but, well, I am afraid I was so mired in my own troubles that I thought nothing much about it, and Cherise took over as if nothing was wrong. She often filled in when Mistress Anne was gone, and was expected to be the next Wise Woman for years."

She nodded and they continued walking. "All very disconcerting. I wonder what Master Carys has to say on the matter? Do you think Lavoussier's papers were in order, so that Carys would know about Mistress Anne, or was Lavoussier so obsessed with you that he left all else go?"

"I am not really worried about that, " William said, " so much as I am worried that the new Wise Woman might be the next target."

"Well, then, we shall just have to resolve it before she gets here," Tasmin said with determination, but absently, so William sighed and said, "My dear, she already is here. And she has a habit of walking around alone at night when she told her long suffering husband that she would not."

"Oh." She frowned at him. "But why me?"

"Why any of them?"

Master Carys walked back slowly, taking advantage of the time to think, the cart quickly passing him on the way to its destination. He was lost in thought, but he nodded at the people who greeted him kindly as he went on his way.

*Finally, I got to meet the infamous Captain and Mrs. Almsley.* He adjusted his hat after a gust of wind knocked it askew. *Not exactly what I had in mind, when I read Lavoisier's rather incomplete notes.* He was unsure what he thought of them, and his predecessor's files had been raided so he did not have a great deal of information to go on. It was impossible to say what had been stolen, but the picture remained incomplete. Master Carys did not like incomplete pictures. His wife used to tease him about it.

William Almsley seemed sturdy enough. He still had the look of the sea about him even though the wind-burnishing was fading from his skin. It was in the way he held himself: straight, calm; quite at odds with the description Lavoisier had written in his own files. But it did not take a great detective to know that he had detested the man.

Lavoisier had not really hated Herb Mistress Tasmin, formerly Tasmin Bey, he recalled. The notes had said she was a university trained Herb Mistress, and that was something that Carys thought made her worth keeping an eye on. She seemed calm, too, a little cool but not hard, he thought. She seemed quite no-nonsense.

The cart was making the turn around the grand fountain and towards the barrack gates. He could see people looking at it with curiosity, but he had no intention of giving any information out just yet. He liked to play his cards close to his vest. No sense people knowing what they did not need to. It was another thing that his wife had teased him about, but unlike the former fault, this one had harmed their marriage.

*Just because the spell chooses the best match, it does not always mean that things will be easy.* He shook the sudden wave of pensiveness that overtook him. *Perhaps there will be a letter, when I get back.* His wife had promised to come when she could.

*Best turn your attention back to the case at hand.* He mused about what he'd read about Tasmin: though she was university trained, she had also traveled for a few months with elementalists, and that made it obvious that her powers were somewhat beyond those of a mere Herb Witch. *Yes. I will watch her. Why would a woman come all this way, give up all that she could have, to live here, of all places?* Because of his own circumstances, the idea of it being because of the Mating Spell alone did not quite cut it with him.

He stopped for a moment to look at the harbor. The House of Almsley had more warehouses than anyone else in the town. *And whatever would possess a man to give up a rather large family fortune to go make chocolate confections?* He had a pretty good idea of the Almsley family worth, and it was not to be taken lightly. *He* certainly would not have turned it down. *Such a strange couple. But the Mating Spell brought them together. There must be some kind of affinity.*

He shook his head. All this was to be stored in the back of his mind, turned over at leisure. Eventually, it would all come together, all make sense. Things always did, if you were patient enough.

His destination was not the most pleasant in the town. It was the basement of the barracks, dug deep and shored up heavily, the rooms thick and dark and dank. He snapped his fingers and lit the various lanterns and candles along his way, until he got to the corpse-room.

The crate and its body were not there yet; even now the contents of the box were being sifted, the body would be undressed and studied carefully. Those tasks had to be done up where there were windows.

So the only thing in the room was the body of another Wise Woman, Anne. Her clothes were folded on a table that was set along one wall. Shoes, slightly heeled with colored hair ribbons for laces, neatly placed next to the bundle. He fingered the stained lilac silk ribbon. They didn't match. The lace on the other shoe was green, and he wondered if the woman had been that poor, or if it had been a fashion statement. Wise Women were recompensed decently, they had a house provided for them by the town, a stipend to make sure they had food and comforts. He shook his head and dropped the ribbon.

The dead body was on the only spelled slab in several hundred miles. The slab, along with the cold of the room, would slow the process of decay. It was old. The carving along the edge was worn from people leaning against it.

The Wise Woman laying on it did not have any marks on her body, or any discernible cause of death. She was simply no longer alive. He reached over to pluck back the sheet, to look upon her face again, but changed his mind, allowing the folds and wrinkles of the sheet to remain undisturbed. He already knew everything he needed to know. They'd managed to keep finding the first body quiet, for now, not wanting to panic anyone when they could not find a cause of death. It could have been completely natural, but today's discovery of another corpse, of another Wise Woman, made him think not.

Anne and Cherise had both been slight creatures, perhaps they could share the slab, at least until he got someone to add to the room's spells to make it colder. *I shall write a letter to the*

*Capital, and to the Marshal Elementalists there. I should have done it sooner, but who thought one would have more than one body at a time here?*

He sighed and left the room, the lights going out as he walked.

"It is still driving you mad, isn't it?" Dr. Havelock looked up from the slight form of Cherise, now carefully laid out on the table. An assistant was combing the woman's hair carefully. "The fact that there is nothing obvious about her death?"

Carys shrugged. It was true enough, the body below bore no signs, no traces. "Learn anything interesting yet?"

"She is much like our guest below. Nothing obvious. There's a small mark, here..." Carys studied the light bruise at the young woman's temple. "Do you recall if the lady below has a similar mark?"

"I do not believe so, but I will look again."

Havelock continued. "This body shows more care taken with it. She was cleaned—no mud under her fingernails, her face is composed in peace. The crate was filled with grasses and leaves to make it comfortable, but the way she was positioned, the fact the blanket was undisturbed on top of the vegetation, tells me she was dead before she went into the box. The killer cared about this one."

Dr. Havelock was the town's best doctor, the most trusted. Carys liked him immediately when they met, enjoyed the man's sense of curiosity, even if it sometimes bordered on the ghoulish.

"Mistress Anne was found in the woods along the road to the Capital," Carys mused. "One of the guards said it looked as if someone had rolled her out of the back of a cart. I thought that made sense. Her body was found down the hill from the road. It was only luck that found her before the animals could get to her."

"As I said. Entirely different. If it was not for the burn marks at her temples I would have been tempted to rule it an accident and say that she had fallen over the hill."

Carys nodded and settled down at his desk. "What do you think of Mistress Almsley?"

"*Herb* Mistress," Havelock corrected, taking the hand up and looking at the fingernails with a magnifying glass. "I don't mind her. Seems to have some sense. Sends patients to me, though I don't know if it's professional courtesy or just that she doesn't want to do the job."

"She can't officially do the job, can she?"

"Not married, no, but she can get away with being the interim Wise Woman, which she is, and doing a fair job. Why? Are you thinking about having her look at milady?" He gestured to the floor. They had not spoken anything about the woman on the slab below them, not her name or title. Few knew she was even there.

"No, not at all. Until I know better, she's a suspect, like all the rest."

Havelock raised his eyebrows, but forebore to comment. "Well, I doubt she is murdering for the position. Now that we know about Cherise, we must send to the closest University Circle to apply for a new Wise Woman."

"I thought the position always went to someone local?"

"If possible, but you must remember, dear sir, that we are in the South. Magic is rare, here. Cherise was an oddity. Anne, her predecessor, came from up North."

Carys looked at the pale face. Adella finished combing the hair and put the comb, and the few things she had found in the box, aside. Carys smoothed the already smoothed hair gently, and nodded. "We shall figure it out, though," he said to her.

# Chapter Four

The trouble was, even though there were mysteries afoot, there was work to be done. Tasmin was doing the washing, the sprites helping her by hanging the clothes. There was not a great deal of space for hanging things and they had opened the small, hidden room and the pantry. When William had started to look grumpy with the mess, she pointed out, "This is the warmest place in the house. The clothes will actually dry." And he had nodded.

It did not help her as she scrubbed on the collar of one of William's shirts. Now she was just trying to find a place to put the last of the wash. A couple of sprites helped, and his shirt and one of her night gowns were now hung close to the ceiling. *I would much rather be out there asking questions, though, to be honest, I am not sure if Master Carys would appreciate my efforts. He seems like the stuffy and prim sort.*

William determined that they had enough stock for today... their dear friend Cecilia was tending the counter, so it was time to get started a little on processing nibs.

"Why do we buy them already out of the pods?" she asked. She had finished boiling the whites, so he could work over the fire in peace.

"Because we do not have a decent place to ferment them, here. They need to dry in the sun, on special mats."

She looked at one of the nibs. It was pretty, more like a cracked and shiny stone than something that would eventually be chocolate. William had pulled up a stool near the fire. He had a roasting pan over it, and he was roasting the nibs carefully, in batches.

Tasmin forced herself over to the other counter, where she started measuring out ingredients for mulling cider. "We'll have people in today," she said. "I think people will be curious."

"They will, but that does not mean that they will buy anything."

"Ailiani didn't hear any gossip. I am surprised. You would think that someone would have heard about Cherise. Azin is not that big."

"Maybe we will be fortunate, then, as I've not heard anything, either."

They worked in silence for a time, and she let it comfort her, the smells of the kitchen. They were starting to work very well together, she knew when to go get a pan for him to pour the roasted nibs in, and she would take it to a rack to cool.

*Maybe I should just let it go. I should be able to go upstairs for a little while, work on my studies. I should not go borrowing trouble. Just finish the mulling spices, and you can go bury yourself in research.* The idea did not please her as much as it should have. She felt restless and a tad itchy.

"Perhaps I shall go visit the new family, it should be a good time to conduct the Mating Spell."

"Do you think you will see the baby's future bride so soon?" William asked, stirring carefully.

"Perhaps. You never know, and it must be done. Do you think..." she paused to reach for the sugar tin, and one of the wind sprites ruffled her hair as they flew past. She paused so long that William shot a look at her, and she fiddled with her words. "Do you think the spell ever chooses someone of the same, well, a man for a man, or such?"

"You would know better than I, my dear, but you yourself have said that the spell is not a guarantee of true love, but the best mate. It's a practical spell, not a romantic one."

She smiled slightly as she worked. "You do listen."

"Just a few doors down from my parent's house there were a couple of uncles who were not really related, and I always suspected that they were intimates. And you do see and hear things, on the sea. I do wonder, sometimes, how people are able to still be together, if the spell, and therefore the law, says that they are to belong to someone else. It seems rather unfair."

A sprite landed on her shoulder...Tatu, she thought from the warm vibration, and because Tatu had developed a fondness for fussing with Tasmin's hair of late...and she dipped a tiny sliver of apple in sugar, and held it out. "I suppose no one wants to look too closely, as the spell seems to work out for the most part." She patted his back on the way to getting the cinnamon out. Tatu leapt off as Tasmin passed, doubtless jumping ship to stick with William.

"I suppose," he said thoughtfully.

She finished her job and felt at loose ends, so she wandered upstairs, gathered her things, and went to visit the new mother. She felt another sprite settle on her shoulder. "Auruch? You don't have to come with me."

He snorted. Somehow the small warrior had a talent for making the puff of air against her cheek feel derisive, so she kept her peace. If he wanted to follow her and be bored, there was nothing she could do.

"Mrs. Almsley, we were just speaking of you, wondering when to send for you!" Joe and his Meggin were in front of their home, Meggin was holding the little boy in her arms, letting him enjoy the sunlight and the neighbors the new baby.

"Well, I am here now, and most willing to be of help." She followed them in. The only table in the home was already bare and clean, and she spread the cloth map out carefully. Meggin's mother, Lettie, wasn't there.

"Why is only Berengeny on the map?" Meggin asked.

"Because the spell only covers the people of this kingdom." She got out the bowl, the oils, and started mixing things.

"But what happens if Kit's true love lives somewhere else? The Stairs of Alessyn? Or, God forbid, Pandroth?"

"Well, the spell is not about true love so much as best match, and I am sure that the mages limited the spell to keep things practical. There is no guarantee that your son would be able to make it to Alessyn, and since we are almost always at war with Pandroth..." She smiled, and started the spell. Part of it was showmanship, part of it real, pricking the finger, seeing the blood go into the mixture, dipping the pendulum and holding it over the map.

"Nothing?" Joe asked. Tasmin could tell that he wanted to ask if she had done it right, and she felt amused rather than insulted.

"Your newborn is a boy, and boys are usually older than their wives. All we know, right now, is that the best match for him has not yet been born."

"But you will come back next year?"

"I will, unless the new Wise Woman takes over." She smiled and cleaned up, dumping the contents of the bowl outside next to the doorway, where the flowers would grow in the spring, putting her vials in their right slots. Joe pressed upon her a nice round of cheese and some dried fruit as payment for the ritual, as well as the other night.

Lettie came in as Tasmin was about to leave. "So, any news?" she asked as she hung her cloak up on its peg.

"No, nothing yet." Meggin tried to sound bright, but she seemed a little down. To Tasmin it made no sense; after all, this was the first year, and they had many years to wait.

William had been seven, for heaven's sake, when the spell chose her. But perhaps she, herself, would feel different someday?

"I thought that it might be so," she said wryly, then said, "Thank you, Mistress Almsley, for coming."

"Not at all. But if I may, would you mind if I ask you about the previous Wise Women?"

Her request made the woman pause for a moment, then she shook her head, gesturing to a chair near the fire. "Not at all. Please, sit a moment." Meggin took her son to the other room, and Joe went out about his business. "I don't know much about Cherise. She was liked well enough, a little, well...like a bird settled on a branch. You never knew when she might fly. Mistress Anne was much more solid. She had been our Wise Woman fifteen years."

The names caught her. Even she rarely put the word Mistress in front of Cherise's name. Few people did. But nearly always it ended up in front of Anne's name. It probably said, more than anything, the differences between the women, and how the townspeople had felt about them. "Do you know anything about where they trained?"

"Well, Mistress Anne trained Cherise. Cherise was a twin, born at some little village about four days ride to the West, I think. They both came to Anne to train, Cherise's sister was a much better student, and went back to her village, while Cherise stayed on. I think she loved Anne like a mother, and I believe she intended to stay on to take care of things as she got older. Poor Cherise, she felt so out of her substance once she became the Wise Woman!"

"I beg your pardon, but..." Tasmin started, because she knew the question might be impolitic, considering there were still some who resented the fact that during the great war, magic had been taken away from the South, and so those with any power at all were very few, while in the North it was much more common. "Did any of them have much of a spark?"

"Anne did, but then she was from the North, like you, though she often lied about it. But neither of the sisters had much. But you know, being a Wise Woman is more about understanding herb and stone lore and common sense than any real magical talent."

Tasmin laughed. "True. Do you remember the other sister's name?"

"Agnes, I think. She was very different from her sister. She was very cold, very certain. We were glad when Cherise decided to stay, thought it would be better for her and the town."

They talked a little more, and after a time Tasmin excused herself, and went back on her way.

Her feet took her in a different direction, towards the edges of the town and well away from the sea.

Mistress Anne's house was set aside from the others, her walled garden forming a natural buffer between her and her neighbors. Tasmin straightened her shoulders and walked slowly down the path, concentrating on looking like she had every right to be there. *I probably do, since I am the acting Wise Woman.* She marched up to the gate and tried it. It opened, but that was not surprising. Wise Women did not often lock their gates. The front door would be another matter, but she had a plan. The wood steps leading up to the porch creaked, the wood feeling soft. Herbs hung where they had been left to dry in the eaves of the front porch. The careless waste—leaving the herbs out all winter—made her wince, as they would be useless now, exposed to the elements for so many months, but she brought down a bunch anyway, crushed some leaves and smelled them. Yes, the strength was certainly less. She abandoned the bundle, they were common herbs and she had plenty, properly stored. She sighed and tried the door. It stayed shut. *No surprises there.*

"Auruch? May I please ask for your assistance?" He did not squeak his acquiescence, he was the most silent of all her sprites, but to anyone who did see, they would merely see Tasmin's hand turn, palm up, and the door slowly opened.

"Thank you, my dear. Again, you have made my life immeasurably better." She crossed over the threshold.

It was not a happy sight. Dust settled everywhere, and the place smelled of abandonment. She hugged herself as a cloak of bitter cold and damp wrapped itself around her, trying to work under her skin like a thing alive.

"This is not good," she said softly. She did not dare disturb things much, but maybe she could go to Master Carys. "The books will not do well in this, we must take them away and warm them up, dry them out before they get ruined, but…" She looked around. The next Wise Woman would have a truly wretched job on her hands. Even though it had only been a few months, some of the labels had fallen off the jars. She bent to gather a few, setting Auruch from her shoulder.

"Something is not right. Look how decayed things already look. The floor feels ever so slightly spongy here, under my feet." She moved away, pulling at drawers. Some of them had already swollen shut. Sea towns were damp, but this was something else entirely.

On the shelves of books a lovely silver mortar and pestle stood, engraved with Anne's name and the date of her graduation. "This is the very university I went to. Do you remember the North, Auruch?" A flutter of papers was her only response. She placed the tarnished trophy back on the shelf. "I don't know what this place could tell us. All I know is that I am quite sad, as if I might weep, the atmosphere here is so oppressive." Auruch sprung to her shoulder, tangling in her hair so tightly that it hurt. She reached up and stroked him, hoping to ease his grip on her strands. The papers fluttered again. *I know that can't be Auruch this time…*The cottage trembled under her, and Tasmin backed into the wall. Movement in the bedroom mirror across from her caught her eye. Between her and the mirror, there was nothing but papers being tossed lightly in the wind that seemed contained in the small cottage. In the mirror she saw something, in profile, glittering wetly, like a figure made of silvery water. She stopped, as if mid-step and turned. Seeing the back of the shade, unable to see the face, what it was doing or saying or if the expression was angry or benign, was somehow worse than anything. Auruch was pulling painfully at her hair, and she followed him out, the figure in the mirror moving its head as if tracking her.

She didn't stop until she reached the gatepost, where she leaned upon it for a moment, trying to catch her breath. "Is it safe?" she asked. Auruch had stopped pulling her hair out, so she assumed so. She rubbed the sore spot.

"That explains the rot. Certain ghosts drain the vitality of the places they hide in, like a leech. It is how they keep corporeal." She backed away from the house, studying it, before shaking herself free of her feelings, heading towards the port. She wanted to see Master Carys.

Master Carys had the distinction of being the first non-naval officer to sit in the chair of port admiral, though, Tasmin assumed, it wasn't really the chair of the port admiral any longer. Port Master, then? Rumors flew around because it was quite unusual. Perhaps he was a master spy in the king's service, retired, some said, others said that he was a lawyer who had saved the king's life or that he was simply a powerful man with powerful friends.

His office reflected none of these things. When Lavoisier's office had reflected his past, his pride in his time as one of the most vicious and daring of all the officers on the sea, Carys had stripped down things to their simplest. The walls had been repainted an off white, the wood work stripped and re-varnished so that it shone dark against the pale paint. Not one scrap of paper was in evidence. The desk was clear, dark wood cabinets dominated one wall, even the book cases had been given doors. Everything was a mirror of their master, sealed up and inscrutable.

It was disconcerting. Even the fireplace seemed too frightened to give off ash.

Master Carys rose from his newly reupholstered chair. "I am gratified that you have chosen to come see me, Mrs. Almsley. Please sit." He gestured to the matching chair. "Mister Saul, would you be so kind as to fetch some tea for myself and the lady?"

She settled into the chair, secretly worrying that some bit of stray dirt would jump off her clothes and onto the fabric. Auruch shifted on her shoulder and she mentally commanded him to remain silent.

"So, the office has much changed since last you saw it, I gather?"

"Yes, it has, though I will own that I was entirely too taken up with my own cares at the time to give it much thought. But it is *neater*, that is for certain."

"Everything has its place, and to be useful, it must remain in its place."

Tasmin looked at him, trying to determine if the words had a deeper meaning. Doubtless. He seemed the type.

"Well, I do not wish to take up much of your time. I simply wished to ask if anyone had considered looking after the Wise Woman's house. She has many valuable books that belong to the town, the Wise Woman merely holds them in trust as long as she is here."

"No one has been allowed in to clean the house as we have not located Anne. Do you have need of something from the house? I hear you have taken over the duties."

"No, I have all the resources that I need, but you may not realize, being new to this area, but the sea makes things treacherously damp, and the weather has been quite bad, adding to it. My husband and I have had to take steps to keep mold and damp from our own house."

"I am aware," he looked almost amused. "I am new to Azin Shore, but not to sea-side living. I shall ask one of my men to look into it, perhaps light a fire to help ease the damp. Will that suit?"

"Perhaps. The books could also be moved, perhaps you have a spare place you could store them here? I would offer my own home but I do not have a great deal of space, where I live."

"I will consider it," he said measuredly. For a learned man his disregard for the fate of the books did not earn him credit with Tasmin.

"May I ask how the investigation is progressing?" Tasmin said. "I did not know Mistress Cherise well, but I had not thought anyone would wish her harm."

"We are following every avenue of inquiry," he replied. "What did you think of Mistress Cherise?"

"She was sweet, well meaning. Nervous. She was filling big shoes."

"Did you ever meet her predecessor?"

"I am afraid not. I received a letter from her once, telling me of my then intended's troubles, but that was all."

He frowned. "Why would she write you?"

"Because it was the Wise Woman's duty to tell me that I no longer had any obligation to marry Captain Almsley."

"Ah, yes. I had forgotten his former position. How fortunate he was, that you did not give up."

Tasmin nodded, but she wasn't sure if she believed that he would forget anything. "I am grateful that all was resolved."

The tea came and she offered to serve it. Tasmin found herself being extra careful. It would simply not do to slop tea on the varnished surface of the desk.

She sipped her tea and wondered, suddenly, how quickly she could take her leave. The conversation was already dying, her avenues exhausted.

"How do you like Azin Shore?" she attempted.

"As much as I like any town, I suppose."

"Do you miss the last place you lived?"

The corner of his mouth quirked, as if her attempts amused him. "I do not stay anywhere long enough to form any deep attachment."

Tasmin cleared her throat. "Ah, well, maybe you will love Azin Shore so much that it will be different. I hardly thought I would like it quite so much as I do." *And now I am babbling.*

"Perhaps."

She sipped her tea again, trying to politely drink quickly. "This tea is quite lovely. You know, my husband..."

He nodded and smiled a little. "Is doubtless wondering where you are," he finished for her.

"Quite." She smiled a little.

"Then, Mistress Almsley." He stood. "Perhaps you should go and let him know where, exactly, you have been."

# Chapter Five

And that was about it, for a time. Any attempt to find out more or to offer help was gently rebuffed. The rumor mill didn't have much to add.

Once Tasmin and William wandered together past the Wise Woman's house, and saw puffs of smoke coming out the chimney, though nothing...nothing at all...could induce Tasmin to walk down that path again. William was not surprised and he did not push.

He worked on his chocolates. They sold some cordials and teas. It made him content, to see that Tasmin's additions to their inventory were popular. He wanted her to be part of the shop, part of its success, because he knew that she could have had a different life and he hoped that the life she had would not make her wish for the one she lost. Cleaning, cooking, research...life was turning neatly as ever, and he was fairly content.

One would say that life went back to normal, save Tasmin couldn't stand an unsolved mystery and William was less than pleased that there was still, possibly, a target on his wife's back. He found himself watching carefully whenever he walked with his wife, wondering if anyone was looking at her with any special meaning. He went with her now when she was called out at night, and though she feigned annoyance, he thought part of her was relieved that she did not have to face the shadows alone.

"Master Carys apparently sent someone to try and find Mistress Anne's relatives," William said as they walked home late one night. "We employ guards at the warehouse to deliver cargo, and he borrowed one of them. You've met him—John Doxen?" She nodded and he continued. "He tells me that they couldn't find anything, so he went up as far as the University where you trained. They didn't know anything—couldn't find a trace of the relatives she was supposed to be visiting."

"Oh, dear. And nothing of the lady herself?"

"It is as if she disappeared when she crossed the town line."

"I suppose they should be looking for a body, then. Soon the thaw will be upon us, and they will be dredging the ponds." Tasmin said softly, leaning on his arm a little. She had actually conducted a fairly serious cleansing spell, and she wavered a little on her feet. He placed an arm around her, stroking her back before settling his arm around her waist.

"Aye," he said.

They were not far from home, and perhaps they would have tea, warm her up and give her a little energy, before turning in to bed.

"The idea of her being murdered doesn't fit, though. There was no reason to kill her. She was fairly well respected, even loved in some circles. She precipitated no tragedy that someone would wish revenge on her for."

"Which sounds a bit like Cherise. Except I don't think she was around enough for people to feel a great depth of respect or affection. She was as innocuous as a daisy."

He felt her nod against his arm. "Ailiani heard that Anne talked Cherise out of marrying."

"That must not have been easy. The laws are fairly clear on the matter, that one must marry who the spell chooses."

"But Wise Women are so hard to find in the South that they will waive the law for those with the right affinity to train. Sometimes they are let go—allowed to become Wise Women, sometimes the would-be spouses petition, and win."

"It seems a bit hard on the rejected spouses. Who are they to marry, then? And if you do not have to have much of a magical spark to be a Wise Woman, how does one really choose to become one?"

William unlocked the door and ushered his wife into the warmth of the kitchen.

"Good questions," Tasmin said wryly. "I don't know, perhaps since most people don't meet until the wedding day it seems less personal? It must be very daunting to realize that you've been rejected." She slipped off her shoes and stood warming her feet on the fireplace stones. "Certainly in Cherise's case, the gentleman was less than pleased, he petitioned to have her still wed him. He lost, and from what Ailiani could gather, he was not very happy. He had several arguments in public with Mistress Anne, eventually got arrested for throwing rocks at the Wise Woman's house and breaking windows."

William took her cloak, and when his offer of tea was rejected, he asked, "How long ago was this? I never heard anything about it."

She wavered a little and he led her up the stairs. "A few years ago. I would think too long for this to be an issue. He was sent to sea to avoid prison."

"I wonder when he came back? That could explain the lapse in time."

She nodded and they stripped their clothes. She was practically asleep on her feet. William resisted the urge to pick her up and carry her the last few steps to bed. "In any case, I am sure Carys knows all this, too, and more."

She hummed her assent, so tired that she dropped her clothes on the floor, missing the chair. He quickly pulled back the covers just as she fell into bed, and she was asleep before he finished covering her. He took a couple of pins out of her hair that she had missed, and kissed her softly before getting ready and joining her.

It would have been better, had he not shut his eyes at all.

He was alone, in a clearing, with a stone throne. The throne was cracked, the manacles that had once held captured a great Sea Witch covered in rust, the seat of the throne was covered in blood that pooled and flowed down the front. He remembered there was a monster, in the woods, and he crept carefully, looking for the woman he knew must be there.

"You won't find me," she whispered defiantly in his ear. "You who could have helped me, you who could have freed me. You won't find me now."

"I don't want to find you. I just want you to leave me alone."

And then, as if the ground had fallen away, he found himself deep, deep in the water. He was being pulled down by a tangle of ropes, and he could see, so far away, the bottom of a ship, his ship. The Sea Witch was there, a woman of delicate beauty, she looked like she was spun from clear glass. "But what if I don't want to leave you alone?"

"Why should you not? If you are free, then why bother with me?"

She laughed. "Because it amuses me." She touched his face. She smiled, her teeth like a shark's. "Drown."

And he did.

When he woke, it was dawn, and his heart thudded in his chest, the weight of his fear crushed the breath out of him. He forced himself to breathe, over and over, one breath, a second breath, until the fear eased and the feeling of the cold water left him. It was not the first, nor, doubtless, the last time he had such dreams, but he could certainly do without them.

He found himself getting up, though, and drawing a robe around him. He crept across the room, carefully removed some things from the window sill, and lifted the sill carefully, popped up and out.

There, in a little space between the sill and the wood work, was a plain gray stone. Once it had been a powerful artifact, but now it was nothing. He stared at it a long moment in the weak light from the world outside, he knew it to be smooth, off-shaped, a soft stone that had been pieced by an iron pin. He could see the hole from it. He picked it up reluctantly, but in his hands it remained just a stone. No voices, beckoning in his head, nothing. It felt cold, and a little damp, like any soft stone.

Once, he'd visited an island that had been the prison of a very powerful Sea Witch. Immortal, half mad, she had been manacled to a stone throne and left. He had not freed her, though sometimes he wondered if he should have. Maybe it was that guilt that fed the visions. But everyone knew that the three sisters of the sea were evil and far too powerful to let free.

Something had happened to the island not long after, and it was said she had poured what was left of her magic into a curse, that any man who had walked on her island would never be free of her. He shrugged it off as superstition, at least until he spent too long in the ocean.

Not too long ago, the stone he held had once spoken to him. It had once held the soul of a powerful Sea Witch, probably sister to the one he'd seen once, not so long ago. But now it was just something they hid because they thought they should. After all, Ithalia had been so frightening that *her* sisters had imprisoned her. It didn't seem prudent to just cast the one-time prison away.

He looked at the familiar and beloved form of his wife, who slumbered on peacefully, then carefully closed the secret compartment. He set the amulet on the table instead, looking at the banked fire and trying to let his mind settle. It took a very long time.

The next day started well enough for Tasmin. She was still a little tired, but she made a full breakfast, stacking flat cakes high on a plate and ignoring the ones that floated away. The sprites had been spending a great deal of time in the pantry, and she reminded herself to take a look later.

"Chocolate shells always do well. Mistress Nugent bought some to send to a friend overseas to the Silver Isles. Apparently she has friends in the Human Court," Ailiani said, and William added to the list.

"I don't think the rose flavored chocolates did well, though." William said.

Ailiani shuddered dramatically in answer.

"It was a good idea!" William protested. "The rose and lavender flavored cookies that Tasmin's mother sent were quite popular with you, after all."

Ailiani shook her head. "But you could make more things with nuts. I swear, you get accused once of killing someone with poison almonds, and you take it as a sign that no-one wants to buy them."

Tasmin tried to keep her expression schooled as she put food in front of them, and poured some more tea. Both of them smiled at her in gratitude before continuing on.

Settling down, Tasmin pointed out, "I do think you should invest more in the cacao from the Lombard—what do they call themselves? A cooperative? Chocolates made from that stock sell much faster than the cacao from Eschavelr," Which of course caused a grave discussion between William and Ailiani. Ailiani had met one of the men from the Eschavelr plantation and thought he was quite wonderful, so of course she was more interested in working with them. Plus they were less expensive.

So Tasmin allowed her mind to drift as she ate. The sprites had been acting oddly, less rambunctious. In fact, she could not remember the last time they'd played slam the cupboard doors or chase the hankie. Or annoyed Tasmin when she was studying.

In the distance she could hear bells tolling. "What's that?"

Everyone was quiet, and William's eyes went distant as he counted the bells. "Not an attack from sea. But still, an emergency. We need to gather in the square."

Ailiani had gotten up and was reaching for the rifle they kept over the cabinets.

"How do you know?" Tasmin asked.

"I can tell from the tone of the bell, dear," he said kindly. "'Tis not the harbor bells, and the timing of the bells tells us that they need us to come, but they are not afraid."

Ailiani shuddered. Tasmin knew she had once been kidnapped by pirates. She took the other woman's cool fingers in hers. "It is hard not to worry. Shall we go and see what they want?"

A puff of air grazed Tasmin's cheek and Ailiani jumped as she was hit by a worried sprite. She reached up and petted her invisible visitor. "No, no, don't be worried. I am just letting silly fears overtake me," she whispered.

"I told you they liked you," Tasmin teased.

"They have been so calm of late, it is easy to forget that they are there."

*We are here*, Nee-no, the Chief and Father of all the Wind Sprites, said in Tasmin's ear as he settled onto her shoulder.

"We had best go and see what the fuss is about," William said, helping Tasmin with her cloak. Ailiani pulled on hers, a bright thing made of every scrap of blue, purple or green cloth she could find, lined with soft fur. It made her look faintly fantastical.

They joined the flow of people heading towards the square. Tasmin listened carefully, but no one seemed to know what was going on. She was not sure what worried her more, the alarm raised to gather them all together, or the fact that Nee-no was with her. He rarely accompanied her anywhere.

Master Carys and Bishop Aberghast stood on the wide edge of the main fountain. The Bishop saw Tasmin and turned to say something to Carys, who nodded. The Bishop turned to address his flock.

"Very well. We have called you all together to conduct a search for Tara Alraziev. Her mother, Magda Alraziev, went out early this morning, as is her wont, to gather shell fish. When she came back to her home, her daughter was gone. The house is secure, there was no evidence of a struggle. We don't know if she wandered outside of her own accord and was lost, or if she were taken, but we need you, good people, to help us organize a search."

There were a lot of murmurs. Sometimes, being a port town, there would be a string of abductions, even though it was very rare. Though Azin Shore had done all it could to prevent it, it was not unheard of for someone to go missing, either shanghaied for a crew or impressed and sold as slaves.

"If she is a shell-fish gatherer, she must live close to shore." Tasmin whispered to William, who nodded.

Master Carys held up his hands. "I know, you are all worried, especially in light of other disappearances, that we are being attacked by slavers. Let me assure you that no ship will be allowed to make way until we are satisfied that the child is not aboard. Azin Shore is rarely a target for such infamy, but we shall do all we can to ensure that no stone is left unturned. Now, the girl is of eight years of age, dark brown hair, green eyes, slight build. If you personally are familiar with the girl, please step forward, we would like you to lead one of the search parties."

As people separated out into groups, Tasmin caught sight of Magda. She worked her way over. Magda was holding a rather large set of prayer discs, strung on a chain heavy with stone beads that clicked and clattered as she prayed. Tasmin had never seen prayer discs, only read of them. "Mistress Alraziev?" she asked quietly.

The woman stopped and looked at her dully. Her light green eyes stood out from her dusky skin. *Pandrazzi. The prayer discs clinched it.* If someone had taken against the Pandrazzi woman and her daughter, things could get uglier.

"Ah. Good. I hoped you would come," Master Carys said at her shoulder. "This is Herb Mistress Tasmin, she is acting for the town Wise Woman right now. She trained in one of the great universities to the North, and I am sure if she can help..."

"I came to ask if you had some of your daughter's hair, perhaps from the last time you brushed it? If I had a strand, I could work a finding spell."

The woman looked at Carys, and he produced a small, threadbare cloth bag. In it was a small comb, wound about the tines was more than enough hair for what she needed. Tasmin took it reverently, "That is perfect." She'd had him pegged for one of the new men, those who wanted to pull away from magic, because they felt it was keeping the kingdom in the past, instead of progressing forward and competing with the rest of the world. He smiled slightly.

She turned her attention back to the woman. "I will go and conduct the spell as quickly as I can."

"It may be best if we came with you?" he said in her ear, and looking at the girl's mother, she could understand why. It would both be more efficient, and give the woman something to focus on. She nodded, and led the way back to the shop. William caught up with them on the way. "Ailiani is with a group going near the sea caves."

"She is a better swimmer than most around here," Tasmin said, trying to reassure herself. The sea caves were treacherous. They seemed to change themselves on a whim, so the path you took in suddenly could not be the path you took out.

William unlocked the shop for them and she ran for supplies. In a moment she had a bowl made out of alabaster in the middle of one of the customer tables. She had a vial of agate, crushed, and a vial of pansy abstract, which she shook into the bottom of the bowl, mixing well. Some water, some essence of Phytolacca. She took a brass needle and wound a hair around it.

"Why brass?" Carys asked.

"Because an iron needle would risk becoming an actual compass. We don't want it to magnetize, this is a compass for a soul's direction," she said.

Carefully, she set it in the bowl, careful not to break the surface of the liquid. It spun, round and round. It did not settle, it did not stop. *At least it does not point down, down would be dead for sure.* But it did not do anything useful.

"I thought you said she was Talented," Magda whispered, pulling her fingers through her wild, dark hair.

"Let us go outside, perhaps the spell would work better outdoors," William suggested, probably more to forestall the mother, who was starting to lose her deadened calm. Sadly, the needle did not work any better outside.

"Did you do the spell correctly?" The mother asked. "Could you do it again?"

"It is a very basic spell," Tasmin said.

"Then you are useless! Useless!" The mother slapped the bowl, sending it skittering across the counter, slopping the contents all over Tasmin, soaking into her skirts. Tasmin grabbed for it, but her fingers were slippery, and it tumbled out of her hands, shattering onto the floor. "Well, that was not helpful."

Magda backed off a few paces, mouth working as if she was trying to say something, whether an apology or more invectives, Tasmin did not know, before running off. Carys sketched a little bow and followed.

William cursed under his breath.

Tasmin sighed. "I rather liked that bowl."

"I am sorry. What will you do now?"

"Change my clothes," she said wryly. "I smell like a florist. Where are you going?"

"Aye. I shall pick somewhere suitably cold and dangerous and join the party, there, specifically so you can worry about me instead of feeling sorry about your bowl."

She laughed. "No, you will choose it because you are not one for searching through tiny cupboards. I will join a party as soon as I have changed." She sighed. "The damnable thing should have worked. 'Tis a basic spell, and impossible to foul up."

He placed a quick kiss on her forehead. "It could not be your fault. Maybe something else was wrong." He strode out to join the search, and she quickly picked up the pieces of the bowl. By some stroke of luck she also found her needle.

Tasmin changed quickly, trying to think of what she could do to help.

Nee-no perched on her shoulder again. *Now we find the child*, the Father of Sprites said.

"Of course," she said, feeling like smacking her head. The solution was obvious. No one could go everywhere as quickly as a clan of wind sprites, for who could defeat the wind?

But obvious did not equate easy. The first step was to have an anchor. That was solved long ago. Tasmin was the anchor for the sprites.

The second step was to put that anchor on the highest point closest to the center of the town as possible.

The Bishop had a church, a lovely, tall spired creation in the perfect place. She borrowed a pair of William's breeches and belted them on under her skirt. It made her feel fat and unwieldy, and by the time she climbed the many, many stairs of the tower, she was sweating profusely and hating everything.

She reached the windows at the very top of the spire and stuck her head out. "Good, you think?"

In response, Nee-no sent a wave of confidence to her, and a mental image of the outside of the spire tower, where bricks had been left pushed out to form steps to the roof. The roof itself had steps of wood on it, as if to facilitate repairs.

"Oh, no." She pushed away from the window. "I...oh, no."

A swarm of warm, confident, loving sprites swirled around her. *Not let you fall!* And, *This is so easy*, were the general messages. "Oh Lord of all that is good," Tasmin whispered, and carefully stepped out onto the ledge. The windows were tall, at least, that made things slightly less dangerous.

But not by much. Sprites whirled around her, pushing her gently up the brick foot holds, lifting her skirts away from her feet, and she concentrated on them, on their warm confidence pushing and coaxing her up and up. Standing at the zenith was the hardest part, she felt like whimpering as she climbed to a standing position using the metal of the finial itself, her feet felt fairly confident on the base of the finial, so she turned and pressed her back to it.

*See?* Nee-no said. *Not so bad.*

She laughed in response. It sounded faintly like a madwoman's cackle.

She took a breath. Then another, calming herself. She tapped into her Talent, into the flow of it in her veins, and let it fill her, let her awareness of the sprites spread into each and every one of her veins them, as the sprites hovered and swirled around her. She spread her arms out. She was steady where she stood. She felt one with the stone, the tile, the metal, and she felt rooted into the spire and from there into the world itself.

*Go! Find the child,* she told them all, and her awareness spread with the sprites as they flew in their different directions. She had a hard time sorting what she was seeing, so she let it flow through her. In some ways she felt as if they were communicating to each other through her, as if right then they were one massive being, searching everywhere. Some of the places they looked were silly, too small for a child of that age (or any age), and she told them so with a tactful thought, and it modified all the searches. Every time she thought, *No, she would not be there,* it stopped any of them from looking in a like place. Soon they were looking in much more sensible places, puffing through hayricks and sending straw to the sky, only to have it settle right back down where it belonged, opening closets and pushing aside curtains and looking through basements and attics, and then a group turned itself to the marshes. *There will be some very displeased townspeople, if they catch on to what happened.*

They reached the marshes, flying through strands of weeds. She saw bright blue and red, and they gathered around the bright color.

"Oh, no," Tasmin whispered. The attachment she felt to the church spire disappeared and she slipped, scrambled for the finial. She screamed and clung to it, on her knees, her weight on her skirts making it hard to find purchase. Somehow she managed to get a knee around the finial, but she shook as she clung to the cold metal. She opened her eyes and saw, way below, that people had gathered and were looking up at her. She raised a shaking hand, pointing towards the marshes, where the wind sprites circled around a small body, weeping and wailing. The sound was so keening, so pained and loud, that the townspeople thought that the wind that whipped through their town, so cold and bitter, was the weather changing to snow or rain, and several went home to batten down.

She waited, clinging to the finial, and finally, the sprites came and got her. They tapped gently at her cheeks, they pushed at her until she was standing, then formed a warm cloud, loving and sad, that supported her as she backed down and went inside again. She shook as she took the stairs back down to the nave, and she could feel individual tiny little bodies attach themselves to her, burying themselves in her clothes. Nee-no alone stood on her shoulder, he did not bury himself in her hair, but rode like the King he was until they made it to the altar, where the bishop was kneeling.

She waited until he looked up.

"Did you find...?"

"Yes," she said.

"She is..."

Tasmin's mouth felt dry. "Beyond our help."

"Oh," he said, and looked away.

"She is Pandrazzi, unless I am mistaken. Will her mother want me here for the rites?"

The Bishop stood. "Who told you?"

"Her prayer discs. Her skin color. Is it a secret?" The Pandrazzi did not believe in Wise Women. It explained Magda's earlier helpless anger.

"We had tried to be discreet about it, as her fellow countrymen are not very popular at the moment. She came to service because she thought it was good camouflage, but she did not believe exactly as we do, so I doubt she will want services done."

"Do you think someone figured out who she was?"

He played with the things on the altar, straightening them. "I would hope not. Besides, why was Magda spared?"

She had no answers.

A thought caught at her. "Do they believe in magic at all, then?"

"Absolutely. Pandroth is huge, and there are a lot of people who believe. The party line is that technology is better than magic, but the Pandroth Empire has never put away a tool that might still have some use," he paused. "In fact, I think Tara's mother wanted to know how we taught magic to people with Talent."

"And was she less interested when she found she would have to send her daughter far away, as we do not bother with schools here in the South?"

He gave her an impressed look, and nodded.

She said her farewells, and trudged home, her mind full of thoughts.

"And what is this that I hear about you clinging to the spire of the church like a madwoman?" Ailiani asked her. Tasmin jumped. She was only half way home and had not expected to catch up with the other woman before then. She looked around her. Some people caught her eye and nodded at her with respect, a few looked a little afraid and uncertain. They had been this way before, when she had first come into town. The sprites had made it seem like she had appeared out of nowhere. She smiled at people, tried to act normally. Her smile faltered when she realized that William was on the other side of Ailiani. *Oh, he is not happy.*

"I had the sprites with me. They would never let anything happen to me."

William shot her a glare.

"Oh, you really aren't happy with me," she said. "But I was perfectly safe."

"Perfectly safe? Ha!" Ailiani said. "And don't you even start, invisible little king!" she said to someone, Tasmin assumed Nee-no. "You and your clan have gotten Tasmin in serious hot water, and for what?"

"At least we all know," William said carefully, through his teeth.

"That your wife is insane?"

"Not helping," Tasmin tried to whisper at her.

"No, I am *not* helping."

"Oh, at least I was not swimming around in the sea caves," Tasmin pointed out, for Ailiani had wrapped her hair carefully in sheeting, the hood pulled tight over the makeshift turban.

"What is your point? He already knew *I* was mad."

"Enough," William said. "You are both making my head ache."

Tasmin wanted to point out it was probably the way he was holding his back teeth clamped together, but reasoned should he unclamp them she would hear a great deal many things she would rather not, so they went home in silence.

Dinner was a cold affair, whatever the three could scrounge. Ailiani was sat close to the fire, where she ate her dinner, and would not be allowed to leave until she was completely dry.

Their meals finished, William was drying the plates and placing them in the cupboard. He clattered them together and winced.

"What are you thinking of?" Tasmin asked, hanging her washcloth to dry.

"Why a little girl? What possible motive could someone have for such a thing?"

"I don't know. I spoke to the Bishop, and he mentioned that her mother was asking around to find out if there was someone who could teach a person with Talent. Perhaps they wanted her for her magic. That is what all the deaths have in common, so far."

"But she is so young." Ailiani was holding a kerchief over the table, pulling it away from unseen little hands. Sometimes whatever sprites were playing would manage to get it out of her hand, and she would chase it and pluck it back. "Does Talent manifest so early?"

"Sometimes," Tasmin allowed. William smoothed his hand against her back and she leaned into the touch. "She is part

Pandrazzi, I know little of them. Perhaps they manifest early? By our rules anyone manifesting this early would be an exceptional Talent."

His hand, warm over her back, paused. "But why target anyone with Talent? Once they are gone, they can't use their powers to help you, though Creighton...and don't stiffen, love, did have a most intriguing story about a wizard who was also a ghost."

Ailiani let the handkerchief go. "And why women? Men sometimes have Talent. Less in the South than in the North, but still."

"And it doesn't follow for certain that you have to have Talent to be a Wise Woman. An affinity, yes. But you don't have to have much power. Certainly not what it would take to be a ghost-warlock," Tasmin added.

"Wizard," William muttered, rubbing her back again.

"As I said."

Ignoring her, William asked, "But how would anyone know that Tara had Talent? She was too young to even be tested?"

"That is the question we must concentrate on, I think," Tasmin said. "If we can figure out who knew, maybe we can figure out who killed her?" She barely resisted the desire to lean against her husband. "Ailiani? Were you tested?"

"The sisters of Shamen are never tested, my dear."

Tasmin tried to make something to reply, and William teased, "That is a bit of a non-answer."

Ailiani shrugged. "They never really test. You either are, or not. Things are not so formal, down by the Stairs of Alessyn."

Tasmin tilted her head and really looked at Ailiani, who studiously ignored her.

"Time for bed," William pushed himself away from the counter he'd been leaning on, and the moment was broken. "Would you like me to walk you home?"

She rolled her eyes. "If you are worried, I will get the boot maker next door to walk me home. He is always looking to be solicitous."

"William is less trouble."

She gathered her cloak. "And less fun."

"Do you think she's magical?" Tasmin asked a little later, as she stripped off her dress.

He hung his shirt up, then took her dress and put it on the next peg. She could tell he was thinking, and did not interrupt. "I have never seen her do aught that one could consider so, no. There were men on the ship who thought she had enchanted Deitson into marrying her, but I knew that to be nonsense." Then he smiled slightly. "In the literal sense, anyway. He was certainly desperately in love. Why?"

Her clean shift was cool against her skin. She sat down and undid her hair, throwing pins into a bowl. "I don't know. I am used to her answers being more direct, I suppose."

"It really wasn't a bad answer. From what little I know her father was very exacting, and she often felt oppressed by the way things where. Perhaps she just doesn't like to speak of it."

She brushed her hair. "I worry. We don't really know why people are being targeted. What if she is in danger?"

He washed his face and settled into the bed. "We will protect her...and you."

"And you." She threw a ribbon at him.

He stretched and snuggled into the bed. "I very much doubt anyone wishes to do me harm. I am completely without merit to anyone but you."

She leaned over and kissed him on the forehead. "I very much doubt that," she said, and soon she turned off the light and joined him.

# Chapter Six

'Well, she probably didn't kill the girl," Dr. Havelock said, pouring them both some very nice whiskey that had been smuggled in from the Silver Isles. They had laid the tiny form out below, on a non-magical slab, and both of them needed a drink.

"And what makes you so certain of that?" Carys asked.

Havelock paused, drank some, started to place the tumbler on the rich, polished wood of the desk, paused, then just propped the glass on his lap. "The amount of effort she put out to find the girl must have been immense. Why would she do that, if she was responsible for the child's death?"

"She did not seem overly taxed by the magic, though. Perhaps she knew, and it was all an act."

Havelock frowned. "When she first came here people called her a Wind Witch, and you can already hear the rumors starting up again. But to be honest, the woman does not strike me as a murderess, much less of children. I've watched her at work. I could possibly feature her killing another person, I don't know her that well...but a child?"

"That is not proof. We don't know." Carys pointed out.

"It doesn't seem logical, or like something she would do."

"That is what makes murder tricky, my dear boy. If the killer was obvious, then anyone could avoid being murdered in the first place." He was staring glumly out the window, the sun was lowering and a fog was already setting in.

"Yes, but if you operate by the idea of who benefits, who gains by this murder, I can't see how Mistress Almsley would."

"Maybe she's mad."

"Now you are just arguing for the sake of arguing," he objected, and Carys smiled slightly.

"So, if not your beloved Tasmin," Carys said, "then who?"

He slumped down in his chair. "Well. As you say, it could be anyone. Any new-comer will be suspected, even you."

"They already enjoy talking about me so much already," Carys agreed. "They speculate constantly as to why I am here. What is my purpose? Why did the King send a civilian to become the Port Admiral?"

"I've often wondered that myself. Not that I am not quite pleased that you are here. You of all people are one of the few people I remember fondly from my school days, but it is, in itself, a mystery." He looked hopefully at his old friend.

"His Majesty is a man of great reason."

"Is that truly your answer?" Carys arched an eyebrow and Havelock glared at him before throwing himself back into his chair. "Bother."

Carys shrugged. "I enjoy the speculations too much to let them end. Perhaps I shall declare a game. You may guess once a week why I am here, and I will tell you truly if you are right."

"I thought we had grown past games."

"Games," Carys said reflectively, "are the only thing I have. So, tell me, was there anything of interest visible on the body?"

Havelock started at this change of subject, then shrugged. "Nothing, really. I will have to see if there is water in her lungs, but there is no visible sign of attack. On first glance it looks as if she just fell over dead. Will you be present when I investigate further?"

"No," he said, staring out at the harbor. "I do not think I need be there for that." They spoke of other things until he could avoid his office no longer.

He walked up to his office, and finally settled down into the depths of his chair. There was much paperwork to go over, but the only thing he wanted to look at was the card that had been laid carefully on top of everything on his desk. It sparkled, faint gold in the candle light. "I could not find the saboteur. I will be there soon," was all it said, in brown ink that seemed to have a sparkle to it, caught by his lamp light.

He sighed, turned it over, and in a moment wrote his answer.

# Chapter Seven

Tasmin opened the pantry. It was a fairly neat conglomeration of bins and shelves, lit by a narrow, rectangular window. Everything was where she expected. Sacks of sugar. William's least favorite molds—the man collected molds and had a collection that would make the most ardent hoarder blush. There was a corner where the wooden shelves did not meet. William intended to extend the shelves so that they met on the corner and continued on, unbroken, but he hadn't gotten to it yet. Tasmin tilted her head and studied the no longer empty corner and thought, perhaps, it was just as well that he hadn't.

A large nest, anchored by the shelf bracing on either side, was being woven even as she watched. A bright blue dress was being taken apart, made into raw materials again, and being added to the nest which already boasted dozens of colors and textures. "Do I wish to know whose dress that is?" she asked.

*Probably not.* Nee-no settled on her shoulder.

"What are you doing?"

There was silence, and finally, grudgingly, he said, *Anchoring.*

"I thought I was your anchor?"

*There are many reasons why being anchored to a woman is not the best thing. We have learned to communicate better, we understand peoples better, but we also understand that things happen to people.*

"If I died, you'd be in danger of scattering. I understand, you are wise to create a new anchor."

*It works. Your home is your heart place. Now we make a heart place in your home. A place to be safe in, instead of disappearing in the walls.*

She looked at the nest. There were buttons woven in, a pair of ear bobs that she had not worn for years. It looked like a honeycomb, in some ways, a large, many-colored oblong with lots of little cubbys in it. "I wish I'd known. You needed this long before."

*We did not have security, before. There was no sense. Now we do. Now we will make an anchor and increase our numbers.*

Tasmin smiled, enchanted by what they'd already built; she studied it intently. "I'll have to get you some more material. You probably should not sneak into other people's places and take their things."

*They had stopped using them years ago. We can tell by the smell.* He sounded borderline offended.

"My dear and beloved Great Chief, people are funny about their things, even things they have not used for years."

*Humph,* he said, but his presence felt mollified.

She walked out, wondering if she could convince William to sneak into the Heir-House and look through the cupboards. Surely there would be an old blanket or two she could give to the sprites to re-purpose. Or a nice, thick down filled comforter. That could provide some marvelous little beds for the cubbies.

William was boxing up chocolates. "Did you see the pantry? The sprites are building a nest. I might go up and see if there's anything we have we can give to the project."

"What kind of things?"

"Anything cloth."

He winced. "That explains why one of my old shirts was floating around the kitchen this morn. I thought they were playing a game."

"Oh, dear. I hope you weren't very fond of it." She thought of the white layer she'd seen near the bottom of the weaving and knew the shirt was long gone.

"'Tis only a shirt," he said, sounding somewhat resigned. "I did not wear it much because it was not particularly fancy, and I was waiting for one of my other shirts to wear out before I started using it." He stacked the green boxes and carried them through the kitchen door.

"I shall sew you another." She followed them out. "Perhaps that is what I shall do, go out and get some fabric."

"You don't have to," he said, putting the boxes neatly on display.

"I would like to." She was not a great seamstress, but it seemed to her that it should not be an impossible task. "I have to go and get some groceries, anyway."

"I might like that, wearing something you made." He sounded almost shyly pleased, and she resolved that she would manage it. She kissed his cheek, gathered her basket and set out.

She was only a few steps from the shop when she felt Auruch settle on her shoulder. Her first stop was the general store, a wide emporium that boasted a rather lovely view of the harbor where it got so many of its goods.

Tasmin wandered the aisles a little, until she got to the bolts of cloth that lay along the back table. She could sew— her mother had taught her. She just didn't have time to sew a great deal, so she felt a bit out of her depth as she looked over the choices. She did do the mending and knew that she was low on white thread, so she picked up a couple of spools, then ran her hands over any fabric that was white and looked like it would make a decent shirt. "I'd like some of this, please?" she asked a young woman.

"How much do you need?"

She had no idea. "Enough for a shirt?" she asked hopefully.

"That doesn't really help much." The shop girl was polite, but far too amused.

"Who's the shirt for?" another voice asked. An older woman was coming down the stairs, her hand careful on the banister. Mrs. Tannel, the owner of the store, Tasmin thought.

"My husband William Almsley?"

"Ah," the shop girl said, and started measuring the cloth by holding the edge of it, stretching her arm out to the side, and grabbing it where it hit about her breast bone. She folded the fabric in and repeated the process. She used scissors to nip the edge, then ripped it down, the fabric parting easily. She folded it up and handed it to Tasmin with a smile. The blush from whatever reproof she had heard in her employer's voice had not yet faded as Tasmin took it, muttering thanks.

Tasmin gathered some other things, such as unspun wool for the sprites, some lovely buttons, sweet-smelling cherries, and by the time she was done, Mrs. Tannel had taken the young girl's place at the counter.

Tasmin placed her purchases on the well-worn, dark polished wood. "Mrs. Tannel, when I first came here, I was told that anything I wanted to know about the town, I should ask you."

"And you should," she said, writing the purchases out in neat, quick hand. "I know all the stories." She smiled at Tasmin to show that there was no meanness in her statement, and went back to tallying.

"Do you know where Mistress Anne came from?"

"She went to university up North...just like you."

"Really?" She said as if she did not already know that. "But I was wondering where she came from before that. Was she a Southerner? From the West?"

Mrs. Tannel tapped her pencil on the counter, turning the receipt towards Tasmin, who started getting out her payment. "I told that nice Master Carys that I don't think she had family in Berengeny at all. She once told one of my friends that she came from across the sea. Now, I don't know the context of the conversation, if she was being silly or not, but it don't surprise me much that no one's found any people for her, I'll admit that."

"Thank you so much," Tasmin said, gathering her change and her purchases. She went into the market, hoping to find something that she felt like cooking for dinner, and saw Magda shucking clams. There was something hunted about her, the way she hunched over the table. She kept looking over her shoulder, studying the faces of the people passing the stall. Their eyes met and the other woman snarled at her. The owner of the stall snapped at her—perhaps he was yelling at her for glaring at a potential customer? Magda tossed her hair and snapped. He raised a hand and she said something, savage and low that Tasmin could not hear. Tasmin started forward, but he lowered his hand and stepped away from her, settling to whatever task he'd been doing. Magda looked at Tasmin again, arching an eyebrow, and Tasmin let herself fade back into the crowd. Fish was cheap, so she bought some nice fillets, and took the long way back so she did not have to pass Magda again.

# Chapter Eight

It took a long time for Tasmin to fall asleep that night. She felt strange, itchy on the inside of her body. When she dreamed, she dreamed of the wind, tearing through her, she could feel it flow through her bones.

William gently shook her awake, and she frowned at him until she heard the bells ringing softly in the distance. "Harbor bells again?" she whispered, still half asleep.

"Aye. Trouble from the sea."

He shifted to get up. She held tight for a moment, and he put his hand on top of her head, comfortingly. If the alarm rang, all able-bodied men had to go and defend the port, and Tasmin knew William was better suited than most to go and fight. She let go.

"It might be nothing," he said, and she could hear him dressing in the darkness, so she rolled over and uncovered the stone light, banged one on the table to brighten it. "I'll get the lantern, you should take one of the light stones."

"Nay, wife, but if you please, give me one of the oil lanterns from the kitchen. The one by the back door should have plenty of oil..."

"But the light..."

"Is better, but I would rather lose an oil lantern than one of the light stones."

Tasmin wanted to argue, but after a moment's pause she ran down the steps. *Practical as always.*

By the door, she helped him into his coat, the oil lantern lit and ready. He checked his pistol and slipped it into his belt, rested his hand on the hilt of his saber without thinking.

"What about Miss Dovlington's? Do you think Ailiani is alright? It's so close to the sea."

"The boarding house is a safe place. They know the dangers, and I would not wish to get between Miss Dovlington and one of her charges." He smiled and kissed her. She clung to his coat for a moment. One of the sprite warriors must have settled on his shoulder as he said, quietly, "No, please stay with her."

She let go, nodded once, and stepped back. "I'll bar the door, and watch for you."

"I'll be back soon." Another encouraging smile, and he pressed his hat on firmly and went into the night.

"Someone please go with him," he heard her say softly, and he was joined by a handful of sprites. He turned and the door shut seemingly on its own, he thought he heard the board slide into place. *Good,* he thought, *she will lock herself away upstairs and watch the streets. She will be safe enough.* The sprites clung to him as the wind got nasty. "Thank you for coming," he said, and he unbuttoned his coat a bit to allow some of them a safer place to hold on. Someone slipped into his pocket, another, he felt the weight of them at his lapel, another close to his collar. He regretted bringing the hat, for the wind kept trying to rip it away, so he clamped it down with one hand. The sprites were clinging to him hard so he knew there was something about the wind, something vile and un-controlled. He could feel it, vibrating in his teeth. The bones of his hand ached harshly as the wind bit into the joints, and he gave up and shoved the hat under his arm.

Roderick Ayers caught up with him near the Angel Street Vista Warehouse. "The wind is wrong, sir!" were the first words he said. "I remember this wind, don't you?" Ayers had served under him when he'd been a captain, and left the sea when he did. William liked the man immensely, and hired him when he could for small jobs. It was good to have him at his side.

They clumped down the cobblestones. Down at the pier people were gathered, looking out to the sea. William could not discern anything, except..."The wind is screaming."

"Sounds like a woman wailing her soul out."

When he was a captain, he and his ship had fought an-other ship, a ship who sailed surrounded by a screaming, vi-cious wind. "Like the Pandora," he said softly. He remembered, distantly, stories of death that followed when that ship put into port. He turned to ask Ayers what he thought, but was smacked in the cheek.

*Not wind. Ghosts. Get everyone inside! That is death!* One of the sprites screamed in his ear. He looked to the sea and saw a dark fog rolling towards them, reaching up towards the partial moon. He felt his jaw drop as dread filled him. He shook himself.

"We have to get everyone inside, now. Break open the door to the warehouse if you have to...that is the best place to get so many people in." He thrust the lantern into Ayer's hand. "Signal the all clear when you're in."

"Aye, Captain." Ayers turned and ran to do his former cap-tain's bidding without pause.

He ran down to the group that had gathered on the shore. "Everyone in, now! Run to the warehouse."

"What's going on, Captain Almsley?"

The man was familiar, but William could not recall his name. "I believe that a ghost wind is heading towards us. We must get inside. Now. Head up to the warehouse!" He could see the lantern, waving back and forth up by the lower doors.

"Ghost winds aren't real," someone protested.

"Don't be stupid. Of course they are," Luisa the cobbler's daughter said. "Everyone listen to Master Almsley! Get inside, get behind as much stone and wood as possible."

Ahead someone was yelling, "And sit on the dirt floor. You'll be safer then."

The word was being passed, but William didn't hear it. People brushed past them as they rushed up to the warehouse, and he knew he needed to join them, but he felt rooted. A wall of rippling fog was swirling across the waters, reaching the outer ring of ships. It was almost pretty, the gold and green swirl that peeked out from behind the black clouds of fog, but as it overtook the ships, one by one the lights disappeared and were replaced by the screams of the dying.

He stood there, frozen, knowing that his old ship was out there, wanting to do something to save the men who had once served under him, to save his ship. "Will it stop before it reaches land?"

*Inside!*

Suddenly, he was being tugged, hard, and William turned and ran up the hill, encouraging lingerers to keep moving. He thought he could see boats bobbing along, desperately heading towards land. If a warehouse was safe, you would think that the deep thick hull of a ship was safe, but it was not so, and no one knew why. William thought it was the connection to land that protected them, walls built in the dirt, stone-bound was even better. He urged people to sit down, to huddle in the middle, where the wood and stone would protect them, as the warehouse doors were shut and barred. *Tasmin is smart. She will be inside, and the shop is stone and wood and strong, and she will know what to do.*

He could hear the sailors screaming, even across the water, and as he sank down one of the pillars that held the massive roof up over their heads, he found himself trying not to weep.

"What's killing them, Captain?" an old salt asked. William saw him, sometimes, fishing in a small boat. His pale eyes glittered in the light from the lanterns that people had brought in.

"Fear."

"It doesn't seem to be getting any closer." Luisa said. He listened and she was right, the noise of the wind did not seem to be getting louder, the buffeting on the building did not seem to be getting any stronger.

He heard banging on the door and he got up, unbarred it despite some protests, and let some men, soaked from the sea, in. A few boats had made shore and he held his heart in his throat as he watched a few more sailors run up the hill. His eyes kept flickering back to the storm.

"You hold that open much longer, we'll all die!"

"It's not moving. We have a minute!" he yelled over his shoulder. A hand landed on his shoulder, and he met the man's eye. "Can you leave them to die?" he snarled. "We're still safe, at least for a moment."

The other man looked away and he yelled to the sailors, "Hurry! We have to shut the door!" And he watched them run, even as he watched the ghost storm, ever so slowly, creep closer to shore.

The bells stirred Ailiani out of a perfectly agreeable dream. She lay there, frozen. *You have to get up. You have to do something.* So she rolled out of bed, her book hitting the floor with a thud. She wrapped her patchwork quilt around her.

She barely had time to shove her feet into slippers before she was out in the main hall, helping to put shutters over the windows.

"We need to go down into the cellar." Miss Dovlington said. "Grab blankets to wrap yourselves in and get below." Ailiani helped her lift the heavy trap door and people were ushered down into the dark hole. No one was entirely dressed, but if they were all packed tightly it should be warm enough.

"Mistress Deitson?" Miss Dovlington started down the stairs. "Come now."

Ailiani froze again, looking down at the frightened, pale faces, and shook her head. But fear was not entirely what kept her from going down. She kept hearing something in the wind, something seemed to be calling her, in the very least inviting her to come out, come take a look. She kept looking out over her shoulder, towards the door, listening.

Ailiani ignored Miss Dovlington, taking a step towards the door.

"We must go below, now. Ailiani?" She looked back, and Miss Dovlington waved at her, held out her hand.

Everything in her being itched. She felt the prickle of magic running along her skin, raising her hair. "Go on. I think…I feel like I can do something, and I must go and see if it is so."

"That is madness, child!"

Ailiani smiled at the other woman. "I will come back if I can do nothing. Go now, you don't need to risk yourself for me."

The wind cut into her immediately, tempting her to turn back. The cellar would be dark, but the press of bodies would be warm, at least, and she wavered for a moment before she shut the door firmly behind her. On the horizon a storm was raging. Despite the colors flickering in and out of the clouds, despite the magnificence of the lightning that flickered through it, watching it made her feel sick with terror. The wind pulled at her, yanked her hair almost painfully, and she followed the pull, stumbling down the path. The wind was getting worse as she neared the edge of the water, and she swallowed heavily.

Her father had seen a ghost storm, once; she remembered him speaking about it in hushed tones as she and her brother sat at his feet. *It rips your soul right out through your eyes*, he'd said. She placed a quilt filled hand over her heart, as if she could grip her soul and fight for it to stay put. The colors, the lightning crashing, the clouds…it was all made up of souls, and she could see it, focusing on the ships that lay in the harbor. Boats were in the water, trying to get away. Men were trying to make the shore.

*It will come here.* She let the quilt drop, it blew away from her and caught in the brush. *And they will never make it. Even if they get to the shore, where will they go?* She kicked off her slippers, never letting her eyes leave the storm, burying her toes in the freezing sand and pushing the pain that cut into her bones resolutely. She wished her brother was here. They had not always agreed. *But it would be good to have you here now.* What would her father do? What would her brother do? Or the wise old women in the village, keeping their mysteries safe from the prying eyes of men, pretending that women had no magic of their own?

She slowly, lowly, began to sing, tapping her right foot out, in, out, and then she drew from herself, pulled everything she had into one shining effort, and danced out a pattern. She had never tried anything so complicated. In her land, women were never allowed to do the higher magics, not like this, it took away too much of what they had. A woman could make herself barren, pulling so much magic from herself, it was said.

The woman on the strand no longer felt cold. She no longer saw the storm that wavered over the ships, as if deciding what to do now that dinner was over. She was in a different place, a place of summer grasses and mountains far away, but the colors were all leached out, the world was in shades of gray, even the high, wide sun. She danced the pattern, and could feel someone with her, someone who corrected her as she faltered, who helped her keep the pattern true.

It was a pattern of everything. *I will protect you,* she told the sailors, she told the women huddling in the cellar behind her. *The storms will not come, not to my land.*

She did not see that the pattern in the sand glowed bright blue, she did not see the line of blue flame that went along the edge of the sand. Did not see the storm falter and fade away as it went back out into the sea.

Ailiani stopped abruptly, shaking. She forced herself to step out of the pattern, taking a couple of feeble steps before she fell, away from the pattern.

"Come now, child." She was being lifted up, shaken gently as someone wrapped her up. She was being rubbed through the fabric of a heavy blanket as someone tried to bring heat back into her. Grains of sand were being dusted off her bare feet.

"Why are you rubbing her feet off? Get her shoes back on!" Miss Dovlington snapped.

"I don't suppose she wants sandy feet, do you?" Phoebe said. She was the young woman who lived in the room next to Ailiani.

Miss Dovlington sighed and shook her gently. "You must wake, we need to get you back inside."

Ailiani opened crusted eyes and tried to ask about the storm, but it came out as a shivery moan. Once the shoes were back on her feet, she was able, with the help of Miss Dovlington and Phoebe, to stand back up. She looked over her shoulder.

"Whatever it was you did, I think it worked," Miss Dovlington said.

"You're a hero," Phoebe added.

"No," Ailiani said, her voice rough and dried out, but this time you could understand her words. "No one must know. It is not for others to know."

"But..." Phoebe said, "The life you could have!"

"Not. For. Others," she said firmly, shivering against Miss Dovlington's formidable bosom.

"We will keep your secret, won't we Phoebe?" She rubbed Ailiani's back again through the cloth.

"Of course," the younger girl said, but her look told Ailiani that she thought her crazed.

She just had to hope that the wind sprite tangled in her hair would keep her secret as well.

Tasmin stared at the closed door for a moment, then turned and headed for the kitchen. Behind her the shutters were slamming over the windows as the wind sprites secured their home. Tasmin barred the door between the kitchen and shop, anyway.

*No sense making it easy on them,* she thought. "Dratted pirates, making trouble in the middle of the night." She slid a chair over to the counter and climbed onto the seat, reaching for the rifle Ailiani had reached for only a few days previous. "People should be asleep, not plundering."

*Not pirates,* Nee-no said to her.

She turned her head slightly towards him. He settled on her shoulder. "Then what?" She asked.

There was a great sadness upon her suddenly, and she knew it came from him, sadness and fear. *Something I do not want to show you, but I must.*

"Very well," she said. "Let me get my cloak."

She took no light, which was fine until they got a little away from town. The trees rose up along either side of the road, and the world got darker and darker. She allowed herself to be pulled by the sprites, herded, picked up and carried even for small, quick bursts, speeding her away from town. The docks were behind her, to the left, and even further away was Miss Dovlington's boarding house.

They herded her off the main road, down a path that led, she knew, to the Pemberton Overlook. *You could have showed me the sea in town,* she wanted to say, instead she walked over to the very edge. The sliver of the moon showed down, cold and hard, onto the fog covered sea. The wind whipped it along, throwing it upon the shore, then pulling back, like the tide.

*The Ghost Winds. It is not powerful enough to come in. Someone is pushing them back, but that will not work for long. If the winds get more powerful they will be much harder to stop. For now the sprites can help push the winds away.*

*But not if they get much more powerful* did not need to be added. Tasmin stepped closer to the edge, considering what was in front of her. She splayed her hands out a little away from her, waist high. "I can undo it, can't I? When I was traveling with my aunt, I could, with your help, mold the wind...I can reach in." She stared at the fog, hard, almost afraid to reach out and touch it. She flexed her hands and thought about the unraveling.

She wanted her box, her herbs, her stones and spells and tools, but they would not work here. She needed help, others to cast with her and push against the storm. "We can take it apart."

*You are not yet strong enough. You will become one of them.*
"Them?"

*The storm will pull your soul right from your body, upon your death the Iechee will be swept away.*

*And then,* she thought, *the town would lose its protection.* The loss of protection would not matter long, for the town would be destroyed. Some of the people would survive, but it depended on how long the storm lingered, how powerful it was by landfall.

Tasmin stayed very still, staring out at the sea, at the wall of fog, reaching out her hands as if by her own will she could break the wall. Rusty, half remembered spell-paths inside of her were forced awake, and she reached out to the storm, felt it.

Tasmin backed away quickly.

"Someone called that thing to being. Do you know who?" Tasmin asked Nee-no.

*No. And it does not feel like the ghost storms we have fought in the past.*

*Well, fie,* Tasmin thought, but was too wise and too polite to say it. She wanted to investigate more…was there a witch out there, now, working the weather? Was someone doing something suspicious, even if it was just to enjoy the havoc they'd wrought? But her main concern was getting home before William. She didn't worry about William being cranky. William would usually sulk in silence for a bit, then get over it. But the self-conscious part of her, the new wife, did not want to risk changing his opinion of her. "Can you take me home?" she whispered. "Or is there more?"

*Is this not enough?* In answer she was lifted a little, and she and the sprites whirled down the slope. She was delicately set on the front step of the shop, and she forced herself to ignore her nausea—she thought perhaps she had left her stomach up on the point—and let herself in. She wondered if she should talk to Carys, suggest evacuating the town as she secured the door and listened.

No William. That was good. She checked the house and took the rifle to her post upstairs. Nee-no and the sprites left her, but she was too taken up with worry to pay much attention.

*Why* no William? Should he not be back by now? She had no idea, really, how much time her trip had taken. *The storm was far from shore. Surely he was nowhere near the storm's reach?*

She went into their room. Maybe she would see him, trudging up the hill. The room was horribly cold, after she checked the street she would stoke the fire.

"There you are. I wondered where you got to. I thought, surely, William will ask her to stay home, surely, she will listen to her husband, who she fought so hard for."

A shade of a woman sat on the bed, but this one did not flicker. She was just a breath of shadow, but Tasmin knew her voice.

"Franny?"

"Got it in one. But you always were such a sharp girl, weren't you?"

Tasmin clutched the rifle tightly. Parts of it were made of iron, if she swung it at the ghost, would it hurt her? Did ghosts dislike iron, or was that some other monster? Maybe it was silver? *Pity they don't warn you ahead of time so you have time to research.*

"Don't you wish to know why I'm here?"

"No," Tasmin said, "I just want you gone."

The shade moved to the window. Tasmin could see her a little better in the dull moonlight. "Pity, I was hoping that we could catch up, since we're practically family and all. Oh, well." She used her chin to point to the harbor. "The barrier won't last forever, you know."

"Why has someone called the ghost storm? What is it for?"

"Fun? Personal enrichment? Revenge?" The shadow shrugged. "I'm just here to tweak your nose. I was so angry when I died and you know, I never really got over it. But it is so powerful. Oh, to know someone who could harness that much power."

"Tasmin?" William was down on the street below.

"I'll be down in a moment," she said, backing away from the window, but unwilling to put down the weapon.

"Well, I'll be off then. Perhaps I'll offer my help to whomever created that beautiful storm outside. Perhaps I'll go kill someone. Pity you won't know how in time to stop me. It'll just be another angry woman in a town full of them." She wiggled her fingers and faded out of view.

Tasmin muttered something unkind before tromping down the stairs, unbarring the doors and standing aside for William. "We are putting in ghost wards. And I don't mean that as a gentle suggestion. Ghost wards."

"Yes," William said, barring the door carefully. "Yes, that would be a good idea. What do you need for them?"

"No questions? What happened?"

"A ghost storm has come to our shores...you know of them?"

Tasmin nodded. "They mention it in the forbidden magic portion of our training. Anyone caught creating or drawing a ghost storm will be held accounted as a murderer."

William looked impressed. "Did they happen to cover stopping them?"

"I have just told you everything I know." She felt quite grim.

"It seems to have faded away for now, but a half dozen ships seem to have fallen silent. No bells. Hailing them from the shore seems to do no good. Some men made it, they either used boats or swam to the shore, but it was too late for the farthest ships. I'll be joining a crew of men going over there in a few hours, when morning comes."

She hugged herself. "Are you sure that is needed?"

"One of them's the *Tregaurde*." He named his old ship. "I have already told my father that I shall be going to see it."

"Oh, William," she whispered, "if the stories are right..."

"If they are right then I will have new nightmares to occupy my mind at night."

"Just what you needed."

He placed his hands on her shoulders and brought her close, kissing her forehead, before bringing her against his chest.

She hugged him back as tightly as she could, pressing herself into his warmth. She felt him shift and reluctantly let go.

Tasmin followed him to the stairs.

"When will you start work?" William asked as he placed a foot on the first step.

"As soon as you leave. I will do the shop front first, before we open, then I shall work my spells as I can."

He nodded. "I am going to go and try and get warm," he said softly, and she stayed put, listening to his tread up the stairs, then stepped back out into the middle of the shop space.

It was very still, out in the shop. She closed her eyes and felt around, spreading her awareness. When you knew a space well enough it became easier. At home she used to be able to find the mice nests, the holes in the wood, though now, because of the sprites, mice did not come to their home. Tasmin concentrated on the sprites, and slowly she could make them out, counting the little sprite heart beats. She thought a couple were missing. "Old Father?" she whispered. "Is all well with your children?" But he did not answer.

She stood there for a long time, thinking. She wished she'd talked to William about Franny, about the warning. She wanted help figuring out what to do, but instead, she stood there in the silence and darkness, and worried.

# Chapter Nine

The fog had a much different texture the next morning, but still, no one wanted to be touched by it. Even William shivered as the perfectly mundane white-gray tendrils brushed his face.

Along the shore, ships sat at anchor, moving with the waves, looking as if nothing were wrong. But you knew there was something amiss. It was too silent, the ships too still. Boats and bodies were bobbing in the water, the only living presence the Navy's narrow, sleek little longboats slipping in and out, bringing men up from the sea.

As some boats and corpses reached the shore of their own accord, men hauled them the rest of the way in. There was a steady pile of the dead in William's warehouse, their faces carefully covered. The rescued boats made a neat line along the shore.

The men on the strand behind him were talking about waiting, see if the sun would burn off the fog. It was, William knew, a way to throw the cost of recovery on the Navy, rather than spend their own money and effort. No one held any illusions. There was no one waiting to be helped. It did not matter.

But it mattered to William. He did not want to wait, spend his day pacing the shore, waiting to be allowed to go see his old command, his old crew.

"They don't get it, do they, Captain?"

"Will you ever call me William?" he asked Roderick Ayers.

"Not likely, sir."

"Well, Mister Ayers, I agree, they don't understand. None of them have connections to the ships out there, not like we do."

"Fairly champin' at the bit to get out there, I am. What about you, sir?"

He nodded. "Champing at the bit, indeed." He looked at his father, standing next to a couple of the other men who owned warehouses along the port. He sighed. The last thing he wanted to do was deal with his father.

Correction: second last. He knocked on the wood of the hull, then turned to join the group, Ayers trailing behind him.

"Father," William said when there was an opening. "I shall take a few men out. There is really no point in waiting."

His father, a grim and demanding man who dominated the circle of fellow merchants, glared at his eldest. He looked like he wanted to form a remark of some sort, no doubt somewhat cutting, as he had not forgiven William anything that he had done in the past year or so, but changed his mind. "If you can find enough foolish souls to go with you, I will not stop you."

William fought the desire to bow, but inclined his head slightly, and marched to the shore. Ayers started gathering up men. There were some who had friends aboard the ships, and were as impatient as the former men of the *Tregaurde*. Oars were gathered from the pile at the shore, and soon they were pushing a boat into the water. He was the first on, the cold feel of the water in his boots familiar and nostalgic, as was the scramble as the men boarded the craft and took their seats.

"To the *Tregaurde*, then," he said to Ayers, who relayed the message. The perks of once having been, and still having the honorary title of Captain, William had to admit, was that no one even questioned but they should go to the *Tregaurde* first.

They passed other ships on the way, each one slowly coming out of the fog, unwrapping like a present. There was no sound but the water and an occasional whisper, the morning seemed sacred and no one wanted to draw undue attention from any ghosts that still lingered in the silence.

Some of the ships were closer to the shore, and their crews had made it to safety, their men had already returned to the ships, now quietly attending to their duties. William tipped his hat to a fellow Captain who was walking his deck, and received a salute back. At another ship, someone was using a boat hook to bring an abandoned boat alongside.

The fog parted and finally, the *Tregaurde* came into view. She was a plain little thing. The stag figurehead was not so fierce as it once was, but worn to a more doleful expression. She could use some fresh paint and new sails, but her lines were strong and she seemed to dance if the right hands were on her wheel. It caught his heart a little, seeing her lines softened by tendrils of mist.

"Ahoy, ship!" Ayers called out. "*Tregaurde*, look lively, there!"

Which, was not the most kind thing to say, really, for no one answered the hallos, and William knew that no one left on the ship would ever look lively, or even peaceful, again. They drew up alongside, and he caught the wood steps built into the hull and pulled himself up. He grabbed the top rail of the deck and heaved himself over, stepping upon the boards and moving aside in case anyone followed him. The *Tregaurde* had been the first to have been hit, and from the longboats still in their places, the ropes untouched, William understood that the attack had been very swift. He forced himself away from the rail and crossed the fresh scrubbed deck. There was a man, his Captain's coat half on, as if he had dressed himself while running above decks. William knelt and turned him over, the look of horror that twisted the dead man's face piercing his heart. He knew that this man was a former first mate he'd proudly promoted to become captain in his stead.

"What happened to them?" one of the men asked, looking a bit green around the face.

"They were frightened to death, if the stories are true. A ghost storm…one of those hasn't hit in years, centuries even." He left the rest off, it seemed too horrid, standing on the deck, looking at men he'd known well. "Pray for their souls, if you would." He pulled the Captain's coat off and placed it over his face, hiding the expression, trying to replace it in his mind's eye with how he'd last seen the man.

"They were a relic of the war, if you pardon me saying, sir," Ayers said. "The angry dead were used to attack the North. It was one of the atrocities that cost us our magic, so it were said."

"Using people's own dead against them is never a wise thing," William muttered, looking at the bodies that lay across the deck, wondering who else he knew, and dreading it.

Ayers came close. "Are you going to check on your father's cargo? 'Tis why they were out, they were to leave with the favoring tide this morn."

"Hang my father's cargo," William said bitterly.

"I understand the sentiment, as it were, but he'll hang you if you don't look."

William smothered a sigh and did not, despite his strong desire, shoot Ayers a glare for his trouble, but rose to his feet and said, "Go ahead and check the other ships if you will, Master Wilkes? I have need to check on some things where we are here." The greenish looking man nodded and all the men, save Ayers, left.

"Kind of you to stay, Master Ayers."

"Well, sir, I can't say that I would feel comfortable leaving you alone. It breaks my heart, to see the *Tregaurde* become a death barge."

William went below, working his way down to the hold. "You don't think they'll let her sail again, do you?"

"No, Captain. They wouldn't dare, you know how superstitious the men are."

William placed a loving hand on the wood work of a doorway. "Then I shall bring her in. When they have checked the other ships over, we can weigh anchor."

"But where will they let us put her? I know we needs must unload the cargo, tainted by haunts as it is, but I can't imagine they will let them so close to shore."

"Then what would they have us do? Burn the ships, the men, at sea?"

Ayers paused. "There are doubtless some here who would prefer it."

Below, there were more bodies, but no other surprises. He stopped, for a moment on the way back above, to look in his old cabin, cramped and neat. "She served us well, didn't she, Ayers?"

"Aye, she did indeed."

Tasmin, for her part, was putting together ghost wards. She had not slept well, and the dawn found her making a concoction in a wooden bucket. She painted the door frame first, then the window frames, determined to get the main rooms done and dried before customers came in.

"I did not know you were making such a hobby out of heights," Ailiani said as she hung her cloak up. Tasmin was on a ladder, trying to paint along the molding, the combination of lavender and garlic giving her a hideous headache. She rolled her eyes, though Ailiani could not see.

"Oh, heavens and light, what is that stench?" Ailiani asked as she got closer. She drew the ends of a shawl over her nose and mouth. "This place smells like sweet rotted onions. We might as well not even open today, who would buy anything from a place that smelled thusly?"

Tasmin got down, carefully, for despite her recent adventures she did not care for even the smallest of heights.

"It must be the moly. Moly and garlic mixed together are really too much." Tasmin stretched. "Only the baseboards to do, and the shop will be sealed."

"May I open some windows?"

Tasmin thought about what she had learned from her readings that morning. "It should be fine, go ahead." She knelt down by the baseboards and went back to work, painting, chanting, painting some more. It faded nicely into the wood so there was no staining for people to stare at, though here and there she could see a few faint sparkles of silver caught in the sunlight.

The shop went from cozy to freezing in a manner of seconds, but Tasmin had to admit the fresh air made her headache feel better.

"Do you feel like explaining the reason for this horrid odor?"

Tasmin looked up at her, struck by how un-Ailiani-like Ailiani sounded. She had never heard her friend sound truly cross before. "'Tis the start of my ghost wards. We had a visitor yesterday."

"A ghost, here? One of the wise women?"

"No, Franny Harker. Of all people to be haunted by."

"I take my objections back. If this will keep the ghost of that harlot away, then I suggest that we all bathe in it regularly."

Tasmin laughed. "Do not worry, I have some strewing herbs put by, you can use them in the shop and it will sweeten it. I'll give them to you before I start on the charms." She stood back up with the help of the counter. "Are you well, my dear? You seem a bit peaked."

"Who could sleep well with the ghost storm going on? We hid like a bunch of children in the cellar of Miss Dovlington's. It was not a good night."

Tasmin studied her carefully. Peaked has been a kind assessment. "Maybe you should go back to bed for a bit. You look like you've not slept in ages."

"No, I will be fine. I cannot help you work your magic, so I will run the shop." There was something very final in her words, so Tasmin smiled and did not push. Instead she made her most restorative tea, adding more honey than most humans could stand, and took it over to Ailiani. She'd prepared herself a brazier and was standing over it, a cold, miserable thing in too many shawls and scarves.

Tasmin continued on, painting, chanting, painting some more. When the bucket was empty she rinsed it out thoroughly and put it outside. Strewing herbs were hung to sweeten the shop and bed chamber. Tasmin started dinner, a stew that she could mostly ignore, save giving it a good stir from time to time, then toasted some bread and spread butter over it. She prepared a tray with some honey, meat and cheese, and took it out to the counter.

"No one has come in yet," Ailiani said. "I suspect this will not be a good day for us." She eyed the tray as Tasmin pushed it over to her.

"I've never seen you look so uncertain about lunch," Tasmin said, only half teasing.

Ailiani shrugged and drizzled honey on some toast, eating it so listlessly that Tasmin forced her to endure being checked for a fever.

"I am fine, just tired."

"But who knows what you might be coming down with. One of those women in the cellar might have had a cold and now you have it, too."

Ailiani shook her head. "Will you offer to ghost-ward other places, too?"

Tasmin shook her head. "I am only trying to keep Franny, or any other ghosts, out. The best thing we could do to protect the townspeople from the ghost storm, probably, is evacuate. During the war whole villages would be abandoned while people hid in caves to put as much stone and earth between themselves and the storms as possible."

"I don't think there is a cave system close enough, save for the sea caves, and no one would want to stay there—the damp and cold would probably kill more people than it saved." Ailiani played with her toast some more. "I explored it last summer.

There are rooms. Some of them are somewhat large, but there isn't enough floor space for the whole town."

"It's also dangerous to get inside of. Why ever did you go exploring there?"

Ailiani laughed a little. "Boredom. I cannot bear to be bored." She shrugged. "Anyway, what do you think Carys will suggest the mayor do?"

"I don't know. It depends on what brought the storm here. There is a good chance that the ghost storm would follow us should we leave." Tasmin stood up and stretched. "I suppose I'd best go to my work room. Perhaps I can find some answers."

Despite her worry, stepping into the small work room was like getting a gentle hug. Someday she would give it up to make it into a nursery, but for now she took comfort in having her own space. It was small enough that the window illuminated the whole of it rather well, especially the broad table that took up a good part of one side. Shelves were crammed in every available space, over-stuffed with books, jars, boxes and assorted trinkets from William's travels.

Normally, the work table was always neat. Habit had taught her to clean up after she was done for the day and place everything back where it belonged, but recently the table was organized in little piles. Piles of Wise Woman stuff sat next to the work box she took with her from place to place. Piles of her research, which seemed to be getting interrupted more and more. A pile from this morning's work. She stretched and took time to clean up what she could and put it away, using the somewhat mindless task to clear her mind.

She reminded herself, as she disassembled a pile of books, herbs, and little jars that she mentally had been calling the "stuff to make for the shop" pile, that the room was small and she could find things that were put away quite quickly.

When the things were all either put away or gone through and re-stacked, she washed the table carefully. Once she was convinced that both she and the surface were ready, she took down a box made up of small drawers that she had found at a rummage-shop. It had been a jewelry box, and had lots of narrow, shallow drawers that were perfect for holding most of her amulet-making supplies. It went on the table next to the window, and was joined by silver wire and some tools. Tasmin ran her hands over the spines of her books and pulled down one on stone lore, making notes. She dug through a couple more volumes until she felt like she had the pieces of the puzzle in her head. That was her day, bending silver and weaving in stone and intention and will. And listening. And worrying about what Franny might be up to. By the time she was finished with half a dozen of the amulets, that was the focus of her thoughts.

She pushed aside the tray she'd been using as a work surface and rubbed her eyes. *Someone angry.* Anger had been a theme with Franny, so Tasmin went and pulled down every source she had on ghosts. But, much to her chagrin, she got nowhere.

Something that William had said to her once, in passing, poked at her. She could hear him reading a passage to her about ghosts. Tasmin hadn't paid much attention to anything but the warm timbre of his voice, but she definitely remembered that it was about ghosts.

In their bedroom William had created a little reading nook, a huge, comfortable (if a bit thread worn) chair and a pair of book cases by the fireplace. Tasmin sat in his chair and pulled down a volume of Creighton's.

The irony of the situation wasn't lost on her as she rested the heavy book on her lap and started looking through. She'd often called Creighton a crackpot, and teased William for his love of the worthless folklore and second hand accounts that Creighton swore was fact. She hated the idea of how his stories and tales changed people's perceptions of magic, how it seemed to cheapen it. Still, she had to admit, it did not take her long to find the information she was seeking. Whether it was right or not was another story.

*It is unsure what started the Ghost Storms,* he wrote, *but it is known that they first emerged during the Great War between the Northern and Southern parts of our great kingdom. Before this time the North and the South had lived together quite peaceably until the war, and it seemed that all kindness that had ever happened was forgotten, and only hate remained, so that there was no trick, no deed, that was too awful to contemplate or commit to. Thus is was said that the South used their magic to gather the souls of the angry dead, the mothers who watched their children die terrible deaths, the husbands who knew their wives died screaming...and set them on their enemies.*

*But, ghosts are souls, and souls cannot be controlled. Fortunately, they can be redirected, and if a fragment of this storm is found, and the way to destroy it not available (See The Forceless, vol. IV) then one must send it back to where there are no people, or at least a smaller concentration. A desert, a particularly unpleasant part of the ocean, all these are safe.*

*In our times, Ghost Storms or Ghost Winds come randomly, drawn usually by what created them. The person who is dying needs to be angry, for the soul needs to be angry to draw the Ghost Storm near. And they have to be powerful, for the Ghost Storm to sense it. Usually a mass murder or war.*

Tasmin looked up from her reading. There hadn't been, she hoped, a mass murder, so what had attracted the storm? She leaned forward, looking at the bookshelves again. William bought his books piece-meal, not in order, so it did not surprise her that four volumes were missing. "Drat it all," she muttered.

She ran down the stairs just as the front door opened. "You're back!" she said to William. He was just shrugging out of his coat, smelling like the sea. "Why don't you have volume four of Creighton's?" She took the coat from him, smoothing it over her arm.

He paused, and for a moment had the look of a man treading on dangerous territory. "Well, you seemed to think the books were so wretched I never bought the rest."

She shook her head at him. "How could you allow your wife to shame you out of buying a perfectly good book?" She started to put on his coat, then shook her head and went over to the pegs and traded his coat for her cloak.

"Because she mocks me constantly as I read it and explains to me why everything he says is complete and utter poppycock?"

"Oh, William. Poor darling." She pinned her cloak securely. "I don't suppose you have any funds on you? I need to go buy that book."

"Now?"

"It cannot wait even a second."

He put his own coat back on. "Well, 'tis a long walk, and I shall join you, and perhaps we can catch each other up on things."

"Lovely idea, dear." She shot an apologetic look to Ailiani, who waved them away. Once the door shut, she said, "I hate to leave her, she does not look well at all. She says it was a hard night for her, of no sleep at all since apparently Miss Dovlington—was there ever a woman more poorly named?—made them all go into the cellar."

"You're worried?" he asked, offering his arm. At her nod, he said, "We shall send her home the moment we return, then, perhaps she can get some sleep. She will need to be well rested. Nothing good can come from recent events. Nothing at all."

"Was anyone left alive on your ship?"

He shuddered. "No."

"I am sorry." She stroked his arm. "I was afraid of that. No one knows precisely what happens inside of a ghost storm, because no one ever survives one. They seem to literally frighten people to death. *It will pull your soul out through your eyes*, Nee-no had said. She shuddered. "I was reading in your book that ghost storms were originally created from angry souls and that more angry souls draw them."

"So, the ghost storm is coming to claim angry souls that we have floating around?" William frowned.

She shrugged. "I suppose that could be a theory, but..." She paused. "There are some holes I need to fill. For one, how does one make a person angry enough to stick around and become part of this storm? Are ghosts naturally angry spirits?"

William directed her down an alley short cut. "I do not see a little girl being a particularly angry ghost. Sad, yes, confused, most certainly."

"How they are murdered must have a part in it. Make them angry before they die?" She shrugged helplessly. "That seems so impossible to predict. Franny, Franny I get."

William stopped in mid step, which caused her to stop abruptly because she was attached to him in more ways than one.

"Franny Harker?"

"Yes." She attempted to smile at him. "I forgot to tell you that Franny Harker visited last night."

"There are so many questions I could ask you right now."

"Like why I waited until now to tell you?"

"But I have a feeling that the answers would just frustrate me."

"Oh, doubtless. Shall I continue, then?"

"Oh, please do."

She swatted his arm lightly to show that she had marked his sarcasm, "Anyway, the important thing, the thing I am trying to unravel, is exactly what Franny was saying. She told me that she was there to tweak my nose. She also seemed to not know who called the storm, but she seemed to admire whomever did. And last, but not least, she said perhaps she would kill someone." Tasmin sighed. "I don't know how much she meant. I don't know how to find her. I am terrified that someone is about to meet their end and I could have done something."

His hand was warm on her back, comforting. "Did she give you any clues?"

"Anger seems to be a big theme with her. She said something like, another angry woman in a town full of them?" Tasmin chewed her lip. "So, someone angry, someone no one would miss?"

He waited for a cart to pass, then started across the street. "Magda?" he asked.

She frowned at him.

"The Pandrazzi woman who just lost her child. She fits the profile that we're forming, a woman with Talent, and someone who is very, very angry."

"Talent?" Tasmin asked.

He opened the door to the Fredeburg Book Shop. "A fire-starter."

"Oh, great. And she's probably angry at me. Lovely. I have a fire starter angry at me." She decided not to tell William how Magda glared at her the day before.

He laughed.

"I wouldn't laugh," she said. "You live in an old building filled with dried herbs and books." This did not sober him, so she asked, "How did you find that out?"

"I asked Ayers on the way back to shore. It was good to have something unrelated to the *Tregaurde* to speak of. "

She paused in the book shop, breathing deeply. It did not have a large selection of books, and so it was not hard for William to find what they came for. "Here we are. Volume Four, you said?" His voice was quite absent as he studied the contents. She felt a little guilty about how she had teased him about his reading and resolved to stop.

"You might as well get Volume Seven too. And that one... there. That matches the spines of your other books, better."

She could feel him studying her. "It costs more."

"Not that much," she mumbled, pulling a book out on flower lore. It was very general and not to her interest, but it was something to pretend to look at. He kissed her fiercely on the cheek. "Besides, since it's for my research for once, I can hardly say anything against him again, can I?"

"Oh, at least for a week. Is there anything else?"

She looked at the shelves. The beauty of being in a port town was that people brought in the strangest books and traded them for others. She could have spent a couple of hours studying it out, but shook her head.

"Should we speak to her?" she asked when they were back on the street again.

"Yes, but I am unsure how to approach her. What do we say?" He dodged around a couple standing in the middle of the sidewalk. "My wife, who is convinced that you are angry at her, thinks that you may be the target of a murderous ghost and her accomplice?"

"Oh, you make it sound so improbable!"

"Tasmin." He waited until she was looking up at him. "I believe you."

She smiled at him. It was only slightly forced. "Thank you." She squared her shoulders. "I saw her at the market yesterday. I think she works for one of the shell-fish mongers."

They headed towards the market. "I am told that she gathers shell fish for a living. It is her main income," William said.

"It does not seem like it would be entirely easy or rewarding." Tasmin said, imagining her out along the shore with a bucket, trying to gather things from the shallows.

They ventured in among the booths. An Ebengene seller, his cart full of the spiced, fried nuts that were a delicacy among the sailors, tried to tempt William.

"I haven't seen those in ages," he said.

"Oh, those are awful," Tasmin stated.

"Awfully delicious," William rejoined.

"Then you should get some."

"Ah, but if I get these licorice sweets, we both can have some."

She brushed her cheek against his arm. "Well, there is that."

Not far down the path, the shell-fish monger was announcing his wares to passers-by. Tasmin caught his attention. "Is Magda here?"

The surly owner shook his head. "Never seen her today. And unless you intend to buy something, you don't need to be here, either."

"My, how ever do you stay in business?" Tasmin asked, never willing to take that much attitude from anyone.

"I am the cheapest and the best." He put a tray filled with fat oysters and clams on the table before her.

She looked at the tray, looked at him, and shook her head slightly as she allowed William to lead her away.

Their adventure took them to the less prosperous part of Azin Shore. The old brick walks were cracked and would be replaced come spring when the upper part of town had walks repaired by new bricks. They never got anything new, in this section, and it made everything look ground down, a little less cared for. Factories and second tier warehouses (none with the Almsley badge) dominated, making streets seem small and oppressive. There was plenty of room to walk through, yet she felt like hunching her shoulders in.

Fishermen kept their houses close to the waters they tended, since smugglers and pirates had made the romantic idea of a seaside home seem quite foolish. So the poor built their small homes on the land left over.

"Ayers lives near here, towards the naval yards. He says it suits his needs. I think he likes being closer to the sea. He sees many of his old friends."

"Why did he quit sailing?"

William paused. "I am not altogether sure. I am also not altogether sure where Mistress Magda's home is. I was only there the once, during the search." He paused, as if trying to discern which street he felt was the most familiar, then turned left.

There was a row of houses, then one, by itself, a tiny yard around it, more sand than dirt, marked by rocks and stones neatly lined up. It was about as close to the shore as one could get without the tide causing havoc to the tiny, ramshackle little hovel. It looked as if she had built it herself with whatever materials had come to shore.

William knocked on the door and they waited, listening closely. Tasmin even found herself holding her breath, hoping to catch the hint of any sign of life. A cup being put down, a chair being pushed back, bed ropes creaking...William tried again, pounding a little louder, while Tasmin walked around, wanting to peek into the windows. They were covered in oil paper rather than glass and she nudged a loose corner aside so she could see. Nothing really telling, except for silence, underscored by the sound of the waves.

She turned and joined William, shaking her head. "She does not strike me as someone who can miss work, at least not without sorting it out with her employer beforehand."

William nodded slowly. The bank of huge buildings behind them made for an extremely overwhelming task. She could be anywhere. "But there is no sign that she was taken. She could very well have just decided to leave."

"Her possessions are still here, as far as I can tell. And apparently there was no sign that her daughter was taken, either."

She looked down the beach, at the jagged rise of the sea caves. "She could have gone down there, to the caves, for all we know. Or slipped and got swept out to sea when she was gathering food?"

"Perhaps we should head along the shore. See if there is any sign that has not gotten swallowed by the waves already," William said.

They started towards the sea caves, figuring the best shell fishing would be away from the busier part of the shore. William looked down the strand. He squinted in the distance, then gestured with his chin towards the slim, dark figure walking down the beach towards them.

They made for her, a slender knife of a woman wrapped in a sand covered blanket, her hair soaking wet.

"What are you doing here?" she said, her imperious tone at odds with her bedraggled appearance.

"Looking for you," Tasmin said, "We thought someone might try to murder you."

"Oh, really?" She let the blanket fall. Her dress was torn, and her skin was ripped, probably from falling against sharp rocks. "Please tell me something I don't know."

# Chapter Ten

It did not take long to realize that Magda would not be the best of house guests.

The sprites disappeared into the pantry, shutting the door with a definite slam, leaving again that eerie, deep, silence. Magda was still in the main shop, so she did not notice. Just as well, as they tried never to advertise the sprites to any but the most trusted.

"Where are we going to put her?" Ailiani asked. The truth was, Tasmin felt as if she were stuck between being a decent human being and doing what she wanted. She didn't trust Magda, didn't want her to have the run of the second floor where all the magic stuff lived, where they lived. It felt too personal.

"We'll make her a nice place in the secret room. If she really is a possible victim, and she gets afraid, she can shut herself in.

It shares a wall with the chimney, so it is one of the warmest places in the house. It still has a bed."

She looked at Ailiani carefully for judgment since she already felt like the worst hostess, or even perhaps the worst human that ever lived, but saw none. Tasmin opened the room. There was an old bed that had no other home, but the mattress was still decent. It was dark and small, but it smelled fine.

Magda came in with her bundle of things. William had run upstairs for blankets. Tasmin pulled out a chair and put it close to the fire. "Here...let's get you warm." They had only stopped to change her clothes and gather her things before taking her to Master Carys. They had sat outside while Master Carys had taken Magda's report, and she emerged quiet and a little shaken.

Fortunately, they'd already discussed that they could not let her go back to her hovel on the beach.

Ailiani made some hot chocolate, giving the first cup to Magda, who was bundled up. "You will like it here. The kitchen is always quite warm, and this quarter gets so quiet and peaceful after dark, you can pretend you live out in the forest, if you wish."

"Really?" Magda said, but the tone, the compressed anger and derision, made Ailiani's spine straighten, the corners of her mouth compress. She swallowed, hard, and Tasmin imagined that she was swallowing some very cutting responses.

"Thank you, Ailiani," William said kindly, "Your drinking chocolate is so much better than any I have ever had."

Ailiani gave him a grateful smile and Tasmin rubbed his back approvingly.

Ailiani picked up her own cup. "The shop is still open, I'd better get back out there."

"Do you want to call it for the night?" Tasmin asked. "We are all here, we can watch."

She shook her head. "And what else would I do with myself? You go on, solve your mysteries, I will be fine."

William tended the fire, trying to coax out more warmth. "It is just as well that you will be staying with us, Magda, I think tonight will be especially cold."

Magda adjusted her blanket so that she could reach her chocolate. Tasmin nudged a plate of cookies closer to her, and she took one, crunching quietly. William and Tasmin exchanged a look. They were both going mad to know her story, but neither wanted to push.

Tired after a busy day, Tasmin decided to sit down. Magda finally began to speak as if all she were waiting for was for Tasmin to settle into her chair. "I was in bed like everyone else was, when the bells started ringing." She stared into the fire and did not meet their eyes. "I'd already let the fire go out, and I don't have anywhere else to go, so I just closed my eyes and ignored it. I thought it was pirates, and I honestly have a hard time caring what happens to me. Being kidnapped by pirates might be an improvement." Magda paused to take a drink. "I heard my daughter calling me. I thought I was still asleep, dreaming, but I went to the window, and there she was." She stopped for a long moment, her eyes going distant, "And I could not help but seek her out. She kept just ahead of me, and I concentrated on her, shimmering in the night. We were near the sea caves when I was hit from behind. I recovered as they were binding me, but it did not stop me from fighting back." She gave a bitter smile. "We are trained, in Pandroth, to defend ourselves, so I fought her. She tried to cast a spell on me but..." She shook her head and fished something out of her bodice. "I am not my mother's daughter for nothing."

"An amulet to protect against spells?" Tasmin leaned closer. "It is wrought differently than I am used to..."

Magda dropped it back into her clothes without comment. Tasmin blushed and took the hint. She was itching to take it apart and learn more, to work backwards and see if she could re-create it, learn the secrets, but she mastered herself and showed great restraint.

"I could not get into the sea caves proper, so I ran down along the shore. They lost track of me, they must have, because I fell and whacked myself a good one, and that was enough to put me out for a bit."

"They?" William asked. "Do you think there was more than one?"

She shrugged. "I was not really paying attention, I was just trying to flee without drowning."

Tasmin rose. "You should let me look at your head. If you were knocked out for so long, I am shocked that you survived at all."

Magda raised a hand, her face and gesture as strong as a worded 'no' as any that had ever been spoken. Tasmin and William's eyes met, and Tasmin knew they were thinking the same thing, that plainly she did not want to talk about what happened, but why?

If she had fallen near the shore, and if the tide had not taken her out, she would have died from the cold. Being cold and wet had taken larger, heartier people than her.

Magic? Just how good was the amulet the other woman was wearing? It could protect her some, but not all. She certainly was scratched up enough, though; that bore her story out, it was the timing that bothered him the most. Tasmin came and leaned against his chair.

Magda looked over his shoulder, where the little secret room door was propped open. "I am not sure," she said, "how I feel about where you would have me stay."

William smiled as comfortingly as he could. "The room does look a bit dark and frightening, but it is warm, being built right next to the stove, and if you close it, no one shall be able to find you."

"What's a chocolate maker doing with a secret room?" Magda asked a bit starkly.

"We found it by accident one day while we were cleaning," Tasmin said brightly.

"Quite a surprise it was," William added. "But we kept it, never know when you might need an extra space for something that no one can find. And you can leave it open, of course. No one will bother you, either way."

Magda sighed softly. "Well, I don't suppose any of you have a reason to kill me, after all, there is little point for you to do so." Tasmin rolled her eyes, but Magda was concentrating on her cup.

"Do you know anything about your attacker at all?"

A simple shrug. "A woman. She fought like a lioness, and that is all I can say."

"I am afraid that there must be a connection between the death of your daughter and this," Tasmin said gently. "Do you know of anyone who would wish you or Tara harm? Her father? Someone who is not pleased to have a Pandroth lady on these shores? Has anyone accused you of anything?"

"I was a slave. Did you know that? A slave. I was in the belly of a ship that broke up off the coast of Daernan, a port just a little larger than Azin Shore. When I recovered I married a sailor who wanted to move here, he said the jobs were better. And he got himself killed, because that's what sailors do." She looked at Tasmin fiercely. "I have nothing. No one would even think to imply that I might be a spy because I make my living sewing nets, harvesting shell-fish, and telling fortunes. If I were a spy, I might set myself up as a business woman. That's where the real information can be found."

Tasmin digested this, and as if she hadn't had a cup of bitterness poured over her head she continued, "What of your fortune telling? Do you have fairly reliable sight? Did someone take your words and twist them, then blame you for the result?"

Magda tilted her head and inspected Tasmin. "Do you have the gift of sight, Herb Mistress?"

"Not really. Which is why when things are settled, the town will need a new Wise Woman." She looked at Magda for a moment, wondering if the other woman would be a good fit. It would give her a better life.

"I have great sight," she said, placing a hand against her chest. "So much so that it was everyone's first suggestion, to use my sight to look for my daughter but I..." she blinked a few times, and then managed, "I cannot see the dead."

"You knew," Tasmin said, closing her eyes.

"They would not look for a dead girl, especially not mine." She looked at Tasmin. "If you are angry that you wasted your time, I had no choice."

"Is that why the spell would not work?" William asked.

"No, if the spell was reading things correctly, the needle would have pointed down-wards," Tasmin said. "I would have known. Did you fox it somehow? To keep it spinning?"

"No!" She glared at Tasmin. "I would not have disrespected you that much."

Tasmin leaned on her hand. "Then something else was at work, for I did that spell correctly."

Magda snorted. Ailiani had joined them again, and she was leaning against the doorway. "She is very good at her craft, very careful. A mistake would be quite unlikely."

Tasmin gave them all a wry look. "It was a simple spell. There are spells that, as long as the ingredients are there, you pretty much can't mess them up."

"But the question still stands, do you have anyone who wished you ill?" William asked.

"No," Magda said. "Nor my daughter."

"Perhaps someone wanted her to use her talents for their purpose. What was she able to do?" Tasmin poured her some more chocolate.

A shrug. "She was not old enough for anything to have manifested. You know that."

Tasmin settled back down. "Then why did I hear that you were asking questions about how people learn magic?"

She sat for a long moment, then as if the words were being dragged from her, "For myself. The magic I know is different from what the Wise Women practice. I thought I could provide a better life for myself and my child."

"Of course. Did you ever approach Mistress Anne? I know she took in Cherise and her sister to train."

Magda tossed her head. "She said I was scum and not worth her trouble."

William and Tasmin exchanged a glace. "That is awfully unusual," Tasmin said. "The South is quite desperate for Wise Women, if you have any Talent for it at all, you will be trained."

"Well, *she* would not. And I did not ask *Mistress* Cherise, either, for why would she be any different from her mentor?"

"You make a good point," Tasmin said, uncomfortably, resting a hand on William's shoulder.

There was a long silence, broken, finally, by Ailiani. "I never understood why everyone assumed Mistress Anne was dead?"

"She was an older lady, and where she went could not be found..." William said delicately.

Ailiani tilted her head. "Older as in, about the age of my mother so I'm being polite, or doddering around with a cane?"

William frowned. "Did you never see her, you were here a year and a half or so before she disappeared?"

"Miss Dovlington's is not located at the most coveted of Azin Shore addresses."

"What she's trying to say nicely," Magda added, "is that Mistress Anne never went into the areas where she could not get paid for her services."

Tasmin paled, and then flushed angrily. William placed a hand over hers to forestall a rant. Everything she was hearing about Anne tweaked her pride and sense of justice.

"But that does go against everything she swore," he said.

"Indeed it does!" Tasmin said angrily.

"Was Cherise any better?"

Ailiani made a gesture with her hand that he took to mean "eh" and Magda laughed. "Cherise was a sheep. A little lamb terrified of everything. Do you really think she would dare go against her Mistress's teachings, alive or dead?"

William nodded. "Well, as interesting as this all is, I doubt she is the murderer. Even if by some miracle Mistress Anne was alive—which I doubt—I cannot fathom that she would have the strength to attack Magda, let alone drag off a healthy young girl."

"He has a point," Tasmin said, deflating somewhat.

"I have a new point. I am quite hungry and I know that Tasmin made a lovely stew that has been bubbling along all day, and I think we should all eat, then we will make up a nice warm bed for you, Mistress Magda." Ailiani said. "We will all think much clearer on a good night's sleep."

William was usually the one with the bad dreams, but that night, it was Tasmin's turn.

She was in a world devoid of color, everything was shades of gray. She walked a stone path towards the ocean, and though the waves got louder and louder, she could not see it, could only see the water as it lapped up around the paving stones. There was a thick mist all around her, and she could see shapes, grabbing shapes that cried out something that was covered by the roar of the water.

She finally forced herself awake. She tried to clear her mind with the usual tricks—building the kind of home she and William would have if they had an unlimited budget, counting William's breaths—all the things that normally put her into that drowsy state refused to work because her mind kept wandering away.

So, she did what any woman would do, she gave up, wrapped herself up in an afghan, and grabbed some books before creeping down to the shop proper. She spread her materials out on the cool marble counter, lit some candles, and settled in on Ailiani's high seat. For a long time the only sound came from the scritch of nib on paper and the turning of pages.

Eventually, a couple of sprites settled near her, one of them crawling into a fold of the blanket she was wrapped in, a cool presence that seemed content to snuggle in for sleep. She smiled a little, and kept reading. The books brought little comfort, because the conclusions she was coming to were not at all pleasing.

Tara no longer fit the victim profile they had decided upon, but her mother certainly did. Tasmin could tell that she was a woman of untamed power, it rolled beneath the surface of her skin. Probably if Magda had been sent to the University that Tasmin herself had attended, or even the prestigious Bourboune, she would have excelled. But it was out of her reach, now, even if Tasmin could think of some way to introduce her to those who would be willing to sponsor her education. She was too old, her magic too set. Any training would have to break what bad habits that could be broken, and work around those habits that could not.

And Magda was angry. Angry, derisive, bitter. Tasmin tried to play it off on the loss of her daughter, but some of it was old, resentments that had been kept as carefully as pets.

She paused in her note taking, the silence in the room once she had left off scratching away with her quill seemed almost oppressive.

"That's why they killed Tara," she whispered. They'd wanted to make Magda angry. She put the quill down and rubbed her eyes. *That ranks quite highly in the category of most horrid thought to ever have crossed my mind.*

*But the idea of the ghost storm being called by creating angry ghosts held up only if you ignored the fact that a) it was hard to create an angry soul. Not impossible, but hard and b) it would be impossible to create enough angry souls to call the ghost storm.*

*But called it someone has. You can't get around that one, either. It is here.* She looked toward the ocean and shivered.

*Pity we cannot make use of the Heart of Ithalia.* She remembered it with a shade of sorrow, for she had used it as a weapon to kill Franny Harker. *No wonder the woman is haunting me. Another angry spirit.* She paused.

*Franny Harker was haunting her. Therefore, Franny Harker was no longer a prisoner in the amulet. That followed that Ithalia might be free, too.*

"But wouldn't we know already if the witch was free?" She tapped the counter thoughtfully with her forefinger, then sighed. *Had Franny managed to free herself, or had she never really been imprisoned in the amulet? She didn't do soul magic...*

it was too black for her, even those who considered what they did for the greater good, Tasmin felt, were going down a very crooked path. Thus, she had no idea what really happened to Franny's soul; she assumed because the woman had died that the stone had done to her what it had done to Ithalia, and basically drawn her soul out, breaking the tether between life and death in the process.

So, had Franny's spirit just been hanging around like an angry miasma? Tasmin shuddered at the thought, wondering if she and the sprites were really alone.

They would have sensed something, would they have not? They are half way between this world and the unseen one. After all, Auruch saw the ghost at Mistress Anne's house.

She hoped so. Franny was bad enough, without a Sea Witch with a vile reputation floating about. An angry Sea Witch, known for her love of destruction? Surely she would have made her presence known by now. Tasmin repeated that over and over, trying to reassure herself.

So, if Franny had been out and about, why hadn't Tasmin seen her before? Where had she been?

Ailiani is right. I need sleep.

So she blew out the candles and hied herself off to bed. She settled on the edge.

William was making sad sounds in his sleep again, and she moved to kneel next to him. She leaned over him, her dark hair falling over his chest and shoulder. She pushed it back and stroked his cheek lightly. "Oh, my William," she whispered as soft as a summer breeze into his ear. "Oh, my love, 'tis alright, shh." He sighed and shifted a little, then went back to more peaceful sleep.

I am not sure if I want to know what goes on in his head at night, but oh, do I wish I could make it go away.

She rolled off the bed carefully and unwrapped herself from the afghan and draped it across the back of the rocking chair, then joined her husband. All night she dreamed of silvery shadows and mocking laughter.

# Chapter Eleven

The smell of rain and the sound of it hitting the glass did not inspire Tasmin to crawl out of bed. William was warm, the rain sounded like it had ice in it, making it hard to convince herself that staying with the former was not better than facing the latter, but William stretched and sat up. She made a sad sound and pulled at him, and he lay back down. Her response was to snuggle back into the crook under his arm, burying her face into his side and wrapping her arm around him, humming happily when he began to stroke her hair. "Doesn't sound like a fit day for anyone, does it?"

She shook her head.

"We have a guest downstairs," he said, hinting.

She shrugged. "You smell good and you are warm," she said, though it was so muffled that she had no idea what William heard.

"Well, maybe a few minutes more," he said softly, turning on his side to face her. She smiled sleepily and kissed him.

A little while later she was brushing her hair by the dim gray light from outside. Laying her brush down she started searching for enough pins for her hair. Underneath a neck cloth lay the Heart of Ithalia. She jumped back as if she had discovered a rabid rat.

"Sweetheart," William said as he came back into the room. "What are you about?"

"Testing a theory," she said absently as she reached in and picked it up. It felt weird, in her hands. She didn't remember the heart feeling quite so damp. It wasn't wet, it just felt like clay, or even plaster, that cold dampness that only a soft rock could have. She remembered the heart being much harder. *When I used it to defeat Franny, I damaged it, I poked a hole in it—what did that mean? Did a soul go in, or did one go out?* She peered at it closely, leaning nearer to the window. There was something off about the texture of the surface, about the pin-hole near the edge with its ring of blood. She frowned more, and did something she could not have done, back when she and William had first set this rock in this strange resting place. She ran her thumb nail along the rock, bringing up a flaking curl of plaster in its wake.

"William?"

"Mm?" His head was tilted back slightly as he tied his neck cloth, his eyes focused on the reflection of his fingers in the mirror.

"Husband, how long has the heart of Ithalia been made out of plaster?"

He dropped the neck cloth and crossed to the window. "What?" She slipped it into his hands and he cradled it, much like she had.

"I like this not at all," he said softly. "Someone knew where we hid the stone, someone broke into our home to get it." He pursed his lips and placed the offending stone on the table next to the window, then reached for the sill board, which was leaning against the wall. "The other night, I had it out, and I thought something was off. I couldn't hear anything when I held it. I think it's been gone for some time."

"As much as those first two statements bother me, the one we must resolve first is why?" He pushed it back into place, pounded one corner with his fist to make it go in. "And what mischief they can do with it."

The morning did not improve after that.

Magda was sitting where Tasmin had perched the night before, reading over her notes. She did not have the look of someone who was enjoying herself, quite the opposite.

"See anything of interest?" Tasmin asked.

"I don't know." She shrugged. "You may have some interesting ideas, but what I find much more interesting is why do you have wind sprites living in your pantry?"

Tasmin straightened her back a little. "Because they love me?"

"How simple of you," Magda said with a slight smirk. "And I do not think it is wise to keep an elemental being trapped as a familiar."

Tasmin was aghast. "You think they are my familiars? They are like children to me." She heard a hiss and a clatter, and forced herself to calm. If she upset the sprites, they might just lob something at Magda, and if anyone was going to hit the wench with a book it was going to be her.

Magda arched an eyebrow as if she heard them and knew what it meant, flipping idly through the book. "Yes, I'm sure they are."

Ailiani came out with a tray of chocolates and started putting things in order. Tasmin helped her, taking the chairs off the tables and placing them neatly where they belonged. If a couple of them hit the floor a little louder than usual, that was better than one of them hitting their guest.

*Lord of Light, what is it about her that makes her get under my skin so?* She sighed and placed the next chair on the floor very quietly.

"I am interested in your theories on the ghost storm, but I do not understand why you think the amount of angry dead is a problem." Her voice was oddly conciliatory, and Tasmin drew in a deep breath, counted to five, then let it go, turning back to the woman as if they were friends, determined to have mercy and remember that she was newly bereft of her daughter, a refugee in a stranger's home. *None of this can be easy. I am almost ashamed of myself. Lack of sleep must be making me less charitable toward my fellows.*

So Tasmin explained it, quoting from Creighton's. William would either be impressed or shocked.

"So, you are sure two deaths is not enough. But you are only counting dead mages. You aren't counting the other people who end up dead, freezing to death under the quays or the other hundreds of horrible, stupid ways people die every day?"

"But it's the anger issue, really. Someone who dies in their bed is not half so likely to be angry, are they?"

Ailiani scooted Magda aside so she could fuss with the display case. "You know, I went through this terrible desire to become a magician," Ailiani said, closing the case. "Not a mage like you, but a stage magician. William taught me about a dozen card tricks and some silly sleight of hand when we were at sea." She smiled. "Isan," she named her husband, "thought it was very silly, but it was harmless and kept me occupied. And I've spent time with every penny magician and actor who passes through this town, if I can."

"Your point?" Magda said dully, and Tasmin would have kicked her, had the counter not been between them.

"The point being, if I wanted to do a lot with a little, I'd find a way to magnify it." She jabbed the notes to prove her point.

Tasmin laughed. "Of course. And now, we have something to look for!"

It didn't take long to gather the materials to conduct the spell. It took much longer to find a place to actually do the spell, since it was one that required a lot of drawing on a lot of floor space as no table was large enough. Magda and Tasmin ended up rolling the rug up and shifting furniture around in the bedroom upstairs.

Straightened her back, looking around the room, her eyes focusing on the blue hangings around the bed, Magda said, "It is very nice." Magda said, her eyes focusing on the blue hangings around the bed.

"Thank you," Tasmin said awkwardly, remembering the cramped hovel with its dirt floor by the sea. She had copied some spells from her books, fragments that she wanted to use to create a tracking spell. She drew an outer circle, and Magda drew an inner circle and started scribbling what Tasmin assumed were sealing runes. They looked different, being from Pandroth. Tasmin wondered if it would still work, but figured as long as she kept the components of the spells consistent it should be alright.

"This is just a magic-map spell," she said. "I'll work on drawing a map of the town. Please feel free to fill in anything I'm missing."

The two women worked in silence, scribbling down the details of the town until they had a good map. At the end they checked the double circle for gaps, as it was to serve as the boundary to keep the spell well contained, and a map of the town, surrounded by runes to make the components do what they wanted.

"Now, for the expensive part of the spell," Tasmin said, as she began mixing powders, silver, and a touch of iron and crushed amethyst.

"Perhaps you could ask the Governor to give you some funds. You are acting as the town Wise Woman, you should not be out of pocket."

Tasmin blushed. "I had not thought of that," she said uncomfortably.

"Well, now you have the idea. Best mark down exactly what you've been using, why and when, maybe if it is presented neatly and efficiently you will find yourself reimbursed for your expenses."

"Thank you," she said, and she poured the powder into Magda's hands. She took up the bowl and poured the remainder into her hand.

"Do I say anything?" Magda asked.

"No, just concentrate on the feel of magic. On the essence of it." She closed her eyes and did so, letting herself fall into the feeling of it, like a river running through her soul. "One," she whispered, "Two...three..." and she and Magda cast the powder upon the map.

The powder gathered in some interesting places. Around the chocolate shop, of course, a touch of it around Magda's home...light traces here, and there. A little around the port admiral's, but then, she reasoned, there would be magic artifacts stored there, and residual magic from the previous tenants. Traces around the haberdashery down the way, but Tasmin suspected they had been selling love possets. If she could get proof she'd have those sisters by their ears. Love possets were not only somewhat illegal, but quite cruel in their way.

The largest cluster of it gathered around the sea caves.

"I heard that you spend much time there," she said, "Is it where you do your own castings? Did you see anything?"

The other woman looked angry, and opened her mouth up to deny her involvement, and Tasmin raised a hand to stay her. "I believe you. I believe you had nothing to do with what happened to your daughter. But I still need answers."

"No. I do not do a great deal of magic," she said. "And I certainly did not see anything different at the caves, though I must admit, I have not been drawn to them lately. When I go towards them, I am filled with dread and unhappiness."

Tasmin looked at the sealing spell that locked her own spell into place, but forbade herself to remark. *If she did not do a great deal of magic, then why is this seal drawn so intricately?* "That sounds like a variation of a spell that I did once," Tasmin said. "Someone doesn't want people around. Which, of course, means that we must go to it immediately."

"Not too immediately," Magda said, straightening. "We won't be able to get into the caves by boat right now because the tide is too low. We'll have to wait until we have a little more tide on our side."

"But too much tide..." she sighed. "Well, we shall just have to time it right. William can help, if you don't already know, from your own experiences, when we should go." She went down the stairs and into the shop.

"I am absolutely certain that there is no cross contamination, Miss," Ailiani said with the air of someone who was trying, very hard, to maintain her patience.

The girl on the other side of the counter from her was sliding something back and forth on the marble surface, Tasmin could hear it scraping, but whatever it was was tucked firmly under her palm. Maybe a glove button? "But are you sure? A woman as strong in magic as yourself...don't you ever wonder if your herbal concoctions don't just naturally get imbued with your power?"

"That would not be a problem even if I had power, but I am not magical at all, Miss." She smiled kindly. "There is the lady who makes our teas and herbals—Mistress Tasmin."

Tasmin quickly painted a smile on as the girl turned. Her hand leapt a little, as if touching something hot, then fingers deftly pocketed whatever it was she had been sliding on the counter. The seeming of youth was quite believable, the bright blue scarf over messy brown hair, the young clothes with their large buttons over a small figure. The clothes made her look like a young girl just growing into them, though close scrutiny showed the cleverness of the tailoring. Close scrutiny also revealed the slight wrinkles at the corners of her large blue eyes. She reminded Tasmin of a bed doll that had been allowed to grow up.

"I am she," Tasmin said. "What is your concern, Miss? I am always most careful to keep a clean work space."

"Not that kind of cross contamination," the girl-woman said earnestly. "Just the natural touch of magic from your preparations."

Tasmin placed her hand on the counter where the item had rubbed, feeling for more than just scratches in the conscientiously polished surface. "I am afraid that it doesn't work that way. You have to work with intent, and do things that will bring magic to the project." It was not the best explanation she could come up with, for it was far too simple, but she hoped it would work.

It did not. "But the magic is there, in the herbs, the properties are already there."

"Very true, and because of this we must be careful how we combine herbs and in what amounts, but there is a difference between natural properties and magical ones. Magical ones require time and preparation and training."

"Otherwise anyone could be a mage," the woman said softly, trailing off her words. Tasmin and Ailiani met each other's eyes.

Magda cleared her throat. "If wishes were horses, eh?"

The woman blinked. "Thank you for your help." And left so abruptly that the three women standing around the counter blinked at each other in confusion.

"What do you think she was after?" Tasmin asked Ailiani.

The other woman shook her head. "She came in, looked at the chocolates, then at the teas, and started asking me if the tea had magic properties. At first she seemed to think I was you."

Magda walked over to the window and looked out. "Have you seen her before?"

Tasmin joined her. The woman was no longer in sight. "Nay. You?"

Magda shook her head, and Tasmin was left with the impression that it would not be the last time they saw her.

"Excuse me," she murmured, following the cooking smell to the kitchen.

William was carefully removing candy from molds. She joined him, putting them on a sheet in groups of twelve. They were chocolate shells, the first candy he had ever sent her, and she smiled for a second.

"How are your investigations going?" he asked her as they worked.

"Horrid," she said honestly. "There seems to be a concentration of magic by the sea caves. Do you think there is a safe time to go and explore them? I should like to see what is there."

His expression was less than thrilled.

"Yes, I know it's dangerous and you worry terribly about me, which is why I am asking you to come along."

"How generous of you," he muttered.

"Because you know all about the sea and will know exactly the right time to enter. And..."

William held up a hand to forestall any further words. "I am sufficiently complimented; besides, I see no real choice."

"You don't think we should leave the matter for Carys?"

He shook his head and took the molds over to the counter to be washed. "I worry about the fact that the last two Wise Women of this town have been murdered. I am somewhat more concerned over the fate of the current one than I believe Master Carys would be."

"Well, true, you do like me a bit more than he does, I imagine." She smiled sweetly up at him.

"And I did promise Magda protection, she could well be a target, too."

"It would be a terrible breach of etiquette if we let her get murdered."

"So, I suppose needs must. I'll check the tidal chart and ask Ayers to get a boat."

"Thank you," she said fervently, and he kissed her forehead.

"We have time before the tide will be right. What do you propose to do?"

She chewed her lower lip, thinking. "I suppose that we need to start over. I must have missed something at Anne's house. I shall go there, and see what I can find."

"I'll do the wash up later," he said. "I shall go fetch my coat."

The last place Tasmin wanted to be was in the Wise Woman's home again, but there she was. This time she had William and a half dozen sprites to accompany her to the house.

"Where is the guard Carys promised?" Tasmin asked. She had prepared an entirely believable cover story.

"He probably does not have the funds or the desire to leave a guard here all the time. They will probably patrol through and check the doors and windows. So, we best get in and get started before they arrive."

A sprite or two took care of the door for them, and she sweetly smiled over her shoulder before stepping over the threshold. First things first. She took something from her pocket and unwrapped it, then cupped it carefully in her hands. It was a home-made spirit detector, a length of crystal that she had marked with the correct runes. She circled the room, but felt nothing.

"What is that supposed to do?" William asked.

"Glow, according to the books. If it's a good enough quality crystal...I need to get some better crystals in, but they are not exactly inexpensive...it will change color to tell you the ghost's intent towards you, but if it's too impure, well, we will just hope that it warns us that there is a presence about, and worry about the rest as we go."

"I'd rather know the intention now," William said softly, and a meep from the direction of his shoulder proved that the comment was not directed at her, so she decided to ignore it as she walked around the house, her cupped hands before her.

"I guess I am satisfied," she said at last, looking again at the mirror where she'd seen the ghost. She shivered. The unknowable, the unreasonable, these things worried her.

"Herb Mistress Anne should have kept a book, you say?" William asked. "I assume that would be at her work desk?" He crossed to the over-crowded table, and she followed. The rooms were still damp, it seemed that Carys had not taken her seriously. Tasmin shook her head. Everything would be ruined if something were not done.

"Go through her shelves, if you please, dear. If you see any books that might relate to the troubles we've been having, please put them in my basket. I think if they are not going to take care of her books, perhaps someone has to, but we don't really have the room." She cast her eyes at the book cases.

"And we would need the cart. I would do it, though, these volumes were collected by the town to help the Wise Woman strengthen her knowledge. This waste makes me feel quite ill."

Tasmin started at one corner of the desk, lifting books and shaking through the pages gently. "To be honest, I fear what Master Carys might do if I were to start wholesale hauling these books away. I warned him of the possible damage to the books, though." They smelled cold and damp.

"What makes you think she kept any records? For the Mating Spell the parents arrange for an appointment, so she would not have to keep records of that."

"I have been keeping a little journal," Tasmin admitted, "because I want to make sure I remember things, but the Wise Woman is able to get funds from the town to cover her costs. I very much doubt they would let her have just anything without a proper accounting."

William made an absent- minded sound of agreement. He was lost in whatever he was reading. He shut the book and slipped it into the basket.

Tasmin found the record-keeping for reimbursement, basically a tally sheet of dates and items.

*Jar. Saph. Bottle of ground horn, bull.*

*(Illegible) Ground rosemary*

And on and on. Nothing that was particularly telling. She frowned over the list, trying to match up ingredients with problems she knew people had been having. "This is a waste of time," Tasmin groaned, her head on the now much cleaner surface of the desk.

"Well, perhaps there was a record-keeping book of some sort, and Cherise lost it?" William put yet another book in the basket. Perhaps putting a book and curiosities addict in charge of the shelves had not been the best idea. "Or Anne kept it with her, so that she could update it right away?"

"I update mine at home," Tasmin admitted, "I hate to write in front of patients, it seems so intrusive. But maybe she did not mind."

And then she paused, and looked at the desk again. "You know, there is not one sign of Cherise at this desk. No different hand writing, I mean. Maybe she placed some of the books on the desk, but if I had to hazard a guess I would say she did not work here."

He looked around. "Then where?" She looked, too. The desk was situated in the very best place for one, near the largest windows and the fire. There was no other place to work. It seemed strange that Cherise would not use the desk. *Maybe she was that afraid of her former mistress?* But the thought did not feel right to Tasmin.

She got up to look. Both bedrooms were sparse, the one belonging to Anne slightly larger and nicer, but again, no sign that anyone else had lived there. A few clothes hung on pegs, a book gathered dust on the bedside table.

Cherise's bedroom was much the same, for the most part. The clothes were much younger, much more like the woman who had tried to take Anne's place. The only decorations were a small box, which held a few pieces of cheap jewelry, and a tiny miniature portrait. Tasmin used her thumb to gently clean away the glass and saw a handsome man. *Wise Women do not marry. Was this the man she gave up?*

"Tasmin?" William called softly. "I may have found her work space."

Tasmin followed his voice to the kitchen.

William was carefully working a thin knife into the crevice of a drawer. The table that Cherise had worked at was scarred but very clean, a long drawer running under the top.

"It doesn't look like a locking drawer." The wind sprite left her shoulder, and behind the drawer she could hear the little sounds of the sprites trying to push it.

"Indeed," William admitted, "But it is not coming open." He pounded the bottom and wiggled the drawer, the sprites pushed, Tasmin helped wiggle and pull. Finally, it gave away, creating an unfortunate waterfall of papers, dried herb packets, a couple of acorns, some roots, and assorted other detritus.

"Oh dear," William said, as Tasmin settled down on the floor next to the scattered mess. William placed the drawer on a clear spot, and they sorted things together.

"Well, at least we know her twin sister's name is Agnes. Agnes and Cherise. What a combination of names." Tasmin waved a letter at him. "It says that she looks forward to Cherise's visit, and not to forget to bring some of that new shop's delightful chocolates. Hah! That dates this a little."

"Perhaps we should take her some of my 'delightful chocolates'," he said, quoting the letter with a little bit of relish. "After all, someone should see how she's doing." He took the letter and read over it. "But we don't know when she was expected, really, or where her sister is."

"Well, the phrasing leads me to believe that Cherise was going *to* her sister, so we shall have to hope that it was in her home town. If we keep digging, surely we will find some paper with an address on it."

William handed her a folded piece of paper. "Here's a partial letter from her sister."

Tasmin opened it up and read it out loud. "Dearest Sister, how is...stuff about people we don't know and their ills...stuff about animals that apparently her sister has...worthless reminiscence...and finally, accusation."

He leaned over her shoulder. "Do tell."

"Every time I see Jared I am reminded again of my poor choices, and my sorrow that I allowed you to persuade me from my desire."

"Excellent work!" William declared. " Jared is not such a terribly common name, and we should be able to go through the records at the Court and get what we need."

"Yes, Jared is high on my list of people to speak with." She set the letter aside to go in the basket, and kept sorting.

William walked to the beach with Tasmin on his arm. The storm's dead had been collected, the boats put away. The only boat was theirs, and the only sign of what happened was off the mouth of the harbor, where fires flickered in the pre-twilight.

"What is that?" Tasmin asked as she took Ailiani's hand. William steadied her as she stepped into the boat.

"Ships that were attacked. No one will sail upon a curse-ship, so we took them out to sea with their dead crews and burned them." William settled into the boat.

"The *Tregaurde*?" It was Ailiani, not Tasmin, who asked.

"Safe for now," he said. "My father had it towed in, the goods are on another ship and already away."

Ailiani sighed in relief, and nodded. "I was happy there," she told Tasmin.

She smiled at her friend. "But why are they treating the ships like they have the plague? Surely the families would want the bodies?"

"Because it is a plague, Mistress," the second sailor, Dresden,said as he started to pull at the oars. Between his and another sailor's work at the oars, while William steered, they slipped across the water. "Fear is the worst plague of all, and no one really knows what taint the ghost storm leaves behind."

Tasmin opened her mouth to object, and William caught her eye and shook his head slightly. To his relief she caught on. "I did bring lanterns," she said, changing the subject. "They are cold lights. Probably not the best cold lights ever made, for my Aunt despaired that I would ever manage to master them, but better than nothing."

"We brought candles, too," Ailiani said, and Tasmin sniffed, even though it were she who spoke against her cold lights first.

"I am sure the cold lights will serve us perfectly," William said, and he saw some tension leave his wife's frame. She was scared, he realized, and he was unused to seeing it.

They slipped into the caves, the light from the lanterns lived up to its name, cold silvery light illuminated the sharp, barnacle covered rocks.

"Up ahead, to the right, there's a ledge where one can walk. That's as far as this boat can go," Magda said.

"Ayers and Dresden will stay here, at the boat," William said, wanting someone he trusted to be guarding the boat, too.

"Should the tide change, Ayers will blow his bosun's whistle. Any whistle, we all come back here should we get separated."

"I would suggest we avoid getting separated," Magda said. "The cave is a dangerous place. In fact, I think you, Herb Mistress, should stay with the boat as well."

"I have no intention of doing so. If there is anything magical up ahead that is not in Pandroth script..." and her tone conveyed that there bloody well better not be, "then we will need my expertise."

"But no swimming," Ailiani said. "You swim like a slightly talented stone at the best of times, I would prefer that you stay dry."

"I would prefer to do so. We shall have to see. There's not really enough warming balm, but you might need me to go look."

Ailiani arched a glance at William, then at her, before stripping down to what she was swimming in, thin breeches and a shirt.

William, too, stripped down to breeches and a shirt, but hoped that the shaking of his hands was hidden by the shadows that the light created. The cold light seemed to strip all the darkness away and compress it, the shadows were unrelieved blackness. They all dipped into a pot of warming balm, they had rubbed it over their bodies before dressing, and now, with Tasmin's help, they coated their hands, feet, necks and faces. It was greasy and smelled uncomfortably of sulfur.

The next step was the potions. The balm was to protect them from the cold of the water, the potion was to heat them from inside. Ailiani raised a toast and chugged it quickly, grimacing. William soon realized why, as the thick fluid burned its way down and made his stomach churn with acid.

"It won't last very long," Tasmin said, stowing the bottles and jar in the boat. "But it will help." She gave him a concerned look, searching his face, and he grinned and kissed the top of her forehead. She pulled away, nose wrinkled, rubbing the balm off her forehead. "Really dear, was that absolutely necessary?"

"Aye!" *It got you to stop looking worried.*

Tasmin shook her head, then went to the edge between the water and the rocks. A long step took her to a ledge that disappeared into the depths of the cave. She stepped with care, Magda behind her, and William wished the other woman was not following so close. Magda had not earned his trust, not yet, and he could not help but worry about Tasmin getting pushed into the water. He hunkered down next to Ailiani, whose own eyes followed the women as they cast their senses into the cave.

"I sense nothing," Tasmin said. She picked her way back to them. "If you see anything in the next cave, you will come and get me?"

William started to remind her of how poorly she swam, and she shook her head, "I can hold my breath and you can lead me. I trust you. And I need to see the marks first hand." She unwrapped an amulet from a bit of waxed cloth and handed it to him. He dropped it over his head, slipping it under his shirt and Tasmin stooped down to hand Ailiani one.

"Stop fussing," Ailiani said to her. There was a small splash as she slipped into the water. "Iyeah!" Ailiani squeaked. "So cold!" She disappeared under the water and came back up, trying to equalize.

William took two of the cold light balls and tossed Ailiani one. She caught it neatly, swimming backwards.

This was the dangerous part. If the lights died too soon, they would be in trouble.

William did not let himself pause. He'd had time to contemplate, on the way in, what he was about to do.

He had almost drowned, once, and ever since he heard a voice, slithery and cruel in his head, whenever he touched the sea. The other day he'd been quick, jumping into the ship before the water could do more than touch his boots, but now he would be immersed completely.

*Stop acting like a madman. You used to love the water. Ignore your fears and do what must be done.*

He took a breath, and eased himself in, under the water. He saw the cold light, and a bit of Ailiani, bobbing in the water before him, and he concentrated on that, concentrated on following her. For a while, he heard nothing, and he followed the cool light ahead of him as they worked their way through crevices to the next cave. They both surfaced. There was nothing but an arch of rock above them, so they smiled at each other, took deep breaths, and went back into the depths again. For a moment, all seemed to be well. But it was only a moment.

*There you are*, the voice said. It sounded so very far away, but still it filled him with fear.

He ignored it with a will.

*Oh, don't you remember me?*

He did. He remembered the island, he remembered her sitting on her throne, chained forever by men too frightened to kill her, too frightened to let her be free.

*You could have let me go. You could have set me free. But you did not.*

He did not answer her, but it seemed to him as if the water around him had become churned and murky. He held the stone away from him, looking for its twin. Nothing but dirt and muck.

*What is wrong, my sweet? Feeling trapped?*

He moved forward, feeling for stone, trying to find something that would give him some perspective.

Cool hands patted him, causing him to jump. The hands tugged at his clothes, giving him direction.

"Did you get lost?" Ailiani panted, as they pulled themselves up on the ledge. "You had me worried."

The water seemed to pull at him, seemed to want him to stay. "No, I was just looking." He crawled out with every ounce of his will, resting for a moment on the ledge. He took a deep breath, trying to gather himself back together. Now the challenge was not to show fear, but to be completely normal.

Ailiani was not buying it. She huffed a sound of disbelief as she walked along the water's edge. He hauled himself up and joined her. The caverns were not pleasant to walk along.

Sea smoothed stones sometimes became rough and sharp from barnacles making a home. A couple of times Ailiani made a little sound as she stepped on something unpleasant, and he steadied her. "I would have liked to have brought some shoes," she said, as they wended their way around a stalagmite and into the next cavern.

The path opened to a much larger room. Cloudy gray light came in from a couple of holes in the ceiling. William could make out some green growth around the holes, water smoothed curves marked the floor where rain and condensation had gathered and dripped over the years. Ailiani gasped, and he followed the direction of her eyes. She was looking up, and just out of the light William could make out four shadows hanging from the ceiling.

As his eyes got used to the shadows he could make out the shapes of the four. No, there was a fifth, hiding behind the others, wrapped tightly, as tightly as if a spider has woven them into a cocoon. The idea of a spider that large rattled him, and he shuddered. They crossed the floor, and their lights picked out the white glow of symbols drawn in a circle, each of the bodies had a silvery cord connecting them to a point in the pattern. There was something dreadful about it, Ailiani's lips were pinched in distaste, and the light in her hand shook a little. "Well," he said quietly. "I guess we found our signs of magic."

"Are you going to go get Tasmin?"

He looked at her, making sure she could see his expression in the light.

She laughed. "You are horrid. She will not be pleased."

"Well, we can study it as close as possible, describe it to her. We will bring her if she absolutely must see it. I am certain, between the two of us, we can reproduce the pattern. There is not much to it."

She nodded. "I think that I can remember it. I am not sure if I want to drag her into the water, or make another trip to do so. The balm and the potion seem to be working, but swimming in this bears no resemblance to a pleasure swim. Shall we go to the next cave?"

"Yes, of course," he said, hoping he sounded normal. The water was not nearly as murky as it had been, and he wondered, again, if it was his imagination. He could not believe that the witch he had seen on the island would have such a reach. It was said that she had died, that the island itself was gone. Surely, dead or imprisoned, she could not touch him? He slipped back into the water.

*And there you are again. Can't keep away from me, can you darling?*

Ahead was solid rock. He could feel a current and knew that this was not the end of the tunnel, but as both of them groped for a way to continue on, he could feel his lungs protesting.

*No answer?* The voice in his head purred.

William has had enough. *I don't understand the question. I don't understand why you haunt me. I'm nothing to you.*

*You could have freed me,* she sulked.

*I'm not the only one. Hundred of people visited that island over the years! Surely I was not the only one. Go haunt one of them.*

*What makes you think I don't? You are hardly special.*

Ailiani signaled him with the light, he could see it bobbing back and forth. He followed it. She had found a passage, finally, and when he broke the surface again, filling his lungs with musty air, he was sure it had never tasted so sweet.

*And, dear boy, some of them are haunts now, themselves. You'll join them, someday.*

He decided, firmly, to ignore her. The cave opened into a room a couple of feet above them, too high to pull one's self up without help. He and Ailiani started looking for hand holds.

"I have a couple of hand holds, here," she said. "Can you wedge yourself against the tooth of rock, here, and give me a push up?"

"You can use me as a step. I'm wedged in." There was a tooth, as she called it, of rock jutting from the water, only a few feet away from the wall of rock that led to the room. He was grateful that the barnacles that had made earlier going painful were not here, as he wedged himself as high as he could, then let her use him as a ladder to crawl up. He pushed under her foot with his free hand and there was some scrabbling, but, after a moment, "Alright. Now. How do we get you up here?" Some more sounds as she shuffled around the room above, and then he saw a long length of cloth come down, not unlike what had wound the bodies in the previous room.

"Don't be squeamish," he heard her say, and he sighed, took hold, and climbed his way up the wall.

The room was actually rather beautiful. Like the other room, natural light filtered in through a hole in the ceiling, but this one was somewhat rounded, in the center of the main area. William, was looking at the tall, smoothed walls, the flat expanse of stone shelf that formed the cave chamber. A small alcove was the only flaw in the roundness.

Ailiani knelt, stroking the smooth, nearly clean floor. "I think I see flecks of silver, and there's a faint circle, here, but nothing truly intelligible. I think they did work here, but they cleaned up well, too. "

Along one wall there was a wooden work bench. It was clean, but the planks that made the top had clearly been scavenged. There was a basket with a needle, thread, scissors. Otherwise, it was all quite clean.

"Drat, I was hoping for walls covered with obscure diagrams and symbols, tables covered in melted wax and herbs and skulls..."

"You read too much lurid prose," Ailiani said.

"You should know, you provide half of it."

She laughed and he held out a hand to help her up. "There is the William I have known for so long. I wondered where you went."

He shuddered a little, her words echoed the woman in his head so closely. "I thought I would deal better with the confined spaces."

She tilted her head. "You, King of the Sea? Claustrophobic? Ah, well, I won't tell Tasmin. She must always think of you as her brave and mighty warrior, undaunted by anything."

"Really?" he said, amused. "I figure, as long as I am able to get rid of spiders, I will be dauntless enough for Tasmin."

There were fifty steps between the boat and the end of the stone pathway. Tasmin knew this because she walked it, back and forth, thinking. Sometimes she would stop and listen carefully, and when she was still everyone had learned to be still, as well. She walked every inch of the cave slowly, tilting her head this way and that, holding the light at different angles. "I am not convinced that the only way into the inner chambers is by swimming," she declared to Magda, when the other woman joined her.

"Why not?"

"One, ingredients." She went back and stole another cold light from the lantern. "There are some things you can't risk getting wet. They would be ruined. Or useless until they dried, and how do you expect to dry anything out here?"

Magda nodded as if she had a point.

"Two...warmth. William and Ailiani will be *blue* by the time they get back, spell or no spell." She worked her way forward, exploring every inch of the cave.

"Perhaps they have a spell that warms and dries them immediately."

"That would take a lot of energy, really, and they are doing such high magic I would think they would want to reserve every drop for the main spell but...point. You are right, it is possible."

There, across the way, was a crevice, a shadow. She knelt and studied the water, frowning, trying to see in. Finally slipped her hand into the water, feeling around. She pulled her freezing hand out and shoved it up under her arm. She stood up abruptly, kicked off her boots. "You just have to have a little faith." She stepped into the water. She hadn't lifted her skirts up quite enough. The water came up around mid-ankle.

"Mistress Almsley!" Ayers called from the boat. She waved at him. "There's a ledge in the water, leading to the crevice, there," she said, feeling her way carefully with her feet as she worked her way across. She heard Magda hiss a curse behind her as she followed Tasmin. The water *was* cold. It made her bones ache, and she wished she had taken some of the warming posset, too. There was a sort of stirrup shaped wedge in front of the rough, v-shaped crevice, so she put her foot in it, and pushed herself up, into the v, and down on the other side.

It was a narrow alley, the water had smoothed the narrow, long space, and she worked her way through it, around the curves that pressed in and threatened to crush her. At least that's how it felt as she slipped through narrow bends, ducked to go under low arches, taking deep breaths to fit around corners. Eventually she came out in a room.

The room was high above the tide mark, in fact, there was only a little dampness around the lowest corner of the room, the only place where the tide came up, not that it came up much at all.

"Nice," Magda said, turning her face up to the holes and their graying light. "This would be a place of great power, where I come from."

"Which is?" Tasmin asked, investigating the ground. "I know you are from Pandroth, but, well, Pandroth is huge." The cavern was too clean. It had been swept, and her fingers encountered nothing but a little dust.

"Alathrea."

Tasmin's hand, which had been sweeping at the floor, stilled. "Alathrea. What a lovely name," she said, proud that her voice sounded perfectly normal.

"I am sure you, with your university education, have heard of it."

"They grow Weather Witches there," Tasmin said softly, straightening, dusting her fingers off on her skirts. She had heard tales of wild nomads who could call the wind, scour their enemies to bone with sandstorms, cloak the stars so that caravans could no longer find their way across the vast desserts of their home. She felt quite as if a tiger had come into the cave, and now crouched, waiting to attack. She had to hide her wariness from the other woman, taking a deep breath, holding it, then slowly letting it go as Magda continued to speak.

"It is the most magical place in the world," Magda said, as she made one, then two, then three cold fires appear, as simple as breathing, and sent them to hover above their heads. "I like this place. I would set my place of working here."

"Where is your place of working?" Tasmin crossed to the holes, looking up at the graying light. "You were not working in your home."

"Nowhere."

Tasmin looked back, and Magda wiggled her fingers and the cold lights turned golden, rather than common silver, and started to slowly orbit around them. "I have not worked anything in years. It was the promise I made to my lover, as long as I had our daughter, I would not work magic."

*Oh. And now…*"What an unusual promise. Did he have something against magic?"

"And now," she continued as if she hadn't heard Tasmin, one single tear track glittering in the light, "Now that they have taken my daughter from me, there is nothing to stop me."

*I do not know if I am more afraid of her now, that I am convinced that she is a grieving mother focused on vengeance, or a few moments ago when I feared she may be one of the people calling the storm.*

"The killer is someone who knows you," Tasmin said abruptly. "They knew how angry you would be."

Magda laughed. "No one knew how angry I would be."

*Oh, goodness, I am stuck in a cave with a mad woman.* Tasmin froze, having finally looked up into the shadowy alcove high against the ceiling. "Well, this was certainly a place of working," she said, walking closer to the bodies.

"Five bodies." Magda said softly. "Your friend, Master Carys, will be less than thrilled."

"I am less than thrilled. That much death…that much power. What can it be for? And how did we not miss five people, in our town? 'Tis not that large a place."

"People miss more than you would like to think, or, rather, they don't. Sailors. Joy girls. There are many who come to this port, and many who get swallowed up, never to be heard from again."

Tasmin drew a small pad and a stub of pencil from her purse and tried to copy what she could see off the wall. Ailiani and William had been there, she could tell from the wet foot prints.

"How did they get them up there? If it were not for how orderly they are, all lined up, I would have thought them the victims of a large spider."

Magda gave her a look, and Tasmin said, "I am not entirely serious."

Magda turned and said something that sounded suspiciously like "Madwoman," but Tasmin decided to ignore it. *She should talk.*

"Well, we are making progress, anyway. I think I have found another exit. Do you see, how the rocks are stacked over by the small hole?"

Magda tilted her head. "No, I do not."

Tasmin crossed over. It was her type of magic, a hiding spell. "I probably saw it because I have been willing myself to see Berengeny magic." She touched the edge of the spell, and the entrance shimmered. "Shall we see where it leads?"

"There," Magda said. "Would you like me to push you up?"

"I think I will be fine, but if needed I'll gratefully ask for the help," she said, simply because *If you touch me I will scream* was probably too rude.

She didn't need help, even though the hole was at an odd angle in the wall, almost like it had once shunted water down into the room they were in. With some scrabbling she was able to push herself up and in. Her main problem was her blasted skirt, getting stuck under her knees, so she had to shift and contort until she was able to move the fabric out of her way. The down side was that she was now crawling down the passage way with nothing but stockings between her knees and the rock.

The hole widened shortly afterwards, and she found herself on a precipice that half circled the room below, like a balcony.

"There is really not much to report to Tasmin," Ailiani said under her.

"And you should probably get back to the boat before the heating posset wears out," Tasmin informed her and William. She was clinging to an outcropping, half hanging over the edge to see them.

Ailiani made an 'eek' sound, which amused Tasmin a little too much as she thought people only said 'eek' in stories. William looked up, and said, "I did not know the boat was so close, since you had plans to stay by it."

She rolled her eyes and forwent pointing out that *he* was the one with such plans. "May I point out that I am perfectly dry, and if you were to find a way up here, you would most certainly be able to avoid another dunking in the sea."

"Oh, I am all for that," Ailiani said eagerly.

"Over here," Magda said, "There's a ladder. It looks a bit like someone stole a rope ladder from a ship." She tossed it down. Tasmin inspected the ends.

"Look," she said. "Whomever used these caves planned on being back and forth quite a bit, the rope has been bonded to the stone."

Magda ran her fingers back and forth over the joining. "No rot between the stone and the rope. That can happen, you know, and I don't think they treated the ladder against moldering."

"Careless of them," Tasmin said, "They didn't mean to use these caves long, then." The rope ladder swung and shook under Ailiani's weight as she scampered up.

"Didn't?" Magda asked.

"I didn't feel the dread you mentioned, the desire to stay away. And mostly, everything is cleaned up. They are done with this place. Do you think you scared them away, when you escaped?"

Tasmin held her hand out to help Ailiani up over the ledge edge, and her fingers were like grasping icicles.

"You are sent from heaven," Ailiani said, starting to shiver a little. Tasmin took off her jacket and wrapped her in it, rubbing her hands up and down the other woman's arms to try and warm her.

"The spell is fading, so your timing is marvelous indeed," William agreed from below. He came up onto the shelf easily, then pulled the rope ladder back up with quick, practiced motions.

"Did you see the bodies?" Tasmin asked him quietly.

"Aye. I will seek out Master Carys as soon as we get back into town."

"I rather think you mean as soon as you are back home and in dry clothes. You will catch your death if you wander about too long."

The walk back was much faster than the walk into the caves, and it was with great relief they got back to the boats. Tasmin and Magda held up a blanket so that Ailiani, starting to shake, could strip her clothes off. William disappeared into the darkness to change.

Tasmin, for her part, was glad to reach the shore again.

Once they took a few steps away from the shore, she could hear another sound. Music, the thrumming of drums, the high trill of pipes. A flash of light, and cheering.

"Elementalists!" Tasmin said. "I can feel the magic, even from here."

They climbed the hill quickly. A crowd was gathered around the central fountain, and Tasmin gently pressed her way into the crowd, looking for a spot she could see from. Her aunt, a famous Ice Elementalist, had not written her to say she would be coming, and it was too soon for that troupe to be back in the area.

It was not her Aunt or her troupe. Tasmin, even though she, herself, had traveled a season with a troupe of elementalists, did not recognize anyone, at least not yet.

In the center a man, his blond hair pulled back to reveal a handsome—if scarred—face, was working his magic. He drew out wonders from the glow of fire in his cupped hands. Dragons of fire fought each other, twirling in the sky, whipping in and out above the crowd. Paper phoenixes passed out to the children were tossed into the air, where they disappeared and became phoenixes of fire. Blues and greens and purples mingled with gold and red and orange. *Neatly done*, Tasmin admired. Adding colors was not as simple as one might think. To use such effects in mere advertising told Tasmin a lot about his power.

A woman, dressed in loose, feathery clothes, rolled a large silver hoop into the square. She placed her feet and hands firmly along the inside edge and used her body to move the wheel, riding inside of it, spinning and weaving it around the Fire Elementalist. At one point it spun like a coin and she lifted her feet up and held on only with her hands, so she looked like she was flying. He sent a dragon flying through the hoop and around her, trailing sparks.

The spinner on her wheel spun around the fountain. The air shimmered over it, and a woman, slender and dark, appeared from clear air as if dropping a cloak away from herself. She balanced on the very top of the fountain, her poise and presence striking everyone silent. She looked exotic and she played up to it. She had long golden fingernails, wrists over-filled with bangles, a neck heavy with chains threaded with various crystals that were somehow *less* gold than her eyes. Her velvety dark skin seemed to make the gold glow all the brighter.

"Ladies." She paused and smiled at the crowd. "Gentlemen." She emphasized the titles fondly, as if she were greeting old friends. "I am Olonah de Vane, and I am very pleased and proud to present to you my troupe. I bring you acts of fire, acts of air! Feats and wonders both delicate and dangerous. Meet us tomorrow night at the gathering hall..."

"This is not good," muttered Tasmin.

"I would think you would be delighted," William said back. "You were looking forward to a traveling show coming."

The announcement finished while they spoke, and Olonah alighted from her perch and led her troupe towards the huge meeting hall where they would perform the next night.

She gestured at them. "But our killers have just been provided with a target rich environment." She pointed at a small, elfin girl. "She has power, he, over there, with the tigers...the main woman, the lady who was on the gyre wheel..." She made a gesture to suggest that she was giving up because there were just too many people.

"They had to ask the governor first if they could perform. Would he have warned them?"

"I strongly suspect he does not even know the correlation between magic users and murder."

"And I cannot imagine warning them would be easy," he said with a sigh. "I think I will cross the square, see if I can catch up with Master Carys. He will need to be prepared to enter the caverns early."

Tasmin sighed heavily and looked up at him. "Hopefully he will not require your presence there. At any rate, do not linger too long, you and Ailiani will need to get warmed up. I will see if I can catch up with Olonah. We might be able to find enough mutual friends that she can trust me. After all, I was a traveling elementalist for a short time."

Ailiani shuddered. "If you do not mind, I shall take my leave and go on to my rooms. I shall see you both tomorrow."

"Drink something hot," Tasmin said. "And make sure you place some hot rocks in your bed!" Ailiani waved and disappeared into the crowd.

Tasmin kissed her husband and followed the elementalists. It would be impossible for her to catch up along their route to the meeting hall, so she took a longer path that would take her around the back of the hall. As she walked, she wondered what she should tell them. About the ghosts? No, they would think her mad. She looked out at the sea, and wondered when the next murder would come, to draw the ghost storm in, and if the sprites would again be successful in fighting them off?

*Keep it simple*, she said. *Possible death should be enough for anyone to take seriously.*

She got to the meeting hall well before the actors, though the doors were thrown open and a couple of young men were setting up camp in the large lawn behind the hall, caring for the horses. There were living wagons as well as carts, and she smiled a little, thinking of the vardo she had briefly shared. The small, homey space could be so comforting. The paint was bright and perfect, even in the swiftly failing light, and everything she saw spoke of prosperity.

One of the lads finished combing down the white steed he was working over, and walked over.

"I am Mistress Tasmin Almsley, and I would like to speak with Mistress de Vane. I promise not to take long."

He shrugged a little. "Have a seat over there. That's her wagon."

The wagon was not at all what she imagined the Mistress of the troupe would own. It was a simple red wagon with blue trim—not heavily carven, not gilded, no large, grand windows—but a humble tinker's home. She pulled a barrel closer and sat down upon it, studying the vardo that stuck out from the crowd by its very virtue of plainness. The main living wagons would be pulled inside the large building, where it would be warmer and drier, and moved back out if needed to make space.

The music grew louder and louder, slowly died as the musicians reached the yard and stopped playing, people separating from the group to grab cups of water or put away their gear. In the center was Mistress de Vane, gesturing here and there, as if planning out the layout for the next day's work. Tasmin rose, and the act caught the other woman's eye. She stopped for a moment, then smiled and said something to the Fire Elementalist, who nodded and departed swiftly. Olonah did not walk so much as glide over, every movement easy and fluid. She had not performed any acts of power, but she did not have to. Magic radiated from her, much as it did from Tasmin's Aunt.

"Good evening. How may I help you?"

Tasmin introduced herself, adding, "My Aunt is Eyrnie, she is an Ice Elementalist, she travels with a group that specialize in Light Day celebrations and ice houses."

She smiled. "I have heard of her. Do you wish an audition? Do you have a talent to add to my repertoire? If you are related to Mistress Eyrnie, you must have many things to offer."

"That is very kind, but I am afraid not," Tasmin said, her cheeks heating. "I am here to tell you something and either convince you to be wary of the town or wary of me. May we sit?"

Olonah sat on one of the steps of her vardo, looking at Tasmin expectantly. The hall doors were being closed, fires and torches lit. It was already becoming a warm, peaceful place. Tasmin sat on a crate, facing her.

"So. Why are you mad?" The other woman prompted.

Tasmin gave her a dry look. "I'm not. But, we have had women of Talent go missing. I just thought since so many of your ladies are Talented, you may want to take extra precautions. We do believe that they have been murdered. It may mean nothing, and you may leave here thinking that I was extraordinarily silly and that perhaps you would rather perform somewhere else next time on your rounds, but I would rather you forewarned."

Olonah smiled. "I appreciate the sentiment, but we are always cautious anywhere we go. You are all mad, as far as I am concerned, and the safety of all my people is of upmost importance."

Tasmin was not sure what she made of this. You would have thought she had warned the woman of a cake shortage, rather than possible death. No questions, just acceptance and a brush off. "Well. I am glad my dire portents have not unsettled you. I am so looking forward to the show."

"It will be worth your time, I assure you." Olonah tilted her head, looking at her while Tasmin smiled and rose, shaking out her skirts. Her feet were freezing, she couldn't wait to get home and put them up by the fire.

"Mistress Almsley, what do you do?"

"I'm a Herb Mistress, and acting as the Wise Woman until we get someone more suited for the position."

She shook her head. "Affinity, Mistress. I wanted to know your affinity."

"Wind, air," she said. "I am good with air, though I have help."

Golden eyes met hers. "Air is the hardest, you know, even with help." She nodded, and looked back at the torches. "Very well. You may be assured, I will keep your words in mind."

# Chapter Twelve

It was late by the time he got back to his offices, and Carys was looking forward to getting a drink, slipping into his chair, sitting in front of the fire and perhaps allowing himself to fall asleep there rather than his usual wont.

It was a surprise to see her there, lounging back in his chair as if she were a queen, gold—gold earrings, necklaces, eyes—glittering in the fire light. He'd known she was in town, he'd watched her, but had not expected her to visit so swiftly.

He came around the desk, and she slanted a glance at him as he dropped his bag with an ugly thump on the desk top.

"You were supposed to write more often," he said gruffly, as he bent to kiss her cheek. She laughed, like gold bells chiming, and he smiled slightly, walking around and slumping in the remaining chair.

"Horrible night, love?" she asked. Olonah crossed over to the buffet where a chocolate service sat. She held her hands over the pot for a moment, concentrating.

"I now officially have more bodies than I have space for."

She flexed her hands slightly, then touched the side of the pot, nodded, then took the lid off and stirred the contents. "And you took this post because you thought it would be boring and you would have time to catch up on your studies." She poured the contents and brought two cups over. They sat opposite of each other, he looking dolefully at the cup in his hands.

"Yes, that is chocolate, from your new friend's establishment."

"My new friend is the one who found the bodies. Five of them in all, trussed up as if ready to be shipped."

Olonah paused. "Did he...?"

"He and his wife discovered five bodies hung like bats in a cave. There was some magical notation. I'll have to let you look at it, my dear, if you are so inclined. He has promised to provide copies in the morning."

She pursed her lips. "You know I hate to be involved in such ugly matters, and you know why."

He gave her a wry look. "Indeed, I do. And so I would not even consider asking you if I could at all help it."

She took a sip of her chocolate, then nodded. "There are strange things afoot. A Mistress Almsley came and warned me that women of Talent were going missing. Did you send her?"

He slanted her a look and she chuckled. "Interesting, though," he said, "that she chose to warn you."

"Your last letter was warning enough. And getting here, that was such an adventure I wondered if someone was trying to keep us away. We broke six axles. Six. At once."

"But you are here." He touched her arm, laying his hand lightly on her warm skin. She smiled at him, a great wealth of tenderness in her expression. "That I am. And I will help, though I rather hoped that someone else in the troupe would be doing the actual helping, and I would be doing the actual getting to spend time with my husband."

"You could stay," he said wistfully.

"For a little while," she said, and turned her hand palm up. He laid his gently in her grip, pulling her hand to his lips so he could fervently kiss her fingers.

The next day was not nearly so pleasant. The bodies were retrieved and the netting carefully cut away. A boy arrived with a sheaf of papers containing notes of what Mistress Almsley and her husband saw in the cave, and notes, carefully annotated, as to what the different parts of the spell could mean. His frown deepened the more he read it, and thought, perhaps, he would spare his wife looking at it.

The five bodies lay on tables in one of the armory storerooms. Sketches of faces were being made to take around the town, especially the docks. Two men, three women. One man was covered with elaborate tattoos. He was huge, his feet hung off the end of the table, the blond braids of his hair were knotted and filthy. He would not have made a useful sailor, certainly not someone you'd send, fleet footed, up the riggings, but he had every mark of a soldier.

The other male was also very tall, but thin, his face so pretty that it was only a look at him unclothed that really confirmed his sex. No scars, no tattoos, not even callouses on his hands. Carys studied him, and his clothes—plain, mid-grade wool and linen—with much thought. The man was an enigma because he was hard to place. A scholar, perhaps. But there was no ink on his fingers, again, no callouses from writing. "Make sure Havelock takes a look at this. Someone cut out this one's heart, I wager. I cannot tell without looking in the cavity, but..."

His assistant hummed her assent and kept scribbling.

The next body was of a young woman, everything about her seemed soft. Her features, her figure. Carys was told that she was a virgin, and her hands bore callouses and ink stains. Her softness made the angry red burns around her face and along her arms and legs even more wrenching.

Next, a woman of indeterminate age, her body had been hard lived in, a prostitute. She had been beautiful once, but a life servicing strangers in the poorest part of the town was not one that let one age well.

The final woman was raw boned, large hands that had seen rough labor. Her hair was cropped close, and he saw, faintly, marks at her temple. Temple, inner arms—swollen like a bite. Interesting.

Shannon was copying one of the drawings. Five of each, with a short description to be sent around town, and beyond if needed. "I have an appointment. I shall be back as soon as I have tended to the governor's business." At the top of the steps he looked back down into the room, at the bodies.

*It will be easier, when I know their names*, he reassured himself.

He did not believe it.

# Chapter Thirteen

Tasmin was not positive exactly how she had planned to spend her day, but it certainly had not included sitting in the Port Admiral's office, waiting for Master Carys. *Brought it on myself, I suppose,* she thought, resigned. She had taken Magda's advice and written out a list of expenses that she had incurred since starting as Wise Woman. It had taken a couple of hours, and several times she had tracked down William or Ailiani to ask them if they remembered anything. Ayers, too, was helpful, remembering a trip out to a farm that she had quite forgotten.

The letter had been carefully written,

*As I am unsure who to ask these questions to, and feel that addressing the Governor's office directly would be a possible breach of protocol, I have written to see if you know what I should do...*

In most towns, it would be quite simple, but in Azin Shore, the structure of government was so messed up that she hadn't the foggiest notion who to press for help. *Besides, it gives me a chance to speak to Carys. If nothing else, getting a better idea of the man would be of service to me.* Though to be honest, she hoped to find out something, anything, about their progress on the murders.

Finally, she was called in, and she was surprised to see that Master Carys was not alone.

Both men rose. "Mistress Tasmin Almsley, this is Master Robert Cavendish. He is the Governor's secretary, and the gentleman who is in charge of the purse strings, as it were."

"A pleasure to meet you." Tasmin settled into a chair so that the men could do so, as well.

"I was just telling Master Cavendish that you have served Azin Shore very well in its time of need."

"Still, Master Carys, she should have contacted us sooner, we like to have a much better picture of spending before the fact, as it were." Master Robert was slender and young but his face was already becoming strained and carved by the work, which he obviously took very seriously.

"I apologize," she said, trying to be kindly and innocent in her mien. "It never occurred to me to ask before."

"And why are you asking *now*, then?" The younger man sounded vastly insulted, and Tasmin wanted to remind him that she was not asking for money out of his purse, but wisely refrained. Instead, she flashed Master Carys a look and then turned her attention back to Cavendish.

"I am sorry, but some of the ingredients that I have had to use are quite pricey. If I am to continue to serve during Azin Shore's time of need, I require help."

"But you are not officially our Wise Woman. There is no documentation."

Master Carys cleared his throat. "I am afraid that Master Cavendish makes very good points." His tone conveyed a wealth of regret that did not quite match his eyes. "Well, there is only one other choice. We shall do without a Wise Woman. Mistress Tasmin, I am very sorry, the best I can do is announce far and wide that the Governor's Office does not wish to employ a

Wise Woman at this time. Perhaps that way you will not be bothered by as many people needing help."

"But Master Carys..." Tasmin did not like the expense, but she did not wish to abandon people, either. She looked at the two men, trying to form words.

"They can just go to an Apothecary or the doctor, right Master Cavendish? And if they need any help with magical rituals...well. I am sure there is a Wise Woman within a few days drive." She caught the gleam in his eyes, then, and smiled sweetly.

"Perhaps you can get her to visit!" Tasmin said brightly. "I am sure that people will be willing to wait a few months."

"Oh, yes," Carys added, "People are very understanding when it comes to the future of their children."

Cavendish did not look amused. He sat there, fingernails digging into the arm of the chair before he caught himself, hands absently smoothing away at the fabric. "Very well. You may take this draft to the bank and get reimbursed." He started writing it out. "It will be reimbursement only on a monthly basis, until you finally take the vows."

"Unlikely, as she has already spoken vows to her husband," Carys interrupted.

"Or we find a new one," Cavendish finished. He signed the paper in the angriest way possible and slid it across the table to Tasmin, who forebore to take it up until the ink was dried. She was not going to descend on the paper like a hungry vulture after all; though the quick glance she had afforded herself assured her that it was fair.

"Thank you for helping us resolve the matter so civilly," Carys said. "Mistress Almsley will submit her invoice directly to you on the last day of each month from now on."

"I will keep very precise accounts and send them over to you," she agreed.

Cavendish rose and grabbed his cloak. Carys rose also, and as he walked around her chair, he said, "You will stay for a moment?" And she nodded, even though she could tell it was not a suggestion.

Carys walked Cavendish out the door and down the hall to the reception area, doubtless to make sure the other man felt important and respected.

She looked at the draft that sat, drying, on the table. *Well, that helps matters and I am very grateful.*

He returned, but this time he sat in the chair next to her, and simply studied her.

"When the last Port Admiral stared at me like that he was trying to decide whether to seduce me or kill me," Tasmin said with a touch of primness.

He smiled. "I am contemplating neither, I assure you."

"That is a relief. Thank you for straightening things out. I did not expect you to act so swiftly."

"Well, we do need a Wise Woman." He paused, rubbing the spot under his lower lip. "And, of course, it gives us an opportunity to converse. Your new house guest is of great interest, as is how you came upon the bodies in such an out of the way hiding place."

*Oh, dear. I am not the only one here looking for information. But at least it saves me the trouble to bringing up the topic.* "Out of the way, yes, which is exactly why that would be such a good place to hide them."

"And work magic."

"Even so," she shrugged. "It seemed like a good place to go and look." She explained briefly about the spell she cast, leaving Magda's help out of it.

"Do you think this Miss Magda knew about the bodies before you got there?"

Tasmin thought about it. "No, I don't. She wasn't shocked or horrified. Truly, she seemed to take for granted that they would be there, but I don't think she was the reason they were there. Does that make sense?"

Carys blinked at her a moment. "No."

"Well, I am fairly certain I am not giving shelter to a murderess. Mistress Deitson lacks magic and is afraid of heights. My husband and myself have no motive, and I still believe the killer of those people is the same as the person who killed Magda's child. If I don't believe anything else about the woman, I believe her grief."

He tapped his finger on the desk. "Start from the beginning, then."

Tasmin did, trying not to leave anything important out, not obsessing over telling him every scrap of information, either. She was still leery of completely trusting the man, but she wasn't so selfish that she didn't want to genuinely help.

"And so Mistress Magda has taken up residence. She must be a pleasant house guest." His tone, of course, implied otherwise, and invited confidence, but she smoothed past it.

"Well, we are merely helping the poor woman...and I do emphasize poor...in her hour of need."

The finger that had been tapping on the desk pointed at her. "You think she's a target."

"I really don't see any reason to have killed the child, was there? And unlike the others, well, we found her body." She paused. "Unless you found something?"

"We found signs that her neck had been snapped."

"It would take some strength to do such a thing..." she started.

"A child like that?" he said in a 'you know better' tone of voice.

She shrugged and looked away. "Healing her seems out of place. There are already several souls on that person's conscience. What is one more?"

"It is hard to tell, with the truly mad." She had nothing to say to that. After a moment, Carys continued. "So, why do you think the mother is the target? Who would want to murder *that* woman? She has nothing, in point of fact, to most people in our town she is the epitome of nothing."

Tasmin frowned at that, but said, "Because someone wants to bring a ghost storm onto the town. You saw it the other night."

He sat forward, looking up at her. "I have seen things, I would say things you would not be able to fathom, but I suppose fathoming the unknown is part of your job."

At this point Tasmin would have usually protested, but she stayed silent, slightly hypnotized by his voice. "Ghost storms feed on anger and pain. They need souls who have died furious and screaming, which is, thank God, not usually what happens here."

"Yes, and if enough souls die that way to bring the storm, surely we would have noted it, aye? But what if they are magnifying what they have?" Tasmin posed.

"Alright." He sat back. "How?"

"That, I don't know. I wish I did, but…" She shrugged. " A magnification spell is a huge working, it needs a space, it needs to be set up and left."

"And you have looked for this spell?"

She nodded. "To no avail. We could not find anything in town. The spell in the cave was, well, it was not for that. I am unsure what the spell was trying to accomplish. It seems to me that instead of trying to erase the spell by washing it away, they scribbled over it with other markings. Very dangerous, but it does confuse anyone trying to decipher intent."

He nodded, but she felt like this was not a great surprise to him.

"In town. Well. Naturally. No one would want to create such a huge undertaking right under your nose. But out of town. Have you considered that?"

William was trying to not think too much about the murders, because his first and most important responsibility for the day was to turn out some chocolates, but he was already distracted. Tatu was perched on his shoulder, clinging to his ear lobe or curled in his collar. When he tried to engage her he got nothing but silence, so he just let her stay there.

Sometimes she unbalanced and pulled on his hair, but mostly she clung to the shell of his ear. Even when he held a chocolate covered spoon up she did not shift or take some of the tempting treat, which worried him even more, because generally the sprites couldn't resist it.

He finished making raspberry filled truffles, and moved on to making chocolate truffles. He kept looking at the pantry, where the sprites seemed to center themselves. They usually surrounded him in a gentle, warm cloud of chaos, but the nest seemed to be taking all their time.

He turned his head and asked Tatu, softly, "What is going on with all of you?" Her answer was to just cling harder to his ear.

He patted the space where he felt her very gently, and kept working. When he didn't have company, he would take Tasmin away from any invisible ears (if he could) and try to come up with a plan. He did not like what was going on. *Perhaps it is just Magda*, he thought, but he feared that the ghost storm, sitting off shore like a gray smudge, was scaring them.

Point of fact, he did not care for anything that was going on. A letter from his brother was well over due, his sister-in-law was sending pitiful notes from her prison, making him feel guilty for neglecting her.

Then, the bodies. He dreamed of them, hanging from the ceiling, quietly whispering to him. One of the bodies held a hand out to him, whispering things in Tasmin's voice. It did not take a dream reader to tell that he was frightened for his wife. He sighed softly, stirring the chocolate over the fire constantly, anxious that it should not stick. He did not wish to curtail her movements, but he was worried. She had magic, was female, and abroad and unprotected often. Exactly as a Wise Woman would be and exactly, William had in mind, the reason why they were dead. He took the chocolate off the fire and started pouring.

Tasmin came into the kitchen. "A letter from your mother has been delivered," she said in a falsely bright voice.

"Oh, how lovely!" he said, attempting to sound at least as cheerful. He wiped his hands and took the paper and opened it, while Tasmin grabbed a cloth and used it to pick up the molds and gently tap them to chase the air bubbles. "She wishes you to accompany her on a visit to Bonny."

She leaned slightly away from the letter, which he laid on the edge of the table in case she wanted to read it. "Does she explain why?"

"Because it is appropriate for you to visit your sister-in-law."

"My sister-in- law who is in prison because she is an adulteress, who somewhat helped the people who were trying to kill you?"

He tried not to smile. "That would be her, yes. I don't have any others."

"Are you sure? Can we make up one?"

"I thought you *liked* Bonny." Bonny's greatest sin had been allowing her romanticism to override her sense.

She sighed. "Oh, I do, I do, but, you see, it's the going with your mother that actually puts me off."

"It will not be a long walk out with her. You should not have to spend much time actually alone with her." He tried to be comforting. He didn't really want to force Tasmin to spend time with his mother, after all, he knew that Henriette could be trying, which he also had to admit, was putting it lightly. But there were things that one must do, and he thought Tasmin probably could not really get out of it.

"Why do you want me to go? She's just going to harp and harp about how horrid I am and that I need to start having babies."

"I don't really want you to go, but you've made your excuses twice already, I am not sure that you can really get away with a third and still keep an illusion that you and she get along. And... really? But we've only been married for a few months...surely she won't be..." and he stopped talking because he saw Tasmin's face and knew he was being unrealistic about his mother.

"Well, fie on it then," he said. "Perhaps you can tell her that because of your duties as Wise Woman and my duties with the warehouse that we are seriously behind on chocolate making and that I cannot let you go."

"Really?" she said, lacing her hands together, her eyes going all big and soft. "You won't be disappointed?"

"Yes, and never," he said, kissing her on the forehead. She turned her face up for a real kiss, and he obliged her cheerfully, ignoring Ailiani's upraised voice.

"Ahem," a new voice said from the doorway. "I do hope that is not the dress you intend to visit your sister-in-law in."

They both froze, not just from mortification, but from the ice of the glare that came from the woman next to them.

William recovered first. "Ah. Good morning, Mother, I was just saying that…"

"Family duty is not nearly important to you, but then," she gestured to the shop, "I knew that already." She turned and looked out the door. "You may make me a cup of chocolate while your mistress changes into less worn attire."

Tasmin hastened off, walking past Ailiani who shrugged and said, "I tried!" apologetically. Tasmin petted her on the shoulder but did not stop.

William smiled at his mother. "She might want to spend more time with you if she actually thought you felt she was part of the family."

"Oh, but I wouldn't wish her to feel pressured."

This put William and Henriette into a staring contest, which lasted a long time, and he let her win simply because he had better things to do. He shook his head and broke contact. "You could try."

"So could she." Henriette smiled sweetly.

He took the molds and walked them over to his cooling shelves to let them set and harden. When he turned around his mother had wandered back out to the front room. Ailiani nervously placed a cup on a saucer in front of her and gave an unpracticed curtsey. The older woman nodded her head and then reached over and scratched at something on the table with one well done nail. She flicked her fingers to clear the imaginary dirt away and looked unimpressed.

"The table is quite clean," William said, peeved because he could see how this affected Ailiani, who looked on nervously from her post, surreptitiously straightening her apron over her bright blue dress.

"Is it?" Henriette asked.

He joined her. "Have you heard anything of interest of late? Have you heard from Andrew?"

"Yes, but only briefly. I know that he is alive." She took a sip of the chocolate, and gave a slight shrug as if to say it wasn't too bad. William knew she would rather die than admit that she liked it or anything about his endeavors. "You know, the Heir House has been boarded up and empty since Andrew left. You might want to consider taking up residence until his return. In fact, you can probably stay even afterwards, at least until his wife is free."

The Heir House was a small, but very lovely home that huddled in the shadow of his parents' much larger abode. If he had not retired from the family business, he and Tasmin would be there now.

"I think that Tasmin and I should probably stay near our place of business."

"Well, I think you should ask her about it, before giving your answer. After all, if we lived closer, you never know, Tasmin and I may become famous friends."

Ailiani ran into the kitchen, where she had a coughing fit. Henriette cast an annoyed look at her departing back.

"We are careful to never cough anywhere near the goods we have for sale," William lied dryly.

"So I see. How very admirable."

"We make every attempt." *How long does it take for one woman to change a frock?*

Another sip. "Your father is very grateful to you for your help while Andrew is gone. He is very impressed that you are able to balance both tasks so well."

He felt as if he were in a boat, and that boat was heading for a whirlpool that had developed out of nowhere. Figuratively trying to paddle backwards and away from it, he said, "It is not as easy as I make it seem, I assure you."

"Here I am!" Tasmin bounded down the steps and into the room. "I am so sorry that I kept you waiting, and poor Bonny!" She smiled. "She's been waiting for lunch all this time. I am dreadfully sorry."

He imagined, he was sure, the half regretful glance Henriette spared for her partially full cup, but she rose. "Of course." She said. "We cannot keep her waiting any longer. But I thought you were going to change your dress."

Tasmin smiled. "Of course I did. I put on a less worn version." She turned as if to display it. To be honest, it was a completely different dress, at least, it was a different color and that was pretty much where William's ability to identify clothes ended.

Ailiani handed Tasmin a small bag of chocolates, and William smiled his thanks at her.

The door closed, and both women were handed up into the coach. Henriette wouldn't walk to the prison like a commoner, after all, and both Ailiani and William—and maybe even Tatu, still on his shoulder— let out a sigh of relief.

"How long was she standing there?"

"Not very long, I promise, I tried to call out in a completely natural way to warn you but..." She shuddered. "That woman. I still bear scars."

"You were only a servant in that house a handful of days."

Ailiani was not impressed. "Deep, painful scars."

"I grew up there. I feel great pity for you, but you will not win this argument."

Ailiani shuddered, and reached over and gave his arm a pet.

"Don't even say it," he warned.

"Say what?"

"'Poor William, it explains so much'," he said in a half decent imitation of the cadences of her voice.

She smirked in response.

Since Bonailia of the House of Almsley was a lady of one of the richest merchant houses in town, she was afforded the use of one of the meeting rooms for her visits. A table had been set out, and her personal servant was putting out plates on the soft green fabric that graced it.

Bonny was led from her cell, which, if Tasmin remembered right, was small, with a tiny window and a brazier that was being constantly tended. It had one narrow but comfortable bed (the maid went back to her own bed at the master house at night), covered in thick blankets. It was as nice as a prison cell could be, but it would be no competition for the bright cheerful room they lent them for their lunch.

Bonny crossed the room and hugged Henriette first, then Tasmin. "I am so glad you made it today," she said with such sincerity that Tasmin felt guilty. She had visited a thin handful of times since the young woman had taken residence here.

"Come, let us sit and eat," Henriette said as her servant and Bonny's started putting out the food. "Before the food gets any colder."

"If you had given me a little more warning I could have created a heating charm, to make sure everything stayed warm," Tasmin said. Henriette took offense, as she was meant to, and arched an eyebrow.

"Oh, please. I do so hate it when you two fight," Bonny said, which forestalled any further words, even from Henriette.

"I received a letter from Andrew," Henriette announced as she smoothed a napkin on her lap.

"Does he ask after me?" Bonny asked, a little too eagerly, but it was to be expected.

"He mentions that he has visited the Stairs of Alessyn. Tasmin, I do think your servant is from there?"

"She's not a servant, really," Tasmin felt forced to explain yet again.

"Shop girl, then. You can't argue with that."

She nodded and used a forkful of salad to keep her from talking any further.

Bonny swallowed and looked at her plate. "They say the women are very beautiful there. It's on one of the trade routes, is it not?"

"Yes," Tasmin said. "William used to buy fruit there, but it is also where they get a wonderful blue-green mineral that they crush up to make paints and make ups. 'Tis hard enough to carve into beautiful little beads."

"Do you think he might send me some?" Bonny sounded wistful. She had taken a sledge hammer to her life, but Tasmin's heart hurt for her.

"Perhaps next time he is through there."

A few weeks back, Tasmin had asked her why Andrew had left, "I thought the two of you were doing so well," she'd said.

And Bonny had teared up and said, "He is hoping to come back a better man." And then started to cry so that it seemed like she would never stop.

Now, at the table she said, "I do not know why he does not write me." She sounded so disconsolate.

Tasmin said. "Mayhaps he has, and the letter was lost. William never wrote much to me, it takes so long for a letter to get here. I was lucky if I heard from him four times a year."

Bonny looked hopeful.

"Letters do get lost," Henriette said ruefully. "And his own letter to me was quite short, just so we know he is well. He knows if he did not I would make him pay most severely."

Bonny coughed a laugh, and Tasmin half smothered a grin, unsure if she could laugh with the other woman or not. "There you go then. If our mother says so, then you know we are telling the truth."

Bonny beamed at them both and started eating, and Henriette and Tasmin met eyes. It was an odd moment, to be in accord with her mother-in-law, and she smiled a little.

"Have you seen the traveling elementalists?" Bonny asked after a little while. "I heard that their promotional display was quite lovely. Did they really have someone who could make dragons out of fire?"

"Yes, I saw him. And they had a woman with a gyre wheel," Tasmin said.

"I wondered when they would finally arrive. They spent two months in Dalmaca," Henriette pointed out. "I have never heard of such a thing."

"Maybe they were able to winter there easier for some reason?" Tasmin considered her point. Dalmaca was the next closest town, about two hours easy ride up towards the Capital Road. Anyone who wanted to cut down to Azin Shore would go through Dalmaca. She mulled over what she said, it was very unusual for a troupe to not winter at a decent port, where there would be more patrons.

"That does not seem like a very salubrious place to winter. Dalmaca is a stop, not a place of rest and convenience. They should have come down here, the Governor might have paid them to perform occasionally as well as offer them a safe place to winter." Henriette said.

"Interesting," Tasmin said.

"It's not like he hasn't done so in the past. Do you remember the troupe a couple of years back, with the fortune teller?" Bonny smiled at the memory.

"My dear, I do not waste my time with fortune tellers," Henriette said, but Tasmin was far from the conversation.

*There are some angles for me to chew on, after all, you cannot get much farther out of town than Dalmaca.*

"One of my friends from the Garden Club brought me a book to read," Bonny said, changing the subject. "I have been obsessively reading about the three Sea Witches."

"Sea Witches? I would think, young woman, you had had enough of witchcraft and such silliness."

"Maybe," Bonny gave her a bright smile. "But I want to know everything about them now. It's not as if I have a busy schedule and cannot indulge myself."

Tasmin clamped her teeth to keep from cheering at this sweet show of backbone. "It sounds interesting. Will you tell us about them while I cut the cake for our dessert?"

"There were three sisters," Bonny said. "There was Ithalia—she was the first born, and the coldest. The next youngest was Sorvalia—they said she was chaotic and mad, one moment she could be kind, the next cruel. And finally there was Thanlia, compared to the others she was kind, she was fair, and could be reasoned with."

"I heard of Ithalia," Tasmin said, not elaborating further. "She was so evil that she was locked away by her sisters."

"That would have been very hard. Nearly impossible," Bonny said. "She was known as the most powerful of her sisters, calculating, cruel, but never stupid. The three of them had a tight bond. The bond was what made their magic so powerful. Each had a different focus, but they could feed off each other. Ithalia, for example, could not be killed because she regenerated far too fast. Anything she touched would be stayed from rot. It made her sisters immortal."

Henriette took a sip of wine, then said, "Well, that would certainly be handy. There was a rumor, about our William, that he'd found an island with a terrible witch imprisoned on it. I always wondered how she would manage to stay alive, chained to a throne like that, outside and exposed to the elements, but that might make sense."

"William found an island with an imprisoned witch on it?" Tasmin asked, feeling slightly amused. "He never told me." *And he would skip that fact, too.*

"Perhaps he did not wish to insult you, he knows how you feel about people being called *witches*." She rolled her shoulders into a casual shrug. "In any case, it was only a rumor, found only whispered in sailors' taverns in the less pleasant part of town."

"And how did you hear of it?" Tasmin asked.

"Because the rumors were spread shortly after William came back and gave up the sea. We were desperate, his father and I, to discover why all of a sudden he decided to give up the life he loved and settle down to being a merchant."

Bonny was picking listlessly at her food. "Of course, because everyone knows it couldn't possibly because he wanted to settle down and get married," she muttered.

"Don't start developing opinions now, dear. It is much too late," Henriette said.

"I think she was agreeing that it was a perfectly reasonable response, because he could have certainly married and stayed at sea." Tasmin stepped, gently, on Bonny's foot. "But I must own that I am fascinated by the idea. Did you hear anything else about it?"

Henriette shook her head.

"They all had elements, that is interesting," Bonny said. "Sorvalia was the sea, Ithalia was the land, Thanlia was air."

"What ended their partnership, I wonder?" Tasmin asked. "Ithalia was put into an amulet, Sorvalia was put on an island...whatever happened to Thanlia? Did she get tired of her sisters and do away with them?"

"I haven't read that far," Bonny said ruefully, then she brightened. "But next time you come and visit, I will. Now you'll have to come."

"As if I need an excuse," Tasmin said, though to be honest, she could come more often. *After the murderer is caught, I will.*

# Chapter Fourteen

The shop smelled wonderful as always—new chocolates cooling on the rack were transferred to green and gold foil boxes of several different sizes. Even the sprites seemed a bit happier, ruffling waxed paper and zipping around the kitchen.

"I never realized how the traveling performers would affect our sales," Tasmin said.

"It feels like a holiday out there," Ailiani agreed, shaking her cloak a little and hanging it to dry.

William packed another little token-box. Sales of the small, present sized boxes of chocolate told William that many gentlemen were taking their ladies out this evening. He closed the box and carried it to the counter, carefully stacking it and the others into a pleasing display. "We will have to close early, even so," William said. "Since I will be taking you to see them."

Ailiani perked up a little, but, nonchalantly said, "But you'd still have me to watch over the store."

He gave her a fond look. "As if we would not include you."

Ailiani bounced on her heels a little, and Tasmin hugged her, one armed. "I am beyond excited," Tasmin said. "I've not seen a decent Fire Elementalist in years." In the North, elemental magic was common, and she found herself missing it.

"Do you think you can find a way to introduce me to him?" Ailiani asked. "He is quite handsome, I should like to see if he has need of an assistant. You can use your elementalist connections to convince him that I am absolutely essential."

William started to point out that elementalists did not need assistants, but at Ailiani's fake wide eyed innocence he busied himself helping a customer who probably did not need it.

"What? Are you planning on leaving us to run away with the elementalists?" Tasmin smacked a hand to her chest, much aggrieved.

"Well, I am just a shop girl!" Ailiani said, joining the dramatics. "What else can I do but wait to be rescued from my mundane existence?"

William ignored them, counted out the change to hand to the customer. When the customer left he shook his head at them, and they collapsed into giggles.

"Away with you, Mistress. Go ahead and get yourself ready, we'll meet you on the way."

"At the clock shop, as usual?" Ailiani grabbed her cloak and threw it around her shoulders.

William closed early as promised, turning the sign on the door over and locking up. Tasmin was in the kitchen preparing his bath.

When he was clean, he dressed in his best;freshly polished boots and everything. Tasmin was braiding her hair into a crown about her head, fastening it down with pearl headed pins. She had so few chances to dress up that she was putting on all her best.

"Did Carys speak to you about the bodies, or the information we sent him?" she asked, turning carefully to make sure that every stray hair was caught.

"Nay. I saw him, briefly, this morning on the way back from the docks, and he tipped his hat and kept going. I fear Magda may be right, that the victims were people no one would miss. I asked Ayers, and between him and Ailiani there is very little one can't find out. He says that no one is missing, say, from a family. But he did say there were rumors around the docks."

She tugged on the clasp of her necklace to make sure it was latched. "I wonder how they managed to take people. One of those bundles, at least, seemed fairly large. How does one capture and take someone that large away?"

He shrugged. "Magic? I was of a mind to ask if you could test them for Talent, but I suppose Carys has his own ways."

Her eyes widened. "That is an interesting thought! No one is ever tested for Talent after they are dead, are they? Because it no longer matters—it is a moot point. I wonder if anyone has a way to do that?" She itched to go look at her books. "The long held argument, you know, is whether magic is a part of the body, or of the soul. Scholars, philosophers, mages have all debated this for years."

"Let us not think of it now. Instead, we will go out, meet up with some friends, and watch magic, and when we come home you can tell me if they were really any good or not."

"Alright," she said, as he guided her down the stairs. She did not even notice him settle her cloak over her shoulders as she thought over the problem. *Would a ghost know? Franny had Talent. Maybe she has power, now that she's a ghost.*

"I wonder if non-talented people become ghosts. What makes a ghost?" she asked William as they made their way to the shop.

"Commonly it is about unfinished business. Even anger is just a form of unfinished business, aye?" He tipped his hat at some regular customers. "At least that's what they say. If someone in a story asks a ghost why it is here, it says 'Because my son murdered me,' or 'because I watched the man I love die horribly.'

Sometimes there is a curse that keeps a spirit here to wander until the world ends, but not a real purpose that you can identify and say, 'Here, if I follow these steps, I will have a ghost of my very own."

She grinned at that. "A pet ghost? We have enough problems with the sprites. But, there are points of comparison, enough that we can say, yes, unfinished business. Curses. But how many people really die feeling content and ready? I would say that if unfinished business was the only thing, that the world would be so full of ghosts you'd not be able to see an inch in front of you."

"What other condition has to be in place? Is it Talent? Are all ghosts people who were Talented in life, which is why the killer is going after them?"

Ailiani saw them and waved. She grabbed Tasmin's arm and the previous discussion faded away. Instead they spoke of other acts they had seen until they got to the hall.

William presented their tickets to the usher, and soon they were in and Tasmin felt her heart lift.

Normally, the meeting hall was a plain place, but through clever magic it had been transformed. Outside it looked like a warehouse. Inside, it looked like a palace. Rows of red velvet padded chairs circled the space for the actors. The walls were now blue with gold and white moldings, chandeliers made of ice and fire decorated the ceilings. Tasmin smiled and poked at her seat before sitting down. William tilted his head in question. "To see if the padding is real or glamor," she answered.

He stayed standing, looking for Ayers. Tasmin slipped her hand comfortably in his, looking around with an expression of pure joy. She and Ailiani exchanged excited grins as they adjusted their things and got comfortable. Elaborate framework had been set up. Not everything would be done by magic, but the line between magic power and physical skill would be erased. Ayers came in with his red-headed wife, Vicka, a woman that Tasmin knew very little about except that she was very quiet and sweet. "Are you sure we shouldn't have brought Magda?"

Tasmin asked as William finally settled down next to her, now that their friends had joined them.

"I wished to, very much, but she made it sound as if I were asking her to stand outside the shop naked," William said. "It was not a pleasant conversation."

"So few of them with her are."

"I agree," Ailiani said, leaning in. "But it must not be easy for her, she has not had a pleasant life."

"Of course, and I wish to be as sensitive and kindly about that as possible. I don't wish to hurt her pride or treat her with pity, but she could be a little less thorny," Tasmin said. "Perhaps one of us ladies should have offered?"

"William was as tactful as can be, but it would not be easy, mingling with people who think you are rubbish, and most of these people here would look down at her."

"But still," William said, as the lights dimmed and the audience slowly ceased to speak. "It might have distracted her for a while." Magda had spent the day reading Tasmin's books, the only time she left the kitchen was when Tasmin chased her out so she and William could heat water and bathe.

It was a shame that Magda had refused the invitation, for the show was well worth seeing. They had a lady who spun through the air, attached to the frame work by slender lengths of silk that sparkled and looked as fine as starlight. During her performance the air froze along the paths she took, forming exquisite patterns as she spun and twirled.

The Fire Elementalist came out, bare chested, his blond hair pulled back. Ailiani whispered something appreciative in Tasmin's ear. Tasmin covered her laugh with a cough.

The reason why he wore no shirt was soon clear. He sent dragons and phoenixes spinning and flying through the crowds, and they would come back and twine around his bare skin, disappearing beneath it. The creatures he created were intricate and beautiful. At the end he used fire to tell the highlights of a classic love story, while a couple sang the songs that accompanied it. Tasmin nudged Ailiani, who nodded. The woman was the same who had visited the shop the other day, asking such weird questions. *Why was she so obsessed with magic on her visit the other day? Especially since she is surrounded by people who live and breathe it?* She put it aside as the couple left and the elementalist conducted acts of daring, accompanied by the lady on the gyre wheel.

The elementalist departed the stage, leaving the lady on the gyre wheel to perform subtle, amazing feats, and then she was followed by a pair of shape shifters who put on a mock battle, changing as they fought from tiger or wolf to human again. They bounded off the stage and the couple came out again, he played an elaborately carved stringed instrument that made images shimmer in the air while she sang, pulling things out of thin air. Nothing she did was magic, Tasmin realized.

And then there was a ghost. Tall and stately, she walked over the stage, hovering a few feet above it. The tiny singer turned to throw scarlet rose petals into the air and screamed. Her partner knocked over his chair as he reached for her.

"Do you see her? Oh please tell me you see her," Tasmin whispered.

"I do," William said numbly.

The ghost tilted her head and looked at the couple on the stage, then she turned and studied the audience. Her face was blank, an oval space devoid of anything, hair floating around her like a veil. She settled down onto the floor, and where she walked, the wood crumbled and rotted and aged. At first people were not sure if it were part of the show or not, and sat, confused and upset, in their seats. The ghost paused and turned that featureless plain towards Tasmin and Ailiani, giving a slight nod. William's arm went across his wife, as if he could somehow shield her.

The doors of the hall were thrown open, and the ghost disappeared out into the night.

"Ladies and gentlemen…" Olonah stood on the floor next to the stage. She stared at the mark in the floor, then looked at Tasmin, her face unreadable for a moment, before the *bon vivant* mask fell into place. "That was not how we meant to conclude our performance, but sometimes the supernatural opens a window and comes through of its own accord. We do hope that you enjoyed our presentations of magic and wonder. We wish you beautiful dreams and a safe journey home." She bowed elegantly and went backstage again.

"Is that all she's going to do?" Tasmin hissed. "That was a *ghost*. You don't just wish everyone a nice evening and go on your way."

The tone of the crowd was no different. "Mistress Tasmin, do you have anything to protect us from ghosts?" a man asked, coming up to her. Tasmin, the closest thing the town had to a Wise Woman, found herself surrounded as the now desperate crowd pressed in. William snaked an arm around her, and looked at Ailiani. Ayers was gently pulling both his wife and Ailiani back from the crowd with an apologetic grimace, which was rewarded by a nod from William. He also mouthed "Magda," because he was hoping that they would go that way, make sure she was safe. There was no sense in them being there.

Tasmin tried to speak but the building noise of the crowd surrounding them was too loud.

"William, help me up," she said, and he helped her stand on one of the chairs. "Ladies and Gentleman," she said in a tone that must have put the fear of God into the hearts of her former students, "I understand your fear. She did not touch any of you, and so we know you do not have to worry that you are ghost marked. If you are really frightened, look at your hands." She stripped the gloves off her hands and held them up, palms out, then turned them, showing both sides unblemished. People followed her example. "Good, good," she said, looking around. "Now, when you go home, get out the salt. Before you are to take to your beds, run a line of salt in front of the window of your bed chamber and the door way. If you have a fireplace, run a line there, too. If you prefer you can run a circle of salt around your bed instead, but this should be just as effective. If you have garlic, place it on either side of the bed. You should be safe enough for tonight.

If you are still worried, come and see me in the morning and I will make you something better, but for this night you and your family should be fine."

She got down off her chair as the crowd scattered, eager to go home and draw a line of salt. The Fire Elementalist was there, tilting his head and staring at Tasmin oddly. "What?" she asked boldly.

He looked around, as if making sure that no ears were too close, and said, "I don't know if you are a very, very good Wise Woman or a very, very bad one."

"The worst thing that will happen is that they will all waste a great deal of salt. None of them are in any danger. But you and your troupe, every single one of you are, and not all of the salt in the world will help keep you safe. You are all very powerful. Why would the ghost fool with them, when it could have you?"

"Or you."

"Or Magda." She looked at William. "We must get home. You, Bran, I think they said your name is? You need to get your friends under protection. Leave this stuff for tomorrow."

It was a very long walk home. She got stopped constantly by people, and she made reassurances, checked faces, wrists and the backs of necks, whatever they needed to feel secure again. Ghosts were rare and the stuff of tales of fear. Some people were wondering if the ghost was even real, or if it had been some prop created by the travelers to create a sensation. Whatever it was, it was not good for making any speed.

But it did not matter. Magda was in the kitchen, drinking tea and reading a book.

It was Ailiani that was missing.

Carys used the confusion of the crowd to go backstage.

Olonah was barking orders. Aristel, the singer, and her husband Merin were in one corner, her tiny hands stroking her husband as he shuddered and coughed.

"Is he alright?"

Olonah looked at Merin blankly for a moment. "No, but no worse than usual. Aris will take care of him." Her fingers sought out his, cold as ice. "Nora is missing. She was supposed to go on next, but then the ghost appeared. Maybe she fled, I don't know."

Merin stood up, gently pushing his china doll of a wife away. "I have to go find her."

"But you are unwell!" Aristel insisted.

"Merin, Aristel is right. Bran and the others are looking for her. If you go out and have another fit, people who could be looking for your sister will be forced to attend to you," Carys said, mostly so Olonah would not have to.

Merin gave him a hateful look. "What does an outsider know?" But he allowed Aristel to pull him back down.

Carys pulled his wife a little aside. The damage the ghost created was immense. "Her caravan?" he asked, pointing to a small wreck of a thing, once bright blue paint peeling, it looked as if it had sat abandoned in a field for years.

"Yes. She always meditated before she went on, to connect her to the earth."

Olonah shook her head. She had stripped herself of all jewelry, save for her long gold nails, and dressed in a plain dress. Any second, they would leave and start the search.

"Was she very powerful?"

"Not really, neither of them are. She's empathetic, she can read energy and make good guesses from what she sees."

"Ah. She's the mentalist, she goes out into the audience and tells people what they want to hear," Carys said, and Olonah sighed at the derision in her husband's voice.

"It is a popular part of the show, and it makes the audience feel a part of things. The whole performance can't be all bright lights and extraordinary feats of body and magic. The mind and heart needs to come in, too."

"As you say," he grumbled. "And everyone is familiar with her habits? To reconnect with the earth? Why the earth?"

"She said it was so that she did not float off into the aether." Olonah smiled.

He reached out and stopped short of touching the rotting caravan. Cold radiated off it still. "I have never heard of a ghost so destructive."

"Or angry. It radiated off of her."

Carys looked at his wife thoughtfully. "Mistress Almsley mentioned that the ghost storms were drawn by angry spirits."

"This is true." Olonah was staring at the caravan thoughtfully. "Do you notice anything odd in the decay pattern? The door is untouched."

"My dear, even I know that ghosts don't need doors."

"But Nora would. And if decay follows everything she touches, why have we not already found a dried up corpse somewhere?"

"Why would a ghost need to kidnap a woman?"

Olonah nodded. "And who helped her do so?"

"We may still find a dried up corpse as you so elegantly put it."

His wife's shoulders sagged, and she looked very tired. "Ah, yes. But I am hoping not. Shall we go and see if we can help look?" He nodded and took her arm.

The town was unearthly quiet. Carys raked his hands through his hair. *They are all hiding behind their doors, doing what Mistress Almsley suggested. Normally that would be splendid, but how am I to track her?*

Olonah looked around. "This is the very center of town?"

"As close as we can get," Carys said.

Bran held his hands over the paving stones, as if feeling for heat. "You are right, a ley runs right through."

Olonah had a feather in her hand, she was wrapping another strand of Nora's hair around it, murmuring something as the wind picked up. Bells started to toll.

"The ghost storm is returning," Carys said.

Olonah hummed ascent under her breath. Bran said, "Two steps forward and, I think, three to the left will get you in a good spot on the line."

The heels of her shoes clicked loudly as she followed the instructions. Carys counted the bells without meaning to, worrying.

The feather balanced on Olonah's palm, then slowly rose up, standing. And that was all it did. Her brows furrowed, her jaw locked as she concentrated, more and more. Bran even came over and carefully cupped his hand under hers, but all the feather did was remain in place, frozen, not even spinning slowly or indicating anything.

Finally she stepped back, letting out a gust of pent-up breath. He'd never heard anyone exhale with such anger before, and he waited for her to finish calming herself before speaking. "Is there another place we can try?"

"No." The word had a great deal of snap to it, but Carys did not mind. "No," she said softer. "The line is the best place for such a spell. Like calls to like, the power of the earth to the power in her. We should have found her in seconds."

"I've seen the spell fail, but usually the feather spins, or floats. It does something," Bran added. "But for it to be frozen, it has to mean someone is blocking us."

Carys thought about Tasmin's failed finding spell. Had someone blocked it, to make it impossible for her to find the girl? He discarded the thought, concentrating on Nora, possibly in great danger, if she was even still alive. "Well, Azin Shore is not that large. We might as well get started. I'll go to the barracks, see if I can rouse anyone."

Of course, the first thing Tasmin did was go into the wind sprites' nest in the pantry, to see if there were any that would help her. Still, the place was empty as a tomb, the room oddly cold and silent. She could hear Ayers outside the room. "She got pulled from us, in the press. We looked and looked for her, it was only a second, and she was gone."

"There was nothing you could have done," William said. "Take Vicka home, we shall send for you if we need, but I am sure we can find her." Tasmin paused only long enough to take a heavier cloak, and they were out the door again.

The walk to Miss Dovlington's had never been longer. William was grimly silent, and Tasmin had nothing to speak on aside from fear, so they walked as fast as they could.

Miss Dovlington met them at the door. She never let anyone in without a thorough interrogation.

"Good evening, Captain, Mistress. How may I help you tonight?"

The parlor was plain. You would expect a certain amount of fussiness from someone called Miss Dovlington, but there was none to be found. A couple of long couches with embroidered pillows, some tables, a fireplace with a painting of a ship being torn apart by a kraken. A tapestry of a battle on the edge of the sea between mer-folk and women mounted on unicorns caught Tasmin's eye, as it did every time. It looked very, very old. She'd looked for the subject matter in books but could find no stories or hints as to what had inspired it.

"Mistress Deitson came out to the elementalists tonight," William started. "There was some trouble."

"A ghost. I heard." Her mouth formed a thin line.

"And we lost her in the crowd. We just wished to make sure she got home safely."

"I shall show you her room. I did not hear her come in."

Her room was what you would expect, narrow, if you sat on the bed you could reach the opposite wall if you stretched out your arms. She had one trunk, which she also used as a table, a basket overflowing with the sewing that she sometimes took in for a few extra pence, a shelf with some odds and ends, pegs with clothes on them.

*I feel like we are wasting our time.* It wasn't until William coughed quietly that Tasmin realized that she had said the words out loud.

"One must be thorough." Miss Dovlington said.

Tasmin looked out the narrow window. She could see the distant flickering on the horizon, and shivered.

Unnatural colors shot along the line between sky and sea, growing closer. "I think the ghost storm is returning." Tasmin pushed past them both and ran down the stairs, heading for the beach. "I need to get closer to the shore so I can see it better, determine if it is closing."

Gravel crunched under their feet as they rushed down the path.

"Her cloak!" William let go of Tasmin's arm and ran for the rise, taking up the fabric. He stopped abruptly, and when she got to the edge of the hill, Tasmin saw why.

The darkness seemed to be looming closer to the shore, the keening wail made her insides turn to water. "I don't think it is coming closer. Should we warn them anyway?"

"The bells have just started," he put his arm around her and drew her close. "Between the show that happened tonight and those, everyone should be inside."

*Except us* was left unsaid. Tasmin felt a familiar tug, and walked towards the bend in the shore.

And between them, where a fragment of moon silvered the water, Ailiani danced right along the very edge of the shore, where the water lapped the land. The sprites were there, Tasmin could not only feel them, but see them lift Ailiani as she danced, slowly and gracefully, in a cloud of air. Ailiani spun in place and threw her arms out, staring into the distance. Tasmin approached her carefully, her eyes seemed to be looking inward.

*Stay back, stay back*, a small voice commanded. It was Nee-no.

"What is going on?" Tasmin asked.

*They are weaving a wall. She will not be harmed*, the Chief promised soothingly.

"Great Father, I do not understand what has been going on."

"We will fight the ghost storm," Ailiani whispered. "We will keep you safe." It was her friend's voice, but she was not certain if it was her speaking.

Tasmin fell silent. *There will be a lot of conversation. A lot of conversation, and very soon.* She was worried about the sprites, about Ailiani who seemed to be acting as a conduit for them.

*Maybe there is something I can do. No wonder she seems so tired. She has always intimated that she had no Talent, and if that is true, this could be killing her.*

"Look at it," William whispered. "The storm is being held back."

"But it means something else is being held back, too."

He looked at her, and she said, "The storm was being drawn in. Someone else is dead."

They spread out Ailiani's cloak and sat on it, huddled together for warmth, while they watched the ghost storm rage against the wall, crashing against it like waves of blackness that flowed up and blocked the moon.

And finally, it backed away, and faded, receding into the darkness again, and the sprites slowly let Ailiani go, and she sunk slowly to her knees.

Tasmin knelt by her head, gently lifting her shoulders. "Sweetheart, are you alright?"

"So tired," she whispered. "Can I not just lay here?"

"I am afraid not," William said as Tasmin wrapped her in her cloak. "Tide and all."

Ailiani smiled weakly, her eyes struggling to stay open. "William?" Tasmin whispered, and he nodded and picked the slight woman up.

"I am greatly relieved that you are here, else the townspeople would take great delight in reporting around that I am carrying an unattached woman to her bed chamber," he said a bit wryly.

"Well, I am sure that they will leave my presence out, and tell the story anyway," Tasmin said, smoothing Ailiani's hair out of her face.

She preceded him into Ailiani's room and pulled the bed covers back. William set her on the edge of the bed so Tasmin could wipe as much of the sand off of her feet and skirts as possible, then departed so Tasmin could help her change and get into bed. Ailiani was asleep. She sighed and moved a little with coaxing, but could not open her eyes or respond.

Tasmin then crawled in next to her, trying to warm her. The bed was treacherously narrow, but she managed, and William adjusted the edge of the blanket. "It is best not to leave her alone," Tasmin said, and he agreed, taking the one chair and placing it against the door. The wind sprites settled along Tasmin's hip. She could feel their familiar presences, Tatu curled up on William, as did Arix, a warrior sprite who seemed to be as protective of Tatu as Tatu was of William. Nee-no was perched against the headboard, between the two women, and the others, all settled in soft valleys along the folds of the blankets.

The next day Ailiani seemed perfectly normal, if a little tired, a little gray around the edges. Her tattoos stood out starkly against her skin, making them almost extra dimensional, but she seemed absolutely herself.

Except for the fact that she didn't remember anything. "This is very nice, but why are you in bed with me?" she asked, patting Tasmin's hair.

"Because you and the wind sprites were doing something, a spell, I am not sure, the Great Father called it 'weaving a wall'—and then you collapsed, and William had to carry you home."

"Ooh, the scandal!" Ailiani said, winking at William.

"We did not wish to leave you alone," William supplied. "Are you sure that you don't remember a thing about it?"

Ailiani scooted up against the headboard and shook her head. "No. I got lost in the crowd and could not find any of you, so I came home and went to bed, and then I woke up with your wife drooling on me."

"Hardly!" Tasmin said, embarrassed.

Ailiani grinned. "Well, perhaps not precisely."

"Not even a hint of a memory? What did you dream of?" Tasmin persisted.

She shrugged her shoulders elegantly. "Ask the sprites?"

Tasmin shook her head. "They were with us when we fell asleep, but I don't feel them now, except for Tatu?"

"Aye," William said. "She is here, against my shoulder."

"Tatu, sweetheart, can you tell us what is going on?" Tasmin held out her hands to the little sprite. In response, she felt little hands tapping gently along her cheek, and then she swerved back and hit William hard enough for him to jump.

"I gather she would rather not," he said.

Tasmin nodded, troubled. "I think that the sprites must be using you as a conduit to help focus their power to push back the ghost storm. If your body was not made for magic, then I fear you may burn out. It could damage you."

Ailiani paused. There was almost a delicacy to the way she picked her next words, as if walking through a house full of traps. "I am not worried. I trust the sprites. And if I am indeed helping the people of my adopted homeland and protecting them from a horrid death, well, that is a good thing."

"Not if you die!" Tasmin said.

Ailiani patted her cheek. "I feel weak with hunger. Could we speak more of this later? If we do not get to breakfast soon, there will be none left."

Tasmin opened her mouth to accuse her of avoiding the topic, but William scooted the chair nosily as he got up. "We will leave you to it, then. I must take my wife home. I suspect business will be quite brisk today, and not for chocolates, oh Wise Woman mine."

Tasmin felt rebellious for a moment, then kissed Ailiani on the cheek and shook out her skirts. William placed his hand on top of Ailiani's head, and the two looked each other in the eyes for a moment. She shook her head slightly and William turned, offered his wife his arm, and left.

# Chapter Fifteen

One of the side effects of the ghost storms was that it seemed to drain the color out of everything. Granted, it was the part of the winter where everything looked dreary and old and gray, but things that William expected to see look bright and cheerful had a sad cast, as if something had been drained from them.

*Maybe 'tis just me.* He yawned hugely. The chair had not been the most comfortable thing in the world to sit in, and as grateful as he was that everyone was safe and sound, he really just wanted to go to bed and forget the world. He had gone out to the warehouse, reckoned with the books, stopping only at the fish market to bring home something to cook for dinner.

Tasmin was chewing on the end of her stylus, looking over her notes, which were spread all over the one of the tables closest to the kitchen. Bits of wire, a canister of salt, crystal beads and tiny bags told him that the table had seen a lot of amulet work that morning, too. "But someone must be dead." William eased down into one of the chairs at the table, careful not to jostle things. He'd have to take the fish into the kitchen but for now he was content to sit with his wife.

"I've been all over the place. No one has seen anything or heard anything at all," Ailiani said. Magda, who had been reluctantly rousted onto the street, nodded in agreement.

"The elementalists?"

"Even they say that all is well."

"I am glad to hear it, of course, that there are no new deaths, but it does not make sense," Tasmin said. "The theory that I have cobbled together says that ghost storms are drawn by angry ghosts, right? Our ancestors must have sent the ghost storm out to sea."

"Instead of destroying it like a sensible person would," Magda interjected.

"I have to agree with you, after all, destroying it would be immensely preferable, but sadly it doesn't seem possible."

Magda threw her hands up. "How do we know that? Books? You are relying on Creighton's, for Light's sake!"

"Point taken, again, but sadly I can only go by what I know. And for hundreds of years, we have thought that the ghost storms were a terrible weapon with undeniable side effects. It is well documented."

"No one in Pandroth would have created a weapon that could not be undone!"

"Well, if you know any Pandrazzi magic that will help, you will find me a willing student." Tasmin's voice brought down the temperature in the room by a few degrees.

"Please, not another hour of this," Ailiani said, slumping in her chair.

Tasmin felt like going back to bed and pulling the covers over her head. Instead, she said, "Perhaps, Magda, you will find a solution if you think upon it. You cannot be the only Pandrazzi mage in the kingdom. Is there a way to put out a call?"

Magda looked like she would say no, but she took a breath. "Yes. I will think on it." Magda nodded.

William looked at Tasmin and shrugged a little. She nodded, and smiled. "If you need anything, let me know."

# Chapter Sixteen

Since Carys was fond, as ever, of keeping things to himself, Tasmin and William knew nothing of the missing woman.

It was driving Tasmin crazy, not doing anything, not being able to find new clues, so, remembering what Carys said about perhaps the spell being done outside of town, they packed their bags and headed out of town, to Dalmaca.

"Have you been to it before?"

William nodded. "A couple of times. As I said, it is a place where merchants stop along the way to the Capital. The inns are cheaper, the warehouses less damp..." He smiled at her. "And a merchant who does not try to save himself a coin or two is no merchant at all."

She smiled a little then, "I don't much care for the idea that Olonah and her crew are involved. They seem fairly nice, really."

"I don't know if the fact they decided to spend some of the winter in Dalmaca is really enough to condemn them," William said. "After all, they pulled up stakes and came to Azin, just a little later. Perhaps they had an emergency."

"True enough. But the troupe I traveled with would never have stayed far away from a steady income for so long. Especially one like Olonah's. They are quite diverse, the income from private shows at parties, fortune telling, even going to taverns must be quite good. Why would they geld themselves by staying somewhere so out of the way?"

William shifted in his saddle. They had borrowed two horses from the stables. William had offered a cart, and Tasmin had rolled her eyes and assured him that she was fine. She was only slightly regretting it now. In a cart she could have wrapped herself in blankets.

"At least we also have Cherise's sister to go and visit. It will be good, to get it all over in one trip," Tasmin said. According to the map, Dert—what a lovely name—was only a little bit further.

"Have you convinced Magda to see if anyone knows any Pandrazzi mages?"

"Well…" She adjusted her skirt. "She said she would, but I have a feeling that if she does not wish to do something, she won't."

He seemed amused by this. "You don't seem to care for her overmuch."

"I don't really dislike her per se, 'tis just that she's prickly, and I am prickly enough all by myself without having someone try to out-do me."

"I would not call you prickly."

She smiled. "I see."

"Of course, being that you are the woman of my dreams you are absolutely perfect in every way."

"I am sure."

"Flawless, patient…"

"Oh, do continue…"

"And absolutely able to tell us what we are looking for when we get to the town."

"That," Tasmin sighed, "I am not quite so sure of."

The town was much as William had described it. Large buildings dominated the right, some inns, a couple of general supply stores and some other buildings squeezed in on the left. William went to the warehouses. His job was to determine if any of them had space where a spell could be laid with no one knowing or disturbing it. Fairly straightforward. His secondary job was to see if the elementalists had rented any of them.

Her job was less straightforward.

The inn she entered was not the nicest one she had ever seen, but while it looked worn, it also looked clean. A woman was scrubbing some of the tables, so Tasmin crossed over the floor, waving a little in greeting as she approached.

"Can I help you, Miss?"

"Aye, I am trying to track someone down. My sister ran away with a troupe of elementalists, and I wonder if they have been through here?"

The woman nodded. "We had a group come through. They stayed on a bit. Six of their wagon axles broke. Six. Can you believe it?"

"All at once?" Tasmin asked.

The woman nodded, drying the table and carrying both rags towards the back. "They only had enough spares to replace four, so they had to wait until they could make suitable replacements. Can you believe it? They looked for magic but didn't find any traces."

Tasmin followed her. "How utterly bizarre!"

The hotel worker stood in the doorway to the kitchen and tossed the rags lightly into the sink, then turned, wiping her hands on her apron. "It was. The head of them...goodness, what was her name...oh, she was fit to be tied. But we didn't mind. People from Dert came to get tended by the leader, who seems to have some Wise Woman skills."

"I thought they had a Wise Woman, up in Dert?"

She leaned against the door frame and shrugged. "No, not for years. Azin Shore is just far enough to be inconvenient for most folk. There's a decent Doctor at the end of town, or wait for someone traveling through."

"What were they like, the elementalists?" Tasmin probed.

"Nice enough group. Kept to themselves. The bard and his lady, they were a hoot. She doesn't have any magic, but she can sing pretty. What did your sister look like?"

Tasmin described Magda for the heck of it, but the woman shrugged again. "Didn't see her in the group. I'm sorry."

She thought it all over. The fact that the bard's woman didn't have magic was vaguely interesting but not worrisome, many elementalists groups included non-mages with other talents, and often those non-mages were exceptional at sleight of hand. "Do you recall where they said they were going?"

"They headed towards Azin, I think. They stayed in the woods at the edge of town, so I don't really know."

"Not in a warehouse, to keep warm?"

She shook her head. "They seemed alright. Put their horses up at a local farm. Prices the warehouse owners charge, you'd run out of your life savings before the end of winter."

Tasmin parted ways from the young woman amiably. She was the best source, and even though Tasmin had been lucky enough to get a great deal of information, she still had to work her way down the street. The woman at the general store had quite the crush on the Fire Elementalist, and so spent more time talking about his part of the act than anything Tasmin needed to hear. In the next store, the man and woman in charge plainly hated the elementalists so nothing that was said could be held as useful. Tasmin ventured into Wise Woman territory, though. "I hear that there is no Wise Woman around here. What do you do when you need one?"

"Mistress Cherise comes, sometimes."

"Really? I heard she..." she substituted her words, noting that Cherise was too timid to travel, "I had heard that she did not much like to travel."

"You heard wrong, Mistress!" the woman said. "She's always going up to help out her people in Dert."

"We see her more often than weever saw Mistress Anne. Personally, I just think Azin Shore is too small for two women like that," her husband added.

Tasmin blinked, and said, slowly, "Like what, may I ask?"

"Headstrong. I wouldn't get in either of their way, not for all the money in the world."

Which, of course, didn't sound like Cherise at all, which was exactly what she told William, when she caught up with him.

"Well, that is interesting. And completely at odds with what the other people had to say." He looked down the street, but his eyes were distant as he considered. "We may need to go look for their campsite. I've been through the buildings, and the warehouses are all either too crowded, or entirely abandoned. I got into one that was abandoned on the pretext that perhaps my father might wish to buy it." He pointed over to a warehouse in roughly the middle of the row. "'Tis not a particularly bad place. The beams seem solid, it has some nice dividers, and the roof seems sound."

"But?" Tasmin prompted.

"Dust an inch thick. No one's been inside it for ages. I scuffed the floor, to see if anyone had written anything on the boards, but it seems quite unlikely."

She nodded, taking his arm. "They kept their horses at a farm. I'd wager it wasn't far from where they camped."

"The woods at the edge of town it is, then."

The people who defined the elementalists' campsite as at the "woods at the edge of town" had a poor idea of what 'edge of town' meant. They trudged out through the woods, seeing nothing, the ground too rough and narrow for them to ride over. They finally found a track and remounted their horses, but there was no evidence of broken ground or camp fires.

"We're getting into cleared land," Tasmin said after a while.

"Aye, the farm must be up ahead. Shall we go and see what they have to say?"

She followed, but she had to admit she was starting to get cold, and a bit cranky, as they approached the farm house.

"Shall we look at the barn, then?" she asked, dismounting. William slid down and gave her the reins again, and she held onto them as he walked around the farm house.

"Sealed up tight. It doesn't look like anyone has messed with it. I thought I saw some water damage. The roof may be gone."

Tasmin peered in as best as she could. "You are right. I see a beam hanging down, I think. Hard to tell in the gloom, though."

"The fields don't look as if they have been worked recently, from what I can see. A bit over grown."

He took the reins, and they headed for the barn. "Look, do you see? Wear marks, from ropes." He walked closer to the barn, and pointed out the marks along the beams. "The grass is well destroyed, here, and it looks as if someone hung an awning."

They tied the horses to the railing. "The paddock looks well cropped, too." She crossed to the barn door, eager to see what was inside.

Clearly, the elementalists had lived there. The dirt floor still showed signs of living, from where people had shoved or dragged tables and such from their vardos. She looked around. "There wouldn't be any room for a magnifying spell. It's just one big space, but people were living in it. Not exactly conducive to magic work, especially if they wanted to hide it." She searched the dirt for marks, as William worked his way along the stalls.

"There's something on the wall, here."

Tasmin took a small note book from her reticule as she joined him. "That is strange," she said, looking at it. It had been partly erased, made with sharp blue chalk against the aged, slightly damp wood. "I've never seen anything like that in our magic." She sketched it carefully, trying to copy the exact lines and curves, making sure the spacing was right. "It looks somewhat similar to some of the symbols Magda used..."

William tilted his head, studying the symbol and her own work. "I always thought that magic was a more universal language."

"People do," she agreed. "But the people who created the symbols that are used in casting came from different cultures. Spoke in different languages. Pandrazzi magic is particularly hard because the empire took over so many different little countries. There is a strong undercurrent against magic there, so it's not clearly defined."

He nodded, and helped her over the sunken threshold of a stable. "They might be putting more of their money and effort into technology, but they are very interested in anything at all that will give them an edge."

"True enough." She turned slowly, looking at the space. It did not look like a comfortable place to live. While it was true that where they lived now didn't really look much better, there was something dreary about it. *Maybe it was warmer, when they were here with their fires.*

They had certainly cleaned it up fairly well, which she approved of.

"We didn't really gain much, did we?" she asked quietly.

"We know more than we did," William reassured her. And that was about as good as they were able to make of it.

"'Tis too far to make for Dert tonight," she said, looking at the setting sun.

He nodded. "We will stay in town the night, then head for Dert on the morrow, if that suits."

She allowed her husband to lift her up into the saddle. "Perfectly, my love. Shall we see what kind of cuisine this fine town offers?"

With a name like Dert, it was almost impossible to have high expectations. It took much longer than expected to get there, thanks to a landslide that blocked the road. The men shoveling the dirt aside to create a path refused William's help, so they ate their lunch and tried not to go mad from boredom. By the time Tasmin, sore and tired enough that she pretty much fell into William's arms rather than getting off the horse with any real decorum, arrived there, all she could think of was a hot bath and a bed.

"I'll brush them down, sir, and give them a good mash to warm them up after their travels, get them ready to go again," the head of the stable was saying to William as Tasmin hobbled out towards the town, travel bag in hand. She stretched her shoulders carefully as she studied the town in the sunset.

"We will be staying here tonight," William objected.

"As you say, sir," The owner of the stable said, doubtfully.

The gloom of the oncoming snow storm did not do the town any favors. *But at least we made it before the snow did. I would not want to have ridden in that nonsense.* Everything about the town was clean but slightly worn. She could see where new paint was needed here, or a little repair on the woodwork on a door frame or window was needed there. The town was a little too far off the merchant route to the Capital to be prosperous, but surviving.

"Not the sight to lift one's spirits, is it?" William said quietly to her.

"Not at all," she agreed. "I had hoped to begin accomplishing something when we got here, but I am simply too tired. All I can think of is food, bath, bed."

He offered his arm, and she took it gladly, leaning on it a little. "If I remember correctly there is an inn just ahead that can provide us with just that. Would you like me to take your bag?"

Tasmin shook her head. "You have your own."

"I can carry both, I am quite sure."

She pressed her face against his sleeve, briefly. "I can carry my own bag, sweetheart. You have enough carrying me."

Already boys were out, taking the covers off the torches that lined the main street. After they removed the covers, they climbed up again, and lit the wide basins.

"That's unusual," William said as the smell of coal smoke filled the air. "I haven't seen a street lamp that was part coal in years."

And it was unusual. Mostly people used special stones that were heated and raked over a hot fire during the day, then added to the torch basins to provide light at night.

"They are poor, here," Tasmin said, understanding the implication.

As they approached the inn, they saw something that had once been quite opulent. A wide stair case led to a columned porch. A dark brick face was covered in white framed windows, and someone was even now lighting candles in each one. William opened the door. The latch was unpainted iron, which made her eyes fall to the floor. Between the sides of the door frame, bisecting the floor completely, was a bar or iron. The old threshold had been ripped out, and the bar had been implanted so that no one would trip over it, but it was quite obviously a newer addition, and sloppily done.

A lady smiled at them from the hotel's reception desk. "One moment..." she said. The wall behind the desk had pigeon holes with keys in them, and a mirror hung from a nail in the middle of them. She checked herself out in the mirror, patting her blondish-red bun, looking this way and that before turning and giving them a very genuine smile. "How may I help you?"

"How long have you been worried about Fae sickness?" Tasmin asked.

"I have no idea what you mean. Fae sickness? What is that?"

"You checked to see if we were real," Tasmin pointed out. "That's why you looked in the mirror. And the iron bar at the threshold, that's to deter the Fae from coming in, right? Is there iron, then, at every window, every chimney, too? Do you leave out offerings at the town square?"

The woman blinked at her for a moment. "Do you wish a room for the night?" she said, as if she hadn't heard Tasmin's questions.

"Yes, please," William said. "May we request a bath?"

Tasmin wanted to point out that this, in no way answered her questions, but William shook his head very slightly, worry pinching his eye brows as the attendant turned to fetch a pair of iron keys.

She held out her hand for payment, and studied the coins he laid in her hand a long moment before she nodded and pocketed them. "This place used to have a large hot spring, so we have a bathing room in the back, near the kitchens.

Follow the red carpet. Your room is on the second floor, towards the river, the number is on the key. Make sure to lock yourself in the bathing room and in your bedroom at all times." She leaned in and looked at Tasmin. "People have been known to disappear," she announced in a stage whisper.

"I see," Tasmin said archly.

"Mostly from here. Which is doubtless why the Stable Master suggested that you consider moving on once your horses are rested?"

William held up the key. "We've paid for the night."

She held the coins out again, expressionless. "'Tis not like I've had time to spend it."

The woman had one hand on the counter, Tasmin reached over and placed her hand on the wrist, feeling how slender it was, how fragile the bones felt, how cold the skin. "Who did you lose?"

The woman pulled away, pocketing the coins again. "Shall I have your bags taken to your room, then? Dinner is in an hour, we can have a tray made up for you if you prefer."

"We shall take our things to the bath. No sense going up only to come back down, eh?" William shot the door a longing look. If there were anywhere else to go, Tasmin had a feeling that he would be on his way.

"You may send a tray up, if you would be so kind." Tasmin said.

The woman inclined her head and turned away. To her retreating back, Tasmin added. "I am a Wise Woman, if you need any help." The other woman did not seem to hear.

William and Tasmin exchanged a look. "This way, I believe she said." He took both their bags, and followed the red carpet to the bathing room. The tarnished beauty of Dert now made sense. The place had once been an elegant place for travelers to come and immerse themselves in the hot springs. When the springs failed, they used the plumbing that was in place. The large marble pools had been blocked up with much less elegant wood and stone to create "tubs" on the shallow end, but one could fill them with the simple, delightful ease of turning a handle, so Tasmin thought they were wonderful.

William filled the time with stories of a bath house he had been able to visit a few times when he was at sea.

"And the mosaics were really made of gold and fine jewels?"

"Aye." He said over the noise of the pipes as he reached in and tested the water. "They had guards in every room. You could leave your clothes and valuables on the benches, no one dared to even consider theft in that place."

"Hmm. I see." She looked at the windows to satisfy her curiosity. Yes. Bars of iron were inserted into the seal. They made a mash of it, chipping away at the marble. "This place must have been nearly as lovely." She finished undressing, leaving her clothes folded on a chair.

The main color in the room was a veined white marble, the expanse broken with large mosaics of flowers every so often.

"Would you like me to wash your hair?" William asked.

"Would you?" She was delighted at the prospect of the treat, but not so much that she did not watch the door with half an eye. That was why she was able to catch it when the latch turned, stopped because the door was locked, and was slowly let go.

When they were in their room, fed a decent enough meal by a quiet young man who smiled shyly when they complimented the food, William wedged a chair against the door while Tasmin tested to see if both windows were locked. "Locked and nailed shut," she whispered to him. "Iron nails, of course."

"So what, exactly, is Fae sickness?"

"A bit like ghost sickness. People fall sick, they don't understand why because it is not like a real sickness. No physical symptoms. They just...the person they were just shuts down and they walk around without any real life. They say the Fae kidnap them and take them away to their world, but they leave the body because they no longer need it."

"They spoke of missing people. I wonder what sort of people are missing?"

Tasmin looked at the chair and shuddered.

"It's wedged tight," William assured her as he sat on the edge of the bed and took off his boots. "But I could move a dresser in front of it instead, if you like."

She shook her head. "But I am torn between wanting to be comfortable when I sleep and ready to run."

He hung his sword off the head board on his side. "Indeed."

It was almost disappointing that the next dawn came with no mishap. They broke their fasts and William went left and Tasmin went right.

It took some time, to track down any information.

A seamstress who also ran an odds and ends shop was the first to give a glimmer. "Cherise and Agnes grew up with their Aunt," the lady said, sewing on Tasmin's cloak. The hem had been coming a bit loose, and so Tasmin borrowed William's knife, and like magic, a repair job needed to be done. "Tragic story. Not sure I should be telling you this, I wouldn't want to hurt Cherise's standing."

"I promise, you won't. She mentioned not getting along with her sister, and I was curious. I hate to pry, but..."

Tasmin had measured the other woman right. "Well, it never hurts, and I'm just relaying what everyone knows." She paused for a moment, gathering her thoughts, her needle moving swiftly to repair the hem. Tasmin could have repaired it almost as well, and she hated to spend the funds on something she could do easily, but it had seemed like the best idea to get information at the time. "They were a tragic family. The father left, the mother died in childbirth. The Wise Woman could only get the spell to work for one of the little girls."

Tasmin was taken aback. "I don't know that I ever heard of that." It was true, she never had, and she wondered if there was a record somewhere, why the spell wouldn't take effect. She pushed the idea aside, determined to gather everything she could.

"Oh, yes. They tried it several times, with different Wise Women. They always said that Cherise was the one, though Agnes always was certain that they were lying. Cherise's intended lived on a farm just outside of town, so they ran into each other."

"Jared?" Tasmin asked, hoping to add to the idea that she and Cherise were confidants and keep her going.

"Yes. Did she tell you what happened to him?"

She shook her head.

"Not a surprise. He ran away to sea, instead of marrying right away."

"I know how that is," Tasmin muttered.

Fortunately, the seamstress hadn't heard. "When he came back he wasn't really right." She didn't say anything else, seemed to be concentrating too much on knotting the end of the thread.

"I am sorry to hear that. Cherise seemed very fond of him."

"She loved him. They both did. She visits him, you know, out at the farm. She was here just the other day."

Tasmin carefully shelved that. "Do they know what happened?"

She shook her head and handed the cloak back. Tasmin, in turn, handed her a few coins. "I know she comes up and acts as Wise Woman, sometimes."

"She does. Becoming a Wise Woman did her a world of good, I think." She stood up. "Well, I have some other projects to attend to. Thank you for the company."

Tasmin took her leave as suggested.

William was waiting outside. "Did you learn anything while I was spending perfectly good funds on a task I am perfectly suited to do?" she asked him.

"It was not a waste if you found out something of use," he assured her. "I have found little save that Cherise has no living family outside her twin, except for a cousin no one wants to talk about. Her Aunt passed away a few years back," he shrugged. "The local Magistrate is about as forthcoming as our innkeeper. I asked him about the disappearances she mentioned, he made out as if it were idle talk."

"Perhaps Master Carys can get more out of him?"

William nodded. "If he wants to. I shall ask."

They stood together for a moment, observing the odd town. Finally, Tasmin broke the silence. "I would like to visit a farm at the edge of town. Do you think this farm will be any closer to the actual edge of town than the last one we visited, or should we pack a week's rations?"

"It was not that bad. We didn't starve to death, after all. Now, fill me in on what else you learned."

Dert's idea of where the edge of town lay was much more accurate than Dalmaca's, but then it's possible that was because the farm in question was not that large. It was quiet. A vacant-eyed man was listlessly sweeping the porch as a woman, thin and tall, came out to meet them.

"Can I help you?" she asked in a soft, deep voice at odds with her frame.

"We're looking for Cherise. Have you seen her? We're told that she came to visit your son, but she had not returned to her home."

Tasmin was studied by the vacant-eyed man, the woman gave him a little push and he turned in another direction, sweeping as he went.

"She's not here." She tipped her chin up, as if daring them to say anything else.

"Thank you," William said. "We are sorry that we troubled you." William gently took Tasmin's elbow, and she took the hint, dissatisfied.

When they were a decent distance away, she asked, "Are you sure we couldn't get anything else out of her?"

"I think we got what we needed." He did not look happy.

"Pray do not keep me is suspense."

"I am thinking. When you are at sea, you hear all sorts of things. It is, outside of running the ship, all you have to do, really, talk. Play games, read if you can, and talk. When you are at port, you gather more things to talk about. You don't know what is truth or what has been blown out of proportion for the sake of something to talk about."

"Alright," Tasmin encouraged.

"Sometimes, if a ghost storm is sent away soon enough, people survive. Some of them survive completely, others, well, it's as if the soul was sucked right out of them, but the body remained alive."

Tasmin stumbled, William steadied her. "You are saying that he's ghost-sick."

William nodded, once.

"Oh dear. But, that said, how was the ghost storm chased away?"

"The Pandrazzi, apparently. If they encounter it, they do something to counter it. It is never really known what, just that if you see a ghost storm and a Pandrazzi vessel, you don't attack. And it is also known that they will help anyone if they are in the clutches of the storm, let them go on their way instead of attacking."

"That is uncommonly kind of them, considering the Pandrazzi reputation."

He was looking up at the sky, considering.

"Do you think there is enough light to get us home?" she asked.

"No, but there is enough for a good start."

# Chapter Seventeen

Ailiani did not mind being alone while they were gone. Magda was annoying, but she had started to leave for large chunks of the day, which meant that the sprites would come out and keep her company. Of course, she knew the woman could get taken and needed to be watched, but Ailiani figured Magda knew it too, and if she was going to go out anyway, that was her business.

"I suspect," she told an unknown wind sprite, who was tangling itself into the curls of her unbound hair, "that she is trolling. She wants to be taken, that she thinks if they attack her she can do something against those who killed her daughter. God help them if she succeeds." Magda was coming back later and later.

Ailiani did not want anything to happen to Magda, but she could not protect her. And she was certainly not going to put herself in the way of the killers. If they wanted magical women, giving them another target would not be wise. *Particularly now.*

She washed the counter, put the chairs on the tables, and locked up. William had prepared ahead, but when he got back he would need to spend several days replenishing his stores.

She would grab a meat pie from a vendor on her way down the hill, keeping to the crowds and lights. She took the longer ways—before she had taken short cuts through alleys, sure she was safe, but now she took the longest route, paying attention. Two sprites usually rode her shoulders, and she payed attention to the tension, or lack thereof, in their bodies.

Sometimes she made it to Miss Dovlington's before it happened. Sometimes she woke, tucked in bed, sand on her feel and in her bedding, with no memory how she got there. Sometimes she did not. Sometimes nothing happened at all, she could remember a peaceful evening of sewing or singing to herself before going to bed like a sensible woman.

*Today, I shall make it*, she promised herself. She could see the steps that led up to the front door.

But she could also see a flicker along the path to the shore. She stopped, saw a woman flickering along, the wind blowing the weeds, but not touching her.

"Not today," she said. "I am so tired."

*Needs must, child. We have work to do.*

She felt betrayed by the sprites. *They never tell me that she's here.* They petted her, as if hearing her thoughts, and she waved an annoyed hand towards them.

*Now, now, Ailiani, do not be angry with them. They are mine, after all. Creatures of the air.*

Ailiani followed the ghost down to the beach. She found herself, as usual, unable to look too closely at her. Half her face was beautiful, half a skull. She did not understand why a ghost would not look less horrifying. Which sounded silly, but, weren't ghosts spirits? Why would a spirit look like that?

She stepped close to the edge of the water. The ghost had commanded her to never touch the water, and she took care to stay back from the tide's probing, cold fingers.

The haze of the ghost storm's clouds tainted the horizon. She hugged herself. "It's coming close again, isn't it?"

*It is. And my sister with it. This we must not allow.*

"I don't understand."

*She is dead, a ghost. But once she touches shore she can begin to rebuild herself. If she finds me...*The ghost flickered, which Ailiani figured was as close to an approximation of shuddering as a ghost could get.

"Can you not rebuild yourself?"

*My body is not gone. They ripped my soul out, put it in a prison. They hid my body, but carefully be-spelled it so it would stay alive. As long as there is a body, somewhere, I cannot create a new one.*

Ailiani sighed. When she was with the ghost, there were no blanks in her memory, and she knew what would come next. "Well, as long as you keep giving mine back to me."

*I would be tempted, you are beautiful and strong, but we are not compatible, you are not an air element, you are earth and a little water, which is why when we come together we can chase away the storm.*

She felt a cold, cold presence at her back as the ghost stepped behind her. She closed her eyes, took a breath and tried not to be afraid. "Well, then. Come on in."

The ghost slipped inside of her, filling her. Ailiani felt cold and light, the world looked different when she opened her eyes. She saw things as thin, blue-tinged. Nothing looked real. The sprites had fled her, gathering a short distance away. Ailiani could see them clearly, blue and white and glowing. She centered herself, and started to dance the circles. It was easier because she floated just over the sand, trailing her toes in, dancing and swirling gracefully through the pattern, leaving a trail of blue light wherever she went. It was effortless in her body, the pattern drawing swift and sure. Pure, perfect, and a wall. It was a wall that spread along the coast, and the sprites lined up, and they pushed the wind with all their might, pushed the breeze from behind them out to the ghost storm.

As they worked, she could hear the Ghost Witch singing softly, her voice ringing through. They reached out, together, towards the storm, and Ailiani could hear the screams and moans of the dead as they wept and railed against their fate.

"And who are you, that pushes me away?" The voice made the ghosts silent, quiet and mocking.

Like a shutter, all sound was closed off, all feeling, as they concentrated on the spell.

The storm retreated back. Sometimes it retreated a long way, sometimes only a little. It depended on many things, how tired Ailiani was, and if someone had recently died. Last night had been bad, but tonight the storm faded a little more. The town was safe again.

The ghost stepped out of her, and she fell like a discarded doll onto the sand.

"Who was that?" Ailiani felt so very cold. Cold and empty.

*My greatest fear. Come now, crawl just a little more. We shall speak of this more later.* The ghost encouraged, a gentle wind pushing her towards the path to the house. She got up on her hands and knees and crawled through the cold sand. The ghost stayed inside her to complete the task, but never seemed to be able to stay once the spell was cast. Instead she coaxed, the wind sprites prodded, and sometimes she could make it all the way back. Sometimes she even had the strength to walk through the door like nothing was wrong.

Tonight was not one of those times. She fell against the sand.

Blearily, she remembered a blanket floating over her as the sprites wrapped her up and surrounded her with their warmth. She recalled waking up for a second to see the ghost sitting next to her, staring out at sea; the Northerly wind from the shore blowing around them both, North but not touching her at all.

But she did not remember any of this, when the morning came and the breeze that had avoided her all night cut into her like a knife. She scrambled to her feet, clutching her blanket, and trying to remember how she got to the beach. The tide had washed away most of the markings. She studied what was left and hoped the tide would take the rest as she took her tired, freezing self up to the house.

The door to her room was open. Miss Dovlington was putting a cup of hot tea on the table next to her bed.

They looked at each other a long moment. Finally, Miss Dovlington said, "Careful, I put a warm brick in your bed."

Ailiani asked, "Why? I would think you would not approve of me, being out all night."

Miss Dovlington looked over her glasses. "Young woman, I don't know what you are doing, but I think that you are trying to save us."

Ailiani wrapped her fingers around the mug, and whimpered. "Do you think, if you are willing, you could check to see if I make it to bed, then? And if not, send someone to get me? I can be found at the end of the shore path."

"I can do that. I thought you stayed out there because you had to. I won't interfere in what you are doing. I am not sure I want to know what it is, exactly, but yes I will come and get you." She looked a little embarrassed as she pushed Ailiani to the bed.

"Thank you," Aliani said, drinking the tea. *And I hope, whatever it is, I don't have to do it for much longer.*

# Chapter Eighteen

Tasmin sat in her office, where she could most easily escape everyone. Several days' travel had made her cranky and out of sorts. The only person she had the slightest patience for was William, and he had decided to not test it by going to the warehouse to catch up on work.

Even the wind sprites were leaving her alone, except for one, present right there, quietly sitting over the door lintel.

She opened the window a crack, letting cold air in to try and clear the cobwebs from her head. Everything ached, adding to the foulness of her mood, and she wrapped herself up tighter, smacked the light stone on the table, and took out some paper that had been spoiled when the sprites, in a more gleeful moment, had accidentally knocked over a tea mug onto it. It was perfect for what she wanted, which was just a place to scribble her thoughts.

*What do we know?*

She wrote, clear and bold, at the top of the page.

The first few responses contained too many words that would shock her husband, so she tapped the end of the quill on the paper, trying to sort out.

She wrote a list of missing or dead. Good start. She tried to mark whether she knew if they were dead with a tiny little D.

Nora she put a question mark by. Carys had told everyone that she had run away with some sailor, but the story was so thin she doubted anyone believed it. A magic woman disappears and she was expected to believe it an elopement. Not bloody likely.

All the missing had magic of some sort. She assumed the five bodies they had discovered had magic, as well. Her overtures to find out more were being ignored, so she wrote "Person 1, Person 2" and so on down the paper. *Really. And after we handed him those nice clues from Dert, all wrapped up in a bow.*

It was quite frustrating. As the town Wise Woman, there was no reason, none, why she should not have been called to help. It was understandable if Carys wanted to hold the information close, but it was also foolish. Tasmin could help if she knew more.

Take a breath. Focus.

She looked at Cherise's name, then added Agnes next to it. *I wonder if both of them are really dead? People have seen them far too recently. And people have remarked on how she has changed. Could Agnes have stepped into Cherise's place? If so, she must be one of the killers.*

Ghost sickness. Jared had it. *What would I do, if William had come back ghost sick?* Probably nothing, to be honest. Perhaps come and visited, seen what she could do, then went on with her life. She would have felt badly, for through his letters she had learned to care for him, but she would have gotten over it.

She wrote the words. Drew a little ghost. Started to draw the ghost throwing up, but thought better of it. *But what would I have done if he'd come back ghost sick when I actually knew him? Say, the other night?*

Cherise had known Jared. If she loved him as she said, then she would not have just accepted things. She was a healer. She would have tried to heal him.

"Alright then. How do you heal ghost sickness?" The chair scraped across the floor as she leaned back, pulling some books down and setting them on the table with a satisfying thump.

The thump was the only satisfaction she got. The answer was, basically, no, you are done for, and too bad. *Time for a bit of tea*, she thought.

In the shop there were a few customers, so she kept on going to the kitchen. When they were gone she reappeared, bearing two cups of tea.

"Ailiani, has the ghost storm been back since William and I left for Dalmaca?"

She gave Tasmin an oddly hunted look. "I don't believe so, no."

"Alright," Tasmin said, pacing. "I wish Carys wasn't being so stubborn. I need to know if Cherise is among the bodies they have found. Maybe she is still alive. Maybe she was the first to die. Who knows?" She threw up her hands, whacking a shelf hard in the process. She shook her hand to get rid of the pain and kept pacing.

"Tasmin?" Ailiani sounded pained.

She stopped and turned to her friend. "I want to feel the storm. I want to get closer, see if I can understand it better."

"Why ever would you wish that?"

Ailiani shrugged, frustrated. "I want to know if the spirits that make it up are still separate. Are they still their own being, swept up by the storm, or do they become part of a greater mass. In short, can you still pull a soul from a ghost storm?"

Ailiani's eyes were aimed towards the counter, but in reality whatever she was seeing was much, much further away.

"They say my father could do such a thing, but I was never..." she stopped, looked up. "I never saw my brother do it."

"Blast," Tasmin muttered, but reached out and petted Ailiani's hand, missing and mostly petting counter.

"What are you thinking?"

"Cherise was the second to disappear, right?" She didn't wait for a nod. "But people still see her, just not in Azin. She was displeased that her sister convinced her to be a Wise Woman instead of marrying Jared, but the point was moot anyway because he came back from the sea ghost sick." She spun and stalked away from the door. "But why be unhappy about not getting to marry your intended, if he's come back from the sea a shell of himself? I think she thought she could fix him."

"That would take a lot of power, even were it possible."

"An insane amount. And Cherise was never noted to be all that powerful."

Ailiani leaned on her arms. "I think I understand where you are going, and I would support this if it wasn't the very opposite of everything we know about Cherise's character. She was a mouse, not a hawk."

Tasmin joined her, leaning against the counter with her head on her hand. "You mean, prey, not predator?" Ailiani gave a little nod, and Tasmin sighed. "I wonder, then, what category Agnes would have fallen into?"

"I am far from convinced."

"I can tell."

"I would far more likely believe Magda the culprit, despite her daughter."

"But what motive would she have?"

"Perhaps someone was forcing her to do something, using her daughter as a hostage. Something went wrong." Ailiani shrugged. "She is supposed to be here for her protection, but do you ever see her?"

"Containing her is like trying to contain the sun," Tasmin muttered. But it was an interesting thought. "We only have her word for when her daughter was taken." She considered it.

"She does make an alluring suspect."

Tasmin laughed. "But is it because we really don't much care for her?"

Ailiani pushed away ruefully as the door opened and a customer came in. "Sadly, you are probably right."

Tasmin went into the kitchen and cut a chunk of bread. She chewed it moodily, tossing small pieces into the air and watching them swirl away. The problem was that she felt as if she was banging her head against a wall and hoping it would magically become a door.

*I could go to Carys. Demand he tell me what he knows.*

She eyed the back door.

*And then I can come home after he's politely laughed at me. Or plucked all information I have out of my skull while replacing it with nothing.*

She tossed the last crumb. *Maybe I can go stand on the shore and see if the ghost storm is close enough that I can sense something.*

*Maybe I can do more reading.*

*Maybe I...*

There was a banging on the back door. It made her jump because people so rarely came that way. She opened the door. "Joe? What is it?"

"Can you come, Mistress? Something wrong with the baby?"

"Oh, no! Have you spoken to Dr. Havelock? I'll come with you, but you should send for him as well."

Joseph was shaking. "Already done. Can you come?"

"I'll go get my bag."

He raised a hand as if to stop her, but she ignored it, when she saw a glance of him again through the stair rail, he was hugging himself tightly.

It only took a moment to grab some things and throw it in her bag, and soon she was drawing her cloak around her shoulders. She waved at Ailiani but did not want to interrupt her, as she was with a customer.

"What's wrong with the baby?" she asked when they were well under way.

"A fever. He's so very hot. He won't stop crying."

*Absolutely more of a case for Dr. Havelock,* she thought. Though she could, perhaps, cool the child, if she remembered enough of her Aunt's elemental training, she could create a cloud of cold air that would help bring the temperature down, and it would be less dangerous than ice water. If Havelock was already there, she could offer her assistance. The mental planning came to an abrupt halt as she neared the end of the bridge and saw a familiar figure striding down the street, opposite the way he was supposed to be going.

"What's Dr. Havelock doing? He should be heading the other way." She turned and looked at Joe, sliding her hand into the decorative railing and holding on.

Joe shrugged. He stared at her, frozen.

"I have no intention of moving another inch," she said.

"You have to come!"

"To see a sick baby? Why isn't Havelock on his way there? If the news was the worst, he'd still be there. If he needed something, he'd have sent someone else, or at least be going faster than a leisurely stroll."

"Maybe he did not get the message. Tasmin, we have to go."

"Alright, I'll go. You must go get Dr. Havelock. He is the best help for your baby." Her voice was flat and calm. She no longer believed Joe, and as she spoke, she took a step back, then another.

He was hugging himself again, shaking, but he did not seem vulnerable. For the first time she realized that he was a large man. Tall. Muscled from tossing cargo around. "When was the last time you saw your husband?"

That stopped her. "You don't have him." She threw every ounce of her disbelief into it.

He twitched. "Do you want to risk it? Can you afford to? Just one more missing person."

She pressed her back against the bridge and slipped past him, keeping her eyes on him as she finished crossing. He followed her.

"Prove it. I don't see how you could take my husband alone. William is a most excellent fighter and no fool."

"But Joe isn't alone, is he?" a woman said, and Tasmin felt something cold snake around her wrist. She looked at the chain, all fine silver and gold braid that tightened and bit in.

Slowly she lowered her arm as her thoughts faded, and the woman took her arm and pulled her away.

William was not at the warehouse, but nor was he in danger.

Mostly.

He was in the cold room, looking at the dead bodies laid on the tables. Only one was on a cold slab, the rest were just trestles. "My wife should be here," he said to Carys. "She could figure this out better than I."

Olonah shook her head. "We do not need her."

"With respect, madam, I do not know you. How do I know you had nothing to do with the reason these bodies are here?"

"Because I trust my wife implicitly." Carys said, putting down a box he'd gone to fetch. "You have helped your wife, perhaps now you can help mine."

William didn't have an answer to that, so kept his mouth shut.

Olonah stretched. "I looked over the files from your Doctor. He found very little revealing. So, I shall conduct some experiments of my own."

Soon it was obvious that William was needed as manual labor. Partly because he was strong, partly because Carys correctly guessed that he was not of a squeamish nature. William found himself lifting the dead bodies, helping to partly undress the corpses, holding them on their sides so Olonah could use her unguents and crystals to investigate the flesh on the back, holding limbs steady so she could sprinkle powders or blow smoke and study whatever it was that she saw. She saw a lot, he could tell, because she kept stopping to make quick sketches, studying blank skin intently. He saw nothing at all, and had to take it on faith that the patterns she threw onto the paper were appearing on the corpses.

"Why do you do that?" she asked him as he straightened the clothes on one of the bodies, his hand gently tucking and removing creases.

He frowned, his head dizzy from the smoke that lay heavy in the room. "I suppose I should want someone to do the same for me?"

"But why? The bodies are simply vessels. These certainly were…a vessel for power, emptied and discarded."

"Why were some of these hung up in the caves?"

She shrugged. "Boredom? To make a statement? I do not know. There is no magical reason for that part. Did you see anything, spell wise, when you were there?"

He went and stood over her drawings. He tapped on one. "Some symbols like this? Tasmin provided copies of her sketches to Master Carys."

"So, someone wanted the magic that these bodies contained. But why? They even tried to tap the child."

"Can magic be stored? Could they be building up for something large?"

She shook her head. "I do not think you can store magic, not without a very powerful amulet. Perhaps then, yes. But, I know this girl in my troupe. Girl, I call her, she's older than me, but she seems so young. She wants magic more than anything. If she had it, she would be using it to save her husband, I wager. She looks at us all as if we are the greatest of all wonders, and her eyes get so sad, because she wishes she were like us."

William thought, *That sounds horrid. If that were me, I would have left that world altogether. Why remind myself, every day, of what I could not have?*

Carys returned, his steps almost silent. "I sent word, as you suggested. My man should be back before sunset tomorrow, if the weather holds."

"So quickly?"

"He will ride hard, and he can be persistent. Obstinate even, with people who are keeping information from him."

Olonah was hugging herself. All of her elegance was stripped away. She did not have her husband's detachment, and looking over the bodies was wearing on her.

"What do we have?" Carys asked gently. He placed a hand on his wife's back, and William saw her lean into it.

"They are all so different. A man with his heart cut out. A woman with severe burns. The magic on some of these bodies is much the same, but I am having a hard time making connections."

William cleared his throat. "If someone was creating a spell to take magic, maybe they were learning how."

"You're suggesting that the killer was practicing?" Carys asked.

William nodded.

"I need away from these bodies," Olonah said, walking from the room.

Carys watched her leave, and he sighed. "Thank you, Captain. If you like, you may go home, now, with my thanks."

"Will she be alright?" William asked.

Carys looked at him thoughtfully, almost as if he was weighing the other man. Finally, he said, "She used to help me more often, but one day we investigated a murder so gruesome that it gave her nightmares for months. Anything even remotely like it will bring it all back to the surface. This, what I made her do today, will give her nightmares yet again, make her relive it all over again."

William nodded grimly. "I see."

"You think me a monster?"

This was not as easy to answer. "I believe you will try and do what you must to protect the people in your care."

He smothered a half of a laugh. "So I am a monster."

"I don't know. I don't really think so."

William started to cover the bodies.

"No, no. I'll do that." The other man pulled a chair into the center of the room. "I need to have a think."

William went up the steps. When he looked back, Carys was in a pool of light, staring at each body in turn, as if wondering what they could tell him.

Tasmin did not know where they went. She felt floaty, and she knew enough of this kind of magic—after all what was the chain around her wrist but some sort of amulet?—to know that the chain was draining her energy and will away. She was being led through the streets, she knew that much, but she had no concept of where she was being taken. If you asked her to retrace her steps, to say what the buildings looked like, anything, she could not. She just could not focus.

She was pushed down into a chair, and she waited, quietly. Joe tapped her wrist and caught the chain as it fell away. He studied her closely for a second as she blinked. "I don't think we left it on too long, she seems to be coming back," he said, his voice miles away. The chair was set in the midst of a broken circle. Tasmin recognized the spell from her own studies, and was not surprised when he grabbed a stub of chalk off the stone floor and closed it with a few sure stokes.

He backed away, dusting the chalk from his hands. The pieces snapped into place, and she was back, as Joe suggested, all her senses clear again. The circle was possible to cross. She studied it from her seat. It would not hurt her body. Her mind, her soul, her magic, however...

In front of her was a table, and at the table, a woman was dealing cards, ignoring Tasmin completely. Now she had to make a choice. The woman at the table was definitely Agnes or Cherise. She considered what she knew, and took a breath. Tilting her head, she said, "All the magic in the world isn't going to bring back Cherise. Or heal the man you love."

She flickered her eyes up, then back to the spread before her. "You are a very powerful woman. Not who I sent for, but powerful all the same."

Joe approached her shyly, stopping when Agnes' eyes cut to him, staring him down. "People will miss her." She hissed.

"I thought you wanted her. The ghost asked for her."

"Did she?" She tapped her finger on the wood. "Interesting. Well. I suppose she will do well enough."

Tasmin reached a cautious hand out towards the barrier. "I am sorry to disappoint. If you just let me go, I can be on my way, and home before anyone thinks to look." A solid wall of air met her hand, flexing a little, but stopping firm.

Tasmin heard a voice, not much of a sound, but a sound that scratched at her ears. She couldn't make out what was said, but Agnes didn't seem to have any problem. She nodded. "I see. That is rather clever. And you know how I adore trouble."

More scratching sounds. It was like trying to make out words through splinter filled cotton. *A spell, blocking me?*

"But you must give her power to us. We must not fail in our mission. I will let you wreak havoc as much as you like, but keep that in mind." Agnes sighed. "Alright. Let me consider it."

Tasmin looked over her shoulder. A glimmer of a ghost attracted her. Again, like with the voice, she could not focus.

"Well?" Agnes said. "You heard her."

Joe gave Tasmin a sad look.

Agnes tapped at a card on the table, shook her head, collected all the cards up then shuffled them again. She did her spread again. "You are right. The probable outcome is more in our favor. Very well then."

She picked up a wrapped bundle, and threw it at Tasmin. The cloth fell away mid-flight, the object passing through the barrier easily. Tasmin grabbed for it without thinking, almost fumbling it. It was stone, damp, soft, but not chalky. The real Heart of Ithalia. "How did you get this?"

Agnes shrugged. "Everyone knew you had it, that you used it. Did you really think such a thing could be kept secret? The hiding place was clever, but, well," she shrugged, "Magic is useful, and it's not like the amulet was that hard to create a fake of.

Now. I am going to give you a very tiny knife. I wish you to cut your wrist and press the amulet to the blood."

"I do not even need to pretend to consider. The answer is no."

"Your husband…"

"Is not here. If he was you would not have needed to use a snake bracelet to make me pliable." She looked at the little pin pricks around her wrist with disgust.

"Does not need to be here to be threatened. Why should I keep him within these walls, feed him, guard him, when he is just as much in danger from me in town? Joe could approach him and shoot him right in the chest, or knife him in the back while walking through a crowd. Spells can be cast. People disappear all the time, in this town."

Tasmin's mouth was dry. "That's not very certain."

"Of course it is. He won't leave town, not while he has no idea what happened to you. He is caged to do with as I will. And I could kill him, right now, if that was my desire. In any case, if you do not do what I wish, I will kill you, instead. There are so very many ways that I can make you useful to me."

Tasmin held out her hand, palm up, for the knife. *Maybe I can grab it, stab that lousy traitor, instead.* Joe gave her a tenuous smile. "Last time I help you. You better hope you didn't ill-wish that baby," she said, "lying to me like that." That made his smile fade, and he grabbed her hand, pulled the wrist forward, and cut her across it.

"Don't need to kill me, you oaf." She yanked her wrist back and cradled it. He shrugged.

"You will be fine. Just press the amulet against the wound."

She'd dropped the amulet, and now she looked at it, remembering what had happened with Franny. *Is that what will happen to me?*

"Come now. You are running out of time, Mistress." Agnes said. Tasmin reached down with a trembling and blood stained hand and wrapped her fingers around the stone. She sat down, and pressed it, resolutely, to the wound.

There was a sound like the ocean, and she lost her ability to see. She heard nothing but the surge of waves, saw nothing but light-speckled darkness. Her body went numb and she ceased to be able to communicate with it. It was as if she was being pulled away, and she fought, tooth and nail, remembering what happened to Franny all those months ago. *I will not die, I will not.* Something brushed past her, and she could feel, distantly, her hand let go of the amulet, and she could almost hear, very far away, the sound of it falling and rolling across the floor. She did not tell herself to rise, but she did, stretching. "I think it worked." She heard Franny say just before the words were echoed by her own voice. "I am in control."

"Are you certain?"

Franny laughed, it echoed madly inside her head, then flowed out of her own mouth. Tasmin wanted to hug herself, to move to the side, scream, do something, but she felt disconnected from the world, as if she had immersed herself in the ocean. She could somewhat see through the eyes of her body, somewhat hear through her ears, but she knew that, instead of water, she was drowning in the presence of Franny Harker.

*Franny Harker is in my body.*

There was a flicker, and she brought forth cold lights, carefully, slowly, using Tasmin's power.

"She is so very untrained. I doubt she knows any of her potential."

*Oh, this will not stand.*

# Chapter Nineteen

William was disheartened when he got home, his mood made worse by the news that greeted him.

"Tasmin is not with you?" Ailiani was pacing, Magda was lounging in one of the chairs, drinking chocolate.

"No, should she had been?" *Did I pass her on the way? Was she looking for me?*

"I tell you, Tasmin went out to check on a sick child. These things take time. If you would listen to me, you would not be so worried," Magda said. "I was in my little closet, I heard everything."

"It's been hours, and it is fully dark now." Ailiani said. "If she went to Joe's she should have been back by now."

Magda rolled her eyes. "And she is such a miracle worker that she can heal a child like this?" She snapped her fingers.

William broke into the argument. "No, she would call Dr. Havelock if the case was beyond her, but true, she might still be doing what she can. In either case, it would be better for me to go and check on her so she does not have to walk home alone. You are sure it was Joe?"

"She called him by name, and this Joe said the baby was sick, so I assume it is the young man who just had the baby," Magda confirmed. "Do you know where he lives?"

He nodded. "Enough. It is in the direction that you have to walk for home." He said to Ailiani. "Shall I escort you?"

She nodded and slipped out from behind the counter, cloak in tow.

The door opened, and Tasmin walked in. "Finally!" Ailiani enveloped her in a hug. It must have surprised her, for she stiffened and pulled away. Tasmin was not an extremely demonstrative woman physically, but she had gotten used to Ailiani. "Are you alright? Is the baby...?"

There was a moment of blankness, and Tasmin recovered. "Oh. Yes. The baby is fine." She smiled at everyone, and William relaxed. "Sorry, it was such a long walk and I am quite tired."

He reached over and stroked her hair. Her back went straight for a moment. He drew his hand back quickly and she relaxed, bit by bit. She gave him a reassuring smile.

"We're all tired. Have you eaten?" William wondered if she was put out with him, but could not see what he might have done.

"I am not hungry. They gave me a bite at..." She paused, waved her fingers. "Joe's home. I just want to go upstairs and read. If you will all excuse me?" They watched her walk away.

Ailiani shuddered. "For a successful return, she seems a bit out of sorts."

"Perhaps Dr. Havelock was rude to her. Men of Science are not always welcoming of people with magic," Magda said. "As if I am less because I learned different things. He can be such a bother."

"He's usually not so bad," William said softly as he listened to her pace upstairs, doors opening and closing as she made her way around. *Looking for ghosts, my love?*

"We both ate before your return. I will let myself out." Ailiani patted his arm on her way past.

"I shall walk you home," he said to Ailiani, who shook her head vehemently.

"I am to meet someone on the way. I will be fine. Magda?"

"I am going to read some more then go to my bed. Fare thee well."

"Would you like anything from the kitchen?"

Magda shook her head, opening her book. She had papers, drawings, books spread across the counter.

"Are you really comfortable? This doesn't seem ideal." He looked around. The shop was dark, the only light from the stones Tasmin had lent her. The tall stool creaked as she shifted.

"It's fine." The smile was slight, but so rare that it felt quite valuable. "I am content as I can be, considering. Best you get something to eat."

He went into the kitchen and set out chocolate and milk and bread crusts for the sprites. There was no squee of delight or food disappearing. He put it in the pantry, with the nest. A feeling of disquiet was building, and as he checked the doors and windows to make sure the place was secure for the night, a feeling of things not being quiet right intensified in him. *Usually there is at least one sprite around. Where could they have gone?* Back in the kitchen he stared at the stove for a long time before deciding that bread and cheese would be good enough. He fixed a tray of food for himself and Tasmin and walked it up. She was in her study, he knocked gently to warn her before going in. Papers were scattered more than usual. "Is this where the wind sprites ended up?" he joked.

She gaped at him. "Oh? Um. No," she said. "I don't know where they are."

He placed her plate on the desk. "You must eat something." *There must be some way to counter your humorlessness.*

"Thank you," she said, smiling a grim little smile up at him until he left.

He beat a hasty retreat, setting the tray on the open surface of his desk, which he'd stolen from his ship's cabin. He picked up the Creighton's and fumbled for the book mark, forcing himself to relax into his chair, reading while he ate. There was a strong sense of disquiet in his soul. He got up, meaning to approach Tasmin's office. He rattled through things to say in his head and discarded them. There was nothing wrong he could point to, just a grave, unsettled feeling. Tasmin's reactions, the way she wore her face this evening rather than living in it. Finally he sat down again, and forced himself to read. Usually Creighton's was an easy escape, it could pull him along in a world filled with wonders and curiosities.

Finally, he put the book down on the desk, book marking the place he was up to and sliding it away from him, sighing loudly. He played with the inkwell lid, snapping it open, snapping it shut.

A glance at the clock. *Much too early to go to bed.*

He got up and listened at the wall. Normally he'd hear the rustle of papers, or a murmured comment under her breath, but even with his ear pressed to the wood he could hear very little. He put his hand on the bare spot of wall, where, on the other side of the wall would be a large bookcase, and then Tasmin's chair, her back to him. He slid his hand down the wall as if sliding it down his wife's back.

*Enough of this.* Normally he would treasure this time to read or even just stare at the fire and day dream, but he just couldn't. He shook his head, and did the normal before-bed things: Washed, changed. He lingered over each thing, wishing he knew why he felt so out of sorts. *You are tired. Everyone should be abed and tomorrow will be so much better.* He wanted to discuss his afternoon with her, wanted to get her thoughts on what he saw, but felt almost as if he would be unwelcome. And he'd never felt unwelcome before.

He left one light out to guide Tasmin to bed, and covered the rest and crawled under the covers.

She woke him up, crossing the room. She was careful, at first, slipping into bed as if she did not want to wake him. Normally he would turn towards her and pull her against him, but tonight he shrank away the tiniest bit, trying to give her room.

Warm and sleepy, he drifted away, until she flopped over in bed, sighing loudly and restlessly. He drifted away again, waking to the feel of her fingers tangling in the lacing of his nightshirt, working her way in to stroke his chest hair.

He turned over and faced her, giving her a sleepy smile. She had not covered the single light, and she was looking at him, large- eyed in the golden darkness. He stroked her cheek and shifted so he could kiss her.

It was as if he'd awakened a fury. Her return kisses were hard, pressing him back onto the bed as she pushed up his night-shirt, and there were claws on his skin, tracing fire where they went. She kissed him so hard he could barely breathe, and then she bit him.

He pushed her away, touching his lower lip. His fingers came away red. She pushed in again, and he quickly grabbed her arms, keeping her at a distance. "Why the teeth and claws, sweetheart?"

Her expression shuttered. "If you didn't want me, you should have just said so." And she rolled away from him, scooting to the edge of the bed and placing her back to him.

He moved so he was against her, and he kissed the bare skin of her shoulder that her gown had slid away to reveal. "I didn't say I didn't want you. I always want you. I just needed to understand why you bit me."

He pressed a kiss against the side of her neck, placed a very light hand on her arm, stroking it. She lashed out with claws, scratching long marks into his hand. "You are vile," she hissed. "Go away."

He looked at his hand. It shook a little, but he couldn't see any blood. "I see," he said softly. He reached over her and she shrank into the mattress, as if afraid, and he covered the light, leaving them in darkness.

He blushed and rolled away from her, wrapping himself with one of the covers and trying to push the hot feeling of humiliation that burned at his cheeks away. *What kind of monster do you think I am?*

He slept poorly, so close to the edge of the bed that a light breeze could have thrown him off, and as soon as he opened his eyes when the sky was light, he got up and dressed quietly.

He stared down at her for a moment as he did up his buttons. *She looks like my wife.* He wanted to cup her cheek, see if a good night's sleep had brought her back to him. He dropped his hand and went out the door, his heart unusually heavy.

Magda was already up, as well. "What happened to your lip?" was the first thing she asked. He felt it, then went and found a shiny surface to inspect it in. "Tripped and fell against the bed post. I must have bit myself when I did it." It was slightly swollen, though it was hard to tell in the surface he'd chosen. The dark scab was not hard to see. Drinking anything hot was sure to be a miserable experience.

Magda was still staring at him, and he arched an eyebrow. "I don't believe you," she said.

"It does not matter to me."

"Oh, joy. Your wife's wonderful mood has spread, I see."

He swallowed the cutting remark he'd been about to make so hard that it made his throat hurt. "I perhaps did not sleep as well as I would have wished. I think I shall go to the warehouse and finish my work."

"What shall I tell the sunshine of your life?"

He slammed his hat on his head. "Whatever you wish."

He was in a foul enough mood that he forced himself to stop at a little pastry shop for breakfast, hoping that a treat would lighten his spirits. As predicted, the hot tea could only be drank when it had sufficiently cooled, and even then from the corner of his mouth.

Last night bothered him quite a bit, partially because he felt guilty about being bothered at all. Everyone had off nights. He aimed a a piece of pastry toward the corner of his mouth, but even that caused the bite on his lower lip to throb. But that was the problem…biting was so unlike her. *Perhaps she was just frustrated and was taking it out on me. Or perhaps I am a terrible lover…could it be that I am not fierce enough for her?*

But he thought that he was reading her needs accurately, she previously seemed content afterwards, kissing him and holding him. She had never been one to use her nails as claws.

*I don't need to leave a mark on you to know that you are mine.* She had said those words once. He forgot the context.

# Chapter Twenty

Franny loved her new body. Love was actually a weak word for it, having been without one for three months, not being able to eat or sleep or feel the breeze on one's face. The sheer joy of it was utterly captivating. She could barely stop smiling as her skirts swished around her legs.

The only pall was William. She still despised him, and now she was married to the dolt. Sort of. *Eric, wherever he ended up at, is either howling in anger or laughing himself sick over the irony.* She could never tell; sometimes he'd enjoyed a good twist of fate.

Last night had been a severe lapse in judgment. She had felt a warm body and wanted to experience a man again, and had been a mottled emotional mess of lust and resentment. Any man would have done, just unfortunately she had a great deal against that one in particular.

*Any man might still do.* She stopped and looked at herself in the window, trying to make out her face in the early morning light. Tasmin dressed in practical clothes, did her hair in a practical way. She had managed to find one pot of lip rouge that was so old that the paste inside was cracked, so makeup was not acceptable just yet. She rubbed her cheeks. *But not now.* She was laying the foundations carefully. Last night felt like a terrible mistake, but she had managed to hurt William, make him doubt. That was good. She would break them apart slowly, carefully. Just enough to make him miserable without it being too obvious.

*And after I have had just enough fun, I shall kill him and sell his damned shop.* She nodded to herself and kept walking. She was on the hunt. There were still parts of the deal she'd struck to be finished.

The beach wasn't much further. She cut down the strand, avoiding Miss Dovlington's House for the Pathetic and Worthless, walking swiftly to the figure that slumped on the bench facing the sea.

Ailiani looked up. She was gray. Franny had often marked her as extremely beautiful, but now you could not see it. Even her tattoos seemed lackluster.

"Tasmin?"

"Where is she?"

Ailiani blinked and shook her head. "Who?"

"Why, your little ghost friend. The Queen of the Sea or whatever she thinks she is. The one who keeps helping you send the storms away."

Ailiani started stuttering and falling over her own words, and Franny watched her, amused, for a moment.

"Now, now, I know you've been sending the storms away. You know, you're even more powerful than I am." She placed a hand over her heart. "Isn't that interesting?"

"How long have you known?" she asked, her shoulders slumping.

"Positively ages, darling. A blind man could sense it."

"Then why didn't you say anything?"

She leaned close, until they were almost nose to nose. "I don't know. If you wanted to put up a charade, who am I to stop you?"

And then she leaned in, and kissed her. "Not bad. A little soft." She bopped noses with Ailiani, who was looking confused. "A better kisser than William, that's for certain."

"You're not Tasmin." She said it with sad certainty.

Franny grabbed her throat. Ailiani's mistake was that she did not act. She was not sure that her friend was not somehow present, and that gave Franny an edge. She sunk her claws in a little, and leaned close to Ailiani's ear. "Tell the Sea Witch Franny Harker thanks her for her freedom. And tell her that she should run, because the storm will come and no one will be able to stop it. You I'd kill, but you could still be of use. So stay inside, and out of my way."

She ripped backwards with her hand, not ripping out skin, but ripping out the essence of Ailiani's voice. She backed away and held out her hand, showing the other woman a shining emerald. "But I don't want you telling anyone else. There is still ever so much fun to be had."

Ailiani was trying to speak. She stood up, gesturing, yelling at the top of her lungs, but not the slightest sound came out. "Maybe I'll straddle her husband again tonight. Hear her scream." She gestured. "In the back of my head. She's screaming right now, for all the good it does her."

She turned and started back down the beach, and heard Ailiani run towards her. A gesture, and the other woman flew several feet, falling with a loud thud on the sand. Franny had had power, when she was alive, but she had been poorly trained. But her spirit, in Tasmin's body, with all of Tasmin's power, that was something unprecedented. She flung out her hand and a boulder lifted and flung itself over the water, skipping like a flat stone.

She would bring the ghost storm. She would bring it right down on top of Azin Shore. Forget selling the shop. She would loot the wreckage, take what she wanted, and disappear. Start over somewhere new.

The emerald flipped in her hand and disappeared. She felt like she could do anything.

Ailiani did not go to the Chocolate shop. She grabbed some bread and some hot milk and ate quickly, cleaned herself up so she did not look like a mad woman, and walked, swiftly, to the warehouse.

She would not be able to get in the normal way, walking up to the guard and asking to speak to William, so she wandered nonchalantly around the back. She waited, patiently, until the back gate was not being watched and slipped in. The two large doors were open, so she straightened her back and walked in like she belonged.

William was seated at his desk. He looked tired and quiet, buried in his work. She tapped the desk edge to get his attention.

"Ailiani!" His smile faded quickly. "Is all well?"

She pointed at her throat and tried to speak. She couldn't even squeak.

"What happened?"

She wiggled her fingers as if she was casting a spell. He frowned and shook his head. She took a freshly trimmed pen from his hand and patted around for paper, and he slipped her something. She wrote: *Someone disguised as Tasmin stole my voice.*

He looked over her shoulder as she wrote, and she looked at him. He started at the paper, shaking his head. "I don't..."

*It's not Tasmin. I do not know who it is. But someone has stolen her body.* The quill ripped the paper, she wrote so fiercely.

"I still don't understand," he said gently.

A dramatized and silent sigh, and she dipped into the ink and started to write again. A warm hand came over hers, stopping her. "Ailiani, dear, you are writing gibberish."

*Very well, we will make a game out of it then.* She put the quill down and took a breath and pointed to his ring finger, but her gestures were as useless as her writing, or her voice. She tried to communicate until she finally slumped into his stool and started to cry in frustration. That language he understood, and he handed her a clean pocket handkerchief and stroked her back. "There, that's alright. I know it is some spell, and I know that if we go to Tasmin, she will help us figure it out."

She shook her head so hard she was sure she had done herself some damage.

"I know she has been acting a bit off since last night."

She snorted. It did not make any sound, but that, with the eye roll, made her intention obvious.

"Did you two have cross words this morning?"

She paused. Not really would have been the right phrase, but keep it simple. She nodded her head.

"Ah. Well." He leaned against the desk. "She didn't do this, did she?"

She tried to nod her head, but the way he looked away, she could tell she had not communicated well at all.

"She is not herself. Last night after...well. She is very much not herself." His cheeks pinked a little, and she felt a little ill. *Maybe I'll straddle him again,* she'd said. Ailiani stroked his cheek, finally noting the swollen lower lip. It looked painful. *Don't make love to her. Don't waste yourself on her,* she thought.

He smiled gently at her and petted her hand, and she let it drop.

*What are we going to do?* She wanted to ask, and he was looking up at the ceiling, thinking. "Go back to the shop," he said, as if he heard her. "Get Magda to stay with you. You don't want to be alone there, now."

She nodded. He looked at her, looking very tired and a bit sad. "I will be along in a bit. I need to work on something."

She went out the front. When she looked at William one last time, he had his face in his hands. She wavered, wanting to go back—he and Tasmin were the only family she still had—but she kept going.

Ailiani did not go to the shop, not directly. First, she returned to the sea, and tried to call on her "friend" as Not-Tasmin called her. Nothing but silence. Could she only come out at night? She was always gone before the fullness of dawn, and never came to her before complete darkness settled in. She danced the pattern, scared that someone would see her and even more scared that the Sea Witch would not come.

No one saw her, which was good, but sadly the witch did not come. Ailiani smoothed the path away, and, shoulders down, went to work. *It is the very first time I have not been eager to get to the shop.* And it was true. Usually her steps were light and quick, but today they dragged.

Magda was in the shop, her face sour enough to ruin the confections on display. "Where were you? There were people, I had to serve them."

She sighed heavily and went through the pantomime of not being able to talk, which Magda seemed to enjoy a great deal.

"Well, have fun serving the customers with your lack of speech."

She brushed by Ailiani, and Ailiani snagged the other woman's earlobe. She pinched, hard, and pulled her back around the counter, letting go only to press her, not too gently, onto the stool.

"No. I will not deal with people. If you think I enjoyed speaking to anything that breathed, do you think I would have lived in a hut on the beach?"

Ailiani gazed murder at her, her hands on the other woman's shoulders.

"I hate people," Magda said quietly.

Ailiani held up her finger. Then she pointed at the clock and circled the face.

"A whole day? I shall die, and haunt you forever." If she had continued sounding angry, Ailiani would have smacked her, but she sounded resigned and a little overwhelmed.

She kissed Magda on the forehead, and received a squirmy push in response.

"One day. As thanks for the shelter." Ailiani reached for Magda, who held out a hand. "Do not touch me."

She patted the counter instead, and went to the kitchen. The food William had put out for the sprites was uneaten, and she looked for them. She did not have Tasmin's bond with them, so she could not sense them, but the kitchen and pantry seemed far too still, dead, in fact. She abandoned her search for the sprites and went upstairs. She searched the rooms for any sign of Tasmin, then went into the workroom and started raiding the shelves.

She stood there, flipping through the pages. This was not her first language, and she was frustrated by her slowness. She had learned a great deal of how to read Berengeny Script from her husband (long may he rest) and William's habit of passing along every lurid penny dreadful he bought had helped, but she was tired, and some of the writing was archaic. Sometimes the phrasing took time to get used to. It was frustrating, and she was not helped by the fact she did not believe in book-magic, everything she had been taught was a different set of mechanics.

In short, she was not having an easy time.

Tasmin had books on stone lore, herb lore...really, how many books did one woman need of herbal magical properties? Amulet making—Ailiani spent some time with those, hoping to find something for protection, but even if she did, she was not sure she could make those small, delicately wrought pieces that Tasmin seemed to throw together as easily as breathing.

She had very few books on ghosts. *Even I know when you start referring to Creighton's, you are at the end of your rope.*

Magda said something, loud and taunting, in greeting to the ringing of the bell, and Ailiani quickly backed out of the work room, creeping to where she could just see the room below.

"I have no time for you," Tasmin said. "I am going to get myself something to eat." She stripped her gloves off, looking even more out of sorts than she had yesterday.

"Get me something?" Magda asked, her tone so endearingly begging that Ailiani was shocked. *Didn't know she had that in her!*

"Some poison, maybe," Not-Tasmin muttered as she strode towards the back. Magda grinned at her retreating back, then slid a glance up the stairs. Ailiani waited for the kitchen door to shut, and slipped down the stairs, heading for the door.

"She did not ask why I was here," Magda observed quietly.

Ailiani shook her head a tiny bit. Magda looked at the kitchen again. "I see."

*Do you?* Ailiani wanted to ask.

Never removing her eyes from the direction Not-Tasmin had gone, she merely flexed her fingers, telling Ailiani to go, and so she did, sliding out so quietly that the bell over the door never even wiggled.

*Who are you?* Ailiani thought. She'd glanced a little at Tasmin's notes. They were scribbles, easy enough to read but not sensible, they had obviously been written strictly for an audience that lived in Tasmin's head.

*Lived in Tasmin's head. That's rather appropriate. But who is living in Tasmin's head, and is Tasmin still there?*

Yes. That she could answer. Not-Tasmin has said so, threatened to seduce Tasmin's husband to upset Tasmin. *I can hear her screaming in the back of my head.* And she had screamed when Not-Tasmin had hurt Ailiani, which, she knew she should not find gratifying, but she did. But what had hurt worse was the kiss. She would have given up much more than her voice, her sight, anything, than to have Not-Tasmin kiss her.

Ailiani paused, trying to decide which direction she wanted to go. Olonah was powerful. Could she help? Going to the elementalists' encampment might be a good start. It was telling what the problem was...that was where the trouble came. She could communicate if she skirted the issue, but that was hardly helpful.

But, it was a direction. She turned to it.

Ailiani loved deeply and powerfully. She had a lover, back home, who had died under what could best be called mysterious circumstances. Isen, she had loved deeply, and she still thought of him, his easy laugh, his love of the stars. She danced for him, always, on his birthday, on the day they met, on the day they married, on the day he died. She danced under the stars and turned the patterns of rest and blessing and she was sure she always would. He had been good to her.

She loved William, quietly, because he was good and strong and loyal. He made her feel safe. She loved Tasmin, because she was hard and stern and so very fragile—a shell, and when the shell cracked what was underneath was so beautiful.

It made her sick, to think that someone else was laughing and talking and walking with Tasmin's body, and all the while she was trapped inside, unable to do anything, while someone made a mockery of her life. Of her.

*I have to do something. But what?*

This was not far different from Tasmin's train of thought.

She wanted to do something. Anything. She found herself wandering the empty blackness that represented where she was, but suspected she was only imagining that she was wandering, that in fact she was just nothing and nowhere.

*So, what would Franny have done to prepare her better for this situation?* She had been in the amulet. *Would that I had smashed it into a million pieces.* So, what would she have done, to keep herself sane?

Tasmin concentrated on creating a little circle of light. Slowly, like the sunrise, it came, a little gray flicker, growing. It was not very comforting, so she tried to focus on creating a chair. Again, it took her a long time, the effort was like trying to move through frozen mud, so she concentrated on something familiar and beloved. Eventually the worn, over-stuffed chair that William sat in to read at night appeared. She thought about walking towards it, across the smooth gray of the floor, and she sat herself in it. Looking down she saw the green velvet of her favorite dress, envisioned her hands smoothing the wrinkles out.

Beneath the hem she could see her bare toes peeking out. That seemed like it would be cold to her, so slippers appeared. The hands stilled their fussing, without her directly considering them. She looked hard at them, and a wedding ring appeared in its proper place. It became easier as she went.

Now Tasmin felt a little more real, but she was merely a figment, she knew, staring out into the darkness.

*I need to see the world outside. What is she doing with my body? What time is it? Is William alright?*

She stifled any fear sharply. Now was not the time to worry. Anger, fear, none of these emotions would serve her now, only distract her.

Distraction would end her for good. There was no way to know what had kept her tethered to her body. Perhaps it was sheer force of will. But Tasmin would not allow that will to weaken, her chance to go to waste.

She worked. Tasmin did not tire, did not feel any pain of effort, it was like feeling one's way along a dark tunnel, lined with soft walls that gave but a little. She sensed her way, seeking the light, seeking her vision.

And then she was at her desk. It was a distant feeling, a suggestion of her hands on papers, a blurry picture of shelves and workspaces that drew themselves in through familiarity more than actual seeing.

*Work. Reconnect. Feel the truth.*

As her body rose, she heard the chair scrape back. Shadows moving in front of a mirror as hair was brushed and plaited into a braid. The familiar ballet of undressing and dressing and preparing for bed.

She nearly lost it, when Franny attempted to seduce William, banging away at the invisible glass wall, screaming words that William did not know she had in her vocabulary. But she forced herself to stop. To detach. Her husband was not playing her false, he did not know. This was not Franny's body, it was still hers.

But still, she was relieved when William pulled away. She wanted to reach out and stroke his back, tell him that she loved him dearly, but, of course, she was not able to. Yet.

The next thing to do was to try and talk to Franny. She tried to reach out to her, tried to sense the other woman. The visualization she kept getting back in return was of a wall of glass. She was cut off from Franny, that spirit and the majority of Tasmin's functions were all on the other side of the wall.

The chair and the light had disappeared when she was busy looking and listening outward. There was no more to see, Franny's majority of the body was plunged in sleep and darkness. Tasmin imagined waving her hand across the way in front of her, turning. As she did so, the corner of her bedroom appeared where William's chair and shelves where, where the fireplace sat. *It is getting easier.* With a snap of her fingers she tore away the wall between the bedroom and workshop, so she was surrounded by shelves of books and curiosities, with the imagined warmth and light of the fireplace and the comfort of her husband's favorite chair. She took three steps from the chair and imagined a large mirror in the place of some of the shelves. She backed into the chair.

*If I did not have power, I could not do this.*

One of the greatest controversies over magic was where power comes from. Even Creighton weighed in. Does it come from the inside of a person, or does a person draw it in from the outside? Was it attached to the body, or the soul that resided therein? Now, Tasmin thought, now she of all people might know the answer.

*If I were disconnected from my body, I would not have access to my magic.* She glanced at the fireplace. The flames had stopped flickering, they resumed again as she stared into the flames.

*Though, to be honest, if I were completely disconnected from my body, I would not be here at all, but dead and solving an entirely different mystery.*

She tested the limits of her magic. She could not do much, but the power was there. There was no pause between her and her sight and hearing, it was immediate.

But beyond that, she felt something else. More power. This power felt different from anything, foreign. It did not belong.

*So, Franny brought power with her soul when she moved in and set up shop.*

Living in her head as she did, she could tell that magic ran along pathways, that it created pathways through the body, much like the blood through veins. There were connections between these paths throughout her soul and body. An educated man with a knife and a great deal of patience would not find them, they were not visible to the eye. But they were visible to the soul. Now that she knew where to look they shone out like a path through the forest.

*Franny intends to use my power. Else she would have pushed me out by now.* And she could have, back when Tasmin was disoriented and weak. Now, however, she knew how to keep her grip.

She started exploring the pathways, looking for connections, looking for a way to use Franny's magic against her. Franny had to sleep, had to move with care. Tasmin did not.

*The whole thing is nonsense.* William threw down his pen. He had buried himself in work. Correspondence, orders, paying bills and demanding payment of bills. He was annoyed. "If I'd wanted to do this, I wouldn't have angered my family by quitting to set up a chocolate shop."

Ayers, doing some sweeping, wisely kept his mouth shut. William glared accusingly at the letter that sat, propped, on the desk against some ledgers.

Curiosity got the better of him, and he broke the seal and opened it. His brother's writing was spidery and dark across the creamy paper.

*Brother,*

*I write to tell you that I am well. Word comes that you are dealing with my absence with great competence, I would have expected no less. Soon you may be moving into the Heir House, and why should you not? I do not know that I ever wish to return there.*

"Oh, for Light's sake," William muttered. Ayers looked at him, and William waved the letter at him. "My brother is being...I don't know. Dramatic. Bugger all."

*I do not know what I will do. Do you think I could make my living, as you did, and never step foot upon the family shore again? I think I should like that. I did not credit your stories about the world, and now I want to see it all for myself.*

*A shawl is enclosed for your wife. Do give her my kind regards.*

William reached for the package and tore away the paper. It was made of a deep pink silk. The border was thick with embroidery. Tasmin would abhor it.

"Bonny would love it, though," he said sadly, stroking the bright yellow silk fringe.

"Aye, she would." Ayers looked at it. "Did he send that for his wife?"

William shook his head. "He says it is for mine." Ayer's eyebrows shot up.

William folded the silk carefully. "This is not a kind place to put me. I have half a mind to give this to his wife. Plainly this is who it should go to. But I do not wish to give her false hope."

"Ask your wife. She has a good head on her shoulders."

"She does," he said absently, shoving the package into his coat. *It would be good to find her.*

It was not hard, the town was not large and he always had a second sense when it came to her. It never took him long to find her, it was as if he had an internal compass that always pointed to where she was. He saw her shadow cross the window of an apothecary, so he waited for her to come out.

She stopped abruptly when she saw him, adjusted the cover on her basket, and smiled at him. "What is it, dear?"

"I just wanted to keep you company." Her actions had been far too much like putting on a mask. He felt, very deeply, like he did not wish to bring up Andrew or Bonny.

She gave him a wry look. "Don't you have a shop to run?"

"All seems to be well." He shrugged. "I know you have been very busy, I wanted to see if I could help."

She paused, gave him an ever so slightly wary look. "I don't think you could." Then, with more certainty. "I am fine. You can go back to whatever it is you need to do." She smiled again.

He offered his arm. Something stubborn had risen inside of him. "Where to next?"

She could not refuse his arm, her hand hooked lightly on it. "Home, I guess."

"Shall we get something to eat, on the way?"

"No."

He patted the fingers that rested on his arm. "I really wish you would tell me what is wrong."

"I would if something was amiss, but William, I am in the middle of research."

"You have not been yourself."

"*Frustrating* research."

An Ebengene seller was set up, hawking his wares from a wheeled cart that steamed in the cold air. Regretting not getting a bag last time, he decided to splurge. He could use the lift. "I'm going to get a bag—do you mind?"

She shook her head and he purchased a small, greasy paper packet, almost too hot to hold. They were best hot, his sailors had always kept a brazier going on deck, roasting them up, every man certain he had the best recipe. "They used to lay bets," he told her, "among the men, who could come up with the best recipe for these."

He threw a couple into his mouth. *Not bad. A little spicier than I like.* He offered the packet without thinking, and Tasmin took some, eating them with apparent pleasure.

By the time they were back home Tasmin had eaten most of the packet. Tasmin. Who hated spicy food. She even licked the spices off her fingers and wiped it off on her dress, which was another absolutely out of character thing for her to do.

He found himself trying not to goggle at her as he opened the door and let her go ahead of him.

"Well, I think I shall go and make some mint and vanilla jellies. They sold so well the last time." He nodded his hello to Magda and Ailiani. "If you are sure you don't need me?"

"Oh, I loved those. What few I could have, since the customers couldn't get enough of them. Save me some, will you?"

William did not dare look at Ailiani. Vanilla mint jellies were one of the few real mistakes he'd ever made. You'd think they would be wonderful, but they were disgusting.

"And then I'll get Ailiani to help me make Babcock Hen. Ailiani made that for us a few weeks ago, you seemed to like it."

Tasmin smiled at Ailiani. "It was wonderful. If you don't mind?"

Ailiani shook her head and gave a charming smile. Magda ignored them all. He was grateful she didn't ask what Babcock chicken was, since he'd completely made it up.

"Well. Up to my researches." Tasmin sauntered out of the room, climbing up stairs. William shuddered.

He pulled a blank receipt paper closer, and a nub of pencil, and wrote, "That is not Tasmin."

"Well," Magda said, "I could have told you that much."

William gave the woman a look that had made cold blooded killers drop their swords.

Ailiani hit her. She hit her as hard as she could.

# Chapter Twenty-One

Some people, when faced with adversity, broke. They wept and cried and prayed. Some became wise and strong, they went on with their lives.

Magda became hard. The list of things in this world that she did not hate became smaller and smaller with every pain. Sometimes she made herself sit at the counter, when everyone was asleep, and she would steal a pencil nub, some receipt paper, and try and list things that made her happy. It was a long time, sitting in the dark, pencil in hand, the light fading away to nothing. The paper remained blank more often than not.

It was not dark, now, but bright day. She slipped off the stool and walked over to the large, sunlit window. "Even the light is cold, here." She wanted to sit in a hot puddle of sunshine and feel it warm her bones. That might make her happy, to melt in the sunlight.

*In Pandroth, the sun is always hot.*

At least it was, in the desert. She remembered wandering the Vikli Deserts, the desert and its ways ingrained in her — how to read the wind and the stars, the patterns of the grains of sand, the hills and valleys – they all revealed great stories to those who knew the language.

They say that you can get lost in the desert and wander forever, but not her people. Her people had always known where they were, the course of the sun, hot and bright, the cold light of the countless stars at night. It had been that way from the times unspoken of; but it changed, of course, once the Pandrazzi had come. The Empire had been afraid of the nomads, of their untamed magic. It had wanted to tap and control, regulate and cage.

And what the empire wanted, it accomplished.

Magda sighed softly. She missed the stars the most. She had never seen stars that bright, that clearly again. Not even on the waves of the sea.

The Pandrazzi did not kill outright. First, they re-educated. Pandrazzi were practical, if you were of use, you lived. You even lived a fairly decent life. There were rules, and they were hard rules, for the Pandrazzi were as hard as they were practical, but if you were malleable, you could forget. You could build a new life there. They would harness you and train your magic for the greater good of the Empire, and you would go home to your husband and children and eat your dinner and think life was fine.

Magda had never been malleable. She resented her captivity, even though it was voluntary. One day they were free nomads, practicing their magic and traveling from oasis to oasis, another the Pandrazzi had captured them, and put swords to their necks and gave them a choice.

The chief chose for them all. Made them swear allegiance to the Emperor, then bent and allowed them to cut off his head, his, and the heads of his sons, because it was known that this new life would be paid for in blood, and he hoped to pay the greatest part for those who had once been under his protection.

Magda never stopped longing for that life, the feel of hot sand and the sight of stars as far as the eye could see.

"Why do I hate you all so much?" Magda asked, and Ailiani, who had been scratching away at some paperwork, looked up. The scritching stopped, and Magda looked over her shoulder. "It is what you wonder, is it not?"

The other woman shrugged, then just waited for Magda. It was not as if she could do anything else.

"I don't know, either," she said, looking back at the window. She finally joined the other woman at the table. She had a sheet of paper laid out, and she was drawing on it. It was a complex knot, circles and whorls with little arrows following their curves, as if telling which way to go. To most it would have looked like nonsense, even though it was intricate and complex. Four patterns, each in a different direction, and one large central one.

"I know this magic," she said, feeling a frisson of interest. "But I can't tell what it is."

Ailiani placed her elbow on the table, at an angle, her hand held like she was about to smack someone. With her other hand she crawled across the counter, until her second hand was under her other hand, which slammed down.

"A trap?"

Ailiani smiled and nodded, and kept working.

"I knew a man from the Stairs of Alessyn. He was on the ship that I was on, he told me about this pattern magic." It was a variation of her own, symbols made patterns, not curved lines, but she knew what she could do. She saw it, a way to overlap her magic on top of Ailiani's, to create something powerful.

"Do you mind if we work together on this?"

Ailiani grinned and shook her head.

"Now I wish I had my scroll book. It is where I copied my family's spells. It was lost many years ago, but I remember much. I think I can make this trap stronger. Can you tell me what we are trying to catch?"

Ailiani made the effort, then shook her head.

"Ghosts?"

A nod.

"Whatever is riding your friend Tasmin?"

Again the struggle.

"I will take that as a yes, then." She made some notes along side of the margins. Broken magic, just a few words to help her keep track. "How large is this spell? The sailor I knew wore his spell as a necklace."

Ailiani stretched out her arms, then walked around the floor, waving her arms a little more as if to say "Bigger than this."

"What are you drawing it on?"

*Sand.* She wrote on a scrap. *The Beach.*

"Oh, you can write. I wondered."

She got a glare.

"So, you are going to draw an elaborate trap on the beach. How are you going to get her annoyance to it? Invite her to walk around a labyrinth with you?"

Ailiani gave a burst of frustrated air.

"You have to admit, it is kind of obvious. Not for ghosts, but for a woman with a ghost riding her. It's not going to work this way."

Ailiani reached for the paper, her hand clawed as if she was going to crumple it up, and received a smack for her trouble.

"I didn't say impossible, I just said we need to tweak this." Magda frowned at it. "I also may need to use Berengeny magic." She looked up at the ceiling. "Will you play look out?"

Ailiani waited for an hour. She served customers, kept her eye on the front door as well as the kitchen in case Tasmin came in through the back.

Magda came down and Ailiani tilted her head. The other woman threw up her arms.

Ailiani scribbled. *I must go. You should be safe if you lock the doors?*

"Certainly. It's not as if I am going to be trapped, alone, with a possessed Herb Witch and her besotted husband."

Ailiani hit Magda's arm.

The water was calling her. Her only stop was to grab a hot hand pie and some cider from a cart as she made her way down to the strand. If anyone stopped her, she would cough dramatically and stick a lozenge that Miss Dovlington had pressed upon her in her mouth. They quickly let her go on her way.

The Ghost Witch joined her when she was almost there, walking, as always, so the ruined half of her face was turned away.

*Can you hear me?* Ailiani asked with her mind.

"What? I didn't catch that?"

*You must have waited a thousand years to use that joke,* she grumbled as she sat on the bench.

The Ghost smirked at her, joining her. "Why do you ask? I know you usually move your mouth when we talk, but I thought that was habit."

So Ailiani told her.

The Ghost stilled. "So that is where she went."

*Who?*

"I believe she told me her name was Franny Harker. She shared my prison for a time. The Heart of Ithalia, I think they called it."

Ailiani felt her blood chilled. *You're Ithalia?* She remembered the stories.

The Ghost Witch laughed. It was not a good laugh. It made the water choppier, the sky grayer. "No, I am Thanlia. Which, give or take your point of view, may well be worse news. Ithalia is out there." She waved out toward the ocean. "The sea and the wind tells me that some idiot sailor accidentally freed her. Her body dissolved in the sea, and now she's rebuilding herself. Someday, someone will be very sorry. But it takes time, to become whole again, so it probably won't be anyone you care about." The emphasis on probably did not comfort Ailiani.

*Why would you be worse than Ithalia?*

"Because I understand them. The women who want to bring the ghost storm. They both want to save the men they love. Franny wants revenge because your friends killed her beloved."

*For good reason!*

"In this world no one cares about a woman's heart. Not even her sisters. I have a great deal of sympathy for Franny and her ilk."

Ailiani sputtered, even in her head.

"At ease," Thanlia said quietly. "If they succeed, then that gives Ithalia a way to get here. I am not ready to face her. Even with your body, I would burn like a cheap match."

*Thank you.*

The sarcasm was lost on Thanlia.

*What about Sorvalia?* Thanlia smiled quietly. "I destroyed her so completely she will never return. Ithalia can remake, but I can unmake. That is my power. But using it weakened me enough that Ithalia was able to capture me. That is what you need. That dratted amulet."

*Do you know where it is?* She shrugged, looking very annoyed for a half-visible ghost. "Do you think place names mean anything to me? It is a place that is old. You can see the sadness of too much time in the walls."

*Will you help me free my friend?*

She gave her a fond look, and shook her head. "I shared my prison with Franny for a long time. Why would I turn against her? As I said, I can sympathize."

*Then will you help her instead?* The Ghost Witch waved negligently. "I do not wish to be involved."

Ailiani felt a bit used. *How kind of you. But what if Franny wants to bring the ghost storm? What will you do, then?*

"Whatever I must."

When something was lost, William knew, the only way to find it was to backtrack. So, to find clues as to what happened to his wife, that was what he would do. The last time they knew Tasmin as, well, Tasmin, was just before Joe came and got her.

*God, I miss you.* His heart ached with every beat. He was terrified that he would never see her again, that the heart and spirit he adored would be gone.

*I don't even know what I will do. What if she is gone for good? Do I leave her murderer to wander the earth in her body?*

He didn't know. He didn't know what he would do, if she was gone forever.

*I don't think I could survive,* he thought, looking down the street where the name of his shop glistened in the late sun. *But these thoughts do no good. Right now she is a prisoner in her own body.* He refused to believe anything else, that she was not here anymore. *Or else, they have stored her away somewhere? The amulet, perhaps? And she must be frightened. I have to find her.*

He made his way towards Joe and Meggin's home. *She will doubtless be finding her own way out, but she will also be depending on her husband to at least be trying to help.*

Knowing that his wife was indomitable in spirit gave his own spirit a rise. He wasn't alone, working the problem, not completely. Somewhere his wife was present, and she was doing all she could to make things right. "We'll meet in the middle," he whispered to himself.

It took a while to figure out which house belonged to Joseph, but the right neighbors finally pointed the way.

An older lady answered the door. "Greetings. My name is William Almsley. My wife Tasmin sent me."

"Mistress Tasmin." The woman swallowed this slowly, then said, "Why did she send you?"

"Ah. Well. I wanted to speak to your son-in-law. My wife seemed to think that he needed a better source of employment, and my family business has been looking to expand. I could use some dependable men to help over-see some shipping."

The older woman opened the door. "You'd best wait for him, then."

"How is your daughter?" William took his hat off as he entered the small house, feeling quite guilty for the ruse. *Well. If he is innocent, perhaps I can figure out something for him to do.*

"She and the baby are resting. Healthy little thing. I've never seen a pinker or happier baby."

William sat down in the small, dark room, placing his hat on his knee. The woman dithered back and forth for a moment before finally settling down next to the smoky fire.

"Have you seen my wife, the past couple of days? She said she was going to come by."

She shook her head.

*Well. That answers that. Joe lied. Why?* William thought. "How long have they been married?"

"Oh, five, six years. He came all the way over from the western coast."

William was a little surprised. "How unusual, usually the husband sends for the wife?"

"Lost all his family to the plague a few years back, when he was a teen. He was happy enough to sell up and start over."

William picked this over for a moment. He knew that the plague often made young men go sterile. Was five years a long time to be married without children? He supposed so, but he never really thought much about it because Tasmin had been taking something to put off that inevitability in their own marriage. "You must have felt very lucky to have become a grandmother, then," he said cautiously.

"Yes," she answered simply.

"Did they ask Mistress Anne for help?"

"I suppose. She certainly visited several times, bringing different potions for them to try." She gave a glance that made him realize that any further questions would not be welcome.

They sat in silence for a long time. She did not offer him anything, a terrible breach in etiquette. He knew that in polite circles this was an indication that he was not welcome and should go, but if he did not see Joe his only lead would vanish. He finally broke the silence by asking, "Does he work for someone else?"

"The odd job here or there."

"Could I go and track him down somewhere? Perhaps he and I could discuss my proposition on his way home?"

She shrugged and they sat there together. The silence grew more and more oppressive, and William, despite his best efforts, grew more and more twitchy. The baby cried a couple of times and the woman got up to check on her daughter and grand-child, but the rest was an uncomfortable silence.

When he could not bear to wait any more, William excused himself.

He questioned the neighbors. Some people thought that Joe already worked for him in the warehouse. Some people thought he worked for the new foundry out along the main road to the Capital. Another thought he spent a great deal of time at the docks, helping to gut and prepare fish.

He walked a bit, considering what he'd found out. The only thing that Joe wanted was a child. *Now he has one. What price did he have to agree to pay to get it?*

# Chapter Twenty-Two

"And what are you up to, today?" William asked, as he handed Tasmin a cup of chocolate.

"Wise Women things." She took a sip, frowned, forced herself to drink it. He had not sweetened it at all, to see what she would do. Tasmin would have asked if he'd forgotten the sugar. Someone who was only pretending would be afraid to.

Magda, kneading dough, was very amused at Tasmin's expression of forced enjoyment.

He felt like a kid, playing pranks. *I don't know if this is merely ridiculous or surreal. I have no proof that the woman in front of me is not merely my wife having a horrid couple of days.*

"And where did you sleep last night?" she asked.

"Where do you think he slept?" Magda said suggestively. William rolled his eyes.

"I fell asleep reading. I do that sometimes. The kitchen is warm, I can spread out my recipes and books and sometimes..." he bobbed his head, let his eyes slide shut. "Can't be helped."

"Hmm," was Tasmin's reaction. Not really speculative, but she plainly didn't really care. She put down her cup. "Well. I am off."

"Me, too." William said. "Work at the dockyard calls. I will probably be busy most of the day."

Tasmin nodded and went out the back door.

"Most of the day? And who will watch your shop? Ailiani cannot speak, and so I must keep going out and dealing with people." Magda whispered harshly.

"I have been paying you the same wages as I pay Ailiani, aye?" he muttered uncharitably. "Anyway," he checked out the window, "I lied. I am going to follow her."

"I shall come with you."

"No, you shall translate for the silent Ailiani. Someone has to pretend that they care about the business."

"I do believe that I despise you," Magda said as he closed the door behind him.

Tasmin had gone through the yard and left, to get out onto the main street. He made it just in time to see which way she turned before she disappeared into the crowd. It was a foggy morning, and people blurred together a little in the mist. He was grateful for it, because he wasn't worried about keeping up with Tasmin, just about being seen.

He tried not to stare too hard at her when the crowd parted enough for him to see her, afraid that the weight of his gaze would make her turn around.

*It isn't her.* As a sensible man, a practical man, he was not sure if the evidence was quite enough. But he knew. Someone was controlling Tasmin's body, her voice. He just hoped, fervently, that his wife was still somewhere inside her own body. If she was, he knew that she would find a way to wrest back control. Not that he wasn't going to help as much as he could.

So, he spent much of the time following the form of his wife's body, the familiar lines of her figure disappearing into shops, coming back out with purchases. He lingered just out of line of sight from the windows, worried that she would go out the back door while he hid.

So far, he'd been lucky.

A flower seller tried to give her a posy, and Tasmin shook her head. His deft fingers reached up and tucked them into the band of her hat, and she looked in the mirror on his cart. She smiled and flirted with him, even reaching out to graze the younger man's cheek with her fingers.

It did not bother William, save to wonder if it was a show for him. Did she know he was there? Or was she really the vision of carefree pleasure that she was showing?

Finally, she ventured past the old Herb Mistress's place. The further away from the main street they wandered, the more William hung back as crowds thinned.

He lost her once, near an old tanning factory, the smell of death and chemicals still sharp enough to be unpleasant. *Is this where they are hiding?* There was a hole in the wall, and his feet were unsure on the broken bricks as he climbed inside. The room was dark and damp, and he shivered as he stood and listened in the darkness, his breath shallow as he tried to hear what was going on in the dark. Finally convinced that there was nothing near he drew a cold stone out of his pocket and banged it lightly to life. No spells on the floor, or convenient spots of blood. There was dust, mostly, some broken pieces of equipment with jagged edges that seemed to be looking for someone to catch on.

William took the stairs leading to the second floor, not out of real hope, but wanting to be thorough. *I cannot believe I lost her.* The second floor was bright enough, so he put away his light.

On the second floor, he looked out through a rounded, low window and saw Tasmin walking through the yard to another disused business next door. He turned and rushed down the stairs quickly, swinging himself down using the rails to skip a step or two with every move.

He approached the side that did not have windows, working himself across weed-choked yard filled with rusted junk. He slipped past the half-rusted form of a cauldron, ruined by a hole large enough to fit a horse through. The sheer size was impressive, and he realized that he was about to enter the old rendering plant, which had closed due to a rather terrible fire that had taken the lives of many workers.

*What better place to start a ghost storm than where so many people lost their lives?*

He wondered if the ghosts had somehow lingered, or failing that, the sheer pain and fear and anger had seeped into the walls.

No longer worried about keeping up, his movements became stealthier. This had to be the place. Like the previous building, there was plenty of rubble to pick around, sometimes there were puddles of water. *The roof must be gone.* The puddles slowed him down, forcing him to go around if they were too wide to step over.

He picked his way through the rubble, pausing only to cover his tracks when he had to.

Finally, he got far enough in that he could follow signs of activity.

"All I need is a little help." Tasmin's voice echoed from below. He hid in an alcove, tracking the sound as it came to him. Ahead of him was a railing, and he carefully crossed to it.

The rendering room was a large and dark space below, lit only dimly. He could see a woman at a table, resting her head on one hand while she played with a quill, brushing it back and forth over the candle flame.

"Can you make me something to connect more fully?" Tasmin asked. She was pacing right under him. "I have looked and looked for a way in, but she is so damned stubborn. I can feel her power just at the tips of my fingers, but I cannot grasp it."

"Where have you looked?"

"At every book she had. There is nothing about bleeding power out of a soul when you are in the body with it."

William was afraid to breathe. He did not want to spook them, so he stayed as still as humanly possible.

"Our amulet work taps into the power and feeds it to the person we direct it to," the other woman said. Her face was nothing but shadow. William recognized the voice, but could not place it. "But the weaving taps into the soul and sends the magic to another body. I cannot figure out how to make it bridge between two souls. Perhaps we should try and drain her power and give it back to you that way?"

"No," the woman who possessed Tasmin said a little sharply. *Oh ho, don't trust them to actually give you the power, or not to at least tax a little for their own purposes?* William thought as he watched them.

The other woman's expression must have said the same thing, because Tasmin's voice said, "I need every little drop of magic. I cannot afford to risk even a little bit being lost. We can finally bring forth the ghost storm."

"If you bridge it."

"Does the amulet need something potent? Blood? The finger bones of her husband? I could bring you his whole hand?"

*You can try,* Willian thought ruefully.

"I do not think we could make use of that." The voice was a bit leery now.

"Oh, but it would be fun to see."

There was a long moment of silence. He wished he could see more than shadowy figures. "You had best resume your normal life. I am going to go about my business. Aris is busy with the elementalists. She thinks that Olonah is suspicious, so she is staying in camp."

"You are not going to guard our prisoner? What if someone comes looking?"

"Why? Do you think someone is going to find her? No one else has ever been found here. They think everything happened in the sea caves."

He leaned back ever so slowly and lowered himself to the floor, careful, careful. He closed his eyes and waited while they bickered a little more before finally they took their leave.

*Her. Someone else is here, not being guarded. Well.*

He waited until he was sure they were gone. Until they would not turn back because they had forgotten something.

He waited until the silence made his heart beat very, very loudly in his ears, and then he made his way down.

The space was huge in the near dark, swallowing much of his light, but he kept his eye focused, made sure to pick up his feet so he did not trip, and kept going. In the corner there was a table, and something was laid upon it.

If he had a mage's eyes, he would have been able to see the silver threads of power drawn around the woman who lay on the rough boards. But he did see the weave of threads, real threads, and silver wires that wrapped around her. He put his hand over her mouth, and soft, warm breath, so shallow he had to leave his hand there for several moments, reassured him that she was alive.

*Will I hurt her, if I undo this mess?*

He had no one. The sprites were gone. His normal boon companion was not herself. Ailiani was out of reach. He placed a hand on her cool forehead. *Olonah might be able to help. Not Magda, I do not think her advanced enough.* "Who are you? Can you hear me?" Her eyelids fluttered open, she struggled for a second, then they shut again. The pull of the magic that held her under was too strong. Normally he'd just pick her up and take her away, but he didn't know if he could just pull her free of the things that held her.

*Very well. Leave and come back with reinforcements.*

But he was scared. What happened if they moved her? Or did whatever it was that killed the others before he could return? So now, he would just risk moving her.

The first thing was to search the space. There was a satchel, hidden deep in the shadows, behind a pile of rubble. The leather itself was clean, he didn't see any marks. He opened it with the care of a man expecting to have a wild monster jump out, but saw books. Books could contain clues to help the woman behind him, he couldn't risk leaving them, so he drew the strap over his head. There wasn't much else. Chalk stubs that smelled strongly of sulfur and iron, some herbs, some twine and some wire. He returned to the woman, and looked at her, listening in the darkness for sounds of someone returning, thinking it all through.

Threads attached her to various things, and he followed them carefully. One led to a jar, which he carried back and placed on the table. Another led to a black shard of onyx, slick and sharp. There was a rag next to it, he took the hint and used that to carry the shard to the table.

The final one led to the Heart of Ithalia.

He sighed deeply. He already knew what would happen if he picked it up, and he did so gingerly, practically dropping it on her stomach. He tucked the items into her clothes, wrapped the connections at her hand and wrists so he would not jar them, and gently picked the top half of her up, putting her arm around his shoulders as best as he could before picking her completely off the table. She murmured sleepily, and he jounced her just a little to make sure he had a good grip, and went back the way he came.

The last place Olonah expected to see her lost performer was in William of Almsley's arms.

True, he was carrying her with the glazed-eye determination of a man who had been carrying a heavy weight for a long time and was hoping to soon be rid of it, but it was still a lovely sight.

"Nora?" Merin stepped out of his caravan and attempted to take Nora from William, but William stepped back. The other man looked too frail to hold Nora's still body. William said, "I need a table, or a bed. She is enchanted."

Olonah gestured. "To me. This way." He followed her to a shadowy part of the warehouse, where two caravans formed a 'V' shape, blocking off the main part of the building from view.

A trestle table was there, and Olonah grabbed the crystal ball sitting on the table with one arm, then gathered the table cloth with its odds and ends and swept them off the table, putting the bundle and ball on the top step of a vardo. William carefully placed his burden down, Olonah and Merin helping ease her onto the table. He stepped back a few shaking paces, then sat on the step of the other vardo.

"I found her on a table in a warehouse. I was afraid to leave her. She was attached to various things, so I carefully gathered them and took her away."

"Better that you had sent for the Wise Woman." Merin said.

"No, I do not think so," William said quietly, and Olonah gave him a glance. "Merin, could you send someone to fetch Master Carys?"

She carefully retrieved the things from Nora's clothes, laying them out on the table around her. Olonah tapped the table next to Nora's body thoughtfully, tracing the woven threads to pins stuck under Nora's skin. "That amulet is like nothing I have ever seen. A simple, misshapen lump, but you can feel the importance of it, the power."

William opened the satchel on his lap. "They call it the Heart of Ithalia. A woman I once knew thought it would give her great power."

Olonah blinked at him, and he nodded, gave a tiny smile. "Yes, that heart."

"Oh, my," she whispered.

"I just hope it is still the prison it was made to be."

She felt her stomach sink. She shuddered, then concentrated on the mystery before her. William had damaged the spell, no question about that. There was a network of silvery writing that she could not recognize around Nora's temples and wrists, some of it fading and becoming gibberish.

"And we cannot send for your wife?"

"I wouldn't." William was hunting through the satchel, stacking its contents on the step next to him.

"Any particular reason why?"

"I do not think that she is currently herself."

Olonah nodded. "Well, then. We shall discuss that later." He came over with two books and a large folded paper he had put in the satchel when he removed Nora from it. He put the books on the table, and unfolded the paper.

"Blank," he said with disgust.

"No. This is good. I can see the writing." She lay it on the woman. "Oh. That is clever." She looked at William, who shook his head, lost. "It is a stencil of sorts. They used it as a template to trace the spell exactly right. I can't read the spell work—I don't recognize any of the markings or symbols, but if you had this, and wanted to cast the spell that they were using on people like our Nora, you would not have to."

"That is interesting. But from what little I gather, it won't help you undo the spell?"

"No." She carefully folded it again, putting it aside. The silvery lines called to her, she wanted to study them.

Nora was breathing so softly Olonah could not even see her chest rise and fall. The power sinks sat on the table, connected, glowing ever so faintly. *That's her life, flowing into them. Being stolen.*

She straightened Nora's blouse and skirt while she thought. *If magic can be taken and used, then we can return it. We can give it back.*

*But how? If we wait until we figure that puzzle out, she could be dead.*

"William?"

He was frowning at one of the books. He looked up. "Aye?"

"Stand on the other side of the table, opposite me."

He did as he was asked. Olonah took a breath. "Do you see the needles under her skin, that they used to connect the items to her?" He nodded, and she continued. "Do what I do." She took one set of needles in hand, then reached for the set in her temples. She nodded at William, who, after a moment of hesitation, did the same.

"On the count of three..."

He seemed to want to say something, but he took a breath and nodded instead. She rewarded him with a grim smile. "One...two..."

The needles gave a slight bit of resistance, then slid out. Black threads of fluid leaked out of the holes they left behind. William squeezed her wounds carefully, pressing in to push the black fluid out until the blood ran bright red and clean. There was not much of it, Olonah was grateful to see as she imitated him with shaking hands.

Nora took a deep breath, after a moment she sighed it out again but made no further move towards wakefulness. "She's breathing better." Olonah placed her hand against her cheek. "And her color seems better." She looked up at William. "What else did you find in the bag?"

He held up a book. "This seems to be about weaving. I do not recognize the writing, but I suspect it is a lesser used dialect of Veridieran." Not unlikely, it was a small country, across the sea and to the North, and one of Berengeny's closest trading partners. He held up another book. A flag graced the cover. "Because that is their arms. This seems to be a journal about airships. This, I suspect, is hidden because every country hides the secret to how they make airships work. I am shocked that I seem to be in possession of such a thing."

Olonah took it from him. It was indecipherable. As she flipped through the pages she saw a few drawings. "It's not a published book. It's a notebook."

He nodded. "The fact that someone was able to smuggle that out of the country is huge."

"I did not think Berengeny had air ships?"

"We don't. The experiments always fail. It is one of the few things we have in common with the Pandroth Empire, and a reason why they have not much interest in us, as of yet. We are too strong to fight easily, and we don't have anything they really need." He eased the book back out of her hand, leaving her with the weaving book. "I would like to study it later. I suppose that we should give it to someone?"

"Perhaps." Airships interested her little. "But now, you need to tell me about Tasmin."

Franny was asleep. She had shut down, and her mind was dreaming, colorful, odd fragments that Tasmin could not see clearly, just sense over *there*, on the other side. Her new connections were giving her a lot of bits and pieces, but much of it she could not use.

The best way to proceed, she'd decided, was to concentrate on one goal at a time. Currently, she was trying to move the smallest finger on her right hand. She wandered around, trying to find the right connections, trying very hard not to wake Franny up. Just move one finger. That's all. One.

It was a different way of thinking, trying to convince her body to listen to someone who was not, well, directly attached to it, but she thought she was almost there.

The twinkling barrage of colors from Franny's side became an alarm. Tasmin threw herself into the seeing chamber, as she had started calling it.

The eyes opened to a view of her bedroom. Franny shook off someone's touch, and after a moment she was finally able to focus.

It was the tiny, china doll of a woman that traveled with Olonah. What was her name?

"Aristel?" Franny provided the answer. "How did you get in?"

"The last of my magic. You'll have to help me leave." The blond curled her arms around herself. "I think you should get dressed. Nora has disappeared."

Franny had been wiggling out of bed but she stopped, looked at the other woman. "But it is not possible. She could not have gotten up and left."

"She is not there. Cherise is furious. She thinks you had a hand in it."

Franny laughed. "And why would I do that?"

Aristel shrugged and Franny got up and grabbed a dress from the back of the chair. She was distracted and upset, more so when her hands suddenly dropped the dress.

*I did that!* Tasmin smothered her feeling of victory. If she could sense Franny's emotions, Franny might just be able to sense hers. So she concentrated on despair with a touch of fear. Franny looked in the mirror, met her own eyes for a long moment, then shrugged and went back to dressing.

The china doll continued. "Merin told me that William brought her home. So, Cherise thinks that William followed you."

The boil of rage that Tasmin could sense was so strong that it was almost a tangible thing. She no longer had to feign fear.

"Well, well that puts a different spin on things, does it not?"

"You can't just go confront him!"

"Why not?"

"Cherise wants us to go get Olonah."

Tasmin stilled.

"I thought we were supposed to wait on her. She is extremely powerful."

Aristel shrugged. "We are to go and lure her out to the sea caves. She doesn't trust the foundry any longer, she is moving back out to the caves."

Franny was not overly pleased. "We are not ready."

She looked up. "I suppose we must be."

"We lost all of Nora's power, unless Agnes managed to harvest it before she was taken?"

"It is possible, but you know I spend as little time with her as I can get away with."

"Oh, you have other concerns, I forgot."

The smaller woman opened the door and gestured for her to proceed. "He is my husband. I will not let him die."

Franny snorted and went down the stairs. *What to do, what to do?* She had so many horrid things she wanted to do.

"We don't have time," Aristel said, and Franny sighed. At the top of the treads she closed her eyes, put her hands together, and while Tasmin could only suspect what the spell was, she could feel the power flow. She almost thought that if she reached out with her fingers she would tangle them into the silvery and coppery strands. Franny tilted her head, as if listening, then proceeded down to the kitchen. William was face down on the table. The spell had sent him to sleep, and sent him hard.

*That does not look overly comfortable,* Tasmin thought, wishing she could wake him, or at least shift him back.

Franny stepped up on the low stool and felt around the top of the cupboards, pulling down the rifle. "Well. Let's go then."

William was in the kitchen, when Aristel floated in through the window. She could have come in through the front door, to be honest, so intent was he on the book of air ships. He could not make out much, he knew a few words, for cargo, crate, or anything else that might be on a manifest. Veridieran had at least three languages, one for trade, one for formal situations, one for family. All he knew, going over the pages, was that this was not the language of trade, and that sometimes the writing was smudged.

The drawings could be studied. He did it to distract himself. It had no bearing on any of the problems he needed to solve, but thinking about air ships was more comforting than thinking of his wife's body, which even now was sleeping upstairs. He wanted to do something, but he rebelled against locking his wife up. *Patience. We need to see what she is up to.* He hoped he had made the best choice for her.

A word stopped him. The Veridieran for crate showed up a few times, and on the next page there was a diagram for a crate. It looked more like a coffin, in some ways, though the sides were not sloped, the inside was padded, with what looked like a pillow. He moved the light closer. *Berths? Do they think that sleeping in a box would be safer somehow?* Fascinated, he kept turning the pages, desperately wishing he could read Veridieran. *There. An illustration of a woman sleeping in the box. I was correct. Not that I would like to sleep in such a tiny space.*

But as he studied, he saw that he was wrong. The diagrams showed things being attached to her, much like they were attached to Nora, earlier. The weavings were diagrammed, as were the needles, a set of three, the middle longer than the others.

He lay the book down for a moment. His good liqueur was upstairs, but there was no way he was going up there. He rummaged in the cupboards quietly, assuming that Magda was in her hiding place, and finally found the cheap rum he had bought to experiment with for his chocolate making. He had read about adding the liquor to flavor truffles, and wanted to experiment with the less expensive stuff before trying with better. He threw some in a mug and drank it quickly, holding the empty cup in his hands for a moment before carefully putting it back down.

Obviously, he could not—would not—allow this book out of his possession. *And when I am done with it, I shall destroy it.* The diagrams told him very clearly how the air ships were powered in Veriderih. Women were placed in the boxes, bound, their magic powered the ship. They were enslaved to the wood and metal and cloth that made up the vessel, and they never left it.

*Now we know how they figured out how to steal the magic from people. Though how they came across this repulsive volume, I cannot imagine.*

Ever since he was just starting out on the waves, he had heard about air ship travel. The Silver Lands had it. *But they have the Fae. Surely their secret is much less reliant on slavery and more focused on simple magic?* Though for all he knew, and it was very little, the air ships were merely hulls carried around by Dragons. He'd loved the idea that one could load a ship up and fly it right over mountains and straight to where they wanted to go rather than taking long routes around continents and through possible hostile waters. He'd fantasized about it, even when he got older. He had been secure in the idea that it would be ingenuity, not cruelty, that would bring the gift of flight to the world.

So to see this journal—he would not call it a book—on the table in front of him, filled with secrets that all came at too great a price, he felt deep disappointment.

There were voices upstairs. He thought about going and checking, but he felt heavy. So heavy. His knees could not hold him anymore. He slumped into a chair, and grabbed some recipe books and slopped them over the journal and weaving book before sleep rippled in and took over.

William woke with a hideous neck ache and the knowledge that someone had cast a spell on him. Despite what he had told False Tasmin, he was not in the habit of falling asleep at the table. He rubbed his forehead and winced. Especially not when he'd been interested in what he was reading.

He looked at the mug, a little rum still on the bottom of it, and gave it a sniff. He couldn't tell if it had been drugged.

The little room where Magda was staying was still closed, so he knocked on the door, listening. When he heard nothing he opened it. Empty. *I've not seen her, nor Ailiani, since the shop closed.*

The rest of the building was empty as well, and Tasmin's cloak was gone. He shoved the journal in his coat, making sure it was secure, and put on his sword belt.

He circled the buildings quickly, trying to find them. Again, he wished for the wind sprites, and again he worried about them. *They are wisely hiding from the woman who is not Tasmin, I hope.*

He placed his hand over the lump the journal made. Ailiani could not speak to him, and he was not sure showing her the journal would help, though she was clever. Mistress Olonah was Master Cary's wife, so going to her was essentially the same as going to him, and he was not certain he wanted the journal to cross that man's desk.

He forced himself to move forward, to keep going. He knew he couldn't rest, not when someone was walking around in his wife's body. *But I still do not know where I am going. I doubt that they would return to the foundry.* His steps turned towards Miss Dovlington's. At least talking to Ailiani would be a starting point, better than wandering around.

Miss Dovlington met him at the top of the short flight of steps leading to the porch. Men were never allowed inside (the time he snuck in with Tasmin aside) and he faced the fierce woman, wrapped in her shawl as she came down the steps.

"She is not here," she said with no preamble of niceties. "She spends most of her evenings on the beach."

He frowned. "What is she doing on the beach?"

Miss Dovlington glared up at him, studying him. "Well, I think she is using magic to keep the storm back."

The thought of Ailiani using magic stopped him. "You think that she is using magic?"

"Ailiani dances, and as she dances she draws patterns in the sand. She's been spending more and more time out there." She started down the path to the beach, and he followed her down the narrow path between the grasses and weeds. Ailiani wasn't there, nor were her patterns.

"I didn't know she possessed magic."

"I don't know how else to explain it. She is one of my girls, and I watch after the people under my roof." This fetched him another fierce glare, as if she felt William was one of the things she needed to protect Ailiani from. "And I have watched her dance the pattern. That's what she calls it. Dancing the Pattern. It pushes the darkness on the horizon back. I think she's the reason why the storm has been staying at bay."

"I need to find her. Do you have any idea where she may be?" He felt a presence on his shoulder, a quiet, familiar little puff of warm air grabbing his ear. He fought not to react.

Miss Dovlington shook her head. "No. To be honest, I have been worried about her. She stays out all night, sometimes I see her talking to the air."

He almost grinned. *Sometimes I talk to the air, too.* "Thank you, Miss Dovlington. Please tell her that I was looking for her. Please tell her not to come and find me, but to stay safely inside."

*She is, after all, a woman with magic, it would not do for her to be out and about. In fact, I am even more eager to see her and make sure she is safe.*

Miss Dovlington nodded, and retreated up the path, pausing once to look at William over her shoulder. William nodded and smiled at her, then started down the strand. Once he was alone, he said, "Where have you been?"

Tatu was joined by the Chief. *Hiding. A bad thing has taken over Tasmin. We have been helping Ailiani push back the souls, and hiding.*

"But why here? Isn't it dangerous? Don't you need to return to your anchor spot?"

*The Ghost Witch drew us out here and temporarily anchored us. We cannot go far. We dare not move for fear that anchoring will break.*

"Well, you can anchor on me, for a little while? I am going on a hunt for Ailiani."

He was surrounded by wind sprites, petting his hair, tangling into his clothes, whirling around him. For the first time in days he felt happy, loved, content and hopeful.

*We can anchor only a little while. We are still drawn to Tasmin. She is our main anchor, she keeps us together and safe.*

"It must have been a bad few days, being stranded out here." William knew that they could move as long as there was an anchor. They could stay in the shop, because that was Tasmin's home, her anchor. So they could leave and come back in safety. But without touching base with Tasmin, or the shop, their connection weakened. They could scatter to the winds if the connection weakened too much.

"Can you help me find Ailiani without risk to yourselves?"

*You belong to Tasmin. You are almost as good an anchor as the shop.* Tatu petted him again, and snuggled herself in between his collar and neck, just under his ear. He smiled. It was good to have her tucked in her accustomed place.

*The wind has teeth tonight*, Ailiani thought as she held out her hand to Magda, who took it reluctantly. They were climbing up the side of one of the scrub covered sand dunes, and it was hard going. When they finally got to the top she looked out at the sea. Ahead and to the left the sea caves sprawled, broken black rock and crags breaking up the pale sand.

She felt like something was waiting, out there on the sharp line of horizon.

"My dear Ailiani. And you brought a friend." The Sea Witch was hovering behind them. Magda jerked in surprise.

*I tried to explain but could not. Her name is Magda, be kind.*

"I remember you," Thanlia said. "You are the one who lost her child. Do you want to know why?"

"You saw what happened? What are you?"

"I am a ghost. I used to be a great Sea Witch." She smiled, and it was hideous. The eaten away section of her cheek stretched away from the coral of her jaw and cheek bones. If you looked too closely, the ghosts of fish flitted around the cave of her mouth. "Perhaps I still am. I saw your daughter over there, playing along the shore. They gave her sweets, led her away. I don't think they meant to kill her. She fell, running away, broke her neck. They tried to fix her, I felt so much magic being poured into her, but it did not work."

*Your delivery leaves much to be desired.*

Magda was looking at the stars, her head too far back for Ailiani to make out her expression. "Well. Tell me who they are, and they will all suffer accidents as well. Unless they are ghosts like you?"

Thanlia grinned. "I will point you in the right direction and let you have your fun, as soon as we have solved our other problems."

*And what is that?* Ailiani asked urgently.

Thanlia pointed at the horizon. "We have to push that away. None of us wish that storm to come to shore."

"Have they taken someone else, then? They had a Vision Witch, but William told me when he got home that she had been found alive."

Thanlia shrugged. "They have been building up their power. I suspect that they will use it, and they will kill the most powerful mage they can find to trigger their spell."

*Can you sense who that is?*

"Ailiani asks a good question," Thanlia told Magda. "She asks if I can sense who the most powerful mage is. I can. Tasmin is high up there. So are you, Magda. And Ailiani, though your power is not as close to a part of your soul, rather, you know how to tap into the power of the world and bring it into you. If they knew that, you would be the most valuable person in the world to them; why kidnap and kill several women, when you can use one to connect you to the world?"

"What about men?" Magda asked. "Men have magic."

Thanlia shrugged faintly. "I am not sure. The ghosts are mostly women. That seems to be their focus."

"There was one male victim, in the cave?"

Ailiani waved her arms in the air in frustration.

Thanlia nodded. "She's right. We must assume that they are women. Tasmin is out. I doubt Franny is going to give her up any time soon."

Magda nodded. "And we are together. What about the elementalists? Power practically radiates off of their leader."

"I will let myself settle into a drifting trance. Follow me. We will see if we can let the power pull us, otherwise, I cannot track her. If I could track specific people it would be just as well to try and track the murderess herself."

Aristel paced back and forth in front of the warehouse where her fellow elementalists temporarily lived. She stopped, looked around, jittering up and down like a bug.

William crept up, and gently put his hand over her mouth and pulled her against his chest. "Stop fighting, I mean you no harm." He pulled her away from the lights at the door.

She shook and struggled all the more, and he felt guilty, holding someone so tiny against her will, but steeled himself. "I would feel badly for your fear, but I know you intend to lead another woman to her death, and that I cannot bear."

She stilled.

"I doubt you meant any harm at first. Your friend offered you a way to help your husband. Olonah let it slip that you are the reason why the elementalists diverged from their normal path."

"She offered so much. The potion she gave me worked so well, at first, but she made it clear we needed more magic for its effects to become permanent," Aristel said. "But it's alright. Olonah knows. I was waiting for her to tell me what she wanted me to do."

William let go of her. "She knows?" He arched his eyebrow, but realized that she could not see it in the dark, so added. "Why do I find it hard to believe you?"

"Because you are mean?"

"Or sensible," he countered.

He took her shoulder and marched up to the doors. "If you truly had told her all, why were you not waiting inside?"

"I waited where she told me. You don't have to pull me around like a rag doll."

He pushed at the door, which opened quietly. The fires were banked, the vardos silent in the dull glow. Olonah's was as dark as the others, it did not take long to determine that she was not there.

"When did she speak to you?"

"She sent me a note. I had left her a note, confessing all, and her reply was to wait outside for her at a certain time. I was early."

"And she is...?"

"An hour late."

He stared down at her.

"Do you truly want out of this?"

She closed her eyes and nodded.

"Go to your husband, curl up next to him, and go to sleep. Stay out of this, now. Just go and take care of your husband."

She backed away a few steps, staring at him. He never knew what she did, because he turned away and strode out the door.

Master Carys was even less welcoming. "What are you about?" He was rubbing his eyes, trying to get awake.

"Hoping your wife spent the night here."

"And what business is that of yours?"

"None. But as your exceptionally powerful wife is missing, I suspect we need to go and find her."

"She's not..."

"No. Not at her vardo." He removed the journal from his coat, tapped it against his hand. "This may give us some clues. But I swear I will kill you before I let you pass on the information in here."

Carys looked as if he had a particularly sharp barb at the tip of his tongue, but he seemed to see something in William's expression. "Well, then. Let's get some more light."

They leaned over the desk together, William pointing out what he had learned. "So I believe they are using this knowledge to strip magic from the person."

Carys walked away, William could hear him dressing in the other room. "And you do not think they will be at the foundry where you found the woman and this book?"

"No. But I also found a stencil that your wife thinks they were using to replicate the spell. I don't know if they can use the spell without it, if they remember enough to draw it freehand."

"Did you burn it?" He was jamming his feet into his boots.

"The stencil? No. I did not know if I would require it. Sometimes Tasmin looks at magic spells and uses what she sees to take them apart. A good mage can read what they see and make changes."

"Will you, then? When this is over? And that thing, as well?"

William breathed out in relief. "Yes. Yes. I will. I do not wish to see anyone bound to slavery, and that is what that is."

"I can read a little more of that language than you. In another life I was a diplomat. Some of the words I saw denoted punishment. They are using women who were being imprisoned anyway." He held up a hand. "No, do not argue, I already agree with you. It is still cruel, but perhaps not as cruel as we think. I do not want our country to do it, for certain. And so when our ladies are safe and everyone is free of this problem, we will burn everything. Every last scrap of spell, all the things you found."

"Good." He hid the journal again in his coat lining.

"Now," Carys said. "Let us go find our wives."

# Chapter Twenty-Three

*There it is. The key.* After many hours of relentless searching, she figured out how to access Franny's side. She made the knowledge into an actual key, formed her thoughts until she was holding a key made of iron and gold with an emerald at the bow. It was ostentatious, but she was bored. She weighed it in her hand, flipped it, considered her next moves. Things made more sense if she pretended that she was still in control of her own body, just in a larger prison, that things were still, well, real. So now, she stood outside a door. The edges were outlined in bright silvery light, the door was cold to the touch. Years of being figuratively trapped in her own head had given her a strong imagination, and she ran her hand along the edges until a keyhole appeared. The key slid in and turned with a nice, satisfying click, and the door opened.

The floor was marble and her heels clicked as she crossed it to the plinth.

The plinth held a bowl made of simple pottery, terracotta glazed with pecks of brown. Inside the bowl magic swirled. She held her hand over it, hovering.

*Wait.*

The voice was her own, in her head. "Why should I wait?" she asked herself, but there was no answer. She moved her hand along the walls of the room, as if opening heavy drapes. Mirrors were on every wall, showing her everything Franny saw. She snapped her fingers and a large chair appeared from the ground.

She settled in. "Alright, then. We shall wait."

Olonah frowned severely at the bindings at her wrists, as if she could make them loosen themselves out of fear. *Well, at least we understand better why they had that book on weavings.* The bindings on her wrists would not shift, they would not catch fire, nothing she did set her free.

*If I ever again decide, out of the kindness of my heart, to help someone, I shall lock myself away with a bottle of wine until the madness passes.*

The plan, such as it was, had been to allow them to kidnap her so she could get close enough to Tasmin's body to throw an exorcism amulet against her skin. She just had to make contact. It was on a necklace in case she had the fortune to get it over the other women's head, but if she shoved it against Tasmin's clothes, it would do well enough. Better if it made real contact with skin, such as down her back, but...

Aristel had written her a letter confessing everything, so she knew a great deal. About the potion that had made Merin so much better, about the broken axles meant to keep them in Dalmaca. She should have been on her guard. She should not have been tempted by the green and gold foil box of chocolates that sat on the steps of her vardo. It was a good trap—of course the woman who inhabited Tasmin had plenty of access to sleeping herbs and chocolate. But she had been hungry, and had thought the box was from William, a bribe or thanks for help.

So she had not had a chance to fight. To scratch or claw or use magic or sneak amulets or anything. She had just slept.

And now, here she was. Trussed up tight. *God forbid that Carys is the one to find me, should they kill me. Henry is strong, but this would kill him.*

People thought, because she rarely stood at her husband's side, that she did not love him. But she did, fiercely. And now she hoped he stayed far away from here until the worst was over. *There is time. They did not kill Nora right away. They sapped her strength. Maybe William will think to look for me.*

A flare of light blinded her for a moment, but when the spots faded she could see where she was more clearly.

Of course. Now she knew she could make out the ocean beating at the rocks, she could smell the salt a little stronger. She was in the sea caves. Her instincts encouraged her to roll off the table and see if she could find a place to hide, but she did not want them to know she was awake yet.

A cautious move of her head to see if she could find the light source. No one. No shadows, no movement.

She slipped her bound feet off the table and the rest of her followed, balancing perfectly on her toes before she overbalanced and fell. The fall knocked the wind out of her.

She shifted forward, got her hands under her and rose a little, wiggling back and forth, propelling herself on her knees, trying to get to the outcropping of rocks that seemed to create an inviting pool of shadows to hide in.

She made it, leaning against them, letting her breathing slow. No longer concentrating on the noises she was making allowed her to hear other noises, such as the soft scratch-scritch, accompanied by low, toneless humming. She scooted a little closer to the light. A woman was drawing something on the rock with a silver stylus. It was neither Tasmin nor Aristel, so she assumed it was Agnes.

The woman paused and took a handful of dust from a pouch, then blew it over the drawing. A small flare of power as the dust filled the pattern, and the woman smiled. She took items similar to what Olonah and William had removed from Nora and placed them dead in the center. She ran the cords out in two different directions, scooted herself over, and started drawing again.

High, and to the right, there was a crack in the wall with a ladder. Behind Agnes was a long trench and the rhythmic splash and play of water. She turned away from the light and closed her eyes, letting herself get used to the darkness. She could not see any way to escape from her part of the cave, but she knew there must be.

As she looked, she twisted and turned at the ties, trying to loosen them.

"They won't loosen." The woman said absently, sitting back on her heels again to admire whatever her work was. "Not without the right word."

"What is it, then? Pretty please?"

Agnes smirked at her. "Nothing so kind."

Olonah shrugged to herself, and scooted herself closer to the light.

"Do you see that green line, running along the floor?" Agnes pointed with her chin, then took up the stylus and started marking again.

"And what of it?" Olonah did see it, now that she looked, for it was dull green and it almost faded into the ground.

"It will kill you should you cross it. So don't."

"Perhaps I should. It would put a considerable hole in your plans."

Agnes stopped, tapped her stylus against the stone, then shook her head. "You won't."

"You sound quite certain. Did Aristel tell you so very much about me?"

"Aristel? Did she confess of her own free will, or did you threaten her husband?"

"Is this answer a question with a question time? I'm very good at it. I used to be a fortune teller before I actually started studying magic."

"You won't kill yourself because any woman who leaves her husband behind so that she can be in a traveling side-show is far too selfish to end her own life for the greater good."

Olonah hit her chest with her bound hands. "A palpable hit, as they say."

Agnes went back to her work. "So I shall assume that Aristel is no longer able to join us. It is no matter. I will get Franny to help. In her current body she is far more useful anyway."

"I don't know how you intend to take my magic away, since you don't have everything you need?"

"Taking away the amulet didn't stop my plans. Taking away Nora did no great good. It only sped things up. I don't need to contain you, try to keep you alive and store your power. I need to kill you, and I need to make sure you are angry first."

Olonah rolled her eyes.

Agnes stood up and let out a huge breath. She looked over her work carefully, her voice off hand as she said, "Oh, you'll be angry. I will make sure you and William are both very angry ere you leave this mortal coil, and your bothersome husband Carys will be very dead." She stepped back and smiled, nodded at her work with real pleasure. "No sense leaving loose ends."

"The sea caves?" William asked, trying to make sure. "Why would they go back there?"

"No one's been back to the foundry...my men have been sweeping the factory and warehouse areas. Going to Dalmaca doesn't make sense. What else do we have?"

He had a point. "The tide will be too high to get into the caves."

"Through the water, yes. After you found the bodies there earlier I was able to get someone to tell us a much better way in."

"I can hardly wait," William muttered.

"Oh, you'll love it. Hopefully you are not afraid of heights."

Considering that he'd been known to climb the rigging for fun, heights was not what he was afraid of. But as he climbed the steep, narrow path that led to the crest of the hill the sea caves were under, he did wonder how two women…or a woman and a man, or whatever combination of human being you wanted to come up with, had managed it with a prisoner in tow. There had to be another way in.

"Now, we need to squeeze under this over-hang. Be careful. It ends up over water, any water that gets into the caves here goes right down into a crevice and out to sea. You'll wish to push yourself away from the wall and feel for a crevice back to the left," Carys said.

"You're enjoying this." There was more than a little madness in the other man's eyes. He recognized it, it was that odd madness that overtook him, sometimes, when he was doing something dangerous but needed.

"Don't be a fool. Down you go."

So, William let himself down using the rope, holding his breath as the rope creaked but the knots held. There was no light, so he did what he had to all by feel. When his feet were on solid ground again he shook the rope, and Carys joined him.

Ailiani helped Magda prepare the tea. It smelled like scorched garbage, and she was sure, absolutely, that it would taste even worse. *I would not put it past Magda to add something to make it taste even more putrid.* She chafed at the time this was taking, but Thanlia insisted that they had to break the spell that bound her voice. She tried not to look too closely around the hovel that used to be Magda's home. Furniture was sparse—a thick straw tick and worn blankets made her bed, a plank on stones formed a low table. The fireplace, made of scrounged stones and a hole in the ceiling was a fire hazard more than a thing for cooking and warming.

"Everyone knows the secret you were trying to hide, so we can hope that will weaken the spell somewhat," Thanlia said, drifting back and forth like grass in the wind. She made the oil paper in the window frames flutter.

Magda thrust a broken handled mug at Ailiani. It was hot, a steaming, foaming hot mess of olive green sludge. Ailiani whimpered.

"See, working already. Now take it. The cup is burning my hand," Magda said.

Ailiani took it and slung it back, even though she knew she was scalding her mouth and throat.

And coughed, and gagged, and barely managed not to throw it up.

"Here. It's a wad of mint, chew it."

She let Magda shove it in her mouth, and she chewed ferociously, her eyes watering. "I am going to kill that hideous bitch," Ailiani said. Her voice sounded as if it was coming out of a gravel filled cave, but it was there.

"And the name of this hideous bitch?" Magda asked, sounding delighted.

"Franny Harker."

Magda scrunched her eyes thoughtfully. "Isn't it too late to kill her?"

Ailiani stood up on shaking legs, straightened herself out as well as she could. "Oh, that won't stop me." She looked to Thanlia. "And now?"

"We are going as close to the caves as possible, and I am going to teach you a very old song while you teach Magda how to dance a pattern."

Ailiani froze on her way to the door, suddenly quite nervous. Sing and dance a pattern, at the same time? Could she do that? Would it work, splitting her focus that way? She had hummed, sometimes, true, while dancing a pattern, but the idea of a new song being introduced into her old magic made her nervous.

"What? Do you not think I can manage to learn?" Magda asked.

"All chipped ego and insults, aren't we?" Ailiani said, continuing outside, rolling her shoulders. She could do this. "I am certain you can learn it. If you can dance, you can create a pattern. Thanlia, is it a very difficult pattern?"

"Of course it is," Thalia said, proceeding backward so she could look at them. "It'll be a combination of things you already know. I want you to draw a ghost trap merged with a blessing mixed with the ward you've been using to keep the ghost storm pushed away. Parts of the pattern need to be keys to Tasmin's body, to draw her here."

"Oh, so, a completely new and hereto never danced pattern. Well. Might as well start large." Ailiani took a breath to keep herself from feeling faint, and cast a look at Magda, who looked worried despite herself. "We can do it. It's complicated, yes, but not difficult. You will be fine, just follow me."

The sand ran right up to the rise of the crags of the sea caves, but the closer to the caves one got, the more sharp rocks and boulders interrupted the land. So Thanlia set them back away from the caves, as close to the edge of the water as possible. "Get a stick and describe an arc from here to...there. Where that rock is sitting.

So Ailiani did as she was told, marking the boundary, then staring at the canvas, trying to envision the pattern. "To sing and dance and teach a pattern all at the same time..."

"A new pattern," Magda reminded her oh-so-helpfully.

"Thank you for that. A *new* pattern. I do not know if I can do it."

*We help,* one of the wind sprites said, and a chunk of pattern started to appear. The one that they'd watched her do for so many nights, now, the one that pushed the ghost winds back.

As the dust settled she drew closer to the pattern. Magda trailed after her. "Aren't we supposed to dance it?"

"You can over-dance," Thanlia said. "Lay out the least important pattern, and dance the most important on top of it. Add it in—edit and change the pattern as you go."

"I have heard of combining patterns, but I never saw anyone over-dance, as you say," Ailiani said. She was feeling overwhelmed. And guilty. She did not want to fail Tasmin, or William, and suddenly what was expected of her seemed huge and unwieldy.

Magda pulled out the drawing that she and Ailiani had made earlier. She looked up at the clear sky. "Wind sprites. I know you are here." She held the pattern out. "Move the arc that you just drew back. Please?"

Ailiani looked over the pattern. "I thought you did not like it, that we could not draw her into it because it was too obvious?"

Magda gave a feral smile. Ailiani suspected it was supposed to be friendly. "You will dance your part, and I, mine. And you, over there, you will sing your song and if we catch onto it we will join you."

Thanlia looked scandalized. "I..."

"You are a Sea Witch. You are magic. If you cannot get the song to work, it is scarcely fair to expect one of us to."

"I am not trying to be unfair. If I use my magic, I may draw my sister." Her silvery eyes flickered towards the horizon. "I am not sure I am ready for the encounter quite yet."

"I care little for what may happen." Magda said. "But what will happen, is the three of us will work together and free Tasmin. And then we will defeat the magic thieves and murderers. And if there are enough of us left, we will push the ghost storm far away. That is the certainty you both must concentrate on. There is no other future."

She stepped away from Ailiani, then stretched out her hand. Ailiani slipped her hand in the other woman's, both were standing as far apart as they could. Magda's smile had not been comforting, but the light squeeze of her fingers was. They nodded to each other, and Thanlia started to sing.

The sprites surrounded them. Ailiana stopped seeing the sand, the stars, and saw only the pattern and the music, like a green and blue strand she could take up and weave. The wind sprites made her float, she was lighter than she had ever been, and she glided over the pattern, whirled around Magda, whose own contribution was an addition of red and gold into the weave. She plucked the weave, changed it, poured magic she had never felt so keenly from her soul.

"Done," she whispered, after the song faded and the last curve was drawn, the last movement of the dance complete, and she was boosted out of the pattern by the sprites.

She stumbled and collapsed next to Magda.

Now it was time to wait. *It would help if William were here. He could help draw her in, perhaps.*

She had not noticed William on top of the sea cave bluff, and he had not noticed her below.

Something was pulling at her, tugging at her. Franny paced the room, looking at their prisoner, looking at the spell laid out neat and perfect. She should be preparing herself for the final push of magic, but instead something was filling her head, making her feel odd and detached. She did not notice how her right hand clutched at a piece of chalk, held it tight in her fist.

There was a song in her head, one she had never heard. Was it Tasmin, way there in the back? She retreated to the next room in the cave, she did not want Agnes to see her struggle. She closed her eyes, and reached for the alcove where she's pushed Tasmin's mind. *There's no one there. What does that mean?* Where could she have gone? Did she give up and die? Unlikely...she would have felt her spirit leave.

A hand settled over her mouth with strange gentleness, an arm wrapped around her and pulled her tight against a warm, tall body. Every move was as light as love, but there was strength. The man holding her tightened his grip slightly as she struggled. He placed his cheek against hers, and whispered, "Hello, thief. Who are you, really?"

She relaxed, boneless and sweet, and he pulled his hand away. "Your wife, darling William."

"I am afraid I require proof. How did you use to sign your letters to me?"

"Really, William, it's been ages. How do you expect me to remember that?"

"Tasmin would remember." He drew her back further into the second cave, away from Agnes, his hand over her mouth again.

She struggled with renewed vigor, stomping William's booted foot as hard as she could, and was rewarded by the click of a pistol. "He may not wish you harm, but I do not care."

"Carys," William hissed warningly.

"Your wife is dead and gone. Mine is not."

William pressed them both a little closer to the cave wall, as if trying to protect them. "I would know if she was gone."

Franny rolled her eyes and sighed. Next to them, the chalk tapped along on the wall of its own accord.

Carys frowned. "Copper defeats red line?"

Franny gasped and ran her hand over the rough rock, trying to erase the marks, but William pulled her away. She bit the meat of his palm, hard, and screamed for Agnes.

Carys ran back into the main room. Franny fought against William, punching, snarling, the fact that the man obviously could not bear to strike the body of his wife a valuable tool because that body did not mind striking him.

There was a shiver down her spine. She ignored it, reached out with her left hand to run claws down William's face...

And it stopped. "Oh, no you don't." Franny snarled at Tasmin. "No you don't."

Franny turned her attention to the inside of her mind. Tasmin's body, with no one commanding it while the two women fought for control, slumped slowly to the cave floor.

Everything inside of Tasmin's mind looked pretty much as Franny had left it, much like the sea caves, dark tunnels that she could see to pass through. There was no light, she just knew where she was going. She pushed her will, her spirit, through the mind that she had lived in for so many days, the mind that she was slowly taking over, making hers...and came to a stop in front of a door.

*What is a door doing here? There are no doors.*

But she opened it.

It was the chocolate shop.

Tasmin was seated at a table, drinking something from a delicate cup made out of ruby glass. Next to here was a plinth with a bowl on top of it. She reached up and dipped her cup into the bowl, studied the contents.

"You waste your power and time on this nonsense," Franny said. "I thought better of you."

"It's not nonsense. It is reclamation. Ever since you sent me into the back of my mind, so to speak, I have been working my way forward. Exploring. Gaining understanding of my spaces. Marking the territory as my own. It's been quite pleasing, to see whatever fancies I wish come to life. Would that I had that power outside of my own head." She laughed. "I rather think I would have the most hideous eyesore of a castle anyone had ever seen. Which surprises me, to be honest. I always rather thought myself more—simple and practical."

"You're simple, alright. Especially if you think I am going to let you have this body back."

"I guess it shall just boil down to who has the most powerful soul." Tasmin took another sip, then put the cup down slowly. "Do you hear that?"

"Yes. One of your fancies?"

Tasmin shook her head, and Franny believed her. "Too unearthly for me. Too much like sea and salt and silence and being forgotten. Yes. It feels like being forgotten." Tasmin stood up and tucked the chair back under the table. "Now. I wonder who wants you to be forgotten? Lost forever on the tides of non-existence."

Franny flexed her hands and smiled. "I have the power of three mages running through me."

Tasmin dumped the contents of the cup on the table. "I have been looking out at the world, seeing what my friends have been up to. You have a limited gift for Sight that I have been tapping into. Thank you." She drew her hand through the liquid, raised it, palm up, admiring the green and red and gold and blue lines that shimmered, dripping off her fingers and trailing down her arm. "I can see what you have. Untrained mages who barely knew their potential. I have a Pandrazzi, an"—she blinked, gave a slight smile and said, "Alessani, and, of all things, a Sea Witch. I could tell you to give up now before I blow what's left of your rotted soul into the pits of oblivion..." She threw her first spell. "But you touched my husband, and made him feel rather badly."

Franny threw up a hasty shield. The spell bounced off the wall and Tasmin caught it again, plucking it out of the air as if it were a ball. "The wonderful and upright Tasmin Bey, out to kill me because you're a jealous beast?"

Tasmin smiled at her hands, juggling two balls of magic between them. She stopped one of the balls, raised it, and met Franny's eyes. She, Franny, felt a frisson of genuine fear and made a grab for some magic of her own. Tasmin signed. "Well, none of us are perfect." She changed her stance abruptly, as if she knew what was coming and avoided the hail of iron thorns Franny sent her way with a flick of her hand. "I am sure I'll find a way to forgive myself." She grabbed the bowl off the plinth, and smashed it on the ground. The bowl had been the key, the symbol of the containment of the magic that ran through Tasmin's body and now it was shattered.

"That was meant to be mine," Franny whispered as Tasmin stepped into the circle, her skirts trailing in the liquid, which started to climb the weave of the cloth.

"If dying is the price to keep you from such power, then I welcome it," Tasmin said softly. She did not gesture, did not even flick her an eye, with her next spell.

The light was blinding. A thousand prickles of pain took over. Franny did not know a soul could feel pain, but she did: the pain of being squeezed tight. She did not know if she could fight it, and, desperately, she looked for a sliver of hope.

William lowered his wife's body gently to the floor. She did not seem unconscious. Her eyes were open, and while nothing really moved, muscles flexed, her breathing was hard. He stroked her head. "Sweetheart. Come back to me."

He heard shouting in the next cave, and frowned. He kissed her forehead. "I shall be back for you." He leapt to his feet when he heard the pistol shot echoing through the caverns, and ran through the door.

The power sinks were glowing. Agnes rushed over to one and pulled at it, but the spell held it tight. "Franny is ruining it...she's pulling our power."

Carys was fighting Joe, who was bleeding, but not enough to stop the larger man. Olonah was in the mouth of a pocket cave, trying to get out. "How are you being held?"

"There's a spell, don't step any closer! It's agreen line, if anyone crosses it...William, leave me, stop Agnes!"

William turned. Agnes cut herself, palm to forearm. He thrust his hand into his pocket and threw the contents of his pouch towards Olonah. Coins...some silver, and one or two gold, but mostly copper rolled across the floor as he ran forward. Agnes threw herself onto the floor, pressing her wrist to the cave.

The spell flared up around them as she wrapped her hand around one of the crystals. "You can't have it all, you greedy child. This is mine."

He grabbed Agnes and pulled her away, and she threw him aside like a toy. He rolled to sitting, then launched himself up as quickly as he could. They'd brought a flask of water for their prisoner, William grabbed it and began pouring it over the spell, scrubbing it away with his hands.

Agnes took a few steps forward, claws out. "What have you done?"

"The only thing I could think of." William studied her as he edged towards Olonah, who was trying to wiggle free of her bonds.

"Not you. Franny. She's taken all the magic." She fell slowly to her knees, holding her hands over her heart. "I am so empty."

Carys was flagging. They had broken a crate, and William picked up a piece of the wood and knocked Joe as hard as he could. He fell like a pile of rocks, close to the edge of the room. "Are you alright?"

Carys was not there to answer, he'd already run across the floor to his wife.

"Why? Why did you take it all? You could have left something for me. Did I not help you?"

"Don't worry. I am still going to share," a familiar voice said, "I promised you that everyone would get what they deserved, and they will." Tasmin leaned against the opening in the wall. William could not tell if she was slumping because she wanted to or because she needed to. William let himself fall to the floor. In truth, he wanted to re-load Carys' pistol, and he tried to do it without attracting attention.

Agnes lowered her hands. "Franny. You won."

She smiled and shrugged, as if the outcome had been obvious all along. "And now we can do what we wished. Those idiots outside have called the attention of the storm. All we have to do is add our magic and poof." She grinned. "Everyone gets what they want. Everyone who is you and me, that is."

"I can feel the power. It's beautiful." She hugged herself, looking down at the floor for a moment as if trying to gain control of herself.

"And it will all eventually be yours." She winked at William, who nearly fumbled his task. "Now. Follow me."

And Tasmin. Or Franny. Or whomever she was vanished.

Agnes followed.

Tasmin had only been able to transport herself a little ways. She looked behind her. She could not tell where Agnes went, or if her friends were safe.

She could not tell a lot of things, but she did know that she hurt. She hurt something awful. Everything burned, Franny's soul, refusing to give up, was burning and scratching, and the magic of so many people, so many souls, was clawing and pulling and splitting her focus.

"My soul is burning," she whispered. And it was true. She was not meant to hold this much power, and she could feel her essence, her spirit, char like old paper. The damage was not bad, she thought, not yet. Right now it was burning away at what little magic she had. Soon it would be gone, the cold ice and wind that protected her and connected her to the sprites would be nothing but ash. And not even that, really. Not truly.

She walked up the strand to the glowing circle of power.

"I am here." Agnes took her hand.

"So much power." Tasmin wanted rid of it, even as it flowed through her, whispering possibilities.

"Give me some. It is burning you alive. I can feel it. I'll throw it back into the spell—parts of it are still good."

"No." Tasmin shook her head. "Not until we are done."

Thanlia stood in the center, along the top arc of a spell. Ailiani and Magda flanked her. It glittered with so many colors, a trap, a ward. There, in the center, a spirit path blessing. It was beautiful and complex and deep and Tasmin knew that she was staring at her grave.

"I know who you are," the Sea Witch said.

"Of course you do." She let go of Agnes' hand. "And Ailiani. Oh, dear Ailiani. You cannot imagine the surprise Tasmin felt when she realized your true measure. If you ever have a heart to heart again...which you won't because, well, I'm in control now, I'm sure it will be an interesting discussion."

She smirked. "I almost want to let them have it."

"Stop being so full of yourself," Agnes snapped. "The ghost storm is coming."

"I know." She grabbed Agnes's shoulder and threw her into the pattern. It reached for her, grabbing her, and Tasmin took an involuntary step back. She looked up at Ailiani as Agnes was pulled to her knees. "For the record, about your magic: you could have told me, sweetheart. I would not have been upset." She smiled at Ailiani, and took another step back.

"Tasmin," Thanlia said.

"I'm losing," she whispered. "It's my soul that's being burned away, not hers. She just has to bide her time."

Ailiani started to run around the edge of the pattern. "No, Ailiani. Stay back. If she wins all three of you will need to fight. Think of something nice to tell William, won't you? I can't seem to frame anything appropriate right now."

She took another step, into something warm and unyielding. "You can think of something later, when you are being less brave and self-sacrificing."

She turned in William's arms. She beamed up at him, and for a moment nothing really hurt that much anymore. "You mean stupid."

He smiled back at her, then turned serious as he gently picked her up. She wrapped her arms around his neck. "Just go to the edge and throw me."

"That would not be my plan."

"You have to hurry. You are connected to Agnes, and she will use that connection to break free," Magda commanded.

"It will hurt you," she told William. "It will hurt an awful lot and you can't keep it from hurting me, so why should you go through it?"

"I am not even going to bother answering that." He stepped into the pattern. She slipped from his arms onto silvery sands. The pattern was like a wall of lace around them, the symbols and whorls seemed to stretch forever.

There were ghosts in the pattern.

Magda and Ailiani had both stepped in as well. Thanlia had stayed outside.

"She thinks her sister, Ithalia, is in the storm," Ailiani said. William shuddered. Agnes was kneeling in the sand, looking around thoughtfully. Sand came up around her hands and knees, and when she tried to shift, she was locked solid.

Tasmin nodded, stepping away from her husband, using the pattern, plucking the strands like an instrument, gathering the threads where she needed them to be, and drew out a knife.

Magda punched William as hard as she could and he looked at her accusingly. In that beat, Tasmin plunged the knife into her chest. The pain made her fall to the sand. She drove down as far as she could, then tossed the blade aside, and plunged her hand in to her own body, pulling out a wisp of cloth that she flung away. William threw himself onto the sand in front of her, holding her tightly.

"You have all that power, heal yourself now, that's a sweet woman." He chanted, over and over, "Please heal yourself, darling." And she used her magic to make the hole go away. She even healed her dress.

Franny slowly got to her feet, looking at the other ghosts. "You would have done the same," she hissed at them. "And worse, I say, for one hour more of life."

Ailiani raised trembling hands, and red coils of vine reached up and snaked around Franny's wrists and throat. "I do not think we need to hear your voice anymore."

Tasmin grabbed her husband's hands. "Hold your hands, like you are holding your favorite mixing bowl," she whispered to him, as she drew pieces of pottery from the air and put them together swiftly.

"Why are the ghosts just frozen?" Magda asked, looking at the silvery shadows that lined along the spirit path blessing she and Ailiani had drawn.

The bowl was healed, and Tasmin leaned her forehead against William. She placed her hands over the bowl and magic shimmered in it. She carried it around the circle and flicked it on the shadows, giving them some of their magic back.

The twins were first.

"Cherise?" one said, hugging her sister.

"You were right, I couldn't trust her, she takes everything you want and uses it against you. I am so sorry."

"It's alright, really, it is." Agnes and Cherise clutched each other tightly. "You just wanted to heal him."

Cherise buried her face in her twin's throat. "You could have had him. I would have let you have him, I just wanted you both to be happy."

Tasmin's idea of returning magic did not work for the smallest shadow, a little girl ghost that got caught up with the others. Tasmin reached out and pulled the green-eyed little girl forward.

"Tara?" Magda froze for a moment, then placed both hands on her head. She looked up at Tasmin with tears in her eyes, her face stone. Ailiani threw her arms around the other woman and was not rebuffed. She was saying something, fiercely, in the other woman's ear. Tara gave Tasmin an uncertain look. "It's alright. Go to her."

Magda clutched the little girl to her, and Tasmin took a hitching breath and turned away, giving back the magic.

There were so many dead, and they stood in a circle around her.

"I need to send you all away. The ghost storm is coming, and if you are here when it arrives, it will sweep you away and you will never be free. But I must ask that you leave me some of your power, so that I can try and take the storm apart. Will you?"

There was a man, covered in tattoos similar to Ailiani's. He looked towards the storm, a shimmering darkness outside the haven of the pattern. "You must give each of us something. That will break us away from you. In return I will leave you what power I can."

"As will I," the scholarly plump woman with ink stained fingers next to him said.

"And we will take those who caused us harm with us. Why should they be free to float on this plane, while we are away from those we love for what may be forever?" This was asked by a blond giant. Even as a ghost he had a huge ax on his back.

"Alright, then." Tasmin forced herself to imagine something that would make sense to the tattooed man. A whale tooth, scrimshawed with patterns. She held it out. He reached for the whale tooth, but did not take it.

"Now say, 'Take your power and go,'" he instructed her.

Tasmin paused, glanced at Ailiani, who said, "He's a shaman. He'd know."

Tasmin gave the man an apologetic look. "Please. Take your power, and go."

He nodded once, and was gone.

For the twins, roses, one red and one white.

Agnes looked at her sister. "I should have helped you more."

Cherise gave a shy smile. "I did not ask, or want to hear you." She leaned her head on her sister's shoulder.

"We can't reach for them until you say the words," her more practical mirror told Tasmin.

"Take your power and go." Tasmin held out the flowers, and the twins took them.

"There is something else I want to take with me," Agnes said. The sisters flanked Agnes's body and dragged Anne's soul, kicking and screaming, from it. The body collapsed.

"Shall I try and put you back into it?" Anne asked Cherise, but she shook her head. "It's been too long. It would not know how to be alive any more. "

Anne looked shocked. She pulled away, straddled the still form, scrabbling to get back in. She had been a tall, stately woman at one time, all white hair and fine, elegant features, but now she was a creature of desperation.

"Why did you do all this?" Ailiani asked.

Anne gave them all a pleading look. "I just wanted my power back. When it's gone, the emptiness eats at your bones. You no longer have a soul. I could not face it." She looked at one of the twins. "I didn't want to kill you. It was an accident. You were like a daughter to me."

Agnes shook her head. "If you really loved Cherise, you wouldn't have had her own sister murder her, even by proxy."

"That was an awful thing to have happen," Cherise said, each of them had Anne by one arm, and were tugging her away. "I liked how she had Joe bury me, though. It was like a fairytale."

And they were gone.

Tasmin felt lighter with each thing she gave away.

And for each person, she tried to feel them along the connection of shared power, tried to give them something meaningful, even though, to be honest, it probably meant nothing at all. But they smiled or nodded, and took what she offered, and went away.

Finally she knelt in front of Franny. She reached over and untangled the vine from the other woman's throat. "The ghost storm is coming. Do you want it to take you?"

"I don't want to die."

"I am sorry," Tasmin said. And she meant it. She could feel the storm getting closer. Water and sand were being kicked up. "I can't take it back."

"I know," Franny said. "I don't suppose you could put me back in the amulet?"

Tasmin shook her head.

"I hate you," Franny said with enough venom to kill a herd of cows.

"I do not blame you."

The bonds fell away, and Tasmin held out a box of poisoned chocolates.

"Does William know how mean you are?"

"I am not very forgiving. You have taught me a lot about myself tonight. Perhaps the irony of our relationship will be that you made me a better person. Now take your power and go."

Franny snatched the box away. "I hope..." she snarled. "I sincerely hope..." and her face crumbled and she disappeared before whatever curse she had been forming could be spoken.

Tasmin finally approached Magda.

"No."

Ailiani pulled her back. "You have no choice."

Tasmin held a doll, elaborately embroidered, dark hair and dark skinned, her clothes all gold and blue. She held it out to Magda. "She's not held here by power. It's you."

She turned away and let mother and daughter say goodbye without her watching. She didn't think, to be honest, she could bear to. She felt raw. Ailiani joined her, and they were surrounded by sprites. The ghost storm was coming, and it picked up such a wind. The sand was getting into her eyes, her hair. She felt William behind them like an anchor. And she nodded and gathered everything she had left. She needed a good cry, badly. And a very long nap and a bath and a real dinner, and a very long nap and...

And she pushed.

She pushed as hard as she could, and the storm deteriorated under her hands. She used every bit of power she had and ripped the pattern up and flung it at the storm. The ghost trap, the spirit blessing, the wards to keep away, all strengthened by the power she had left. It shredded the storm.

A hand on her back, as she started to flag, and she smelled cold desert air and felt the glory of the stars, and magic flowed into her, and out again. Magda.

Ailiani joined her, a whirl of colors and the smell of the sea.

And another joined them, fire bright. And another, singing in a deep, sorrowful voice. Another and another, and the storm was not pushed back.

Tasmin stared at it. *This cannot be how it ends. There is so much power, so much will.*

*Yes. Yes there is,* a cool mocking voice said. *It is mine. All this power, all these angry ghosts, poured through my amulet, and you did not think I would come?*

*Ithalia.*

Tasmin schooled herself. She could not care. She would not quail in fear. Instead, she studied the situation. Ithalia's storm was a ghost storm that she'd just managed to get swept up in, whether by intention or by horrid fortune.

She could see the little flecks that held it together, and she reached out, and, carefully, experimentally, snuffed one out.

*What are you doing, Wind Witch? Do you really think you have the power to do such a thing?*

*Thanks for the encouragement.*

The only power, the only form Ithalia had was the storm. So, Tasmin forced herself not to fear. She simply reached out and snuffed out each light. And as she did, the storm fell apart. The souls screamed past her, ripping at her, ripping at the people who were around her. The sprites held on, tangled together, pulling at her hair and clothes and keeping anchored.

And then it was done. The storm had come, and it had broken like the waves on their beach. But this time, the storm was truly gone, and thousands of souls were free.

"Where is your sister?" Tasmin asked. "Tell me you can sense her if she is here."

Thanlia looked out at sea. Even a ghost's hands could shake, Tasmin saw, as the spirit raised her hands and reached out. "She cannot come on land. She has fled to the water. I am safe."

Tasmin fell to her knees.

"Does anyone have a basket?" William asked softly. "The wind sprites are too tired, I think, to fly home. I think I can collect them by feel."

"I can see them," Thanlia said.

William took a quickly-emptied basket and handed it to her.

There was an offended gasp. "I am…"

"A very useful friend who can do me a huge favor and help gather up exhausted sprites?"

Tasmin wished she could see the expression on Thanlia's face, but she could not even open her eyes, caked with grit as they were, and her hands were too tired to lift them up to clean it away.

"You. You freed my sister." Thanlia's voice was full of scorn.

William's, in return, was resigned. "I am the one she has chosen to blame for it, yes."

She must have taken the basket, because William was there, wiping off her eyes with a handkerchief. He was the first thing she saw.

"I love you," she said.

"And I, you."

"You helped. You gave me strength. We ripped apart a ghost storm. No one has ever done that. Ever."

He shook his head and pulled her so he could kiss her forehead.

She pulled away and looked around her. She could sort of see the sprites, mostly they were putting themselves in the basket that Thanlia held with an air of resignation that was rather hilarious in a spirit. It was odd, being able to see them so well. An after-effect of the power? She could not tell.

Magda was in a heap on the sand, pounding her fists on the ground, clawing at it, the low keen issuing from her throat was merciless and painful. Ailiani was kneeling beside her, rubbing her back. "It's like losing her all over again, my poor dear. I am so sorry." She turned and gave an exhausted smile to Tasmin. *We did it,* her expression seemed to say. *Oh, thank God, but we did it!*

"Let's get you home." William helped her up, brushing the sand away.

"The sun is coming up. Isn't that wonderfully symbolic."

"Yes, dear," he said, his arm around her. He kissed her cheek.

"You must have been worried. You are not normally this demonstrative in front of...oh, Light. So many people are here."

And there were. It seemed like the whole town had emptied its buildings onto the beach. She worked her way through the crowd.

"I told you she was a Wind Witch. Remember how she arrived here?" someone whispered.

*Lovely,* she thought. *That old rumor will never die, now.*

"Is this how you reward bravery? Spewing nonsense?" Tasmin's head shot up, and she saw Henriette in the crowd. "Anyone who wishes to say anything against my daughter will have to contend with me." She smiled grimly and gave Tasmin a half nod. "Get her home, William," she commanded.

Tasmin gave her a small smile as William said, "As you wish, Mamma."

Olonah, disgustingly cool and elegant despite every single hair on her head being out of place, reached out and pulled a sea bird feather from Tasmin's hair. "My husband and I would invite you and the others to dinner tonight, at his home. I hope you will come." She ruined the formality with a smile.

"If we are awake by then," William said and they continued on, people parting. Ayers patted her arm as she went by.

"Ooh. Sleep. I like sleep. What is sleep like? I somewhat remember it…"

"So you did not sleep while you were away?" William asked.

"Not for days. Is there a way to bathe my insides? I'd like to do that, too."

"We'll have to settle for bathing your outside, for now," he said. "You are coated in sand."

"So are you."

"You did kick up a terrible storm."

"Me? That was not my fault, sandy boy."

She willed herself to keep going, through the crowd. She was starting to shake. "I feel so detached still. And so empty. And nothing sounds right in my head." Tears started spilling down her cheeks. *Oh no, not in front of everyone. Please.*

William picked her up again. "You just need sleep, darling. Why don't you start right now?" So she buried her face in his neck, grit and all, and that is what she did.

# Chapter Twenty-Four

"I did not know people could lose their magic."

Tasmin listlessly picked at her food. Neither she nor William had wanted to go out, Tasmin thought she could bear to sleep another day or so and wanted to do nothing more than hide. People were treating her differently. Men tipped their hats, sometimes, sometimes they crossed the street. Women pulled their skirts away, some of them smiled at her shyly. It would be a lot to get used to.

They could go on with their lives, though, once the whole of the mystery was understood. Maybe she would feel a little less dull and colorless once she'd gotten some more rest, moved back into her own life.

"We went to the former Wise Woman's house this afternoon," William said, when he realized she was not going to answer. "There were not a lot of clues, but there was one book on mages who had lost magic. When she was at University she won awards—so we know she was once quite powerful."

"She was completely empty. I could sense no magic within her at all, when we were all connected," Tasmin said. "I think somehow she became a null."

Olonah touched her chest. "A null? But that is practically impossible."

"The key word is practically. It is rare. I looked up some cases in my own books at home." The word home tasted both like longing and ash in her mouth. "It does happen. Sometimes a spell burns out your magic. Sometimes a sickness." *And sometimes you pour it out to undo a ghost storm.*

Perhaps. Or perhaps she was just tired.

But she did know she was empty. *It'll come back*, she told herself reassuringly. She'd said it so many times already, though, that it was wearing thin.

"Anne must have been so desperate, when she lost her power. She looked for every kind of magic she could. She put out advertisements, she told sailors that she would pay them, and pay them well for any tome on spells. That's how we think she gained the journal on air ships. Someone who didn't really understand what they had wanted to make some gold." Tasmin paused, remembering what William told her of it. "Thank goodness for that."

William played with the stem of his glass. "We found a journal that we'd originally thought was just patient notes. There were lists of what she bought and where it came from and how much she paid. We found a copy of one of the advertisements that she'd run, too. No one would remark, if a Wise Woman wanted to increase her knowledge. That's all anyone would have thought it was."

"As the town Wise Woman, she knew everyone's secrets," Ailiani said. "She knew Aristel wanted to keep her husband alive. That Cherise wanted her lover back. That Joseph wanted a baby. So she used them."

"I do not understand how Cherise would help her," Olonah said. "She did not seem to be a murderer."

Carys tapped his fork on the table. Olonah gave him a look and he stopped, gave her a wry smile. "Love is a strange thing. She must have been desperate. As was Aris. Can she tell us who was directly involved in the murders?"

"If we find her." Now was Olonah's turn to pick at her meal.

"Oh, we will. And she will be put in a nice, safe madhouse. She won't stay away from Merrin for long."

Olonah sighed and looked at her guests. "It is quite certain that, despite her protests, Aris helped to lure and murder people during our time at Dalmaca. It is why she wanted us to stay there. Joe helped as well. Dalmaca was as close as you can get to part way to Azin and Dert, where they started their experiments."

Tasmin felt terrible for Meggin and her child. "What will his family do?"

"He will certainly hang," Carys said. "He is claiming that Anne managed to create a spell—possibly from magic she harvested—and was able to get Meggin to conceive. Then she used the baby and the health of the mother to threaten and force him to help her with her work."

Olonah nodded. "That is much what Aris said. That Anne provided her with a cure for her husband, then threatened to take it away."

"And yet she will get the madhouse while Joe will get the noose." Tasmin started to give Magda a reproving glance, then realized. She was the one who has spoken.

"He did kidnap you," Carys said.

"But it is a hard thing, to know Joe's son and wife will suffer greatly knowing that he has been hung." William said.

Carys was aghast. "I would not have thought to hear mercy from you."

William shrugged a little, and Tasmin put her hand on his knee.

"You said that you could destroy the amulet?" William asked.

Olonah thought for a second as she ate. "The Heart of Ithalia is one of the most important pieces of magic that I have ever held."

"And if you do not crush it to dust you will see my disagreeable side," Magda said. "I have one you know, I just like to hide it."

William and Tasmin exchanged a look. Ailiani snorted, trying not to laugh.

Olonah wavered, but asked, "Have any of you considered whether we should try and return Thanlia to it? She was imprisoned for a reason."

The chorus of 'no' from the other women at the table was emphatic and in near perfect unison. They looked at each other, and Tasmin grinned. Ailiani giggled, and even Magda smiled. For a brief moment she felt almost right again before the emptiness came back. But still, she felt as if her breathing was a little easier.

"That's settled, then. I suppose Azin Shore must live with its resident Sea Witch Ghost, and you, my dear, must destroy the amulet. Anything that can be used to capture souls as well as magic cannot be allowed to fall into the wrong hands." Carys said.

"You will need help with that. I hope you know that you can depend on me." Tasmin smiled sweetly, but she was too tired to make it a genuine request. Dinner was good, Tasmin thought, as she moved the orange-glazed bird around her plate. Normally she would have been struggling not to eat with unseemly speed.

Olonah tilted her head. "Of course. We can do it tonight, if you like."

"And in the realm of things better not known?" William asked.

Carys smiled and put the book on air ships on the table. "We can burn this before you go. I promise on my honor that I did not make any copies."

After dinner, the amulet was brought out. "Do you want to hold it one more time?" Tasmin asked William, and he shook his head. She did it for him, listened to see if there were any echoes of the sea, but there was none. Olonah and Magda drew a circle while she held it.

"If you would place it in the middle," The elementalist asked her, and Tasmin obeyed. Olonah bought out a silver hammer, written over with runes.

"An amulet breaker." Tasmin wanted to examine it closer, but was forcing herself to be polite.

"Sometimes they are useful." Olonah studied the amulet for a long moment, then hit it with the hammer.

"And like that, 'tis finally gone," William said softly. No flash of magic or whispers of revenge. Just dust that Olonah threw in the ash bucket.

"Now that we've done that, does anyone wish to join me in the library for port and journal burning?" Carys asked.

The library couches were comfy. The fire was warm, and the port hit Tasmin hard. She tried not to drowse as William and Carys ripped the journal up, feeding the horrid thing into the fire. She shifted to look at the woman in the chair next to her. Magda stared pensively at the flames, her port resting on the chair arm, untouched.

"What will you do now, Magda?"

"Mistress Olonah asked me if I would like to join her troupe. I will be leaving with the elementalists. Until I learn how to use my magic in an entertaining way, I will tell vicious lies to any-one stupid enough to ask me to tell their fortune."

"You will not have employment long, then," Olonah ob-served, and Magda smiled sweetly at her.

"You won't be leaving too soon, I hope?" Tasmin was sin-cere, and Magda looked surprised.

Olonah took her husband's hand. "Not until spring, I think."

"I need time to build my vardo," Magda said. "I hope you will let me at any scraps you have in your warehouse?" She looked at William.

"We shall see what we can do," he said, which was William-speak for yes. "And I will make sure that some of the 'scraps' actually are suitable to make a decent home from."

"Can I help paint it?" Tasmin asked. "I want to paint stars on the ceiling."

For a moment she wondered if Magda would accuse her of being too deep into her cups, but she smiled and said, "I would like that. And Ailiani will paint a blessing on my floor boards, I hope."

"And until she has her vardo, she will be staying in one of Miss Dovlington's rooms."

Magda groaned "If I wanted to stay in a chicken coop under the watchful eye of a dragon..."

"You will be so happy, there. If you are very nice I will even let you stay in the room across from me," Ailiani said. "It will be much nicer than where you have been staying...no offense to you, my dear friends..."

Tasmin touched the chair next to Magda's arm. "If you change your mind, we can provide you something better than a store room."

"The store room might be better. All those women in a tiny space..." Magda's expression was like one who was looking into the basin of hell.

Tasmin met William's eyes, then feigned nodding off. He took the hint. "I am afraid we have stayed later than we intended. Thank you for dinner."

It was not long until they were all on their way. Magda was a little ahead of them, wanting to be alone, but still in view of the others. They were taking the route to Miss Dovlington's.

"The town needs a Wise Woman, now," Tasmin said, the cold air doing wonders for stripping away the content buzz she'd been experiencing.

"I am sure one will come, now that the danger is past," Ailiani said.

Tasmin sighed. "I was trying to get around to the idea that you could be the Wise Woman."

"What? William, are you handing me the sack?"

It took a moment for William to get what she meant. "No, no, of course not!"

"And goodness knows we will miss you," Tasmin added, "But it would be a good life. You could have Anne's house. It's not hers, it is for the town Wise Woman, and there is a stipend. The town always takes the very best care of its Wise Woman."

Ailiani crossed her arms across her chest, looking so lost in thought that Tasmin worried she would trip on the cobbles. "What makes you believe that I can do such a job?"

"The way you are. You were so good with Magda today. You are good with people. Heaven knows you like them far more than I do."

"And you could do worse for a teacher," William said. "And perhaps you can continue to work until we find someone who actually likes talking to people."

"I am perfectly capable of serving the counter without scaring away the patrons," Tasmin protested.

"Of course," William said. She could have sworn he also followed that by, "On occasion," but decided for the good of their marriage that she must have misheard.

"Perhaps. I will think about it." Ailiani smiled a little. "I never thought I would be allowed to practice. It was something always forbidden to me. Hiding it was a habit. I never thought anyone would understand. A woman dancing the higher patterns, where I come from..." and this was her attempt at an apology.

"I understand," Tasmin said, and that was her forgiveness.

They hugged each other fiercely, and the four fell into a companionable silence until Ailiani was up the stairs and into her lodgings. Magda had waited for them. She said a rather muffled, "Good night," and turned and followed Ailiani into the house.

"Good night!" Tasmin said with far too much cheer.

"Ailiani will be closer, if she takes the old house up," William observed.

"Yes, it will be nice. And much more convenient. For me to pester her."

She took his arm and they turned for home.

"It is a great deal to think of, though." Tasmin said. "She won't be able to marry. But then she won't have to deal with her husband dragging her out to be social at all hours of the night."

William turned her face so he could see it.

"What?"

"Just making sure you weren't Magda."

She punched him, and he said, "Since she likes punching me, that does not help prove it."

Tasmin laughed. "That was clever of her."

"It hurt."

"But it worked."

"She could have said 'William, look here!'"

The nonsense helped get them home. He deflated as he looked at the empty counters of the shop. "I will never catch up."

She patted his back. Mostly. She was also using him as a prop to pull off her shoes. "We will catch up."

"Do you think we can afford one more day off?"

"Probably not." She dropped the shoes and rubbed her cheek against his arm. "But let's do it anyway."

They ended up taking two, one to truly rest. They read together in bed, they held each other and talked about nothing much, and slept. The next day they spent cooking like mad, and the day after that they did a little grand reopening party. Business did not seem hurt by the hiatus; indeed, more people came in than the little shop could easily hold.

And if sometimes someone called Tasmin the Wind Witch, it did not seem to hurt their business at all.

"But I do not think I am a witch anymore," she said to Neeno. The sprites were gathering things again, working on the nest in the corner of the pantry. William was at the counter, waiting on customers.

*It will come back. But it may be different.*

"Different?"

*You see us now, do you not?*

She nodded.

*Different already. But there. You could not see us if you did not have magic. William will never see us.*

"Unless you are covered in dust." She smiled, and he gave her a very dignified scowl.

*We have been changing. You have changed us by being our anchor. You are changing, too.*

"That is all well and good, but will I like it?" she muttered.

As the days passed so did the emptiness, swept away by her studies (William bought her new books as a surprise to cheer her up) and by life. The change crept up so gradually that she did not even notice it.

They were cleaning out the Wise Woman house. She was tired and cranky, cranky enough that William had lost patience and sent her out to the main room so he could finish moving furniture for Ailiani by himself rather than deal with Tasmin's bad mood. This just made her more annoyed because William never lost his patience. Ailiani had been called out—she was helping Dr. Havelock with a bit of midwifery—leaving the two of them to work on the project by themselves.

Tasmin looked at the broom and she looked at the filthy floor and she swept, once, hard. A whirl of dirt came up off the floor, as the front door flew open, slamming against the wall.

The dirt from this action was hovering over the floor, as if afraid to move, so she quietly, gently, made a little ushering gesture with her fingers, and it all sailed out the door. "Thank goodness we already cleaned up most of the papers," she muttered.

"Are the sprites here?" William asked.

She jumped a little, then turned and shook her head.

He smiled slowly, a little bit of wonder. "So my wife really is a Wind Witch, now?"

She wiggled her fingers, then shook herself, folded her hands over her stomach and said, "I think I prefer to stay a Herb-Mistress, thank you."

He kissed her. "I see."

She frowned at the door, and thought about the wind shutting it. The door shut with more force than needed, but it was shut. Tasmin grinned despite herself, then threw her arms around her husband's neck. "Though sometimes it might be useful."

# About the Author

For Cindy Lynn Speer, the pen and the sword are both equally mighty. She has written the novels *Blue Moon* and *Unbalanced*, as well as the book that you are holding right now and its precursor, *The Chocolatier's Wife*. She has also written a number of short stories, most of them collected in her enchanting collection, *Wishes and Sorrows*.

When she is not writing, she studies historical combat and is an adept rapier fighter. Both things, in their own way, are about telling stories.

You can find out more about her at her website, www.apenandfire.com.

# Acknowledgements

For everyone who loved *The Chocolatier's Wife*, this one is for you.  Thank you for your support.

Especial thanks to Mont Bowser for always trying to support me by helping me so I had more time, Cheryl Jamison for being someone I could spill my worries to, and to my mother, Cynthia Speer, for being my boon companion on many adventures.  Love you all!

Cindy Lynn Speer

# More from Dragonwell Publishing:

**Once Upon a Curse**
by Peter Beagle
and other authors

The dark side
of fairy tales and myths.

**Fire and Shadow**
by Imogen Howson

Five enchanting stories
spanning from ancient
Greece's underworld
to a dystopian future.

**www.dragonwellpublishing.com**

# More from Dragonwell Publishing:

**Ashamet, Desert Born**
by Terry Jackman

A desert world.
A warrior nation that
worships its emperor
as a god.

**Lex Talionis**
by R. S. A. Garcia

*"A stunning debut"*
—*Publishers Weekly*

www.dragonwellpublishing.com

# More from Dragonwell Publishing:

**The Princess of Dhagabad**
by Anna Kashina

A princess unwittingly
unleashes a power older
than the world itself.

**Sorrow**
by John Lawson

A child of joy.
A victim of Sorrow.